Take a Chance on Me

by Alexa Land

The Firsts and Forever Series

Book Fifteen

Books by Alexa Land Include:

Feral (prequel to Tinder)

The Tinder Chronicles (Tinder, Hunted and Destined)

And the Firsts and Forever Series:

1 Way Off Plan

2 All In

3 In Pieces

4 Gathering Storm

5 Salvation

6 Skye Blue

7 Against the Wall

8 Belonging

9 Coming Home

10 All I Believe

10.5 Hitman's Holiday (novella)

11 The Distance

12 Who I Used to Be

13 Worlds Away

13.5 Armor (novella)

14 All I Ever Wanted

15 Take a Chance on Me

Dedicated to

Sandrine Gasq-Dion

The MM community lost a fantastic author

and the world lost an amazing woman

with her untimely passing.

I'll always cherish the memories

I have of you, Sandy.

Acknowledgements

Thank you Jera

For all the late-night chats, the encouragement, and the feedback. But most of all, thank you for your friendship

Special thanks to:

Rianna, Melisha, Kim, Ron & Kelly

I truly appreciate your help and support

Thank you to Kristin, who sparked the idea for Mrs. Nesbitt

And thank you as always to my Firsts and Forever group on Facebook for the laughs, the enthusiasm, the suggestions, and for keeping me company every step of the way

Contents

Chapter One 7

Chapter Two 35

Chapter Three 70

Chapter Four 104

Chapter Five 124

Chapter Six 162

Chapter Seven 191

Chapter Eight..216

Chapter Nine 236

Chapter Ten...259

Chapter Eleven 288

Chapter Twelve 322

Chapter Thirteen 348

Chapter Fourteen 388

Chapter Fifteen 411

Chapter Sixteen 427

Epilogue...452

Bonus Recipe: Duke's Sugar Cookies.................................480

Chapter One

"Wait, is that a macaroni Elvis?"

Duke Blumenthal had been startled by several of my treasures, but that one stopped him in his tracks. My new roommate and I were carrying a dresser across my bedroom, and he'd just spotted the dried noodle portrait propped up in the corner, awaiting a place of honor on my wall. "Isn't it awesome? You find the best stuff at garage sales! I got that just last week." He stared at it for another moment, until I said, "My arms are about to snap off. Can we please put this down?"

He shook himself out of it, and as we continued across the room, he said, "Won't that attract vermin?" His deep voice matched his huge build.

I grinned at him. "Your house seems pretty vermin-free, Duke. I wouldn't worry about it."

"I'd like to keep it that way."

We put the dresser down in a corner, near the doorway to the bathroom. As much as I'd liked my old apartment, and especially my former roommate River, my new digs were pretty sweet. The bedroom was nearly twice as big as my old one, and having my own private bathroom was awesome.

The part I was a little iffy on was my new roommate. Duke was nice, but oh my God was he uptight! I went over to Elvaroni and tapped one of the glued-on noodles with my fingernail. "This stuff isn't even food anymore. It's all been shellacked, see? No self-respecting vermin would waste his time on this shit."

Even though he looked skeptical, he murmured, "Yeah, okay," and headed for the door. "What's left in the truck?"

"Just my new bed. It's another two-person job."

I followed him down the stairs and out of the house, then jogged around him and climbed into the moving van. When I pulled off the tarp with a flourish and revealed my latest and greatest treasure, Duke asked, "What exactly am I looking at here?"

"My bed."

"But it's round. And huge."

"I know! Isn't it awesome?"

"I have no words."

"It was only two hundred bucks! I totally scored, right?"

"Where'd it come from?"

"A warehouse sale at a porn studio."

Duke's blue-green eyes went wide, and he took a step back. "You bought a used porn mattress? Are you nuts? Didn't you stop to consider the germs, the bodily fluids, the—" His gag reflex kicked in, and he pressed the back of his hand to his mouth. My new roommate was a total clean-freak, and I probably should have guessed a used mattress would make him squeamish.

"Yeah, but it'd been in storage since the late 1980s. It's not like a strain of mutant, twentieth century herpes has been lying in wait all this time, looking for its opportunity to leap out and infect an unsuspecting host!"

"I still don't want to touch that thing. You shouldn't, either."

"Fine, don't touch it then. I'll do it myself." I had no idea how I was going to get it up the stairs and into my room, but step one was to get it out of the truck, so I wedged myself behind it and pushed off with my legs to get the thing moving. Once it gained some momentum, I was able to roll it fairly easily.

Duke stepped out of the way as my new bed rolled down the ramp and out of the truck. But when it hit the street, I lost my grip on it. As it started to wobble, I yelled, "Timber!"

He tried to scramble backwards, out of its way, but he stumbled and landed on his ass in the street. Duke was a huge guy, probably six-foot-eight and solid muscle. He was also a cop, so he'd probably faced some scary shit in his day. But somehow, that bed was just too much for my quite possibly germ-phobic roommate, and he yelled like he was auditioning for a horror movie. In the next instant, the porn mattress landed on top of him.

I tried to shift it, but the thing was a dead weight. There was no sign of life from underneath the mattress, and I started to panic. What if he suffocated? I made another desperate attempt to haul it off him as I called, "Save yourself, Duke! Don't let it end this way! Think of the headlines: 'San

Francisco police officer smothered by cum-soaked 1980s porn mattress.' Jesus, why is this so heavy? Do you think it gained weight from all the bodily fluids it absorbed over the years?"

Apparently, that was all the motivation he needed to free himself. Duke flipped the mattress up and over and scampered out from under it. The thing landed partly in his driveway, overlapping the street and sidewalk. He shuddered and marched up the front steps, and I called after him, "Where are you going?"

"Shower."

"What about my bed?"

"Burn it." I watched as he disappeared through the front door of the tidy, white duplex, and then I sighed and climbed onto the mattress.

I was spread-eagled on my new bed and staring at the blue September sky when my neighbor came home about ten minutes later, carrying a sack of groceries. Xavier lived in the other half of the duplex, and we'd only met briefly, but I liked him. He was a nurse and seemed like a nice guy. He also looked like a big, blond, ruggedly handsome Viking, which earned him major bonus points, as far as I was concerned. He paused to contemplate the scene in front of his home and said, "Hi Quinn. What're you doing?"

"Moving in."

"You seem to have hit a snag."

"Duke got all squirrelly at the idea of a used porn mattress and went inside. I'm waiting to see if he takes pity on me and comes back to help."

"A used what now?"

"I bought this bed at an adult film studio's warehouse sale."

"I hope you soaked it in bleach."

"Like I told Duke, it had been in storage for thirty years. That means it's perfectly sanitary."

"Yeah, I don't know about that. The squick factor alone would have made me steer clear."

"It probably had sheets on it when they were making the porn."

"I know, but still." Xavier shifted his grocery sack to the other hand and asked, "Did you get anything else at that warehouse sale?"

"Just a couple 1980s porn costumes."

"Seriously?" When I nodded, he asked, "Why?"

"Because they were hilarious. Don't worry, I'm going to wash them before I wear them."

"Where exactly would you wear such a thing?"

"Anyplace, really. You could also stay in and make a theme night out of it: get dressed up and watch 80s porn while enjoying some wine coolers and whatever the hell they ate back then. Oh man, I totally need to do that!"

"You're an interesting person, Quinn Takahashi."

"Thank you."

"Is it insensitive to ask why you're a blue-eyed blond with a Japanese last name?"

"I was adopted," I said. "I've been asked that a million times before, so I guess a lot of people find it unusual."

"Sorry, I shouldn't have said anything. It's none of my business."

I just shrugged. "It's not a secret."

"Still."

We chatted for another minute, and after he went inside, I stared at the sky some more. A little while later, Duke came back outside dressed in a pair of blue coveralls and yellow kitchen gloves. Since his dark blond hair was dry, I couldn't tell if he'd actually showered. As I got to my feet, he produced a tape measure and said, "It occurred to me this might actually be too big to fit through the door."

I studied Duke as he measured the mattress. He was actually a good-looking guy, despite the I-don't-give-a-fuck buzz cut and the frown line that was trying to carve a permanent home for itself between his brows. He had nice eyes and a square jaw, and his nose was slightly on the big side, but it suited him somehow.

Was he always so dead-serious, though? I'd only met him on a couple of occasions before agreeing to rent a room from him, so I didn't know him very well. His former roommate and mine had moved in together, which left both Duke and me looking for replacements. I'd jumped at the offer of a bigger room and private bath for less money than my old place, but maybe living with Duke was going to be problematic. I used to accuse River of being uptight when we shared an apartment, but with this guy, I needed to totally recalibrate my uptightness scale.

He straightened up after a few moments, and the frown line between his brows deepened. "As I suspected, this won't actually fit through the front entryway. Even if we got it into the house somehow, we'd have the same problem with your bedroom door."

"Aw. I was really looking forward to having a big, round bed. Now what am I going to do with this thing?"

"Take it to the dump."

"That's so wasteful, though. Oh hey, I just had an idea." I pulled out my phone and fired off a quick text, then said, "My friend Skye is a metal sculptor, so I'm asking him if he could use the springs. It'd be cool if part of it could live on in a piece of art." A reply popped up a few moments later, and I told Duke, "Skye's stoked about getting to recycle the springs into one of his projects. He and his husband Dare are out of town though, so they can't help me get the mattress into their warehouse. I don't suppose you want to take a field trip to Oakland, so you can help me unload it."

He considered the question before saying, "I need to be back here by five, because I work at six."

"That's perfect! I need to return the truck by five, so we'll definitely be back by then."

"How are we getting into the warehouse if no one's there to let us in?"

"I have a key. I'm in Dare's dance troupe, and that's where we practice."

Between the two of us, we managed to lift the mattress and balance it on its edge, and then with a lot of effort, we rolled it back up into the truck. As I folded the ramp, Duke said, "Be right back. I'm going to lock up."

I called after him, "Thanks, Duke! You're a prince among men!" He just kept walking.

After I pulled the rolling door shut at the back of the truck, I shot Skye another text to let him know I'd be delivering the mattress. I got behind the wheel and started the engine, and I was trying to find a decent radio station when Duke opened the driver's side door and said, "Move over." He was dressed in jeans and a gray T-shirt, and the gloves and coveralls were tucked under his arm. He'd also donned a pair of mirrored, aviator-style sunglasses, as if he needed to look more like a cop.

"Why?"

"Because I'm driving."

I repeated, "Why?"

"Do you want my help or not?"

"I really do."

"Then move over."

"Fine." I climbed over the gear shift and into the passenger seat, and then I tugged down the legs of my red shorts, which were riding up something fierce.

"Fasten your seatbelt."

"I was just about to, right after I saved myself from this atomic wedgie."

Duke frowned at that. I was beginning to realize that was his go-to facial expression. I strapped myself in, then sat there and fidgeted as he spent a solid minute adjusting and readjusting the rearview and side mirrors. Finally, I exclaimed, "You should have just let me drive! I had 'em all where I wanted them." He leaned out the open window and adjusted the mirror an eighth of an inch up, then an eighth of an inch back down again. "That's right where you had it!" He tilted it up an eighth of an inch again, and I flopped back in my seat and groaned.

He asked, "Are you always this impatient?"

"Yes. Are you always this slow?"

"Yup."

"Fantastic."

He wasn't kidding. Eventually, he put on his signal, pulled away from the curb, and started rolling down the street at about three miles an hour. "We only have four hours to make it to the East Bay and back. Go crazy, shoot for double digits on the ol' speedometer there, Duke." He ignored me and kept creeping along. I muttered, "Sweet Baby Jesus, give me the patience to survive the world's slowest trip to Oakland."

When I started tapping my foot, he said, "Could you not?"

"This is making me crazy! We've been driving for twenty minutes, and we're still in our neighborhood!"

"It's only been ninety seconds."

"You're shitting me." He shook his head, and I told him, "If I ever get a terminal illness, I'm hiring you to drive me around. You'll make the last week of my life feel like fifty years."

He chose to ignore that. I reached above him, pulled my yellow plastic sunglasses out of the visor, and stuck them on my face. That only killed about four seconds. My leg started bouncing quicker than ever. He clamped his huge hand down on my knee to stop my foot from tapping and shot me a look over the top of his shades. "You have to be able to drive faster than this," I said as he let go of me. He turned on the signal and looked both ways, then inched into an intersection and made the world's most cautious left turn. "You're a cop. That must mean you go on high-speed chases and are used to driving—" I leaned over and looked at the dashboard, "faster than fourteen miles an hour, otherwise you'd never apprehend any criminals. Kudos on finally reaching double digits, though."

"I'm still getting used to this big truck."

"It's not that big."

"It's probably twice as long as my pickup."

"And?"

"And I'm not going to drive very fast until I'm comfortable with it."

"You should have just let me drive," I said. "We'd already be there."

"That's exactly why you're not driving. I knew you'd be reckless."

"What are you basing that on?"

"Absolutely everything about you."

"That's unfair! You barely know me."

He turned a corner and accelerated a bit, but not enough. Then he asked, "How fast would you be driving on this road?"

"Fifty."

"The speed limit is twenty-five."

"But whoever decided to make it twenty-five was wrong," I said. "It should be fifty, so that's what I'd drive." The frown line got so deep that I could have stuck a quarter in there, and his clenched forehead would have held it for me. He didn't say anything though, and I wasn't a fan of awkward silences, so after a while, I blurted, "Tell me about you, Duke. Were your parents massive John Wayne fans? Is that what happened there?"

"It's a nickname."

"What's your real name?"

"It doesn't matter."

"Why wouldn't your name matter?"

"Because I never use it."

"Is that because it's really bad? It is, isn't it?" He didn't say anything, so I prodded, "Come on, you can tell me."

"I can, but I don't want to."

"If I guess it, will you tell me I'm right?"

"No."

I twisted around in my seat so I could study his profile and tugged on the seatbelt to adjust it as I asked, "Is your name Marion?"

"Why would it be Marion?"

"Because that was John Wayne's real name, and it makes an odd kind of sense, since you call yourself the Duke, just like he did."

"Not *the* Duke. Just Duke."

"Is it Gaylord?"

"Oh my God."

"I think that's actually a cool name. It's like Star Lord from Guardians of the Galaxy, but, you know. Gay."

"You're never going to guess it, so please stop trying."

"Elmer?"

"What, like the glue?"

"Yes."

"No."

"Were they hippies? Is your name something like Wheatgrass, or Kumquat, or Quinoa?"

Duke shot me another over-the-glasses look. "You're terrible at guessing, and you need to stop."

"I'm also hungry, not that any of those foods sound appealing. Hey, can we find a drive-through?"

"Let's just focus on the task at hand."

"Fine. I know where Skye hides his secret chocolate stash, so I can fortify myself once we get there."

Fortunately, he sped up to match the flow of traffic when we reached the Bay Bridge, and I tried to keep the conversation going with, "If you won't tell me your real name, tell me something else about you, Duke."

"Like what?"

"Where'd you grow up?"

"In South San Francisco. What about you?"

"I grew up right over there, in the Oakland Hills," I said, pointing out the window. "I spent my entire childhood staring at the city across the bay and dreaming of the day I could finally live there. A little over a year ago, I made it happen. I would have been here sooner, but I moved to New York for a few years after high school to study with a famous ballet instructor."

"My old roommate mentioned you're a classically trained ballet dancer. So, why are you working as a go-go boy?"

"I just needed a job when I moved back to California. I met Dare Evans when I went to audition for his start-up ballet company, and he referred me to this club. It's actually where he met his husband Skye. Dare's still trying to get the dance troupe off the ground, so at this point it doesn't pay anything. But we're staging our first production in a few weeks, and we all have high hopes for it."

"If it's a success, will you quit go-go dancing?"

"I don't know." I settled back in my seat and said, "Even though it was meant to be a short-term gig, it's a great job. I used to spend most nights dancing in the clubs anyway. Now I get paid for it." He glanced at me, and I noticed the frown line was back. "You don't approve?"

"It's not that. I just can't imagine getting up and dancing in front of a bunch of strangers while wearing almost nothing."

"I'm feeling judged."

"What? I didn't say there's anything wrong with it."

"Your frown line begs to differ." That just made the crease between his eyebrows deepen. I asked him, "Have you ever been to Thrust?"

"That big nightclub in the Castro? No."

"That's where I work. You should come by sometime and check it out. It's just a really fun party atmosphere, not sleazy at all."

"So, you and the rest of your coworkers aren't dancing in skimpy costumes?"

"We are, but everything's covered that needs to be."

"And you don't get hit on every five minutes?"

"Oh no, we totally do. But that still doesn't make it sleazy."

"If you say so."

"So judgmental," I muttered.

"I'm not."

"Yes you are. Come to Thrust on your next night off and see it for yourself."

"I don't think so."

"Why not?"

He muttered, "I'm uncomfortable in places like that."

"Are you straight?"

"No."

"Why then?"

"I just don't like crowds, noise…all of it, really."

"I bet you'd have a great time, despite yourself," I said. "A big muscle stud like you would get a ton of attention."

"Why would I want attention?"

What the hell kind of question was that? "Don't you want to meet people? Have fun? Get laid?"

"Not like that."

"God forbid." The conversation ground to a halt at that point.

When we reached Oakland a few minutes later, he asked, "What exit should I take?"

"Oh. Um, I'm not sure. I always take public transit. Try that one, maybe?"

I was way off. We ended up winding through a part of the city I didn't know at all, for the better part of half an hour. "Why don't you just map it?" Duke asked at one point. When I told him I didn't actually know the warehouse's street address, a muscle started working in his jaw as he ground his teeth. I tried texting Dare, then Skye, but they took a long time to reply. By the time they did, I'd finally gotten my bearings, and we pulled up in front of the warehouse just as the address appeared on my screen.

I pushed my sunglasses to the top of my head and flashed Duke a smile as he cut the engine. "Well, the good news is, we got here," I said. "Sorry about the detour. At least it'll be easy to find our way home, since we can just map our way back to the bridge."

We both got out of the truck and went around to the back of it, and Duke murmured, "Seriously?"

The rolling door was wide open, and the truck was empty. I blurted, "Where'd the mattress go?"

"It must have fallen out. Didn't you latch the door?"

"Oops."

Duke sighed, and as he pulled out his phone, I asked, "Who are you calling?"

"A friend in dispatch." When the call connected, he said, "Hey Anita, it's Duke. Are there any obstructions on the Bay Bridge?" Apparently the answer was no, because he looked relieved. Then he asked if anyone had reported a round mattress in the road anywhere in the city. Another no. "Can you check with Oakland P.D. and see if anyone called it in?" He listened for a moment, then rolled his eyes. "No, someone didn't abscond with my bed. I have a new roommate, and…you know what? It's a long story. Will you please call my cellphone if you hear anything?" Apparently she agreed, and after a brief pause, he said, "Thanks, Anita," and ended the call.

He climbed up onto the tailgate and pulled the door shut, then told me, "Come on, we have to retrace our steps."

"That's impossible. I have no idea how we got here."

"We have to try." Duke got behind the wheel and started the engine.

I unrolled the window and hung out of it like a limp noodle as we drove around Oakland for what felt like days. Duke was thoroughly annoyed and apparently done talking to me. The silence in the truck was deafening.

After maybe twenty minutes, I sat up and exclaimed, "This is impossible! The bed is gone, and it doesn't even matter! It's not like we *had to* deliver it to my friend. Wherever it landed, someone is bound to report it to the city sanitation department, and they'll haul it away. You thought it belonged in the dump anyway, and that's where it'll end up."

All he said to that was, "This is our responsibility. We have to find it."

It took us one hour and thirty-three minutes to locate the mattress. We got lost several times and had to keep finding our way back to our original, circuitous route. But then finally, we rounded a corner in an abandoned-looking industrial area and there it was, overlapping part of the street and sidewalk.

The mattress had company. A tiny, light brown Chihuahua sat right in the center of it, and I exclaimed, "Aw, he's so cute!" Duke cut the engine, and I tumbled out of the truck and rushed toward the compact canine. But when I got within ten feet of him, the dog puffed up, bared his teeth, and started growling at me. "Whoa there buddy, we come in peace," I said as I held up my hands.

When he leapt to his feet and started barking, Duke said, "I'll call animal control." He reached for his phone, but I stopped him with a hand on his arm.

"No, don't do that. He's wearing a collar, so he probably lives around here." I took a step toward the dog and raised my voice a couple of octaves as I called, "Hey, puppy. We need that bed, so how about heading home now?"

The dog snarled and barreled toward us, and Duke and I both turned and ran. We scrambled onto the bumper of the truck, then the hood when the furious little animal took a flying leap at us and narrowly missed my red sneaker. "Wow," Duke said, "that dog hates you."

"Animals never hate me. You must have done something to piss it off."

"Oh no. That was all you." He pulled his phone from the pocket of his jeans and added, "It was probably that high-pitched cartoon character voice you used. No wonder it's so angry."

He started to scroll through his phone, and I asked, "Who are you calling?"

"Animal control, like I said. That thing's a menace."

"You can't do that! What if his owner doesn't find him in time and he gets put down? I'd never forgive you!"

Duke turned to me with his phone poised in midair and said, "It's a vicious animal."

"He's eight inches tall!"

"What if it bites somebody?"

"He won't. I just pissed him off."

"He almost took a chunk out of your shoe."

"But he didn't," I said. "Come on Duke, put the phone down."

"Calling animal control is for the dog's own good. He could get hit by a car if we just leave him out here."

"Then we need to help him get home."

Duke peered over the edge of the truck, and the little animal let out a menacing growl. "How do you propose we do that?"

"Well first, I need to take a look at the tag on his collar to find out where he lives."

"If you try, he'll bite you."

"Not if I establish dominance," I said.

"What are you talking about?"

"Right now, we're acting like scaredy cats, so he thinks he can boss us around. I need to convince him I'm the alpha dog, and then he'll fall in line." I jumped off the truck, and when the Chihuahua lunged at me, I waved my arms to try to appear as big as I could and started barking. The dog stopped in his tracks and stared at me with his bulging eyes, and then he turned and ran. I exclaimed, "Shit, I overdid it! I was going for alpha dog, but I guess I landed on big, scary werewolf!"

I took off after the dog, and Duke yelled, "Why are you chasing it?"

"I have to make sure he gets home safe!"

For an animal with four-inch legs, the Chihuahua was pretty damn fast. I sprinted down the street, then cut through an alley and across a vacant lot in hot pursuit. After a minute, the industrial area gave way to a modest residential neighborhood. The dog was maybe thirty feet ahead of me when it darted into a yard. An old man was watering a weedy lawn, and he exclaimed, "There you are, Tank! I thought I told you not to go out on any more of your adventures!" The yard was surrounded by a waist-high chain link fence, and the man closed the gate behind the little animal.

Because I was watching that interaction instead of where I was going, I didn't notice the curb in front of me. I stepped off of it and into a storm drain, and pain shot up my leg as I fell to the ground. I was cussing a blue streak when Duke jogged up to me and asked, "Are you alright?"

I carefully extracted my foot from the drain and said, "No, damn it! How could I be so stupid? I wasn't watching where I was going, and I just sprained my ankle!"

"That's okay. Sprains heal."

"It's terrible! My dance troupe is just six weeks away from our first performance, and I'm the lead dancer. I'm going to let everyone down!" I tried to stand up, but my ankle wouldn't hold my weight. I cried out in pain, and as Duke put his arm around my shoulders to steady me, I said, "Shit, it's already starting to swell up and bruise. How could I be so careless?"

"Let's get you to the hospital. A doctor will be able to tell you how bad it is." I was surprised when he scooped me into his arms. At five-foot-nine, I wasn't the biggest guy in the world, and Duke tossed me in the air a bit when he picked me up, as if he'd expected lifting me to be more of an effort.

"You don't have to carry me," I muttered embarrassedly.

"It's best to stay off your ankle. You might make it worse." He turned and started back the way we'd come, and I sighed and rested my head on his shoulder.

"I'm sorry about all of this," I said, as I idly ran a hand over the soft, gray fabric of his T-shirt. "I didn't mean to hijack your entire day."

"It's okay."

"I wish I could tell you I'm not always like this, but in all honesty, I'm usually even worse."

Duke grinned, just a little, and said, "I know."

"You do?"

He nodded. "I asked my old roommate about you before I decided to let you move in. Since he just married your former roommate, I figured he'd probably spent a lot of time at your apartment and knew you fairly well."

"What did Cole say about me?"

"He called you a loveable disaster."

"That pretty much sums me up." I glanced at Duke and asked, "Why would you let a disaster move into your pristine home?"

He shrugged and kept his eyes on the path through the vacant lot as he murmured, "We both needed roommates, so…." That really didn't explain why he'd let someone like me move in, but I let the subject drop.

When we got back to the truck, Duke deposited me in the passenger seat and went to retrieve our cargo. I felt bad that I couldn't help him load the mattress. He swung by Skye's warehouse and left the bed leaning against the side of the building before driving me to the nearest hospital.

The emergency room was crowded. We sat on either side of a little table in the corner, at right angles to each other, and Duke lifted my foot onto his knee to keep it elevated. At one point, he asked, "Is there anyone you want to call? Your boyfriend, maybe?"

"I don't have one. The last guy I was interested in turned out to be a big, giant cheater with a live-in boyfriend, which is why I'm now on a hiatus from dating. For a week or two, anyway."

"I'm sorry that happened to you."

I said, "He wasn't much of a loss."

"But it was still enough to make you swear off men for a while."

"I'm just really tired of being lied to, and it keeps happening. It seems like guys will say almost anything to get laid."

"Not all men are like that."

"I know. I've just encountered more than my fair share of liars since I've been back in California."

"And you didn't when you lived on the east coast?"

"I was in New York to study dance, not to find a boyfriend, so I never got to know any of the men I slept with." Duke frowned a little, and I said, "What? Are you judging me for having an active sex life?"

"No."

I crossed my arms over my chest and said, "You totally are."

"No I'm not. I've just never quite understood the concept of casual sex. It's literally the most intimate thing you can do with another human being, and…never mind."

"So, what exactly are you doing? Saving yourself for marriage?"

"No."

He looked embarrassed and broke eye contact, and I said, "Oh my God. You are, aren't you?"

"Of course not."

"Why don't I believe you?"

"Let's talk about something else."

"But—"

He shot me a look and said, "You have two choices: drop the subject, or wait alone."

"Okay, okay. It's none of my business anyway. I've just never met a thirty-year-old virgin, so it threw me off."

"I'm not thirty."

"But you are a virgin?"

He lifted my leg and started to slide out from under it as he said, "I'll be in the truck."

"Wait! I'm sorry. I'll shut up about your sex life, I promise. Please stay and keep me company." Duke studied me for a moment, then sat back down and returned my swollen foot to his knee. After a pause, I said, "Asking how old you are is okay though, right?"

"I'll be twenty-eight at the end of next month."

"Really? That's when I'm celebrating my twenty-fifth birthday, but you seem a lot older than me. I'm surprised we're only three years apart." His expression could best be described as exasperated, and I blurted, "I don't mean you look old or anything. You really don't. You just seem much more serious than most guys your age. Plus, you're a homeowner. How many people in their twenties can say that, especially in San Francisco? Actually, now that I think about it, cops make a fairly modest salary, and the city is crazy expensive. How did you afford that place?"

"If you must know, my father loaned me the money for the down-payment. That's why I work a lot of overtime, and why I need a roommate. I not only have to pay the mortgage, I also make monthly payments to my parents, with interest. Fortunately it's a duplex, so I can rent out half of it, in addition to the spare bedroom on my side. That helps."

"Still, though. Given the housing prices in San Francisco, it must cost you a fortune every month, even with a roommate and a tenant."

"It does."

"That must come with a lot of sacrifices. I guess it was really important to you to be a homeowner." He just shrugged, and I asked, "Wasn't it?"

"My parents felt I should buy a house. They thought paying rent was a waste of money."

"And what do you think?"

He studied a spot on the faded beige wall and said, "It doesn't really matter."

Because he seemed uncomfortable, I changed the subject by asking, "When's your birthday?"

"October thirty-first."

"Mine too! Well, kind of."

Duke glanced at me. "How can that kind of be your birthday? Either it is or it isn't."

"My parents decided to celebrate the day my adoption was finalized as if it's my birthday, and that's Halloween. I have no idea when I was actually born."

"I don't understand. Your birth parents would have included that in the paperwork when they gave you up for adoption."

I fidgeted with the hem of my yellow T-shirt and said, "There's no paperwork involved if you abandon your toddler at a bus station."

Duke's eyes went wide, and he murmured, "I'm sorry. I shouldn't have asked."

"It's okay. You didn't know."

"That's no excuse for being so insensitive."

"Seriously, don't beat yourself up over it. My parents are Asian, so it's super obvious I'm adopted, and people ask about it all the time. I've gotten used to the questions. So yeah, I celebrate my birthday on Halloween, and I tell people I'm turning twenty-five this year, but that's just a guess. The doctors thought I was about three when I was found, but it was hard to tell, because…." I had to pause and swallow a lump in my throat. Damn it, no. I wasn't going to cry about it, not again. I made myself keep my voice steady and finish the story. "It was hard to tell because I was severely malnourished, and a lot of my baby teeth had fallen out prematurely."

Duke's voice was full of emotion when he whispered, "Oh God."

"Don't be upset. I'm alright now, and I totally believe that old saying, it's never too late to have a happy childhood. Not that it was bad after that rough start. I was adopted by an amazing family, and they took such good care of me. I was left with a few challenges, like the fact that I could never sit still or concentrate in school, and they figured out early on that I needed to channel my energy into something physical. That's why they signed me up for ballet lessons, which turned out to be the best thing ever for me." I was probably telling my new roommate much more than he actually wanted to know about me, so I wrapped it up with, "Anyway, I think I'm doing pretty good now, all things considered."

He said, "Speaking of your parents, do you want to call them? You said they live nearby. Maybe you can stay with them while your injury heals, so you won't have to deal with the stairs at the duplex."

"I really don't. My dad already worries about me, and if he knew I hurt my ankle, he'd just worry more. As a dancer, I'm always one injury away from the end of my career, although I'm pretty sure this one's just a sprain. But even minor injuries are stressful when you're in ballet," I said. Then I added, "Besides, I don't need anyone's help. Once I get some crutches, I'll be able to take care of myself."

"You sure?"

The nurse called my name just then, and I nodded. "I'll be fine. I always am." I pulled up a smile and tried to look braver than I felt.

Chapter Two

As Duke held the door for me, I hobbled into the house on my shiny new crutches, and he said, "I want you to use my bedroom. It's yours until your ankle heals. You really shouldn't try to navigate that steep staircase."

He had a point about the stairs, but I still protested. "I can't kick you out of your room. Where are you supposed to sleep?"

"On the couch."

"There's no way! I'm not kidding when I say that's the most uncomfortable couch in the history of uncomfortable couches. Once I make it to my room, I'll be fine."

"You don't even have a bed."

"I'll make a nest out of blankets."

"And when you get hungry? Then what?"

"I have some candy bars upstairs."

"Just use my bedroom. I don't have time to argue with you," he said as he led the way down the hall. "I have to leave in about five minutes, so I can return the truck and still make it to work on time."

"You don't have to do that. The truck's not your responsibility."

He pushed open his bedroom door and said, "There's no point in getting charged for an extra day, not when I can make it to the rental place before they close."

"Well, okay. Thank you, Duke."

"Before I go, do you want anything from upstairs?"

"Yes please." I leaned the crutches against the wall beside the nightstand and said, "There's a big box in my room labeled 'happy stuff'. Could you bring it to me? I think it's underneath the window." He glanced at me with a raised eyebrow, but instead of asking what it contained, he nodded and left the room.

I climbed onto his neatly made bed, dropped my single sneaker onto the floor, and propped my foot up with a couple of pillows. Fortunately, I hadn't done any significant damage when I twisted my ankle, but it still hurt like hell and had puffed up so much that it resembled a watermelon. The E.R. doctor had wrapped it tightly after she'd x-rayed it, and I slipped a fingertip under the stretchy, peach-colored bandage and scratched the top of my foot as I took in my surroundings.

Duke's bedroom, like the rest of his house, was both immaculate and surprisingly generic. The white walls displayed a couple unremarkable, black and white landscape photos, while the pale blue bedspread and the wooden dresser, headboard, and matching nightstands provided the only color in the room. The king-size bed was longer than average, which made sense, since my new roommate was one of the tallest people I'd ever met. But other than that, there was no personalization whatsoever. In fact, it felt more like a hotel room than a home. I had no idea what any of that said about Duke.

Actually, I didn't really know what to make of him in general. It was as if he kept a wall between himself and the rest of the world. Even if we became friends, I doubted that wall would ever disappear. It just seemed like a huge part of who he was.

Duke returned a couple of minutes later with the box, two bottles of water, and a serving bowl brimming with all kinds of healthy stuff, like fruit, packets of nuts, and granola bars. I almost asked him if some squirrels would be dropping by later. He put the food and drinks on the nightstand and the box beside me on the bed, and then he asked, "Do you need anything else before I take off?" I shook my head, and he told me, "I have a dinner break four hours into my shift, so I'll come home and check on you. If you need anything before that, text me."

"Thank you, Duke. I want you to know I really appreciate all you've done for me."

He looked a little embarrassed, and muttered, "Not a problem," as he headed for the door.

It was so quiet after he left. Too quiet. I played some music on my phone, but it didn't help all that much.

I fidgeted with nervous energy. I'd never been able to sit still for very long. I couldn't do it when I was a kid, and I couldn't do it now, either, so lying around with my foot in the air really wasn't an option.

I desperately needed something to distract myself, and Duke's room wasn't helping. Why was it so totally blank? Who lived like that?

What the room did have was a glass door that opened onto the oddly perfect backyard. After a few minutes of sensory deprivation in the white room, I busted open my happy box, pulled out a bottle of rum and stuffed it into the front of my shorts, so I could free up my hands for the crutches. Then I hobbled out to the little cement patio, which contained a perfect table with a perfect umbrella and four perfect chairs.

Being frustrated and in pain had put me in a bad mood, so the whole anal retentive neat freak thing was beginning to grate on me. The lawn in particular was getting on my last nerve. It was flawlessly, uniformly dark green, and every single blade of grass was exactly the same length. I imagined Duke out there with a ruler and a tiny pair of scissors, trimming it precisely. I couldn't really explain why it made me want to scream. It just did.

I flopped down on the lawn and made the grass equivalent of a snow angel. Ugh, it was damp. I felt it seeping through my shorts and T-shirt, but since I was already wet, I decided to stay put. I stuck my injured foot straight up and tried to swing my good leg over far enough to create a proper skirt, but I had a feeling that was going to be one jacked up lawn angel.

Then I sprawled out and stared at the sky for a while. I had no idea how I was going to pass the time until my roommate came home, let alone get through the next several days on crutches. After a while, I sat up and took a long drink from my bottle of rum. It was super gross without its usual Coke counterpart, but I drank it anyway, because I figured being drunk and bored was a hell of a lot better than being sober and bored.

I scrolled through the contacts on my phone, looking for someone who could come over and keep my pathetic ass company. But it was Labor Day weekend, and everyone but me had plans. My friend Ash was DJing a party, and River had gotten married just the day before, so obviously he and his new husband Cole had better things to do than babysit me. Skye and Dare were somewhere down the coast, and I didn't feel like freaking out Haley or the other members of my troupe by telling them their lead dancer had injured himself a few weeks before our first show. I even thought about calling Nana Dombruso, an adorable senior citizen who'd taken me under her wing, but she'd rented a beach house for herself and her family and was out of town for a few days.

Finally, I decided to call my parents. My dad answered on the second ring with, "Are you okay, Quinn?"

"Of course. Why wouldn't I be?"

"Because you're calling me on a Saturday night, and you always have plans."

I said, "It's only five-thirty."

"That's true. Are you working at that strip club tonight?"

"It's not a strip club, Dad."

"You told me you dance around in your underwear."

"That's not what I said. I told you all the dancers wear outfits that are basically like Speedos."

"Speedos are even smaller than most briefs."

I told him, "You should come and see where I work sometime, Dad. It's really not sleazy."

"It's still beneath you."

"No it isn't," I insisted.

"You undervalue yourself, Quinn. You always have."

By that point, I was completely sorry I'd called home. I took another swig of rum and asked, "How are you and mom?"

"You're changing the subject."

"Uh, yeah."

"We're both fine. When are you coming to dinner?"

"Maybe next weekend, but I don't know my work schedule yet." Okay, that wasn't true. I just didn't want to tell my dad I'd hurt myself by doing something stupid and wasn't sure when I'd be off the crutches. I'd actually called my boss on the way home from the hospital and told him I'd sprained my ankle, so I was off the schedule until it was healed.

"Alright. So, how's your new apartment? Did you get all your stuff moved in?"

"Yeah, as of today. It's a nice place, but I don't know how long I'll last here. My new roommate is probably going to drive me nuts."

"Why? What's he doing?"

"He just seems really uptight, and he's such a neat freak. This whole place is way too perfect. He seriously must spend every spare moment cleaning and doing yardwork. It's weird."

"You told me this place was bigger, better, and cheaper than your old apartment. Now you're complaining because it's too clean?"

I flopped back onto the grass. "That's not what I'm saying."

"I don't see how having a tidy housemate could possibly be construed as a negative."

"You know what I'm like, Dad. How do you think I'd get along with a perfectionist?"

"Maybe this person will be good for you. I know you've struggled with getting organized and following a routine, so living with someone who's disciplined might be exactly what you need."

"Or we might end up murdering each other."

"I'm sure you'll learn to get along. Now tell me, how are rehearsals going with your dance troupe?"

"Great. We're down to just six weeks before our debut." I added silently, *and my ankle better fucking heal in time.*

He said, "We're looking forward to seeing the show."

"You get that it's not exactly going to be Swan Lake, right Dad?"

"Don't worry. You already explained that it's a bit avant-garde. I know you think your mom and I are squares, but we're very open-minded when it comes to the arts." The fact that he used the word 'squares' proved he was exactly that, but okay. "After the show, do you think you'll find a job with a ballet company that will actually pay you?"

"This troupe is just getting off the ground. I'm not going to bail on them after one performance."

"But you're so talented, Quinn, and you should be dancing with a top company! I'll never understand why you turned down that position with the San Francisco Ballet."

I sighed and said, "You bring that up literally every time I talk to you."

"That's because I want what's best for you, and it was such a wonderful opportunity."

"I had my reasons for turning it down."

"But you won't tell me what those reasons are, so how can I hope to make sense of your decision?"

I'd lost track of the number of times we'd had that exact same conversation over the last year. It reminded me of a pair of race cars I had as a kid. They sped around and around on their little track, but they never actually went anywhere. I said, "I have to go, but I'll talk to you soon, okay? And I'll try to come to dinner next weekend."

"Alright. I love you, Quinn."

"I love you too, Dad."

I felt a bit depressed after that, but the last thing I wanted was to sit around feeling sorry for myself. I drained the last inch of rum from the bottle, jumped up onto my good leg, and admired my lawn angel. She looked awesome, clearly defined in the damp grass. I gave her the empty booze bottle and my crutches and hopped to the patio on one foot. Then I stripped off my soggy shirt and shorts and hung them from the umbrella to dry. My red briefs were also damp, so I pulled them off and spread them out on the picnic table before hopping into the bedroom.

I fell across Duke's bed, reached up blindly, and felt around in my happy box. The first thing I pulled out was a big tub of hot pink glitter. Excellent! My second round of Go Fish produced a bottle of vodka, and I murmured, "Don't mind if I do." I was already tipsy from the rum, but that was the whole point. I took a big swig of alcohol, then shuddered dramatically and said, "Ugh, needs orange juice." The kitchen was too far away, though. I took another shot and put the bottle on the nightstand, then reached back into the box.

I pulled out a light blue teddy bear and exclaimed, "Yay! You can keep me company, Mr. Fluffers! But be forewarned, we're trapped in the no-fun zone. Look at this place!" I rolled onto my back, held him up, and panned around so he could see Duke's bedroom. I slurred a little as I said, "This is the lair of my new roommate-slash-landlord. He'd actually be kind of hot if you went strictly on appearance. He's super tall with huge muscles and nice eyes. But then, the moment he says or does anything, you realize he has a huge stick up his butt, and not in a fun way. I don't know what I'm going to do about him."

I balanced the bear on top of the headboard, then got up on one knee with my wrapped foot sticking out to the side and peered into the box. "This is one of the best ideas I ever had," I told the stuffed animal. "It was just supposed to be for the move, so I could keep all my good stuff together. But I need a happy box every day of my life."

I clustered six more half-empty booze bottles onto the nightstand, stacked a fistful of candy bars next to them, and transferred the box to the wood floor. I then slid off the bed and pulled the pristine, light blue bedspread off with me as I said, "All that chocolate might get messy, Mr. Fluffers, so I think I should keep this fussy little granny coverlet thingie out of harm's way." I shoved the bedspread into the corner, along with the pillows that came with it, and when I turned back toward the bed, I exclaimed, "Hospital corners! Figures."

I grasped the top sheet and blanket and pulled as I grumbled, "These make no sense. The second you get in bed, you have to untuck it anyway. Otherwise, you're all pinned down. Damn it, these are tight!" I put my back into it, and finally freed one corner of the super-tucked sheets. "Forget what I said about getting into bed and then untucking it. That would literally be impossible! You couldn't even slip a postcard under these tight-ass sheets!" I climbed back onto the bed and finally managed to wrestle the top sheet and blanket free, and then I threw them on the floor.

"Shit, I actually worked up a sweat doing that. I need a drink." I took another sip of the vodka and shuddered again, then told the bear, "Not packing mixers in my happy box was a total fail." I retrieved the box from the floor and muttered, "Oh no," as a bunch of multicolored glitter rained out of the gaping seam along the bottom. It got all over the sheets, and all over me, and I sighed and pushed the box to the foot of the bed.

My ankle was throbbing, and my head was spinning from all that booze on an empty stomach. I fell back and muttered, "I know I need to clean that up, but I don't feel so good right now, Mr. Fluffers." I swung my leg wide and propped my injured foot up on the happy box. That felt a little better. Then I polished off the last sip of vodka, operating under the theory that it would act as a painkiller if I drank enough of it.

I dropped the empty bottle onto the bed and reached for another, but ended up with a handful of candy bars instead. I tossed them aside and tried again, this time managing to grab a nearly empty bottle of gin. Okay no, that was way too gross straight. I cradled the bottle in my arms and let my eyes slide shut. A moment later, Mr. Fluffers fell off the headboard and landed on my face. That was a good thing, actually, because he blocked the glare from the overhead light. I'd probably feel much better after a little nap....

*****

"What have you done?"

Panic flooded me as I sat bolt upright and blinked a few times. I didn't know where I was, or why a huge cop in uniform was yelling at me from the doorway. I looked down at myself and mumbled, "What the fuck?" Why was I completely naked, covered in multicolored glitter, and holding a nearly empty bottle of gin?

My head was pounding, and I blinked again as I tried to get my bearings. After a moment, I realized the cop was my new roommate, and also that my legs were spread and he was getting a hell of a view of my junk. I pulled my left foot off its cardboard perch and winced as I jarred my sprained ankle.

Duke barked, "What happened in here, Quinn?"

"I don't know."

"What do you mean, you don't know?"

"Give me a minute." I squinted against the glare from the light fixture on the ceiling. God, my head hurt.

"Why is there glitter everywhere?"

I thought about that, then tipped the cardboard box and looked inside. "It spilled."

He strode to the open back door and stuck his head out, and then he asked me, "Did you get naked outside? My neighbors can see right into the yard! And what's that on the grass?"

"Oh, I know this one! A lawn angel on crutches."

He turned to me and demanded, "Are you drunk?"

I thought about that, then said, "Not drunk enough." I held up the bottle I'd been cradling in my arms and contemplated the clear liquid, but my stomach churned at the idea of downing straight gin.

Duke snatched it out of my hands. His eyes flashed with anger as he gestured at the bottles on the nightstand. "Did you drink all of that?"

"Am I under arrest?"

"What? No! I just need to know if I should take you to the hospital to get your stomach pumped, so you don't die of alcohol poisoning."

I snapped, "Of course not! I'm not that stupid!"

I tried to get up, but it was impossible to balance on my one good leg, given how much my head was spinning. Duke barked, "Sit down before you fall over!" I did both, falling back into a seated position on the mattress. I looked around, then started to reach for a bottle of tequila on the nightstand.

Duke grabbed it and said, "Are you kidding? You've had enough for one night!"

That really pissed me off, and I yelled, "I decide when I've had enough, not you! I'm a full-grown man, and if I want to get drunk off my ass, then I'm damn well going to!"

"Full-grown men don't sleep with teddy bears, run around naked, trash other people's houses, drink like fish, or toss around glitter like they're at a rave!"

"Yes they do! Maybe not you, Mr. Perfect Uptight Cop, but I do!"

"Then you need to grow the hell up!" He stormed out of the room, and a few moments later, I heard the front door slam.

It took a few moments for the guilt to reach me through my alcohol haze, but when it did, it hit me hard. I looked around at the mess I'd made and the bottles of alcohol and could plainly see why he'd been so upset. After he'd spent all day helping me, this was how I repaid him.

I noticed a bag by the door, and when I hobbled over to it and looked inside, I was hit by a second wave of guilt. He'd brought home a couple of delicious-looking Mexican dinners, then left without eating anything. Oh man. I'd basically destroyed our first night as roommates.

He probably hated my guts after all of that. He should. I'd been a drunken asshole, but maybe I could make it up to him. I limped out to the backyard, got dressed, and retrieved my crutches. Then I went in search of the vacuum.

*****

It was sometime after three a.m. when I heard the automatic garage door rattle open, then close again. I was sitting on a rainbow-striped beanbag in a corner of my room, and I turned off the movie I'd been watching on my phone and set it aside. I fidgeted with the tie on my red pajama pants, which featured an all-over pattern of yellow rubber ducks, and listened intently as Duke came in through the door off the kitchen and went to his room. After a pause, he crossed the ground floor and headed up the stairs. The house creaked just enough for me to follow his progress.

He appeared in my open doorway a few moments later, dressed in a dark blue hoodie and jeans, and murmured, "Hey."

"Hey. Sorry about earlier."

"I'm sorry for yelling at you."

"It was understandable."

"No it wasn't. I never lose my temper."

"You had a lot of provocation."

Duke stuffed his hands in his jacket pockets and said, "Thanks for putting my room back the way you found it."

"I tried. I even watched a YouTube video on how to make hospital corners, but I couldn't get your sheets exactly like you had them. And I vacuumed for almost an hour, but I think you'll still be finding specks of glitter in there for years to come." I looked down at myself and brushed a fleck of glitter off my pink T-shirt. I'd taken a shower after cleaning his room, but somehow it kept reappearing.

"You shouldn't have done all of that on your sprained ankle. You probably made it worse."

"I was careful." I got up and said, "I put your dinner in the refrigerator. Are you hungry? I could warm it up for you."

"You don't have to do that."

"I'm trying to make up for being an asshole earlier. Humor me."

He hesitated for a moment before saying, "Okay then."

I followed Duke out of my room on the crutches. When we got to the top of the stairs, he watched me trying to navigate the first couple of steps and blurted, "This is an accident waiting to happen. Can I carry you?"

"Knock yourself out." He scooped me into a fireman's carry, jogged down the stairs, and deposited me on the ground floor. I murmured a thank you, and he nodded embarrassedly, then led the way to the all-white kitchen.

I heated the enchilada platters one at a time in the microwave, and we sat down to dinner on a pair of barstools at the tiled kitchen island. He was quiet as we ate, and I was, too. I figured I'd gotten on his nerves enough for one evening.

He seemed distracted though, so after a while I said, "I don't know you very well, so maybe this is how you always are at three in the morning. But is something wrong? If you're still pissed about what I did to your room earlier, I don't blame you at all."

"I'm not upset about the room."

"Did something happen at work tonight?"

"I don't want to talk about it."

After a pause, I asked, "Do you want me to make you a margarita to go with dinner? It might help you unwind."

He glanced at me and said, "Actually, I usually do something else to unwind. If you're going to be up for a while, you can join me if you want to."

"Whatever it is, I'm totally down for it."

After we finished our meal, he cleared away the plates and wiped down the kitchen island, and then he exchanged his hoodie for a simple, white apron. He took a bag of flour from one of the cabinets, and I grinned and said, "You bake to relax?"

"It works wonders."

When he reached up and pulled a storage container of sugar off a top shelf, the sleeve of his gray T-shirt slid down two or three inches, exposing a white bandage that was wrapped around his big bicep. I exclaimed, "You're hurt! Did that happen at work tonight?"

"Yeah, but it's nothing."

"It doesn't look like nothing. What happened?"

"A fourteen-year-old drug addict took a swipe at me with a broken beer bottle."

"Holy shit, Duke!"

"It's not a big deal. He barely grazed me. It didn't even need stitches."

"No wonder you seemed rattled."

"That's not why."

"You mean something else happened, too?"

He said, "Most nights, my job is boring. But every now and then...not so much."

"What happened?"

"Like I said, I don't want to talk about it."

Duke pulled some butter from the refrigerator and softened it in the microwave, and I asked, "Are you sure?" When he nodded, I said, "Okay. Tell me how I can help with whatever you're making."

"You can pick out the cookie cutters if you want to. They're in there."

He pointed at what I'd assumed was a broom closet, but when I opened it, I was in for a surprise. The narrow closet was filled top to bottom with narrow drawers. I slid open the one labeled 'Christmas' and smiled. It was subdivided into little compartments, and each held a cookie cutter in a different, whimsical shape. I murmured, "This is the best thing ever." Then I pulled open a few more drawers and exclaimed, "I never in a million years would have guessed you had a cookie cutter collection! Can we make one of each?"

"It's best to limit it to one shape per cookie sheet, so they bake evenly. This recipe makes about four dozen cookies, depending on the size of the cutter, so maybe stick to three or four shapes."

"Do we get to decorate them after we bake them?"

"That's half the fun." He put on a pair of wire-framed glasses and began to carefully measure ingredients into a mixing bowl. Meanwhile, I went through every single drawer and commented on the treasures I found.

By the time I'd made my selections, Duke had finished mixing the sugar cookie dough. He put it in a zip-top bag, stuck it in the refrigerator, and told me, "That needs to chill for at least thirty minutes. An hour is even better."

"An hour! What are we supposed to do while we wait?"

"For one thing, we can plan how we want to decorate the cookies. Let's see what you picked out." I lined up my selections on the counter, and he said, "Really?"

I smiled at him. "I knew you'd say something about my choices." I'd picked out a Christmas tree, sled, Santa, and a six-inch-long dragon.

"I mean, it's Labor Day weekend…."

"And you've never in your life used those cookie cutters outside of the holiday season." He shook his head, and I said, "That's exactly why I picked them out. Go crazy, Duke! Make Christmas cookies in September with me."

I could tell he wanted to protest, but after a minute he said, "Okay. But how does the dragon fit in?"

"He's going to pull the sleigh."

Duke looked a little pained, but he said, "If that's what you want, then sure." He opened another cabinet and pulled out a couple of pastry bags, a plastic box containing about two dozen little metal cones that turned out to be tips for piping icing, and some red and green food coloring. "What color do you want for the dragons?"

I leaned my crutches against the counter, reached into the cabinet, and grabbed as many little plastic bottles of food coloring as I could. I handed them to Duke and exclaimed, "Oh my God, you have edible glitter! That's awesome!" The little bottle of iridescent powder was still in its packaging, and I asked, "Can I open it?"

"Yeah, but be careful. I've seen what happens when you and glitter get together."

I unwrapped it and asked, "What does it taste like?"

"I think it's flavorless, but I'm not sure. I've never used it. I only bought it because the lady at the baking supply shop insisted I give it a try. She was so excited about it, and I didn't have the heart to turn her down."

I unscrewed the lid, sprinkled a little glitter in my hand, and licked my palm. "It doesn't taste like anything, but I don't even care. Can you pick up a case of this for me next time you go to the baking store? I'll pay you back."

"Sure, but what are you going to do with it?"

"I'm going to put it on every single thing I eat!"

"Why?"

"Why not?"

He took off his glasses and returned them to their case as he said, "There's probably a limit to how much edible glitter one can safely consume."

"I'll take my chances if it means all my meals will sparkle from now on."

Duke looked at me for a moment, as if he was trying to figure out what to make of me, and then he said, "Let's go sit down while we wait for the dough to chill. The doctor told you to keep your foot elevated, and from what I've seen, you haven't been doing a lot of that."

When we got to the living room, I stretched out on the wood floor and put my wrapped ankle on the pale green couch. My roommate asked, "Wouldn't you be more comfortable if you sat on the sofa and put your foot on the coffee table?"

"God no. That's like, an April Fool's prank disguised as a couch. I'm pretty sure it's actually a big slab of concrete wrapped in minty green fabric. I don't know what compelled you to buy it."

He just shrugged and said, "It was on sale."

"That's no excuse." I shifted around a bit and told him, "If you want to do something while we're waiting, you can bring down one of the boxes in my room labeled 'entertainment'."

"I'm afraid to ask what's in them."

"All sort of things: games, sporting equipment, dress-up clothes, porn. There's no way of knowing what we'll end up with, so let's just commit to doing whatever's in the box you bring downstairs."

"I don't know about this idea."

"Come on, it's brilliant! In fact, I think I'm not even going to unpack them. That way, whenever I'm bored, I can just grab a box and surprise myself." He hesitated, and I said, "I was kidding about the porn. Just go grab a box. It'll be fun."

He muttered, "Yeah, alright," and I flashed him a big smile as he headed upstairs. Duke was back a minute later with a medium-sized cardboard box, and he said, "Half the boxes in your room are labeled 'entertainment'."

"I know. Open 'er up and let's see what we get to do for the next hour."

He sat on the couch with the box on the floor in front of him and carefully peeled back the packing tape. Then he lifted the flaps, stared inside it for a few moments, and finally said, "I have no idea what I'm looking at here."

I sat up and said, "Oh shit, did you end up with the porn?"

"I thought you said you were kidding about that."

"I lied." I leaned over and peered into the box. "Oh hey, you got crabs in my pants!"

"Excuse me?"

"Did you ever play that game 'ants in my pants' as a kid?"

"I've never even heard of it."

"Really? I have no idea how you missed it! The game came with a plastic pair of pants, and you had these little fake ants that you tried to flip into them."

"That's insane."

"I know! It was awesome. When I found that amazing planter at a garage sale, I knew I had to make my own version." The object in question was nearly two feet high and eighteen inches in diameter, and it looked like a pair of jeans with red sneakers sticking out at the bottom. I had no clue why anyone would ever want to plant anything in it, because it would look like a super creepy cut-in-half guy with a shrub growing from his midsection. But it was perfect for my game.

I asked Duke to position the planter across the room. After he centered it precisely in front of the glass doors that blocked off the fireplace, he removed a trio of weird little ceramic figurines from the mantel and relocated them to the dining table, which was just outside the kitchen. Even though I was curious about the figures, I didn't ask, because I knew my question would basically come out as, "What the fuck is up with those?"

We sat side-by-side on the couch, and I dumped about five dozen miniature beanbags onto the coffee table. Each was about an inch long and printed to look like a tiny crab. My roommate raised an eyebrow and asked, "Another garage sale find?"

"Actually, they're from a cool import store in Japantown. I have no idea what you're actually meant to do with them." I lined up a slingshot, a tiny plastic crossbow, and a pair of mini catapults beside the beanbags as I said, "We can trade off on the crab launchers. Oh, and you have to keep score for us, because I always lose track."

"Can't we just toss them in the bucket?"

"That's too easy. Plus, then we're basically just playing basketball. Or, you know, crabsketball. You can go first."

He held up a little catapult and asked, "Did you make this?" It consisted of a ten-inch wooden frame with a metal spoon held taught by rubber bands. When I nodded, he said, "You have a truly bizarre skill set, Quinn."

"You don't know the half of it. Go ahead, launch a crab." He loaded the device with a tiny beanbag and spent a long time lining up his shot with his brows knit in concentration. After a while, I said, "Just give it a try, Duke. If you miss, it's no big deal. You get about thirty more chances."

He lowered the catapult and shot me a look. "You're distracting me."

"You're taking too long."

"You didn't say there was a time limit."

"There's not."

"Then let me do this."

"Fine. Oh, you know what? We have to decide what we're playing for."

He said, "Loser cooks dinner for both of us, tomorrow night."

"That's a great idea, but I'm a little surprised you'd come up with that. I'd assume the thought of turning me loose in your pristine kitchen would make you all twitchy."

"Oh, it does, but I'm sure I'm going to lose." He positioned the catapult and launched the little orange crab, and it overshot the planter and bounced off the fireplace. "See?"

"But I suck at this, too." I loaded the plastic crossbow, aimed it at the ceiling, and fired. The mini-crab ricocheted and landed on the honey-colored wood floor.

"You did that on purpose to make me feel better," he said. "You didn't even aim at the pants!"

"I was trying to do a bank shot off the ceiling. The crossbow fires in a straight line, but you need an arc to get the crab up and into the slacks."

"That makes sense, actually." He picked up the slingshot and fired a crab at the ceiling, and it bounced off and landed in the planter. He yelled, "Yes!" But then he glanced at me and looked embarrassed.

"Don't hold back," I said as I sent a crab flying with one of the catapults and missed again. "If I ever get one in, I'm totally going to scream and yell and do some kind of awkward, one-footed victory dance."

Duke ended up beating me pretty easily, and it was totally worth losing just to see him smile. "That was fun," he said. "I had my doubts, but I really enjoyed myself."

"I did, too. So tell me, what do you want for dinner tomorrow night?"

"You don't have to cook for me. I only suggested it because I assumed I'd lose, and I wanted to make you dinner so you could stay off your sprained ankle."

"You can cook another night. Tomorrow, it's my turn. Or technically, later today, since it's past four a.m."

"Is it? Let's go make the cookies, unless you're too tired."

"I'm not at all," I said as I got up and reached for the crutches. "Normally, I'd be getting home about now and making myself a late dinner."

"Really? But the bars close at two."

"I usually stay until closing and then go home with someone." He frowned a little, and I said, "I know you don't approve."

"It's not that. I just don't get the casual sex thing, like I said before."

"Haven't you ever fucked someone just for fun, or just because you were horny, without it meaning anything?"

Duke shook his head. "There has to be more to it than that."

We reached the kitchen, and I turned to him and said, "There is. I get to feel another person's touch, and the warmth of his body, and his arms around me. It's short-lived, but I really need that. Don't you?"

He glanced at me with some sort of strong emotion in his eyes, then looked away and shook his head. There was something so vulnerable in that moment that I set aside my crutches and drew him into a hug. He went completely rigid with his arms at his sides and mumbled, "What are you doing?"

"Showing you what I mean." After a moment, he brought his hands up and rested them lightly on my lower back. I put my head on his chest and could feel his heart racing, and I asked, "Doesn't that feel good?"

He let go of me and took a step back. "Sure. But it's a huge leap from that to having sex with strangers." I sighed and let the subject drop.

Duke turned his attention to baking and was instantly in his element. He preheated the oven and placed a big, marble board on the kitchen island, then showed me how to roll out the dough. Once it was a uniform quarter-inch thick, he let me cut out the shapes. He had a method for everything, including the way he positioned the cutters to get the maximum number of cookies out of each slab of dough.

I realized after a while why he liked baking so much. There was a precision to it, and he needed that somehow. With cooking, you could just throw ingredients in a pot and wing it. Not so with baking. Everything was measured out, and I couldn't argue with the results. The cookies he pulled from the oven were perfect. They smelled like vanilla and made my mouth water, and when he let me try one, I exclaimed, "Holy shit, these are amazing!"

He seemed pleased by that. "I spent a long time perfecting the recipe. I think I've finally gotten it right where it should be."

"Do you bake other stuff too, or just sugar cookies?"

I ate another cookie from the cooling rack as he said, "I bake all kinds of things, but these are my favorite. They're a lot of fun to decorate." As I swiped a third cookie from the rack, he said, "But we won't get to do that if you eat them all."

"Just one more." I crammed a Santa into my mouth.

It took a lot of willpower not to Cookie Monster the rest of them while he whipped up a batch of icing, divided it into several bowls, and mixed in various colors. He loaded half a dozen piping bags, and then he put his glasses on, sat on one of the barstools, and carefully drew a green line around the edge of one of the little Christmas trees. I sat beside him and watched as he filled in the outline with icing. When he finished, the surface was perfectly smooth and shiny, and he said, "After that dries a bit, I'll go back with other colors and add details. Do you want to try decorating one?"

"For sure." I slid the cooling rack closer to me and picked up five piping bags at once, then swirled them over a couple of Christmas trees. A parchment-lined cookie sheet beneath the rack caught the excess icing, so I wasn't too worried about precision. Next, I reached for the edible glitter and made it snow. I picked up one of my masterpieces to show Duke and said, "Ta da!" Then I took a big bite and mumbled, around a mouthful of cookie, "It's even better with icing!"

He stared at me for a moment, then said, "That's not how you do it."

"That's how I do it. You go right ahead with your perfect little forest while I make a rainbow tornado."

"Try it my way, just once. You might like it. Here, let me show you how to hold the piping bag, so it doesn't all come flooding out the top." He twisted the top of the bag of green icing and said, "If you hold it like this it won't unravel, and you can control how much comes out by putting gentle pressure here." I watched him as he tried to guide my hands, and when he looked up at me, I smiled.

"Tell you what," I said, "I'll decorate the rest your way if you try my technique, just once. Make me a rainbow squiggle dragon, Duke."

"Alright." He picked up four of the piping bags and used both hands to lightly swirl them over one of the dragon cookies. Then he drew on a blue eye and a red smile and asked, "How's that?"

"Fantastic, but you forgot the glitter."

He sprinkled some carefully over his creation. "Happy now?"

I beamed at him and said, "Very."

When all the cookies were decorated, I arranged my favorites into a diorama. I lined up six dragons, propping them upright with stuff from around the kitchen, followed by a sled with Santa and a tree, layered so it looked like they were riding inside it. I snapped a picture with my phone and exclaimed, "Oh no! Look out, Rudolph dragon!" I leaned in and bit the lead dragon's head off, then said, "The horror! Santa can never make his deliveries now, not with a big giant eating up his team of trusty, mythical, sled-pulling creatures!"

Duke had been cleaning the kitchen while I conducted my shenanigans, and he said, "You're the strangest person I've ever met."

"I get that a lot."

He started to pack the remaining cookies into a plastic storage container, and I said, "You skipped a step."

"I did?" He looked around the kitchen in confusion.

I leaned over the island and held out a cookie. "You didn't eat anything."

"Oh. Well, no. I try not to eat sweets before bed."

"Have one cookie, Duke. Live a little." He hesitated, but then he took the green tree I offered him and seemed to savor it. That made me happy.

The sun was just beginning to rise by the time the kitchen was clean and everything was put away, and Duke said as he returned his glasses to their case, "You can have my bed tonight. I don't want you climbing up and down those stairs more than is necessary, or sleeping in that sad little blanket nest you made in your room. I'll sleep on the couch."

"You don't have to give up your bed. I can sleep on the couch."

"You won't, though. You'll sleep on the floor and complain about how uncomfortable the couch is."

"That's true, actually." I thought about it, then said, "Okay, here's what I propose, since I really do hate climbing the stairs with crutches and I don't want you sleeping on the torture couch: let's just share your bed. It'll be strictly platonic. The thing's ginormous, so you won't even know I'm there."

"I don't know...."

I grabbed the crutches and began to make my way down the hall to his room. "Come on, Duke. Pajama up and let's get some rest." After a moment, he followed me.

He spent a long time in the bathroom. When he finally emerged, he was wearing light blue pajama pants and a T-shirt so white it could cause snow blindness. He looked nervous, and after he slid under the blanket and turned off the light, he stared at the ceiling.

I said, "I had fun tonight, Duke. Thanks for letting me bake with you."

"You're welcome."

"Can we bake something else tomorrow night, after I make you dinner?"

"I meant it when I said you don't have to cook for me."

"I know, but I want to. I can cook while sitting down, so it won't hurt my ankle."

He glanced at me, then returned his gaze to the ceiling and said, "Okay."

He remained flat on his back, as close to the edge of the mattress as he could get without falling off. After a while, I asked, "How'd you get your nickname?"

"It's stupid."

"I'll trade you, story for story. Tell me why you're called Duke and I'll tell you why I'm named Quinn. Just so you know, mine's kind of depressing, so whatever you say will seem like the story of the year by comparison."

He rolled onto his side facing me. When he did that, his sleeve rode up a little, exposing the white bandage around his upper arm. "You go first."

"Okay. Well, you already heard how I was abandoned at a bus station at age three or so. My dad, Hatsuo Takahashi, was the pediatrician who took care of me after the police brought me to the hospital. He asked me what my name was, and I said something that sounded like Kin. He interpreted that as Quinn, so that's what he called me. I wasn't very verbal at that age, so I couldn't tell him what I really meant. I'd actually just been excited about a poster of a baby cat on the wall of the children's ward, and I'd been trying to say 'kitten'. But the closest I could get was kin. By the time I was old enough to explain that to him, my name was a done deal."

When I looked up at Duke, there was heartbreak in his eyes. He said softly, "I'm surprised you remember all of that."

"That day is seared into my memory. I can't recall much before then, including my real name. But I think that's a good thing."

"I'm so sorry about what happened to you."

"I didn't mean to depress you. It's actually funny in a way. I mean, I basically named myself kitten. How many people can say that?"

He watched me for a long moment before saying, "I gave myself the nickname when my parents moved and I transferred to a new school in the fourth grade. I got it from a book I was reading at the time. I should have given it some thought and come up with something better. Who knew it'd stick with me for life?"

"What book was it?"

"It was actually called Duke." He frowned a little, then admitted, "It was about a police dog."

I smiled at him and said, "You named yourself after a dog, and I'm named after a cat. Go figure."

"I can't believe I told you that. It's so stupid."

"No it's not. I think it's great."

"If you say so."

After a pause, I said softly, "Please tell me your real name."

"Promise me you'll never use it."

"I promise."

"It's Ulrich."

"What's so bad about that? It's a nice, strong name."

He just shrugged and rolled onto his back again. He was quiet for a long time before saying, "Somebody took a shot at me today. You asked why I seemed rattled earlier. That's the reason."

"Oh my God!"

"It's actually the third time that happened in the line of duty. This one though…it really got to me, because the shooter was just a kid, the younger brother of the boy who cut my arm."

I whispered, "Was anyone hurt?"

"No. My partner was able to disarm the shooter, and both boys are in custody, so they can't hurt themselves or anyone else. I just didn't see it coming, and maybe that's why I'm having a hard time with it. I thought we were making a routine stop to help a couple of homeless kids. Next thing I knew, a bullet was sailing past my head. I just don't understand the world we live in sometimes."

"I'm so glad you're okay."

He fell silent again. It was a few minutes before he said, "You have an odd effect on me. Normally, I'm nowhere near this talkative. In fact, you're one of the only people outside of my family who knows my real name."

"I'm glad you trust me enough to open up to me."

"That's the other thing. I usually have a hard time trusting people. But you just seem to put it all out there, and…I don't know. You strike me as very genuine, like you always show people exactly who you are, and that puts me at ease, somehow." He shook his head and added, "I'm doing a terrible job explaining it."

"Actually," I said, "that's one of the nicest things anyone's ever said to me."

Chapter Three

"Well, damn. That's not pretty."

I said that to no one in particular as I grimaced and tossed aside the stretchy bandage that the E.R. doctor had wrapped around my injury. My foot and ankle were twice as swollen and bruised as the day before and had stiffened up a lot during the night. Totally failing to stay off my feet really hadn't been a good call.

I had a hard time sitting still, but by the look of things, I was going to have to spend the day on my ass with my foot packed in ice. That was as much for my dance troupe's sake as my own. I still hadn't told any of them I'd hurt myself. I wanted to wait until after the long weekend so I could give them some good news about how quickly I was recovering. But that would only happen if I gave myself a chance to heal.

I swung my legs out of Duke's bed, then got to my feet with the aid of my crutches and made my way to the restroom. After that, I went in search of my roommate. His truck was in the garage, so I figured he hadn't gone far.

Eventually, I spotted him outside. There was a metal shed at the back of the fairly narrow but long backyard, and its double doors were open, revealing a home gym. Duke stood on the cement slab in front of it, glistening with sweat and doing a rapid series of curls with a large set of dumbbells. I brewed some coffee while he kept going and going. No wonder he was so ripped.

When the coffee was ready, I sat on the kitchen island with my mug and the container of sugar cookies and watched him like a TV show. When he finally finished a thousand sets of curls (that was what it seemed like, anyway), he held the dumbbells at his sides and started to do a series of lunges. His back was to me, and I murmured, "Sweet baby Jesus with a lobster bib, will you look at that ass!" The form-fitting, dark blue shorts he was wearing left little to the imagination. Same with his white tank top, which showed off his huge arms and shoulders.

When I realized I was both talking to myself and totally ogling my new roommate, I slid off the kitchen island and tried to find something else to do. Yes, he was sexy and putting all kinds of dirty thoughts in my mind, but come on. I couldn't sleep with Duke and expect to go on living with him. It would be beyond awkward for both of us.

Still though, I snuck another look after I filled a big, zip-top bag with ice and muttered, "Damn." I tore my attention away from Duke and started to assemble a survival kit for myself. It included the pot of coffee, the container of cookies, a box of cereal, the icepack, a box of snack cakes, a half-dozen bananas, a six-pack of soda, a loaf of bread, and a jar of peanut butter. Because I also had to somehow manage the crutches, all of that was a little problematic.

Duke came inside through the kitchen door a minute later. He was drying his face with a towel that was draped around his neck, and he stopped in his tracks and asked, "What are you doing?"

"Laying in supplies."

"Why?"

"Because I need to stay off my sprained ankle today," I said, "so I'm trying to take everything with me that I'll need for the next couple of hours."

"Where are you going?"

"My room. The kitchen and dining room are too uncomfortable for long-term nesting, and when I moved in, you told me you don't want me to eat in the living room."

He started taking things from me and said, "I usually don't want anyone eating in there, but I'll make an exception today. Please don't attempt the stairs while I'm out."

I was disappointed to hear he wouldn't be keeping me company. "Are you going to work?"

He shook his head. "I was scheduled for this evening, but the department requires us to take a mental health day any time we're involved in a situation like last night."

"Do they really think one day off will make a difference?"

"I could have taken a few more days. One is the minimum."

He carried my supplies into the living room and arranged them on the coffee table, then got a sheet and draped it over the couch. While I attempted to settle in, I noticed the figurines were back on the mantel. There were two other clusters around the living room. All were around four inches tall and depicted children in traditional German clothing. I'd resisted the night before, but now I had to ask. "What's up with the creepy ceramic kids?"

"The Hummel figures were gifts from my grandmother."

"They really don't strike me as your taste."

"They're not. I hate them."

"Then why are they prominently displayed in your living room?"

"Because my parents drop by unannounced sometimes, and they expect to see them."

I halted my futile attempt at getting comfortable on the couch and exclaimed, "Are you shitting me?"

"Excuse me?"

"You live with horrible little ceramic people that you hate, just because your parents expect to see them? What kind of bullshit is that?"

"The none-of-your-business kind."

"It's totally my business. I have to live with those cherubic nightmares too, you know."

"Nobody said you had to like them."

"If they mean so much to your parents, why don't you send 'em home with them next time they drop by?"

"Like I said, they were gifts from my grandmother, and that would be disrespectful."

"Is your grandmother off her rocker? I mean, seriously, who gives shit like that to a guy in his twenties?"

"They're collector items, and some of them are worth a fair amount of money. She thought she was doing a good thing by giving them to me."

"But you hate them."

"Yeah."

"How much money are we talking here, thousands of dollars apiece?"

"Not that much." He gestured at one of them, which featured a boy and girl sitting around being really boring, and said, "This one's the most expensive, and it's worth maybe three hundred bucks. The rest are about one to two hundred dollars each."

"Are you serious about hating them, or are you just saying that because it would seem dorky to admit you secretly liked them?"

"I absolutely despise them."

"Then sell them to me, Duke. I'll pay you three thousand dollars for the lot of them, since they might have appreciated in value over time. Your family can't get mad at you for that. It's just good business!"

He raised an eyebrow and asked, "Do you really have three grand?"

"Yup."

"How?"

"My parents give me an extremely generous check every birthday and Christmas. I usually sock half of it away for a rainy day."

"If you have that kind of money, why do you shop at garage sales?"

"Because they're super fun and awesome and you never know what you'll find. So, can I buy them?"

"No."

"Why not?"

"For one thing, it's a waste of money. You could buy a used car for that."

"If I wanted a car, I would have bought one a long time ago," I said. "Out of curiosity, is your grandmother still adding to your collection? In a few years, will the house be full to the rafters with those mini horror-shows?"

"No. She stopped giving them to me four years ago."

"How come?"

"Because I came out to my family, and my grandmother disowned me."

"I'm sorry."

He tried to play it off, but didn't really succeed. "I kind of expected it."

"Given that, doesn't it hurt to look at those statues?"

He broke eye contact and muttered, "Every time."

"Then they have to go!"

"I can't get rid of them."

"But I can if you sell them to me."

"I don't have time for this discussion right now." He left the living room and returned a minute later with a towel, blanket, all the pillows from his bed, and the Ace bandage, and he asked, "Do you want me to rewrap your ankle for you?" When I nodded, he deposited the pillows on the couch, knelt down, and quickly and efficiently wound the stretchy fabric around my left foot. I propped it up on some pillows, and he folded a towel around the bag of ice and positioned it against my ankle. "While I'm in the shower, think about anything you might want from around the house, and I'll bring it to you before I take off."

"Where are you going?"

"Church."

"Seriously?"

He glanced at me and asked, "Is that really so hard to believe?"

"What denomination are you?"

"Lutheran."

"And what do the Lutherans have to say about the fact that you're gay?"

"I don't have time for that conversation either, Quinn."

He started to leave the room, and I called after him, "Thanks for helping me."

He murmured, "Welcome," and disappeared down the hall.

When he returned to the living room about fifteen minutes later, his short hair was damp, he'd shaved, and he was wearing a crisp, white shirt with a pearl gray suit and tie. "Wow," I said, "you clean up good."

He looked embarrassed as he muttered, "Thanks."

"How long will you be gone?"

"About three hours. I always go to lunch with my parents after the service. What can I bring you before I take off?" I told him what I wanted, and he jogged upstairs. When he returned a minute later, he placed my backpack and a moving box beside the couch and handed me a stuffed animal. But instead of rushing out the door, he paused and asked, "Are you going to be alright?"

"Why do you look so concerned?"

"You're doing this puppy-dog eyes thing, and it's making me feel bad about leaving you all alone."

"I'll be fine. I have everything I need."

"Are you sure? I could call my parents and tell them I can't make it this week."

Asking him to stay seemed way too needy, even though I wanted that more than anything. I pulled up a smile and said, "Don't worry about me. I'll probably just take a nap while you're gone. We really didn't get much sleep last night."

Duke hesitated, but then he said, "Alright. See you soon." He cut through the kitchen, grabbed his glasses, and left by the door to the garage.

Once he was gone, I pulled my backpack closer to me, found my checkbook, and wrote out a check for three thousand dollars, payable to my roommate. Then I limped across the room, put it on the mantel, and picked up two of the sicky-sweet figurines. "Sorry dudes," I told the little boys in brown shorts, one of whom was hanging out with a pair of goats, "I need to evict you, but don't worry. You'll find a nice new home, probably with some old lady and a bunch of cats. You make my roommate sad, and I just can't let you keep doing that. He's going to end up royally pissed off at me for this, but it's worth it if he's happier in the long run."

I carried them to the couch and unpacked the box I'd asked Duke to bring downstairs, then carefully wrapped the Hummels in the bubble wrap I'd removed from my novelty bar glass collection. Once all twelve statuettes were packed up, I sent a quick text. As soon as I got a reply, I pulled up Uber and told the boxed-up figurines, "You're going for a ride, kids. But never fear, there's a kind and lovely person waiting for you at your destination."

The driver arrived within a few minutes. She tried to tell me she wasn't in the parcel delivery business. Eventually though, I sent her off with the box, an address, and a fat tip, after convincing her I wasn't actually trying to smuggle contraband or conduct the world's clumsiest drug deal.

Then I returned to the couch, draped the icepack over my ankle, and started to worry. I'd overstepped. I knew that. Was Duke going to be angry with me, or furious? It'd definitely be one or the other.

But I honestly believed I'd done the right thing. Once he got over the fact that I'd bought and disposed of them without his permission, I was sure he'd be glad to be rid of the much-hated knickknacks. In the short term though, I knew there'd be hell to pay.

*****

Almost exactly three hours after he left, Duke pulled into the garage. I'd known he was coming, because he'd texted to ask if I wanted him to pick up anything on the way home. What a nice guy. Too bad I was about to cement my spot in the number one position on his shit list.

He came in through the door connecting the garage and the kitchen, then stepped into the living room and said, "Hey. How are you?"

"Hey yourself. I'm fine."

"That's good. I'm going to change. See you in a minute." He headed to his bedroom.

Duke soon returned, dressed in jeans, sneakers, and a white T-shirt. He was wearing his glasses and carrying a paperback, and he said, "I'm going to read on the patio for a while. I have my phone with me, so if you need anything, text me instead of getting up."

In an effort to be good and help my injury heal, I was sprawled out with my ankle elevated on the back of the couch. I was also holding my breath and waiting for Duke to notice the missing Hummels. But instead, his attention was riveted on the coffee table, where food, cans, and wrappers competed for space with my barware collection.

He just couldn't let it go, either. Duke put down the book and started picking up my trash, even though I told him he should just bring me a garbage bag. When he got to the empty cereal box, he glanced at me and asked, "Did you actually eat this whole thing?" I nodded, and he said, "Without milk?"

"That's how I always eat it. Milk just makes it soggy."

He stuffed some snack cake wrappers in the empty box and asked, "How do you stay so thin with these eating habits?"

"By dancing six hours a day on average, six days a week, and by having the metabolism of a hummingbird."

"That makes sense, actually. Where do you want these bar glasses, the kitchen or your room?"

"The kitchen for now, though I propose setting up a tiki bar in a corner of the living room. I didn't have enough space in my old apartment or in my tiny studio in New York, so my dreams of tiki bar nirvana have always gone unfulfilled. But we could totally fit one in here."

"Why a tiki bar? Why not a regular bar?"

"I can really only answer that with: why a regular bar and not a tiki bar?"

He said, "Well, for starters, we're not exactly in Hawaii."

"But we can pretend. It'd be so fun! We could theme out the whole room with bamboo furniture, tropical plants, tiki torches—"

"We are *not* lighting torches in here."

"I never said we had to light them. In fact, I bet I could find some cool battery-operated ones with plastic fire, like the Statue of Liberty torch."

Duke straightened up with his armload of trash and said, "The Statue of Liberty torch isn't made of plastic."

"The one I got when I visited Liberty Island is. And you know what I mean. I'd buy us torches with a simulated flame, not ones that would burn this place to the ground. I bet I can find them online."

I pulled my phone from the pocket of my T-shirt and started searching for electric tiki torches, and Duke said, "You know, I never actually signed off on a Hawaiian living room."

"I know, but I really want some fake tiki torches now. Even if you nix the downstairs transformation, I can still put them in my room."

He looked like he wanted to offer a rebuttal to that idea, but after a beat, he said, "I'm going to throw this away and be right back for your barware. Since your cabinets are full already, I'll see about fitting them in with my glasses." I murmured a thank you and flipped to another webpage.

Duke returned to the living room a minute later and said, "Okay, what did you do with them?" Since I was totally wrapped up in my search for the perfect tiki torches, I looked up at my roommate in confusion. I'd temporarily forgotten about my Hummel hijacking, but when he walked over to the empty mantel, it all came back to me. He picked up the check and asked, "What is this?"

I slipped the phone in my pocket and said, "Payment in full for your figurine collection."

"I never agreed to that, Quinn. Put them back."

"I can't do that."

"Why not?"

"Because they're not here anymore."

"You're still in your pajamas, so you obviously didn't take them anywhere. Did you hide them in your room? Just tell me where they are and I'll go get them."

"I mean they're literally not here. I put them in a car and sent them away."

He knit his brows and said, "You'd better be kidding."

"Before you start yelling at me, please remember I was only trying to help. You said you hated those things, and they made you sad every time you looked at them. Now they're gone, so they can't keep hurting you. I know you're worried about your parents' reaction, but maybe you can use the money to pay down the loan they gave you. That way, they'll see you made a smart business decision by selling them. In fact, you totally turned a profit. They should be proud of you!"

His voice was a low growl when he said, "I never agreed to sell them."

"I know. But—"

He turned and headed for the garage. "Come on, we're going to go get them. Right now."

I hadn't anticipated that. "Are you sure, Duke? Just stop and think about it for a minute."

"Now."

That single syllable left absolutely no room for argument. I grabbed my crutches and backpack and hurried after him. He already had the engine running when I reached the garage. I put the crutches in the bed of his white pickup truck, and he began backing out of the garage the moment I closed the passenger door behind me.

He asked, "Where am I going?" It was equal parts growl and question. I gave him directions as I fastened my seatbelt.

The silence in the cab of the truck weighed on me like a ton of bricks. Duke ground his teeth and kept his eyes on the road. After a few minutes, I couldn't take it anymore and blurted, "I'm sorry, Duke. I was only trying to help."

"You keep saying that, as if it somehow excuses your actions. But I didn't want or ask for your help, Quinn." His voice was gravel.

"But you need it desperately!" I was surprised by the anger welling up in me, and even though I knew I was totally at fault, I snapped, "I mean, how can anyone live like you do, in your perfect, pristine home, with your perfect, pristine life, surrounded by shit you don't even like, just because you want your parents to think you're a perfect son?"

He hissed, "You need to stop talking."

"Fucking make me! Did I overstep? Yes. But do you know why I did it? Because I care about you, Duke! You told me those stupid knickknacks made you sad, and that broke my heart. So I packed that shit up and got rid of it, after paying you a small fortune for it, by the way! I knew you'd be pissed, but I did it anyway, because I wanted to make your life better."

"You want to make my life better? Stop interfering in it!"

"Fine!"

We both spent the rest of the fifteen-minute drive across town fuming. When he finally pulled into the alley behind the address I'd given him, he muttered, "What the hell are we doing at an old fire station?"

"It's where I exiled your precious doll collection," I muttered as I fished around in my backpack, then jammed a flip flop onto my swollen left foot.

"They're not dolls!"

"They might as well be!" I put on my other shoe, hopped out of the truck with my backpack, and grabbed my crutches. Then I stomped to the back door as much as I could, given the fact that I only had one foot to work with.

After a minute, my new friend Darwin answered my knock. He was a lot younger than me, but he was also twice as mature, so I figured it balanced itself out. As soon as he saw me, he threw his arms around my neck and said, "You're amazing! I just got done looking up the prices of those figurines you sent over for the silent auction, and they're going to bring in a ton of money for the shelter!" Then he held me at arms' length and looked me over as he asked, "What happened? Your foot's enormous."

"Isn't it pretty? I sprained it while running after a Chihuahua." He looked a little worried as he glanced over my shoulder, and I said, "That's Duke, my new roommate. He's usually not quite so homicidal-looking."

Duke said, "Can I speak to you for a moment in private, Quinn?"

I glanced back at him, and Darwin said, "Just come on in whenever you're done. I'll leave the door unlocked." He took another look at my giant, pissed off roommate, then disappeared into the building.

I turned to Duke as he asked, "What is this place?"

"A transition shelter for homeless LGBT teens and young adults, founded by my friend Nana Dombruso. It's called Rainbow Roost, and it's opening at the end of the month."

"They're holding an auction?"

I nodded. "Nana and an investor friend of hers have been pouring a ton of their own money into this place, so a few people decided to hold a fundraiser to offset some of the operating costs."

"Is that boy one of the residents?"

"No, Darwin's a volunteer. Although, if it wasn't for Nana, he might have ended up in a place like this. His family won't accept the fact that he's transgender, so Nana took him in. He's dating her great-grandson."

Duke sighed and said, "I can't take the Hummels back now. That kid's so excited about them."

"Just let them go, Duke. If your parents complain about you selling them, so what? They'll get over it, and you'll get to enjoy a Hummel-free home."

"You don't know my parents."

There was something in his tone, something I'd never heard from him, and I whispered, "Do they hurt you?"

"Nobody hurts me. Not anymore."

Not anymore. Oh God. I stammered, "I totally fucked up. I'll go inside and get the figurines back. I didn't mean to make trouble between you and your family."

After a pause, he said, "No, don't. Let the shelter have them."

"What about your parents?"

"I'll deal with them."

"I'm sorry."

"No, see, it doesn't work that way. You can't do things like this and expect to apologize and make it all better, Quinn."

"I don't know what else to say."

"Me neither. All I know is, I can't live with someone who constantly brings chaos into my life. I really can't. You've been my roommate for *two days*, and in that time, you made me drive all over the city of Oakland looking for a germ-ridden mattress, got drunk, trashed my bedroom, and turned my living room into a garbage dump. Then for an encore, you gave away my family heirlooms without my permission!"

"I'm a lot to take. I know that," I said. "But you wanted someone to shake up your life, and guess what? You got it!"

"Who says I wanted that?"

"You did, by allowing me to be your roommate!"

He exclaimed, "That's crazy!'

"Oh no it isn't. You knew exactly what I was like before you rented that room to me. You'd met me on two separate occasions, when I was every bit the hot mess I am now. Plus, your former roommate Cole told you exactly what you were getting yourself into! He spent plenty of time at my old apartment before he married my roommate. But despite the stories and witnessing Hurricane Quinn for yourself, you went ahead and opened your door, and said, 'Come on in! Come live in my perfect home, and fucking turn it upside down!' And gee, here's a surprise! I turned out to be exactly as advertised!"

"Maybe I just didn't think it through."

"Oh no, I don't buy that for a minute," I said. "You're the kind of person who thinks *everything* through. There's no other explanation for renting that room to me, except this: you wanted some chaos in your life."

"I let you move in despite that, not because of it!"

I knit my brows and asked, "Why would you do that? Why would you let someone like me into your home?"

"I had my reasons. Can your friend drive you home? I have to go."

"Yeah but...I don't understand. What reasons?"

"It doesn't matter. I made a mistake. You and I are one hundred percent incompatible, and I think you need to find a new place to live."

He turned and started to leave, but I said, "I'll find another apartment if you really want me to, but I call bullshit."

He stopped a few feet from his truck and turned to me. "What does that mean?"

"Remember early this morning, Duke? We baked together and had fun, and we talked and opened up to each other. That proves we're not totally incompatible, not by a long shot. We're just different." I took a couple steps toward him on my crutches and said, "Or is that what you're really running from? Not the bad stuff, but the good? I know I'm driving you nuts, but I also know you've been letting me in these last two days, maybe more than you'd intended, and I bet that's really uncomfortable for someone like you."

He crossed his arms over his chest. "Someone like me? You say that as if you know me, but you don't."

"I don't pretend to know you well," I said. "But I know a little. The walls you've built around yourself are way too big to miss."

"Actually, you know what? You know plenty about me. You met me beforehand too, and you spent time with Cole, as you said. I'm sure you heard stories about his uptight, boring, anal retentive roommate. And yet you still decided to move in with me. So you shouldn't be surprised that I too turned out to be exactly as advertised, and that this is absolutely not going to work out."

He got in his truck and drove away, and I sighed as I watched him go. Then I went into the former fire station and locked the door behind me. Darwin was sitting at a long table, cataloging what were probably auction items on a beat-up old laptop, and he asked, "Are you okay? I kind of accidentally heard all of that." He pushed his long, black bangs out of his eyes and pointed at the open transom above the back door.

"Yeah. Day two with my new roommate. It's going great, obviously." I sat on the stool beside him and looked around. "Are you here all by yourself?"

He nodded. "My boyfriend and his family are spending the long weekend at the beach. I needed a little time to myself, so I decided to come back early."

"Are you nervous about Thursday?" He'd been saving for years and was finally scheduled for top surgery.

He said, "The whole thing's freaking me out. Don't tell anyone I said that, though."

"Why not?"

"Because I don't want people to think I'm having second thoughts. I'm really not. I've known I wanted this since puberty. But I've never had surgery of any kind before or stayed in a hospital, and it's frightening. I keep thinking, what if something goes wrong? I know that's irrational. I've read the statistics and countless case studies, so I know there's every chance I'll breeze through this. But...."

"But you're still scared."

"Yeah."

I said, "Instead of telling you what you already know, which is that you're going to be fine, I'll tell you this instead: it's perfectly normal to worry. Hell, I've raised it to an art form. If you want some pointers on how to totally work yourself into a panic for no real reason, then I'm your man."

He grinned at that and pulled his sagging black cardigan higher up on his skinny shoulder. "You don't strike me as a worrier. Just the opposite. It seems like you take everything in stride."

"It's an illusion. Good to know I'm pulling it off."

"So, not to change the subject, which of course means I'm totally changing the subject, but what are you going to do about your new roommate?"

"I have absolutely no idea."

"Well, while you figure it out, you can keep me company."

"You sure? You said you wanted some time to yourself."

Darwin slid off the barstool and said, "I did, at first. But I've been rattling around on my own since last night, and I've started to regret my self-imposed exile. So right now, what I want is to talk to you, and a huge cup of tea. Would you like some?"

"Sure. Can I help you make it?"

"I think you should stay off that ankle. I'll be right back." He went into the adjoining stainless steel kitchen, which had been opened up in the extensive renovations and was now separated from the living area by a long counter. The ground floor had housed fire trucks at one time, but now clusters of jewel-toned chairs and couches, a foosball and pool table, a big TV, and all sorts of other amusements awaited the teens who would soon call the shelter home. Around all four brick walls, a five-foot-wide rainbow meandered like a river, while three brass poles and a row of lockers kept the fire station's history alive.

Darwin soon rejoined me with two steaming mugs of tea and handed me one of them. He then wrapped both hands around his cup and inhaled deeply. "Doesn't that smell amazing? It's called rooibos tea, and it's from South Africa. I'm kind of infatuated with it."

I grinned and said, "Sometimes I have to remind myself you're only nineteen. Do people call you an old soul a lot?"

"All the time." He took a sip of tea and let out a long, "Ahhhhh." Then he gestured at the Hummel figures, which were clustered on the center of the table, and said, "You know, I'll get over it if you return those to Duke. You didn't really take them without his permission, did you?"

"Yes and no. I left him a check for three grand, which is more than fair market value, and I only got rid of them because he told me he hated them and that they made him sad. They were gifts from his bigoted grandmother, who disowned him when he came out." I took a sip of tea, which pretty much just tasted like tea and could have used a ton of sugar, then said, "You really did hear everything, didn't you?"

"You guys weren't exactly quiet."

"I'm kind of glad you overheard us, because now you can help me decide what to do. Duke was furious that I got rid of them, but then he also decided to leave them here. He really didn't have to do that. So, do I take them back? I can find a lot more stuff for the auction, that part's not a problem."

"You should ask him about it later, after he's calmed down a bit. The auction's almost three weeks away, so it's not like we need to know what to do with them right this minute."

"That's true." I took another sip of tea, then said, "Oh man, I just realized we were talking about you, and you must have overheard that, too. Sorry."

"Don't apologize. That actually made me happy."

"How come?"

"Because someone who didn't know me referred to me as a boy without prompting."

"Well, yeah. Doesn't everyone?"

"Nope. Sometimes people treat me like a freak, or ask questions like, 'What are you?' I usually answer that by telling them I'm a human being who shouldn't have to explain myself to nosy strangers."

"It sucks that people have to be so rude."

"I've gotten used to it. Mostly." He took another sip of tea and asked, "Are you alright, Quinn?"

"Sure. Why wouldn't I be?"

"That was a pretty major argument between you and your new roommate, and you seem distracted."

"I knew it'd be challenging to live with Duke, but I didn't expect it to come to a head quite that fast. He actually told me to find a new place to live! That's pretty bad, after just two days."

"Why'd you decide to rent a room from him? He said you knew what he was like before you moved in, so you must have known there'd be conflict."

I gave my standard answer. "Compared to my old apartment, it was a bigger room for less money…." After a moment, I glanced at Darwin and admitted, "Actually, none of that would really have been worth the hassle of moving. I could have just found a new roommate when River moved in with Cole and stayed where I was, but I felt like Duke needed me. I know that's crazy, because I also knew I was going to frustrate him and get on his nerves. But there's just something about him. He's so serious and controlled, all the time, and I just couldn't leave that alone. I guess I'm like those annoying tourists you always see buzzing around the guards at Buckingham Palace, trying to get them to crack a smile. Not that I'm trying to be annoying. He just didn't seem happy to me, and I wanted to do something about that." I sighed and took a sip of tea, which really could have used a big shot of brandy along with the sugar, and added, "But he doesn't want my help. He made that abundantly clear to me."

"It sounds like you care about him."

"I do. There's a great guy under that frown. And I don't want to give the impression I'm trying to fix him, because he's not broken. I just want to help him enjoy life a bit, and to act like a twenty-seven-year-old for once."

Darwin said, "Okay, I totally see your point. I would have guessed he was much older than that, not based on the way he looks, but because of how he comes across. It seems to me like our twenties should be all about having fun, taking risks, and discovering who we are." He grinned a little and said, "That's my theory, anyway. But then, I've never acted my age, so I don't know why I expect other people to."

"Meanwhile, I feel like I'm aging in reverse. I spent my childhood and teen years completely focused on studying ballet. And now, ever since I moved back to California, I've basically been acting like a kid."

"Except for the part where you're endlessly rehearsing for your upcoming show."

"That's fun, though."

"It must be nice to love what you do."

"What do you see yourself doing down the road, Darwin?"

"I don't know, actually. I spent the last few years working constantly and trying to save enough money for top surgery, so my outside would match my inside. I guess I never really thought about any long-term goals beyond that. I mean, college was always in the back of my mind, and maybe I'll look into that now, but I'm not sure what I'll study." He glanced at the array of items on the table beside us and said, "I can tell you what my short-term goal is, though: to rake in huge barrels of cash for the shelter."

I took another sip of tea, then said, "This looks like a big job. Tell me how I can help."

"I don't even know what to do here. The volunteers have done an amazing job collecting donations, but it's all so random. Like, here's a bottle of lotion from a salon. Okay, great, but who's going to bid on that? I know I can put it with, let's say, these scented candles and that gift certificate for a manicure and call it a spa gift basket or something, but that's not very interesting."

I started gathering items from around the table and clustering them together. "But if you put the lotion and candles with this bottle of wine, the silk scarf, and that gift certificate to a bed and breakfast, then add in a couple cheap novelty items like a feather boa and a set of furry handcuffs, suddenly it becomes 'Pauline's Pleasure Package'. Or, you know, whatever. It doesn't have to be sexy. But let's just have fun with it."

"That's exactly what we need to do! Can you stay for a while and help me come up with a few more themes?"

"Absolutely. I'm yours for the next four hours. Then I need to get some groceries and go home to cook dinner for my roommate, but I can come back tomorrow and help some more."

"Um…I'm pretty sure he's not speaking to you right now. So, why are you cooking for him?"

"Because I told him I would, and I always keep my promises."

*****

I returned home late that afternoon with two bags of groceries and a little white flag that I'd fashioned out of a straw and an inside-out snack cake wrapper. Duke was nowhere to be seen when I stuck my head in the front door and looked around. I turned and waved at Darwin with one of my crutches. His rusty beater was idling at the curb, and he waved before pulling away. Then I went in search of my roommate.

As I cut through the living room, I noticed it was back to its usual immaculate condition. Of course. I put the grocery sacks on the kitchen counter and looked around a bit. Duke's truck was in the garage, and his bedroom door was closed. I decided it was best not to disturb him just yet.

Instead, I got busy making dinner. I doubted he had any interest in dining with me, but I was still going to follow through. By the time he appeared in the kitchen doorway half an hour later, my rice cooker was going and sheets of nori were soaking, and I was slicing vegetables into tidy matchsticks.

I glanced at Duke when he said, "We need to talk."

I put down my knife and swiveled to face him on the barstool. "I know."

He was clearly uncomfortable, and he fidgeted as he said, "I apologize for yelling at you. I usually pride myself on my ability to control my temper. I don't know what's wrong with me lately."

"You don't have to apologize. I shouldn't have interfered in your life like that. For what it's worth, I hope you give me another chance, because I really don't want to move out."

"I don't want you to either, but we need some ground rules," he said. "Well, pretty much just one: if you think you're overstepping, you probably are, so don't do it."

"I'll definitely agree to that."

"Okay, good."

"Just so you know, Darwin has no problem whatsoever with returning the statues if you want them."

"I've been thinking about it, and I'm glad they're gone, but that should have been my choice."

"You're absolutely right." An awkward silence descended on us, and Duke glanced at the assortment of bowls, sauces, and ingredients on the kitchen island. After a moment, I asked, "Will you have dinner with me? I know I'm not your favorite person right now, but I told you I'd cook for you, and I want to make good on that."

He hesitated for a moment, then said, "I don't know. I just...."

"I get it. I can be a total pain sometimes, and I don't think I'd want to spend time with me either."

"Don't say that. You thought you were helping me."

"But you didn't want help. I know I keep saying it, and you're right that it doesn't change anything, but I really am sorry, Duke."

After another pause, he pulled out the second barstool and sat down beside me, and then he said, "Maybe this is exactly what we need, a nice, quiet meal together with no drama."

"Agreed. I give you the one hundred percent drama-free guarantee." I smiled and added, "For this meal, anyway. I mean, come on. We both know I can't sustain that forever."

He grinned a little, and as I went back to reducing carrots to matchsticks, he asked, "Are you making sushi?"

"Yup."

"I've never had it before, and I have to be honest, I'm not on board with the whole raw fish thing." Duke wrinkled his nose, just a little.

"Well, good news: I'm not using raw fish. I'm making shrimp tempura sushi, veggie tempura sushi, Las Vegas rolls, and California rolls. So, in order, we're talking fried shrimp, vegetables, smoked salmon, and cooked crab meat."

"That's not so bad." He watched me for a minute, then said, "I'd offer to help, but I have no idea how to make sushi."

"It's okay, I've got this. The nice thing is, it's more assembly than cooking, aside from the tempura shrimp and veggies, but they're easy. I'm not much of a cook."

"You really look like you know what you're doing. I assume your parents taught you."

I shook my head. "My parents were both doctors with busy schedules, so if we wanted sushi, we'd go out. They're retired now, and my dad has actually developed a love of cooking in the last few years, but that wasn't the case when I was a kid. My mom, meanwhile, has pretty much evolved into an Asian version of Georgia O'Keeffe. They're both awesome."

"Did they retire young?"

"No, they're seventy-two and seventy-four, and they both retired about five years ago. They were in their fifties when they adopted me. Now my brothers are in their fifties, and my nieces and nephews are my age or older. It's all a bit skewed."

As I emptied the rice cooker and spread out the rice to cool on a baking sheet, he asked, "If you didn't learn it from them, how'd you get to be an expert at sushi-making?"

"I wish I was an expert. Actually, I just learned a bit through observation. There was this fantastic sushi restaurant right down the street from my apartment in the East Village, one of those places with the little boats. Since I ate there three or four nights a week, the sushi chefs and I got to be friends, and I'd hang out, drink sake, and visit with them while they worked."

"Little boats? I have no idea what that means."

"There was a fake river running through the restaurant, and all the patrons would sit at long counters and wait for the little wooden boats to go by with their sushi cargo. When you saw a type of sushi you wanted, you picked it up off the boat and ate it."

Duke said, "You have to be making that up."

"Nope. It's a real thing."

"There's no way." I just grinned and kept preparing my ingredients.

When I reached the step of pulling a softened sheet of nori out of the pan of water, Duke grimaced and said, "I'm sorry. I know you're going to a lot of trouble here, but I can't eat that. I'm fighting my gag reflex just thinking about it."

Instead of arguing with him, I assembled a Las Vegas roll, dipped it in tempura batter and fried it in hot oil. After I sliced it into bite-size pieces, I slid the plate over to him and said, "Just try one piece. That's all I ask."

He raised a skeptical eyebrow at me. "That's not sushi."

"Of course it is."

"You put cream cheese and smoked salmon in it, and then you cooked it. It's basically a deep-fried bagel with seaweed. You're trying to invent something I won't think is disgusting, just so I'll admit sushi's not bad."

"I swear you can buy this at most sushi restaurants. Granted, Las Vegas rolls were invented in the U.S., but they caught on all over, even Japan. At least, that's what I've heard. Just try it."

"I'll try one piece, but you have to promise not to be offended if I spit it out."

I picked up a pair of chopsticks, plucked the lovely, crunchy end piece off the plate, and held it up for him. You would have thought I was feeding him an earthworm. He held his breath and wrinkled his nose, then gingerly took the morsel in his mouth.

The moment he bit down, his expression totally transformed. His eyes went wide, and he exclaimed around a mouthful of yummy deliciousness, "That's the best thing I've ever tasted!"

I whooped triumphantly, then jumped up on my good leg and did a fist-pumping victory dance. He chuckled at that, and I exclaimed, "I told you! Didn't I tell you?"

"You were right, and I'm absolutely shocked." He picked up another piece with his hand and said, "I know it's rude to eat with my fingers, but I can't use chopsticks." He tossed it in his mouth, and his eyes rolled back in his head. "Oh man, it's *so good*." He picked up the next piece and said, "I admit it, I was wrong. Will you make the other kinds, too? I can't wait to try them."

"Absolutely."

I got to work assembling the California rolls, which might have been a bit run-of-the-mill, but I happened to love them. "I can't believe I've been missing out on this all my life," Duke said. "Thank you, Quinn. You introduced me to something brand new tonight, and it was a revelation."

"Stick with me," I said with a smile. "There's so much more I plan on showing you."

Duke grinned embarrassedly and broke eye contact as the color rose in his cheeks. I wondered where his mind went just then. But I figured I'd stirred up enough trouble for one day, so I didn't ask.

Chapter Four

Maybe I'd gone a little overboard on the balloons.

After being rejected by a cab, an Uber, a Lyft, and the city bus because of the enormous latex and Mylar cloud floating above me, I resigned myself to walking across town with the gargantuan balloon bouquet I'd picked up for my friend Darwin. It was the following Sunday, and he'd finally been sent home after three nights in the hospital following his surgery. He'd come through with flying colors, but he still had to take it easy for the next few days, and I'd decided to bring him a care package and the rainbow-colored balloons to keep his spirits up.

The walk from Hayes Valley to Pacific Heights would take a good forty-five minutes, probably longer because I wouldn't be moving all that quickly. I was off the crutches, but I had to wear an ankle bracc for the next couple of weeks. The physical therapist I'd met with had given me some range-of-motion exercises and told me I was fine to walk on it, which was a good thing, since I was determined to deliver some cheer to my friend.

It was best not to push it though, so when I reached Japantown at just about the halfway point of my journey, I decided that was the perfect place for a break. Unlike Chinatown, which was an entire neighborhood, it was basically an enclosed shopping mall. Just a few seconds after I stepped through its doors, my phone rang. I juggled the balloons and the gift bag on my arm and smiled when I saw Duke's name on my screen, then answered with, "Hey! Come meet me for dessert!"

"Oh. Okay. Where are you? I'm just leaving lunch with my parents and was calling to ask if you wanted anything from the grocery store."

"I'm in Japantown. Park in the underground garage, then look for me in the west mall." I glanced at the two dozen balloons overhead and said, "I'm impossible to miss."

"Alright. I'll be there in about fifteen minutes."

After we disconnected, I left the balloons and their gift bag anchor on a table and got in line at one of my favorite places. The crepe café was little more than a counter and a small kitchen. There was a reason people stood in line for it, though.

I'd just gotten my order when I spotted Duke across the mall. He'd worn a pale blue shirt, gray pants, and a tie to church that day. He had an odd tendency (well, odd to me, anyway), of dressing in muted colors, as if he thought that would make him blend into the background or something. He had to know that was impossible though, given his height and build. I sat down under my balloon cloud and waited for him to notice me. As soon as he did, his face lit up.

He joined me at the table, ducking under the balloons as he sat down, and said, "Subtle."

"Isn't it, though?"

"As if the rainbow balloons weren't enough, you're dressed to match. Was that intentional?"

I was wearing bright red jeans and a yellow sweater with a cartoon unicorn and a rainbow, and I said, "I didn't even notice, but yay me for color coordinating." I held out one of the pink paper cones and said, "I went ahead and ordered for you, since the line was long. If you don't like what I got you, we can trade."

Duke looked perplexed as he took the wrapped crepe from me. "What exactly am I holding right now?" The crepe was rolled up like a cone and held ice cream, berries, and whipped cream. But what made it extra special was the fact that it was topped with a totally edible teddy bear head, rendered out of a scoop of ice cream, candy, and brightly colored cereal.

"That's the berry crepe. Mine's chocolate ice cream with banana. Want to switch?"

"I'm good with berry. But why does it have a face?"

"Why not?"

"That's not really an answer."

"Okay," I said, "here's a longer one. There's a great love of *kawaii*, basically all things cute, in Japanese culture. This café decided to incorporate that into their luscious desserts."

He looked around at the other tables and said, "I would have assumed these are meant for children, but ninety-five percent of the customers are adults."

"Isn't it great? I love it when grownups hold on to their sense of whimsy."

"It's like a whole crowd of Quinns," he murmured, and studied his dessert from every angle, as if he was unsure how to approach it. When he glanced at me, he asked, "Why do you look unhappy all of a sudden?"

My plastic spoon was poised above the round, adorable ice cream chick on top of my cone, and I said, "I hate this part! He's so cute. Look at him!"

I held out the crepe cone to Duke so he could see the baby chicken, and he said, "It's just going to melt, so you might as well dig in."

"I know, but still."

He pulled out his phone and awkwardly juggled it and the crepe cone, then snapped a photo of me with the ice cream chick. "There. Now he'll live on forever, and you can enjoy your dessert."

I licked the cute confection. When I saw what I'd done, I exclaimed, "Ew! Now he's all smeary and looks like road kill!"

Duke chuckled as he scooped up the chick with his spoon and fed it to me. After I ate it, he said, "Can you move on now, or are you mired in guilt?"

"It's better now that his little, beady chocolate chip chick eyes aren't staring at me accusingly."

"Good."

I dug into my dessert as I asked, "So, how was church and lunch with the fam?"

"Same as always."

"Is it always good, or always bad?"

"It just is. What's up with the rainbow cloud?" He gestured at the balloons above us with his spoon before eating a big bite of ice cream.

"I'm on my way to deliver these to Darwin. He's recovering from surgery. Hey, do you have a pocket knife on you?" When Duke nodded, I untangled one of the ribbons in the balloon bouquet and said, "Will you please cut this for me?"

"Sure, but why?"

"You'll see."

He handed me his cone before cutting a balloon free with the miniature pocket knife on his keyring. I then pivoted in my chair and held the balloon out at arm's length. A little boy of maybe five or six with brown hair and freckles, who'd been standing a few feet away and staring at me with big eyes, darted forward, grabbed the balloon, and ran. I grinned and said, "Balloons are like kid catnip. They just can't resist."

We went back to our desserts, and Duke said, "He didn't say thank you."

"He was too shy."

Duke looked skeptical. "Or maybe he was raised by hyenas."

"I always give kids the benefit of the doubt. I could never talk to strangers either when I was that age. They scared me to death."

His expression softened. A minute later, the kid was back. Duke cut another balloon loose and offered it to him. Once again, the boy grabbed it and ran. I flashed my companion a big smile, and he grinned a little.

He ate another spoonful of ice cream, and I said, "You're totally eating around the bear. You feel just as bad as I did, don't you?"

Duke looked embarrassed. "No."

"Yes you do, and I think it's sweet. Let's memorialize him." I snapped a picture of my roommate and his dessert with my phone, then said, "Now I'll tell you what you told me. It's just going to melt, so you might as well go ahead and enjoy it."

"Good advice." He still frowned a bit as he scooped up half the bear and stuck it in his mouth.

I ate another big bite, then told him, "I'm glad we've become friends, Duke. I know we got off to a rough start, but I feel like we've come a long way in a week."

"We just needed some time to get used to each other."

It helped that I'd tried my damnedest not to be a pain in the ass the last several days. I licked the back of my spoon and asked, "What are your plans for the rest of today?"

"I'm going to clean the garage."

"You're kidding."

"Why would I be kidding about that?"

"Because it's already so clean that you could rent it out as a surgical suite."

"Not quite." He plucked a blueberry from his dessert, and after he ate it, he said, "I had my doubts about this crepe thing, but it's delicious. How much do I owe you?"

"It's my treat." He thanked me, and I said, "Very welcome. So, I have a counter-offer for you. Instead of cleaning the already immaculate garage, spend the afternoon with me. I have a couple of errands to run, including delivering these balloons to Darwin in Pacific Heights, followed by dinner with my parents. You'll like them, they're nice people."

"Are you sure I wouldn't be intruding?"

"Positive."

"Okay then, but I should probably wait outside while you visit your friend."

"Why?"

"Because I made a terrible impression on him last weekend, and he probably thinks I'm a jerk."

"Darwin understands why you and I were fighting, and he wouldn't hold that against you."

"Well, alright. Out of curiosity, how were you planning to get to Pacific Heights with all those balloons?"

"The same way I got here from our neighborhood, on foot."

Duke said, "I know your physical therapist told you it was fine to walk on your ankle brace, but isn't that kind of pushing it?"

"I didn't really have a choice."

"Now you do. I'll drive you the rest of the way."

When we finished eating, I gathered up the balloons and the gift bag, and we headed for the parking garage. On the way out, I noticed the freckled boy talking to two little girls. Each was holding a balloon. "Check it out," I told Duke with a grin. "The Kindergartener is a player." He just sighed at that.

*****

Nana Dombruso's great-grandson Josh answered our knock when we finally arrived at the big, elegant home in one of San Francisco's richest neighborhoods. He was a cute kid of about sixteen, who was rocking the nerd-chic thing with his shaggy, dark hair, vintage wardrobe, and chunky, black-framed glasses. I asked if Darwin was up for company, and he held the door open for us as he said, "Absolutely. He's in the kitchen, along with Nana and her entourage. They were supposed to be coming up with some rainbow-themed drinks and appetizers for the shelter fundraiser, but here's a shocker: they've all become completely distracted."

It took me a few moments to stuff the balloons through the big front door and even longer to get them through the doorway into the huge, chaotic, white and yellow kitchen. Half a dozen people were bustling around making cocktails, talking loudly, and in some cases, trying to cook around the mayhem. My friend River and his new husband Cole greeted us, and we chatted for a minute before they both rushed over to something overflowing on the stovetop. They were catering the fundraiser, and it looked like Nana had been offering a lot of input, judging by the huge array of dishes on every countertop.

When I introduced Duke to Nana, she grabbed a pair of big, round glasses from the counter, stuck them on her face, and looked him up and down. The senior was five-foot-nothing, and he towered over her. Nana exclaimed, "Hot damn, you're a tall drink of water! And look at those muscles, lord have mercy!"

Duke got as far as, "Nice to meet—"

But Nana blurted, "You look familiar. Weren't you the strippergram my girlfriend Kiki sent me for my birthday?"

Duke blushed vividly while Kiki, having heard her name, rushed over to us. The little, full-figured senior tipped back her sequined baseball cap and squinted at my companion, then said, "Who can tell with all those clothes on? Let's play some stripper music and see if they fall off!"

She pulled a phone from the pocket of her red velour track suit, which coordinated with Nana's orange one. Duke looked like he wanted the earth to crack open and swallow him whole, so I tried to tell the seniors, "He's a police officer."

"Then that's definitely him," Kiki exclaimed as she poked at her phone. "He started out dressed in a cop uniform, and then he stripped down to tiny little briefs with a badge stuck to the front of 'em. It looked like he was smuggling a double-A battery in those skivvies. That was disappointing. The rest of him though, ooo la la!" A Tom Jones song called 'You Can Leave Your Hat On' started to blast from the phone, and Kiki whooped with delight, then pulled a handful of cash from her pocket and waved it around. Nana got in the act too and started shaking her rear and pumping her fists in time to the music.

Normally, I would have joined the impromptu dance party, but Duke looked like he was on the verge of panicking, so I thought it best to lead him to safety. I grabbed his hand and dragged him and the balloons around the kitchen counter and away from the spirited seniors. Fortunately, an elegant-looking man with salt-and-pepper hair and a lot of self-tanner distracted Nana and Kiki with some bright blue cocktails just then, so we could make our escape.

Darwin was tucked into an upholstered chair in the corner near the kitchen table, and Josh sat beside him, holding his hand. The teens were both watching the kitchen chaos with amused expressions. Duke and I joined them, and I told Darwin, "You look happy."

"I am." He leaned around me and smiled at Duke. "Nice to see you again."

"You too. Sorry about last time." Duke ducked his head and studied the floor.

"Don't give it another thought." Darwin's smile widened when I gave him the balloons and gift bag, and he exclaimed, "Thank you, Quinn! You didn't have to do that."

"You're welcome. How do you feel?" He was pale and thin, to the point of seeming fragile, but that was always the case.

"I'm bruised and achy, as expected. But everything went perfectly, which is a huge relief, and I'm thrilled to be home from the hospital."

"I'm so glad it went well." I helped him free the gift bag from the balloon strings, and he grinned when he looked inside. "That's just some stuff to help you pass the time while you heal, plus something for later," I explained. He unpacked a stack of comic books and paperbacks, and then he grinned at the black, form-fitting tank top. "I know that's not your usual style, but I thought you might have fun showing off your new bod. I wanted to get you a bright color, but you always wear black, so I decided to stay within striking distance of your comfort zone."

"Thank you, Quinn! I'm going to live in it when the weather gets warm. I can't wait, after all those years sweltering in layers and a binder."

We chatted for a few more minutes, and then Nana rushed over to us and exclaimed, "I just had the best damn idea! We need to do a gay homosexual bachelor auction at the fundraiser! You two are both single, right?" She pointed at Duke and me, and I nodded. "Perfect! Let's see, who else…." She spotted a tall guy with shoulder-length dark hair across the room and yelled, "Ignacio! Can I count on you to help with the fundraiser?"

He yelled back, with a thick Spanish accent, "Of course, Nana. I'll do whatever you need!"

She clapped her hands together and exclaimed, "Perfect! I'm up to three hot bachelors already and I only had this idea a minute ago. This is going to be the tits!"

Nana rushed off, and Duke turned to me with a panicked expression and asked, "What just happened?"

"I think you and I both got roped into a bachelor auction for charity. How fun!"

"No." He shook his head. "Absolutely not."

"Don't worry," I said. "If you're nervous about ending up with someone creepy, I'll bid on you. Then for our date, we can just do something low-key, like ordering a pizza and watching Netflix. I mean, if you want me to."

"Yes! God, yes. Do you promise to bid on me? It'd be so humiliating if no one did."

How could he possibly think no one would bid on him? I rested my hand on his shoulder and said, "I not only promise to bid on you, I promise to win. I fully expect to get into a bidding war for you, but I'll come prepared with big ol' piles of cash.

You and that pizza date will be mine!" I flashed him a big smile, and he grinned self-consciously.

*****

As we were leaving Nana's house a couple of hours later, I turned to Duke and said, "I have one more thing to do before dinner, and it should take about an hour. Dare, the guy who runs my dance troupe, called a few of us and asked if we could meet him at the warehouse. We usually take Sundays off, but he's thinking about changing the ending of the routine we're performing in a few weeks. I know it'll probably be deathly boring for you, but maybe you can read or something while we try out the new choreography."

"Actually, that sounds interesting. I'd love to see you dance, as long as the other guys don't mind me hanging around."

"Oh they definitely won't mind," I told him with a grin, as we walked down the street to his truck. "The whole troupe is gay or bi, and you're smoking hot, so they'll love the eye candy."

"You think I'm hot?"

"Of course!"

"I know I'm in shape, but aside from that, I've always thought of myself as plain."

"Are you serious?"

"Well, yeah. With this big nose and square jaw, I'm basically Shrek. All that's missing is a green complexion."

"Here's a newsflash, Duke: you're a handsome guy. People must tell you that all the time."

"I just get comments on my height and my body, because I'm so big."

We'd reached the truck, and he opened the passenger door for me. I climbed up on the doorframe so I was close to eye level with him and said, "You're not plain, Duke. Far from it. I hope someday, you find someone who makes you feel as gorgeous as you are." I smiled at him and climbed into the truck, as the color rose in his cheeks and he looked at anything but me.

*****

When we got to the warehouse, I found the gym bag I kept stashed there, stripped down to just my briefs, and pulled on a pair of stretchy shorts. Then Duke followed me up a creaky, metal staircase at the back of the building. We used the roof of the warehouse to practice, since the interior was taken up by Dare's husband Skye's massive sculptures.

When we stepped through the door at the top of the stairs, Duke murmured, "Oh wow." The roof looked like a dreamscape. Skye had built tall, metal supports around the edge of the roof that looked like undulating tentacles, because he was an artist and couldn't just make a boring framework. Dare had stretched several cream-colored Army surplus parachutes between them as a light, airy canopy, to keep the sun off us as we practiced. What had started as a practical idea ended up whimsical and beautiful in Skye and Dare's hands.

Three other dancers were already stretching, and I said, "Guys, this is my roommate, Duke. He's going to hang out while we practice." They waved and called out greetings, and I turned to Duke and pointed around the roof as I said, "The tall, muscular brunet dressed all in black is Dare, and the guy with blue hair and overalls on the lounge chair in the corner is his husband Skye. Haley is the African-American guy with short dreads and tatts, and Cleveland is the pale redhead in 1970s-style short-shorts, who looks like he might burst into flames if he ventures into direct sunlight."

Cleveland flipped me off good-naturedly as he bent at the waist and stretched his hamstrings, and Dare said, "Welcome, Duke. Pull up a seat next to Skye if you want to, and make yourself comfortable." To the rest of us, he said, "Thanks for coming in on a Sunday, guys. I know it's crazy to keep changing things this far into the process, but we all agreed we need to rev up the ending, so Haley helped me choreograph a new combination."

I sat on the rooftop and stretched as Dare and Haley demonstrated what they had in mind. Both of them were big guys and couldn't lift each other safely, so they talked us through that part. The new sequence involved Cleveland and me crossing the stage diagonally in opposite directions, then being lifted by our partners and thrown into the air. Dare said, "We know we want to do something fresh with this production, and I keep feeling like we're not pushing the envelope enough. I don't know, maybe I'm just second-guessing myself."

"You're right that we need to go bigger," Haley said, "and this might get the crowd on its feet. Let's give it a shot and see how it feels."

Haley and I practiced the toss and catch a few times while the other two dancers did the same. Then Cleveland and I took our positions as Dare started counting in place of the music. I extended one arm above my head, then bent at the waist and brushed my fingertips across the ground as I swept my torso in a wide arc. Across the rooftop, Cleveland mirrored my every move. We both spun in unison, then took off running. We crossed within inches of each other in mid-air as we both executed a *grand jeté*, and when my feet hit the ground, I ran at Haley. He grabbed my waist and tossed me in the air, and I spun three times, moving my body from a vertical to a horizontal position. Haley stooped and caught me about twelve inches from the ground, and I arched my body with my arms stretched overhead. We held that pose for a moment before he returned me to my feet.

Dare said, "That was totally a cheerleader move, wasn't it? All that was missing were the pompoms." He turned to his husband and asked, "Did that look like cheerleading to you?"

Skye called, "I thought it looked hot! Quinn got so much air that he almost grazed the canopy. It was epic!"

Dare wasn't convinced, and we spent the next forty minutes or so trying out different lifts, spins, and catches. Cleveland and I had the relatively easy part, while Dare and Haley had to repeatedly toss and catch a hundred-and-twenty-pound person. Finally, Dare said, "Let's stop here. I'm just not feeling it. Haley, can you stay for a while so we can try to iron this out?"

Haley said, "Absolutely," as he pulled off his tank top and wiped his face with it.

"Thanks for coming in on your day off, guys. I really appreciate it," Dare said, as Skye came up to him, handed him a towel, and slipped an arm around his waist. "Hopefully by rehearsal tomorrow, we'll have something worked out. But if not, we'll keep trying. We still have five weeks to get this right."

After we said goodbye to everyone, Duke followed me back downstairs, and I asked him, "What did you think?"

"You're a fantastic dancer. I was worried Haley was going to drop you though, so that was stressful."

"He'd never do that. Haley would break himself in half trying to catch me, rather than letting me hit the ground."

"You really trust him that much?"

"Absolutely. I trust all the guys, especially Dare."

"He seems nice."

"He is. When I moved back here from New York, Dare was one of the first people I met, and he took me under his wing. He not only brought me on as the lead dancer in his company, he also got me a job at the club where he used to work and found me an apartment with his brother-in-law River. He didn't have to do any of that, but it's just the type of person he is."

"It's good to know he's looking out for you." We'd reached Dare's office, where I'd left my clothes and gym bag, and as I wiped myself down with a towel, Duke asked, "How does your ankle feel?"

I flexed it in its black, neoprene brace and said, "Not bad. I'll be curious to see how it holds up tomorrow. It'll be my first full rehearsal since the sprain."

When I was dressed again, we cut through the warehouse, pausing to admire some of Skye's massive sculptures before leaving by the back door. The alley was wonderfully overgrown with purple bougainvillea vines, and as we walked to his truck, Duke asked, "Out of curiosity, what do you call that flying leap, the one where you take a running start, then do the splits in midair?"

"A *grand jeté*."

"How can you do that and make it look so effortless?"

"Nearly two decades of practice."

He said, "I could try to do that for twenty years and I'd never get there."

"Sure you would. You're an athletic guy."

"I'm built like a tank, and I move like one, too. Forget about the extraordinary stuff you do. I can't even manage the most basic dance moves."

I stopped walking and pulled up a song on my phone, and as Louis Armstrong's 'What a Wonderful World' started to play, I said, "Challenge accepted!" I put the phone on some cement steps beside us and held out my hand. "Dance with me, Duke."

"I can't. I wasn't kidding about that."

"Sure you can."

Even though he looked like he wanted to argue, Duke reluctantly curled his fingers around mine. I raised our joined hands and circled under them, smiling at him as I slipped my other hand around his waist. Duke's attention was focused on what his feet were doing, so I said, "Look me in the eye and let me guide you."

He did as I asked. After a moment, he relaxed a bit and moved with the music, but he still looked worried. "This is an odd song choice," he said. "It's not exactly dance music."

"It's slow and steady, so all you have to do is sway. But if you want to spice it up a bit, we can do that, too." I pulled back as far as our joined hands would reach and did a quick, exaggerated jitterbug, and Duke laughed. He didn't do that nearly enough.

Then he surprised me by picking me up and spinning us around. Now it was my turn to laugh. I threw my arms around his neck and leaned back, watching the purple vines and bright blue sky and all the buildings swirl around us.

A moment before the song ended, Duke exclaimed, "Big finish!" He dipped both of us deeply, and I whooped with delight.

His face was just inches from mine, and his sea blue eyes sparkled with happiness. I'd meant it when I told him he was handsome, but when he smiled at me, he was so stunningly beautiful that my breath caught. We held each other's gaze for a long moment as something unfamiliar and exhilarating crackled between us.

After a minute, Duke straightened up and put me down. We just stood there for a beat, as if neither of us knew what to do with the new, unspoken but unmistakable *something* between us. I finally broke the spell by picking up my phone and saying, "I guess we should get going. My parents are expecting us." Duke nodded, and we headed to the truck side-by-side.

Chapter Five

Duke murmured, "Oh wow," when we pulled up in front of my parents' house.

I turned to look at the elegant, modern structure. Its center was a square, two story atrium with glass walls front and back, so you could look right through it and see the stunning view of San Francisco across the bay. The atrium was flanked by two symmetrical wings, paneled in dark wood and set off by flawless, minimalistic landscaping, including a rock garden and an artfully designed dry riverbed, interspersed with a few drought-tolerant shrubs and small trees.

Most people who saw the house for the first time reacted just like Duke. All they saw were dollar signs. And yes, my parents had done well for themselves. But they'd also bought the land and built the house in the 1960s, before housing prices in the Bay Area totally spiraled out of control. I always felt the need to explain that to people, almost as a way of downplaying the fact that my family had money. I didn't know why I was so self-conscious about it.

I absolutely loved the house though, not because it was an architectural gem, but because it was home. It represented safety and security, and it also held so many wonderful memories, as did the land around it. We were high up in the hills above Oakland, at the very end of a residential area, where manicured lawns and grand houses gave way to open space. It had always seemed to me like the ideal place to grow up, a country oasis in an urban environment. I'd been able to explore and have little adventures as a child, climbing trees, building forts, enjoying nature, the sorts of things city kids usually missed out on.

Duke asked, "You grew up here?" When I nodded, he said, "I can't even imagine. It's like something out of a movie."

"I often wonder why I got so lucky," I murmured, as he and I both studied the house. "I doubt I'll ever understand why they decided to open their home to a random, skinny, little stranger. In my dad's line of work, he often encountered children without families, and he didn't feel the need to adopt all of them. Why me?"

"Did you ever ask him?"

"No. I always thought I might not like the answer."

"What do you mean?"

"I suspect he took me in because I was so much more damaged than the rest, so broken and pathetic that he just couldn't trust the foster care system with me," I said. "I guess I never wanted to hear him describe just how pitiful I was."

"Or maybe he just felt a connection to you."

I shrugged and said, "Either way, it's always felt like this huge debt I can never repay. All my life, I've wanted to make my parents proud and show them they made the right choice by taking me in. They always say they love me no matter what, but I guess I still have this need to prove myself worthy of them. The problem with that is pretty obvious, though. Look at that place! And wait until you meet my family and see how wonderful they are. How on earth could anyone ever be worthy of all of that?"

"Of course you're worthy, Quinn."

When I turned to Duke, there was so much sympathy in his eyes that I wished I hadn't said anything. I tried to keep my tone cheerful as I said, "Come on, let's go inside. My parents are looking forward to meeting you."

"I'd wondered if you told them I was coming."

"Yeah, just as a courtesy. Guests are always welcome, and my dad tends to cook enough food for ten people," I said as I opened the passenger door.

Duke stuck close to me as we walked up the flagstone path, and when I let us in with my key, he wandered into the atrium and murmured, "This is so beautiful."

That part of the house was pure show. Dark, rich stone lined the floor and the central, boxy fountain, which filled the space with the melodic sound of trickling water. The walls to either side of us were dark wood, similar to the outside, with large, open doorways that led to the rest of the house. It was all very posh, but also understated, so it didn't compete with the view on the other side of the two-story wall of glass.

The hill sloped sharply just past the edge of a wide deck, giving way to a breathtaking panorama of Oakland, the bay, and San Francisco. We'd arrived at sunset, and the sky was lit up in gorgeous, gaudy swaths of pink and orange. It was almost too much, too ostentatious. The view on its own was already ridiculously fantastic, and the sunset on top of that seemed over-the-top somehow. I felt like apologizing, which of course made no sense whatsoever.

Duke seemed stunned as he followed me through the doorway to the left, which led to the huge, dark wood and black granite kitchen. My dad was stirring a pot of something disappointingly healthy-looking on the stove, while another family member snuck in behind him and tossed in some spices. As I stepped around the long kitchen island, I said, "Please tell me that's not your infamous quinoa surprise again."

"You loved that dish!" My dad stopped what he was doing to give me a hug. I jokingly referred to him as Straight George Takei, because there was a definite resemblance, especially as both men got older. He had a slight build and thinning hair that was more white than black these days, and a wide, genuine smile that lit up his eyes.

He felt skinnier than ever in my arms, and I said, "Hi Dad," as he gave me a big squeeze.

"Hi, kiddo. How's your weekend going?"

"It's been great." When we let go of each other, I said, "This is my friend and roommate, Duke Blumenthal. Don't feel like you need to tell him every embarrassing story from my childhood over dinner."

My dad and Duke shook hands and exchanged greetings while I hugged the other person in the kitchen. When I let go of him, I said, "Duke, this is Max, my brother Shigeo's son."

Max grinned broadly. The half-dozen piercings in his ears and lip sparkled in the orangey light streaming in through the enormous kitchen windows. He told Duke, "In other words, I'm his nephew. Quinn always feels weird about introducing me that way, because I'm actually a year older and two inches taller than him." He tossed his long, black hair over his shoulder and shook Duke's hand. "Speaking of height, I think you're the tallest person I've ever met! What are you, like six-six?"

"Dude, nice social skills," I said as I rolled my eyes. "He's six-foot-eight, not that you really needed to know that." Duke colored slightly. That was probably because of my clumsy attempt to keep Max from embarrassing him, more than anything else. I changed the subject by asking, "Is Mom in her studio?"

My dad nodded. "When you go back to say hello, please tell her dinner will be ready in half an hour. And by the way, no, it's not quinoa surprise again. It's a new recipe I'm trying out."

"Surprise," Max said with a smile, "it also contains quinoa."

"Of course it does," I said. "Good luck with whatever that turns into. After we say hi to Mom, I want to show Duke my room. We'll be back in time to throw that out and order pizza."

My dad grinned at me and said, just like always, "Don't knock it until you try it." He was used to my ongoing complaints about the health food kick he'd been on for the last year or so.

We left the house and walked along the deck before reaching what we'd always inaccurately called the backyard. It was actually to the left of the house instead of behind it, since the only thing on the other side of the deck was a steep slope. "There used to be a lawn out here, along with a great swing set," I said as I gestured at the rock garden. "It's silly, but I wish they hadn't taken out the swings. I know I grew up and moved out, but still."

As we followed the meandering path to my mom's studio, Duke asked, "Does Max live here?"

"No, but he comes over a lot. He's unemployed and living at home, and he and my brother always seem to be fighting. It's funny. Our parents are fairly open-minded, but somehow Shigeo ended up pretty uptight. He hates Max's long hair, tattoos, and piercings and is always getting on him to 'clean up his act'. Actually, as far as that goes, Dad's not a fan of tattoos either, which is why I haven't told him I'm getting one tomorrow. I mean, I know I'm an adult and it's my decision, but I don't want to argue with him."

"What does your dad have to say about your piercings?"

"He only knows my ears are pierced. I decided the nipple piercings are on a need-to-know basis. Not that he'd care all that much. I can take them out when I perform, so they're not a big deal. Tattoos are another story. My dad's main argument against them is that they might make me less employable as a ballet dancer."

"Why would a ballet company care if you have tattoos?"

"Almost all mainstream companies consider them visually distracting, so they require dancers to cover them with makeup before they perform. That's less than ideal, though. Not only are you prone to sweating off the makeup, but you're probably going to end up smearing it all over your costume, and anyone else you come in contact with."

"I see. So, given that, why are you getting a tattoo?"

I paused outside my mother's studio and said, "Besides the fact that I like them and have always wanted one, I think it's my way of embracing the fact that I don't want to be mainstream and fit the mold of some big, pretentious ballet company."

"Makes sense to me."

I pushed open the door to the studio, and Duke followed me inside. The spacious, octagonal room was lined with windows and skylights, and it contained a dozen canvases in various stages of completion. My mom stood right in the center of the space, totally focused on the canvas in front of her. She was barefoot and dressed in a colorful caftan and matching headband that held back her chin-length white bob. All of that made me smile. She'd been a surgeon before she retired, and I loved the fact that she'd totally reinvented herself in the last few years.

Duke stopped in his tracks and whispered, "Is she painting a…oh, never mind. I just got that it's a close-up of a pink flower."

The flower in question filled a five-foot-square canvas, in a style similar to Georgia O'Keeffe, with a dash of Roy Lichtenstein thrown in for good measure. She painted in bright colors and added black outlines, which gave her macro florals almost a comic book feel. I thought they were fantastic.

She glanced over her shoulder and exclaimed, "Hi sweetie! Come on in and introduce me to your friend."

I crossed the room and kissed her cheek, then made the introductions. Duke seemed even more formal than usual as he shook her hand and said, "Thank you for allowing me to join you for dinner, Doctor Takahashi."

"Call me Toshiko, and you're welcome any time." She turned to me and asked, "Did you stop off in the kitchen, and if so, what's your father making for dinner?"

"I don't really know what it was," I said. "It just looked brown. He wanted me to tell you it'll be ready in half an hour."

"He took another healthy cooking class," my mom said as she turned to the canvas and assessed it critically. "Last week, he came up with nine different things to do with kale."

"I only know of one thing to do with it: throw it away."

"The kale smoothie actually wasn't horrible."

"Not horrible isn't exactly a ringing endorsement," I said, and then I headed for the door with Duke right on my heels. "We'll let you get back to work. See you at dinner! I like your newest giant lady parts painting, by the way. So does Duke."

My roommate looked stricken, and I grinned as my mother clicked her tongue and said, "Why does everyone have such a dirty mind?"

"Because you're painting a giant vag, Mom. It's cool, though. I totally respect your righteous feminist statement."

"It's a peony!"

I called, "Keep telling yourself that," a moment before the door swung shut behind Duke and me.

I chuckled as we crossed the yard again, and Duke said, "Your parents seem so nice."

"They are."

"I'm sorry they got rid of your swing set, though."

"It's my own fault. I told them they could, because I was trying to be mature about it. Good thing I didn't make the same mistake with my room."

I waved to Max and my dad on the way back through the kitchen, and Duke and I headed to the other wing of the house.

When I opened my bedroom door and flipped on the light, Duke exclaimed, "No way!" He looked awe-struck as he wandered into my room and spun in a slow circle, and then he surprised me by saying, "You grew up in a Studio Ghibli movie."

"I can't believe you know what this is!" The walls and ceiling of my room were painted to look like we were in the country. The background was a forest of fluffy camphor trees, and rendered in perfect detail in the foreground were the house and characters from the animated movie 'My Neighbor Totoro'.

He said, "I stumbled across one of their films by accident years ago when I was flipping channels, and it was so charming that I sought out more of them. Who did the painting? It's extraordinary."

"My parents hired a student from CCA. I always wondered what she went on to do after she graduated. I hope she ended up at Pixar or some other fabulous place."

"CCA?"

"California College of the Arts. It's here in Oakland."

"Oh, right."

"I have to show you one of my favorite things," I said. "Well, two of them, actually. For the first one, you need to get comfy on the beanbag." I gestured at the big, dark green lump in the center of the room. He grinned and awkwardly lowered himself onto it, as I went around and turned on every light.

"It's just going to take a minute," I said. "I need to charge it up."

"Charge what up?"

"You'll see. Here, you can play with this while we wait." I handed him my Totoro, a round, grinning stuffed animal with gray fur and a white belly. It looked a bit like a rabbit with short ears and wide-set eyes, but according to the movie, it was a forest spirit. Duke smiled at me and tucked the toy under his arm. After a pause, I said, "Close your eyes." He did as I asked, and I went around and turned off all the lights before dropping down beside him on the wide beanbag. "Okay. You can open them."

Duke drew in his breath when he saw the way the room was transformed in the darkness. The artist who'd painted the mural had added hidden details with clear, glow-in-the-dark paint, and the scene came to life around us with all kinds of wondrous things that had been invisible when the lights were on. There were flowers, cute little animals, a full moon, and a starry night sky. Best of all, a long, wide ribbon of the little puffball dust creatures from the film streamed from a crack in the old house. I put my head on Duke's shoulder and whispered, "Isn't it amazing?"

"It really is."

"The other thing I wanted to show you is the nighttime view outside my window, the one that made me want to move to San Francisco when I grew up. From this distance, the city looks like Neverland."

He took it all in, and after a while, Duke murmured, "You and I might as well have grown up on different planets. All of this is so far above and beyond anything I ever experienced."

"I don't know why I got so lucky."

There must have been something in my voice when I said that, because Duke turned his head to try to look at me in the darkness. After a moment, he said softly, "You feel you don't deserve this."

"I've felt that way all my life."

Duke said, "That's surprising. Growing up with such a loving family, I wouldn't have expected you to be so insecure."

"According to the therapists I saw for most of my childhood, by the time I was adopted, the damage had already been done. Sometimes I wonder if I'm doomed to spend my entire life as this needy, pathetic little thing, desperate for love, praise, and attention."

"You're not pathetic. Far from it. You're just someone who was badly hurt, and you're doing the best you can, despite what was done to you." He took my hand and was quiet for a while before saying, "It's odd. I was convinced we had nothing in common. But I just realized I was totally wrong."

"I'm so sorry you were hurt too, Duke."

"I didn't mean to tell you that last weekend, when I said nobody hurts me anymore. It just came out."

"I know, and you don't have to tell me anything else if you don't want to," I said as I held his hand in both of mine. "I know how painful it is to talk about the things that were done to me before I was abandoned."

Duke whispered, "Oh God. You remember."

"Yeah. Not everything, but bits and pieces." I took a deep breath, and then I got up, turned on the small lamp on the nightstand, and said, "I didn't mean for this conversation to get so heavy."

"It's my fault. I'm always too serious."

"Come on," I said as I headed to the door. "I want to show you the rec room. Maybe we can work up an appetite over a heated game of ping pong." It was a pretty clunky attempt at changing the subject, but Duke was more than willing to go along with it.

As we headed down the hall, he said, "Thank you for letting me tag along today, Quinn. It meant a lot to me."

"You're being nice. I've probably bored you out of your mind."

"Just the opposite. This look into your life has been fascinating."

I pushed open the last door on the left, and Duke murmured, "Just when I thought the house couldn't get any better."

Half of the huge room had been converted into a dance studio for me, with smooth wood floors and a mirrored wall spanned by a long ballet barre. The other half included a pool table, ping pong table, dartboard, and a comfortable seating area. I crossed the room and picked up a pair of paddles, and then I smiled at Duke and asked, "Are you one of those people who holds a grudge when they lose?"

"Doesn't matter," he said as he took a paddle from me, "because there's no way I'm going to lose." There was a playful sparkle in his eyes.

"Oh, it's on," I said as we took our positions at either end of the ping pong table. "What should we play for?"

"Bragging rights."

"That's a given. But what else?"

"You tell me."

I thought about it for a moment, then said, "If I win, you have to bake me cookies when we get home."

"And if I win?"

I smiled at him as I tossed the paddle in the air and caught it by the handle. "That's not going to happen."

"Okay, so when I win, you have to make me dessert, and possibly buy me a sandwich later, because I'm not so sure about whatever your dad's cooking. What on earth is *keen-wah* anyway?"

"Quinoa is a grain. It's supposed to be good for you."

"So definitely a sandwich and dessert."

"You're on," I said as I tossed him the little, white ball. Then I grinned and said, "Let's see what you've got."

When Max came to tell us dinner was ready maybe fifteen minutes later, we were right in the middle of a prolonged rally for match point. I'd been surprised to find Duke was actually a great ping pong player, and we were pretty even. I jumped out of the way when he hit it off the end of the table, and then I exclaimed, "Yes! Victory and cookies are mine!"

We put down our paddles and headed to the door, and Duke said, "That was fun."

"Why are you so good at it? I thought I'd smoke you."

"There was a ping pong table in the rec room at my old church in South San Francisco," Duke explained. "I taught Sunday school, and the kids and I used to play afterwards, while they waited for their families to pick them up. But then our pastor moved to a church here in the city, and my parents and I followed him, so I haven't played in about a year."

Max was staring at Duke as if he'd just said, 'I eat live crickets for the extra protein.' I asked, as we headed to the kitchen, "What does the Lutheran church think about homosexuality? I asked you once before, but I never got an answer."

"The church is divided on the subject. Unlike the Catholic Church, we don't have a single governing body that dictates to the entire organization. Instead, we're overseen by several synods, each with their own take on it," Duke said. "Unfortunately, the pastor my parents are so enamored of is pretty intolerant. If it were up to me, I'd go back to my old church. The person who took over is much more progressive."

I asked, "How is it not up to you?"

"I guess it is, but right now, the Sunday morning tradition of going to church and then lunch with my parents is working for me. If it wasn't for that, I'd be expected to go to their house once a week for dinner, and…let's just say, I'd rather not. Ideally, I'd have liked all three of us to remain at our old church. I think hearing what the new pastor had to say would have gone a long way toward boosting my parents' tolerance and understanding."

"But you're a grown man," Max said. "Why not just go to the church of your choosing and say thanks but no thanks when they ask you to come to dinner?"

I knit my brows and said, "Just like you always stand up to your dad, Max? It's easier said than done, and you know it."

"My relationship with my parents is already precarious, and it wouldn't take much to drive the last nail into that coffin," Duke said. "Anyway, enough about that."

We'd arrived in the kitchen, where my parents were making some last minute adjustments to the stew's seasoning, and my mom said, "It's a nice night, so I think we should eat on the deck. Will you kids set the table?"

Place settings for five were already stacked on the counter, and I grabbed the plates and napkins and said, "On it!" Max and Duke followed with the glasses, placemats, and cutlery. As we worked our way around the long, redwood table, I lowered my voice and told Max, "I'm getting my first tattoo tomorrow. Don't tell Mom and Dad."

"Dude, you have the coolest parents in the world," he said as he tossed a red placemat on the tabletop. "There's no reason to hide that from them."

"My dad thinks tattoos are a mistake," I said as I straightened the placemat and put a plate on top of it. "I don't want him to be disappointed in me."

Max rolled his eyes and said, "Whatever. It's your body. So what if he's less than thrilled? He'll get over it."

"Just don't say anything."

"I won't. Where are you getting it done?"

"At this studio called Artifact in the city. The owner is a friend of a friend. His name's Yoshi Miyazaki."

Max's eyes went wide. "No freaking way! You know Yoshiro Miyazaki?"

"Keep your voice down," I said. "Kind of. Like I said, we have some of the same friends. Do you know him?"

"I wish! He's an insanely talented, nationally recognized tattoo artist. Do you realize what an honor it is to get inked by him?"

I said, "All I know is, he's a nice guy, and I like his work. I've only seen this sleeve of a cityscape he inked on himself, but it's incredible."

Max asked, "Do you suppose I could, you know, just happen to drop by during your appointment? I'd love to meet him."

"Sure. It's at three, and he blocked off four hours. You could also just book an appointment with him, you know. It takes a couple months to get in, but still."

"I've thought about doing that for years," Max said, "but I always chickened out, because I wouldn't just be going for a tattoo. I always wanted to ask him if he'd take me on as an apprentice."

"You totally should! You've talked about becoming a tattoo artist since high school. Come by during my appointment tomorrow, and bring your sketchbook. I'll ask to see some of your drawings, and then we can casually work apprenticing into the conversation."

Max looked worried, and he began to fidget with a silver stud in his right earlobe. "I don't know. Maybe I'm aiming too high. I should probably build up a little experience somewhere else before approaching someone of his caliber...."

"Come on, just give it a shot," I said. "What's the worst that could happen?"

"He could tell me my drawings are terrible, and that I have no business wanting to tattoo my homely shit onto people's bodies."

"There's absolutely no way that would ever happen."

Max chewed his lower lip, and after a moment, he said, "Yeah, okay. I'll drop by maybe an hour into your appointment. But try not to oversell me, okay? You tend to be really enthusiastic about stuff, so don't, like, introduce me as the world's greatest illustrator, or some crazy shit like that."

"I promise to tone it down."

"Good." Max continued his path around the table and asked, "What are you getting?"

"It's going to be Totoro wearing his leaf hat, right here," I said, touching my ribcage. "How perfect is that? My favorite character from my favorite movie, which was, of course, written and directed by the great Hayao Miyazaki, and I'm having it inked by, wait for it…Miyazaki! Yoshi isn't actually related to the filmmaker. I asked. But still, I think that's oddly perfect."

Max raised an eyebrow and said, "You're such a dork. Also, you know the ribcage is one of the most painful places on the body to get a tattoo, right?"

"I heard, but that's where I want it." I wrapped my arm around myself and rested my hand on my ribcage. Then I glanced through the sliding glass door and said, "Here come my parents. Let's change the subject." Max sighed, and I blurted the first thing that came to mind, which was, "Did you know people thought tomatoes were poisonous in ancient times? I always wondered how they found out that wasn't the case. Like, maybe it was because of some poor guy who'd given up on life, and he staggered into the town square with a tomato, ready to end it all, and was like, 'Goodbye, cruel world!' And he took a huge bite of the tomato, but then he was like, 'Shit.' But maybe he went on to invent marinara sauce and totally turned his life around, and it was a happy ending after all."

A bark of laughter slipped from Duke, and Max just stared at me. My parents put a heaping serving dish of stew and a huge green salad on the table, and I went inside for the basket of wholegrain rolls and the salad dressing. When I returned to the deck, Duke asked me where he should sit. I pulled out a chair for him facing the view and said, "Right next to me."

The stew was surprisingly good, and my dad seemed pleased when Duke and I went back for seconds. We kept the conversation light and talked about the local art scene, which my mom was passionate about. Duke followed the conversation closely but remained quiet for the most part. At one point, I turned to my parents and said, "I meant to tell you we got this amazing artist to paint the backdrops for our show. His name is Christian, but he paints under the name Zane. Have you heard of him?"

My mom looked impressed. "Of course! He runs that fantastic community art center in San Francisco, and his graffiti art has gained quite a following. Some people were calling him the next Banksy, but then he stopped painting a couple of years ago. I heard he'd been ill. It's quite something that he's doing this for your dance troupe."

"Christian is best friends with Dare's husband," I said. "That's how we got him to agree to it."

"I hope you're advertising the fact that he's involved in the production," my mom said.

"I think so. I mean, Dare's handling the PR and advertising for the show, but I'm sure he's putting the word out."

My dad patted his mouth with his napkin, then said, "I read in the paper that San Francisco Ballet is looking to fill a couple of positions. Auditions are invitation-only, and since they offered you a spot last year, I'm sure they'd let you try out again."

I put my fork down and sighed. "Really, Dad? Are we going to have this conversation for the thousandth time?"

He said, "It's just such a fantastic opportunity, Quinn! I can accept the fact that you weren't ready last year. You'd just finished your training and moved back to the west coast, and you needed to settle in. But the timing is right for you to try again, and you can't let this pass you by! It's everything you've worked for, all your life."

"I already have a job that pays the bills, and I'm lead dancer with a fantastic troupe. I know it isn't as prestigious as the San Francisco Ballet, but we're about to stage our first performance, and there's no limit to where we could go from there!"

"I know that," my father said, "and I wish those boys the best of luck with getting their company off the ground. But the fact is, no matter how successful they become, they'll never rival a world-renowned, highly prestigious company like the San Francisco Ballet."

My voice rose, despite myself. "Why does that matter, Dad? Who cares if Dare's troupe never becomes world-famous? What possible difference does it make? I'm proud to be a part of it, and I believe in what we're doing. Our show is going to be important and innovative, not just because all our dancers are gay. I know that's been done before. Wait until you hear the original score Dare commissioned for our show, it'll blow you away! And we're incorporating art with Zane's backdrops, and all the dancers and the choreographers are working so hard to do something spectacular here!"

"All of that is fantastic," my father said. "I applaud the troupe for taking risks and pushing boundaries. But you've already given them a year of your life, and after this performance, I think it's time to set your sights higher."

"Did you ever stop to think that maybe you and I have very different definitions of what it means to be successful, Dad? I don't need a prestigious ballet company to validate what I'm doing!"

"I understand that," he said. "I really do. But at the same time, you're a world-class dancer with an astonishing gift, and you deserve so much better than performing for a few dozen people in a run-down theater in the Tenderloin that used to feature adult entertainment!"

I lowered my voice and held my father's gaze. "I told you the name of the theater, but not its history. Did you seriously go and research it?"

"I was curious."

I sighed and said, "Great. So now you have another way to discredit what I'm doing. But so what if it used to show dirty movies, or whatever? It's just a pretty, art deco theater from the 1920s, and the new owners are trying to start over."

"When have I ever discredited what you're doing?"

"Uh, by saying I work as a stripper, when I've told you a million times that I'm a go-go boy? Every time you say I'm a stripper, it demeans and cheapens it."

My father looked contrite. "I apologize for that, and I meant it when I said I'd come down to the club and see it for myself. When's your next shift?"

"Tuesday, from eight to midnight. You really don't have to come to the club, though."

"It'll be fun," my father said. "Let's meet for an early dinner in the Castro on Tuesday, then go to your club and have a drink before you start working."

"Fine. Are you coming too, Mom?"

"I wish I could," she said, "but I'm teaching an oil painting class every night next week at the senior center."

Max raised his hand and asked, "Can I come?"

"Why? You've been to the club plenty of times."

He smiled and said, "Yeah, but never with my grandpa. I think it'll be a blast."

"Fine. You two can carpool in together," I said. "This is probably going to be totally awkward, but on the plus side, we'll end up with a ton of free drinks."

Duke had been watching the conversation closely while packing away four or five rolls, and he asked, "Why will you get free drinks?"

"Because everyone's going to think Dad is George Takei."

Max and Duke chuckled at that, and my mom grinned as she pushed back from the table. "I'm going to make some coffee to go with dessert," she said. "I bought some nice, ripe berries at the farmer's market, along with a lovely pound cake. I figure we can splurge a little after that healthy dinner. The stew was delicious, by the way." She kissed her husband's forehead before heading to the kitchen. I got up too and picked up my plate, and Duke followed my lead.

Once inside, I put my dishes in the sink and said, "Let me do that, Mom," as she reached for the coffee pot. "Go sit down. Duke and I will put the desserts together too and bring them out to you."

"Alright, sweetie."

I told her, "I'm sorry about all of that. You must get sick of Dad and me arguing all the time."

"He just wants what's best for you. We both do," she said.

"I know, Mom. We just don't seem to agree on what that is." She kissed my cheek and patted it before returning to the deck.

Duke leaned against the counter as I got the coffee going. Once it started to brew, I turned to him and said, "I'm sorry you got caught in the middle of my family drama. That must have been so awkward for you."

He grinned and said, "Actually, that was the most civilized domestic dispute I've ever seen."

That made me grin, too. "In the context of your job, I guess it would seem pretty tame."

He studied me closely and said, "Feel free to tell me if this is none of my business, but did you turn down that job with the San Francisco Ballet because you think you don't deserve it, like what you were saying earlier about deserving a nice home and family?"

I looked up at him and said quietly, "I turned them down because I'm not good enough, Duke."

"The ballet company seems to disagree, since they offered you a position."

"My parents do, too. They just don't get it."

"What don't they get?"

"That I'm a total fuck-up. Sure, I'm a good dancer. Great, even. I've trained hard for almost twenty years, and my technique is pretty damn close to perfect. But I know for a fact that sooner or later, I'm going to make a mistake while performing. I'll lose concentration. My mind will wander, or I'll get distracted by something, and I'll mess up. That's just an absolute given. If I do that as a dancer for a major ballet company, I'm gone. No two ways about it. If I do that while performing with Dare's troupe, I'll feel absolutely terrible and the guys will be pissed, but they're not going to fire me for it. They care about me as a person, and they'll give me another chance. Also, the fact that I feel secure with this troupe takes some of the pressure off, which in turn makes it less likely that I'll mess up."

"Have you tried telling your parents what you just told me?"

"No. They'll just say I'm underestimating myself, but I'm really not. I know my limitations, including the fact that I've always had a hard time concentrating. I can probably force myself to stay focused for a single performance. But to do that day after day after day? It's just a matter of time until I lose my concentration, and when I do, I want to be with a company that gives second chances, not one that'll kick me out on my ass. Plus, think of the big picture. Who would hire me after a major ballet company canned me for fucking up onstage? Here's the chain of events I'm trying to avoid: take the job, make a mistake, get fired, end my career."

Duke said, "It makes sense. Although, just to play devil's advocate, what if you really are underestimating yourself?"

I crossed the room to the refrigerator and said, "I'm not. Will you help me by assembling a tray for the coffee while I put together the dessert? The mugs are in the cupboard to the right of the sink."

"You're changing the subject."

I met his gaze over my shoulder. "Yup."

After a beat, Duke said, "Alright," and went to get the coffee cups.

*****

We lingered over coffee and dessert with my family, and after Duke and I loaded the dishwasher and cleaned up the kitchen, I asked him, "Are you up for a little walk?"

"Always."

I dried my hands on a dishtowel and stuck my head out the open sliding door. My parents and Max were relaxing in one of the comfortable seating areas out on the deck, and I said, "We'll be back soon. I want to show Duke my sky fortress."

My mom called, "Have fun," as we headed for the front door.

Once outside, we crossed the street and started to climb. The land was undeveloped and fairly overgrown, but I knew the trail well, and the full moon lit our way. We soon reached a huge boulder, and I led Duke around to the back of it and scaled it easily. He followed without question or complaint, and when we reached the top, he murmured, "Oh wow."

The view from my parents' home was spectacular, but this one was even better, because it included the house itself. It looked beautiful and warm and welcoming, all lit up below us. Beyond it, the lights of Oakland and San Francisco framed the inky black bay.

We sat down side-by-side on top of the boulder, and as a light breeze stirred our hair, Duke leaned against me and said, "Thank you for an extraordinary day."

"Thanks for being a good sport and going along with all of it."

He was quiet for a while before saying, "There's something I want to ask you."

I turned to study his face in the moonlight. He looked nervous. I said softly, "You can ask me anything, Duke."

He took a deep breath and met my gaze. Then he said, "Will you please go out with me? Before you say no, let me just say this. I know I must seem boring to someone like you, but I'm asking you to take a chance on me. Let me show you there's more to me than what you've seen so far." He broke eye contact. "And yes, I know I shouldn't be asking you this because we're roommates, and it'll probably make things awkward between us. But I'd never forgive myself if I didn't try."

His eyes met mine again when I said, "Of course I'll go out with you, Duke."

He seemed surprised, and he touched my face and murmured, "Holy crap, you said yes." I smiled at him, and after a moment, he leaned in and brushed his lips to mine.

The kiss was pure, and unhurried, and innocent. It made no demands and carried no expectations. It was different from every other kiss that had come before it. All the rest had been nothing more than preludes to sex, delivered by men interested only in what they could get from me. But not this one. It gave instead of taking.

I slid closer to him, and he wrapped me up in his arms and his warmth. Duke's lips were as soft and gentle as his touch. He was careful with me, as if I was something precious, something he wanted to protect. We kissed for a long time, and then I curled up against him and whispered, "I didn't see that coming."

"That's probably a good thing. I'd hoped I wasn't too obvious about the fact that I was attracted to you. I'd intended to keep it under wraps, but in the end, I only lasted a week before breaking down and asking you out."

I sat up a bit and looked at him. "You mean you felt this way for a while?"

He studied his shoes as he said, "Remember when I said I had my reasons for wanting you to move in with me?"

"Oh!"

He risked a glance at me and said, "It's creepy to admit I wanted to be your roommate because I was attracted to you, isn't it? I probably just ruined everything."

I grinned and returned my head to his chest. "You worry too much."

"I know."

"I could never figure out why you'd let someone like me move into your home. It makes sense now."

"It wasn't just because I was attracted to you," he said, "though that was part of it. I also thought you'd be fun to be around, and I was right."

"You're fun too, Duke."

"That's literally the first time anyone's ever said that."

"Then most people don't know you very well."

"Nobody does. I usually keep people at arm's length, but I don't want to do that with you." He gently touched my cheek as he said, "I have to be honest here: I have no idea what I'm doing. My few attempts at dating before this were total disasters. And the fact that we're roommates is a major complication. You'll probably want to move out after this falls apart, which is a huge hassle. It wasn't fair of me to ask you out and put you through all of that. In fact—"

I pulled him down to my height and kissed him again, and he grinned against my lips. Then I asked, "Who says it's going to fall apart?"

"Like I said, it always does. You've already gotten a sneak preview as my roommate, and you know how uptight I can be. You know who wants that in a boyfriend? Nobody."

"You're not all that uptight." He shot me a look, and I said, "Okay, sometimes. But here's a newsflash, Duke: I like you."

"You do?"

"Why do you think I agreed to go out with you?"

"I figured it was probably a pity date. I'm fine with that, by the way. Feel free to pity date the hell out of me."

I chuckled and ran my hand over his short, surprisingly soft hair. "Kind, gentle, beautiful, sexy men who bake cookies don't need pity dates."

"I don't know who you're describing, but it reminds me that I owe you cookies when we get home, since you turned out to have mad ping pong skills."

I smiled and said, "I wasn't going to let you forget."

He traced my lower lip with a fingertip and gazed at my mouth longingly for a moment, but then he shook himself out of his reverie and said, "We should probably head back. It's getting late."

We climbed off the boulder, and as we made our way back down the hill, I asked, "So, when do you want to go out?"

"My next day off is Wednesday. Are you working that night?"

"Nope."

"Okay, good. I'll pick you up at seven."

I grinned and asked, "Are you planning to go outside and knock on your own door?"

"Possibly. We can still do this properly, even though we live together."

"A proper date? I don't know if I've ever had one of those." I'd had plenty of improper ones, but I didn't feel the need to say that out loud.

My parents and Max were still out on the deck when we got back to the house. Their gaze went right to Duke's and my joined hands, and then my parents grinned from ear to ear. Subtle.

"Thank you for inviting me into your beautiful home. Dinner was wonderful," Duke said. He turned to my father and added, "I'd love a copy of that stew recipe when you get the chance, sir." Wow. He was every parent's wet dream.

My dad promised to email it to me so I could forward it on, and Max blurted, "Did I miss something? Are you two a couple? I thought you were just roommates."

"Duke just asked me out. We have a date on Wednesday. Dad, I'll see you Tuesday for our super awkward outing, and Max, I'll see you tomorrow. Mom, good luck with your senior art class. I hope they all paint truly spectacular technicolor lady parts." Dad and Max chuckled while my mom grinned and shook her head.

*****

Everything felt vastly different between Duke and me as we drove back to San Francisco. It was as if a deck of cards had been shuffled, and we'd been dealt a whole new hand. Over the course of a week, we'd gone from strangers to friends, and all of a sudden, there was the possibility of so much more. I watched his profile as he drove, and whenever he glanced at me, the sweetest smile played around his full lips.

When we got home, he went to change while I lined up everything we needed for sugar cookies on the kitchen island, including the edible glitter. Duke was barefoot and dressed in a gray T-shirt and shorts when he joined me, much more casual than usual. I took that as a sign that he was loosening up around me, at least a little.

He put on his glasses and went to work mixing the ingredients while I sat on the counter and chatted about nothing in particular. Once again, the dough came together quickly, and after he put it in the refrigerator to chill for an hour, he asked, "Do you want to watch TV or a movie while we wait?"

I slid off the counter and looked up at him as I ran my hand down his arm. "We could do that," I said, "or you could take me upstairs and fuck me." I was nervous, which surprised me. I'd propositioned countless guys over the years, and they were almost always perfectly willing to take me to bed, no questions asked. Somehow though, I just knew things would be more complicated than that with Duke.

He said, "It's tempting, but I can't do that, Quinn."

Even though I'd predicted it, I still felt embarrassed, and I turned away as I murmured, "That's fine. It was just a thought."

His voice was gentle when he said, "Hey. Look at me."

"Like I said, it's fine. No big deal."

I started to leave the kitchen, but he stopped me with a quiet, "Please don't run away. Let me explain."

I hesitated before turning to face him. He stood right in front of me, and I broke eye contact again. When he knelt down and sat on his heels, I glanced at him and asked, "What are you doing?"

"I'm trying to seem less intimidating, since I'm as big as a house. You're obviously uncomfortable around me right now, and I don't want to make it worse by towering over you."

"Is it a cop thing? Did they teach you to do that when you're dealing with skittish children?"

"It's a human being thing."

His expression was earnest as he looked up at me, and he was still wearing his glasses, which I found surprisingly sexy. It felt awkward to have him kneeling before me though, so I sat down cross-legged on the kitchen floor and tugged his arm, and he sat down facing me. I still had to look up at him when we were both seated, but it was less pronounced.

He told me, "Like I said before, to me there's nothing casual about sex. I know that must seem hopelessly old-fashioned, and in case you're wondering, it doesn't have anything to do with my religion. It's just who I am."

I said, "You don't have to explain."

"But I want to."

After a moment, I asked, "Are you saving yourself for marriage?"

"Not necessarily." He held my gaze and said, "It's about feeling safe enough with another person to totally let my guard down. It's also about trust, love, and commitment. That doesn't have to mean marriage, but those things do take time."

"Am I right in assuming you're a virgin?"

He nodded. "I've never even come close to finding what I just mentioned."

I thought about that, and then I murmured, "None of this should be surprising. There are all kinds of people in the world, right? I guess I've only ever known the one kind, though: slutty like me."

"You're not slutty. You just think of sex differently than I do."

"I need some clarification," I said, "and I'm going to be totally blunt here. Are we just talking about waiting to have anal sex? Do you do other things, or would you, and if so,

when? Oral, for example? Or like, jerking each other off? Or—
"

A quick, embarrassed burst of laughter slipped from him. "Um, I don't know. It's not like I have a chart that says, second date, French kissing, fifth date, below-the-belt contact, and so on. All I know is, I'm not ready to have sex with you today, and I won't be ready on our first date, either."

"Got it. Well, I can handle the wait if you can. It basically just means my right hand and I are going to become BFFs in the days ahead."

He admitted, "Yup. Right there with you."

I grinned at that, and then I asked, "So, what should we do to pass the time?"

"We could keep talking."

"No problem there. I have a lot to say. Probably too much."

Duke shook his head and said, "Never too much. I want to hear anything and everything you're willing to tell me. And you know what? I feel bad for those other guys who were only looking for sex and never took the time to talk to you. They really missed out."

"That's a nice thing to say."

"It's the truth. There's nobody like you, Quinn. Not only are you interesting, but you make me feel like I am, too. I know I'm not, but you make me feel that way."

"Here's something you should know about me," I said. "I have a pretty short attention span. If I don't find something interesting, it's impossible for me to concentrate on it. So, the fact that I'm able to give you my undivided attention for long stretches of time is actual, scientific proof that I find you interesting."

"Scientific, huh?"

"That's right. I can prepare some charts and diagrams clearly illustrating your position as the most fascinating person I know, if that helps."

He grinned and said, "Give me your feet instead." I stretched out my legs, and Duke slid back a little and put them on his lap.

"Is this your version of first base? Start at the feet, then work your way up my legs inch-by-inch over a number of weeks?" He raised an eyebrow, and I smiled and said, "Sorry. I had to tease a bit, but I really am on board with the taking it slow thing. What are you doing down there, though?" He pulled off my shoes and socks, then carefully removed my ankle brace, which was so tight that it left deep, red indentions in my skin. As he began to massage my foot, I moaned with pleasure and flopped back onto the kitchen floor. "That feels *so* good. How did you know I needed this?"

"Because I spent all day with you and saw how much time you spent on your feet. You would have needed this even if that brace hadn't been cutting into you."

"Most people wouldn't have thought about that."

"But I'm not most people."

"Nope," I murmured. "You're a thousand times better."

Chapter Six

Yoshiro Miyazaki matched his tattoo studio. Or, more precisely, it matched him. Both were sophisticated-looking, decked out mostly in black, and had a distinctly modern vibe.

The airy, high-ceilinged space contained eight workstations, four of which held tattoo artists and their clients. That was where the sleek, minimalistic look sort of fell apart. Each artist had personalized their space with various mementos, posters, and collections. I was *not* a fan of the one crammed full of clown figurines. Fortunately, that one wasn't Yoshi's workstation. If it was, I probably would have turned and walked out.

Yoshi greeted me with a smile and a handshake and led me to the tidiest and most sparsely decorated of the eight workspaces. As I perched on the black leather lounger, he said, "I see you brought a friend," and gestured at the two-foot-tall stuffed animal I was clutching.

It was a larger version of the Totoro I kept at my parents' house, and I said, "I thought it'd be good to bring a visual aid for my tattoo. You said you've seen the film, right?"

"I have."

"Okay, good." I showed him a picture on my phone of Totoro wearing a leaf as a hat and said, "Please draw him like this, in full color, as if he just stepped out of the movie." I peeled off my T-shirt, and we discussed size and placement.

After that, he handed me a clipboard with a short form to fill out and sign.

I studied Yoshi while he prepared the inks and tattoo gun. He was probably in his early thirties, with strong cheekbones, dark, expressive eyes, and a flawless haircut, short on the sides, a bit longer on the top. It looked like it fell into place each morning with little more than a rake of his fingers. His only visible tattoo was a beautifully rendered cityscape that sleeved his left arm from wrist to elbow. I wondered if he had more.

According to the rumors I'd heard, he dated a famous singer. I totally believed it. Not only was Yoshi strikingly handsome, he also exuded confidence. It was easy to imagine him poolside at some ritzy Hollywood party with a rock star on his arm.

He was all business at the moment, knitting his brows as he pulled on a pair of black latex gloves and lined up everything precisely on the black lacquer table beside him. But I knew he had a playful side, too. He was friends with one of Nana Dombruso's grandsons, a cute but nerdy guy named Mike, and I'd seen Yoshi at a pool party that summer acting like a total goofball with Mike's three young sons. I'd liked him right away.

Once all his supplies and tools were ready to go, he prepped my skin, and then he said, "I'm going to freehand your tattoo, if you're comfortable with that." I told him I was, and he said, "Great. So, let's get started. The ribcage is a sensitive area, so whenever you need a break, just let me know, okay?"

"I will." I held my breath.

The tattoo gun started up with a low buzzing sound. When Yoshi touched the needle to my skin, it hurt. I knew it would. But the fear reaction that spiked in me was unexpected and totally out of proportion to the amount of pain I felt. As my heartbeat sped up, I pressed my eyes shut and tried to rationalize my way around it.

There was no reason to panic. I took a deep breath, then another. It didn't help. When I leapt from the chair without warning, Yoshi pulled back quickly and swore under his breath. But then he asked, "Are you alright, Quinn?"

I grabbed the stuffed animal, which had been sitting on the floor beside me, and nodded, even though my heart was pounding in my ears. "I just need some air."

Yoshi called, "Take your time," as I forced myself to walk instead of sprinting to the door.

As soon as I was outside, I started running. After a minute, I stopped and looked around. Where the hell was I going? And what had just happened back there?

When I got my bearings, I realized I was close to the Castro. Okay, good. I crossed Market Street and went into the first dive bar I came to. The whole thing was maybe fifteen feet long and eight feet wide, just big enough to hold the bar itself and three little round tables, which were crammed in the back corner. The wall to my right was covered floor-to-ceiling with colorful flyers, which were doubled by the mirrored wall behind the bar.

The place was empty, except for the bartender and a guy of about seventy. I sat down at the bar and put Totoro on the stool beside me, and the barkeep turned to me with a raised eyebrow. He looked exactly like Mr. Clean, right down to the gold earring. I told him, "I need a drink."

"What you need is an I.D. and a shirt, princess. I might let the shirt slide though, just because we're light on eye candy at the moment."

The drunk senior citizen at the end of the bar, who had a big, bushy mustache and an obvious toupee, yelled, "I'm all the eye candy you can handle, Gary!"

The bartender rolled his eyes, and as I pulled out my wallet and riffled through its disorganized contents, he quipped, "Your junior high student I.D. doesn't count, princess. Neither does your Happy Meal punch card or your fidget spinner of the month membership card." When I finally gave him my driver's license and my best exasperated glare, he exclaimed, "Well shit fire and hold the matches, princess is legal!" He returned the license to me and said, "What'll it be?"

"Doesn't matter," I said as I tried to reassemble my wallet, "as long as it's big and loaded with alcohol."

The guy at the end of the bar jumped up and exclaimed, "I'm right here, baby!"

The bartender yelled, "Sit your drunk ass down, Clyde!"

Normally, all of that would have entertained the hell out of me, but I was too out of sorts to fully appreciate it. Pretty soon, a big glass of whatever was placed in front of me. I slammed it down, tossed a couple twenties on the bar, and said, "Keep whatever that was coming."

"You sure? That Long Island iced tea had five shots of alcohol in it."

"I'll take two this next round."

*****

About an hour later, I sent Duke a text, which said: *I'm drunk off my ass, and I don't remember what I did with my shirt.* I glanced at the sore spot on my ribcage and sent a second message: *My new tattoo looks like a tiny dick.*

He texted back a minute later with: *Where are you?*

I turned to the bartender and asked, "Where am I, Gary?" He rattled off a street address, and I typed it in, hit send, and tossed my phone on the bar. "I need another drink."

"Maybe you wanna switch to soda pop, princess," he said. "I don't know how a kid your size is even forming sentences after four Long Islands."

"I'm not a kid or a princess. I'm Quinn, and this is Totoro." I patted my stuffed animal. "I just texted my roommate. He's hot. We're going on a date. He won't fuck me though, because he's a good boy." I blinked and slurred, "What were we talking about?"

"I don't know, honey, but I'm cutting you off. Do you want some coffee?"

"Only if it has booze in it."

"How about milk and sugar instead?"

"Okay." I put my head on the bar. "This is really comfortable. Can I lie down for a minute?"

"Sure honey, go ahead. Not like you're chasing away the rest of the customers."

"Thanks, Gary." I crawled onto the bar and curled up. Then I glanced at him over my shoulder and asked, "Do you have a sandwich I could borrow?"

"Sorry honey, I don't. I think I've got a candy bar around here somewhere, you want that?" I nodded and he said, "Let me find it for you."

"You're really nice." I looked around and asked, "What happened to Clyde?"

"He went home. Here honey, here's your candy bar."

I grasped the chocolate with both hands and closed my eyes. "That's the nicest thing anyone's ever done for me this afternoon. I'm a go-go boy at Thrust, it's just a couple blocks from here," I told him. "You should come visit me. We don't have sandwiches either, but I always keep some candy bars in my locker. I'll give you one."

Gary said, "You're alright, kid. Except for the part where you're drunk off your ass at four in the afternoon. But hey, nobody's perfect." A moment later, he exclaimed, "I checked that kid's I.D., officer. He's twenty-four. You can check it yourself."

A familiar voice said, "It's okay, I'm his roommate."

"Oh," Gary said, "the good boy."

"The what?"

"Nothing, officer."

I raised my lids a quarter-inch and my gaze traveled up the dark blue uniform in front of me. And up, and up, and up. Finally, I reached Duke's face. I sat up and smiled at him as I exclaimed, "Hey! What are you doing here?"

"I decided to check on you, after you texted and told me you were drunk. I thought you were getting a tattoo this afternoon."

"I did. Look." I stuck my candy bar in the pocket of my jeans and framed the black squiggle on my ribcage with both hands. "It's a tiny dick."

"Why did you get a tattoo of a tiny dick?"

"I didn't mean to. It was supposed to be Totoro, but I freaked out like, sixty seconds into the tattoo and jumped up when Yoshi wasn't expecting it. Shit. He probably thought I was going to come back. I need to text him."

"What do you mean by freaked out?"

"I don't know. The needle hurt, which I knew it would, but it wasn't even all that bad. Next thing I knew, I was out of the chair and heading for the door."

Duke held out his hand to help me off the bar. "Come on. Let's get you home."

"But you're working. You had that big-ass double shift today."

"I can radio in and tell them I'm taking my dinner break a bit early."

"You're so nice." I jumped off the bar, grabbed my stuffed animal, and looked at my phone. Then I said, "Yoshi sent me a couple messages. Shit, so did Max! I totally forgot he was coming to the studio."

I sent them both a quick, awkward apology while Duke asked the bartender, "Did he pay for his drinks?"

The man gestured at some bills on the bar and said, "Yup. There's his change."

I called, "Keep it. You're awesome, Gary!"

"Come back any time, honey!"

I waved to him as I meandered out the door. There was a black and white police cruiser double-parked in front of the bar. "This is awesome," I said as I climbed into the backseat. "It's just like being arrested! Can we turn on the siren?" I noticed Duke's partner behind the wheel, watching me over his shoulder with an amused expression, and I exclaimed, "Hi Finn!"

"Hey, Quinn."

"It's a good thing I'm going out with your partner and not you," I said, "because our names sound really stupid together. Finn and Quinn. Quinn and Finn. We could never have one of those celebrity couple nicknames, like Brangelina. We'd just be Finn. Or Quinn. See? It totally doesn't work. Wait, what are Duke and I then? Dinn? That sucks ass. I guess that leaves Quke, as in cucumber, but with the spelling all fucked up. Hey, did you ever wonder why cucumbers have a cute pet name? You don't see other vegetables with that. They're all just carrot. Or squash. Then again, I suppose squash is a cute name all on its own."

I rambled on like that until we pulled up at the curb in front of the house a few minutes later. Duke had to let me out of the backseat, because the doors didn't open from the inside. I paused in front of him on the sidewalk and slurred, "You're sexy as hell in that uniform. Wanna make out?"

"Not now, Quinn."

"You're annoyed with me, aren't you? I'll have to remember not to text you next time I get drunk. Will you remind me?"

Instead of answering, he said, "Come on, let's get you inside so you can sleep it off."

"I can take it from here. You should go back to work so you don't have to use up your dinner break on me."

He walked me into the house anyway. I flopped down on the couch and grumbled, "Damn it, this thing is harder than the floor. Why, Duke? Why must you have such a joyless couch?"

That didn't get an answer either. Instead, he asked, "Is this where you want to be, or should I help you get upstairs?"

"You don't need to help me. I'm fine."

"No you're not."

"I'm still forming sentences, and I haven't puked or passed out."

Duke knit his brows. "That's your definition of fine?"

"It is when I've been drinking."

He turned and headed for the door. Even though he was clearly less than thrilled with me, he said, "Text me if you need anything, and be careful please, especially on the stairs. I'm going back to work."

"Thanks, Duke." The door closed behind him.

I took off my shoes and jeans before curling up in a ball with my stuffed Totoro. I needed a nap, but climbing all those stairs to my room seemed far too ambitious. Fortunately, I was drunk enough to fall asleep pretty much anywhere, even the torture couch.

*****

My neck and shoulders ached when I awoke a few hours later. No surprise, given where I'd been sleeping. I sat up and looked around as I stretched my arms. I didn't know what time it was, but it was dark out, and I'd transitioned nicely into the hangover portion of my impromptu booze fest.

I slumped against the totally unyielding couch and scowled. What was it stuffed with, bricks? Curiosity got the best of me, and I picked up one of the surprisingly heavy, square seat cushions and unzipped it. It took some effort to wrestle off the light green fabric cover, and I was swearing under my breath by the time I tossed it aside. When I unzipped the plastic inner liner, nothing happened at first. But the moment I parted the seam to look inside, hundreds of feathers burst from it.

I jumped up and exclaimed, "What the hell?" They'd been packed in tightly and apparently were under tremendous pressure, so when the upended cushion bounced on the floor, a huge cloud of feathers shot into the air.

I blinked in disbelief. The living room looked like dozens of chickens had exploded in it. How had the manufacturer gotten so many feathers in there? And why? I'd heard of down stuffing, and some of them were small and airy like you'd expect, but most of them were actual, full-size white feathers. They were accompanied by a strong, gamey smell, just to make them worse. I had to wonder what kind of seedy, bargain basement, cheapo emporium had sold Duke his chicken coffin of a couch.

There was absolutely no way I was going to get all those feathers back into the cushion. I knew that for a fact. So basically, I'd just murdered Duke's sofa. I also knew I had to clean up the mess I'd made, which was going to suck. I doubled over with a big sneeze, which kicked up a cloud of feathers, and scratched my left arm.

When I sneezed three more times in quick succession, it became obvious I was allergic to the damn things. My eyes started to itch and water, and I upgraded the diagnosis to *severely* allergic. I decided the best course of action was to put some distance between myself and the source of my allergy, so I rushed out the front door in a swirl of feathers. I was vaguely aware of the fact that I was dressed in nothing but a skimpy, red jockstrap, socks, and an ankle brace, but I didn't really care. After all, I wore little more than that when I worked at the nightclub.

I went around to the side of the house, turned on the hose, and splashed some cold water on my face, which soothed my eyes a bit. I had a pounding headache, thanks to my earlier one-man Long Island iced tea party, and every time I sneezed, it made my head throb. Plus, I was breaking out all over in itchy hives, so basically, I was a total mess. I turned off the hose and ended up stretching out on the cold cement walkway leading to the side gate, just because it felt good on my bumpy, red skin.

After a few minutes though, I started to shiver, so I got up and went around to the front of the house. I stopped and smiled at the sight of a tabby cat running up the steps, and I called, "Hey kitty, where are you going?"

I got my answer a moment later, when I reached the foot of the stairs and peered through the front door, which was in the process of swinging shut. The living room was filled with at least a dozen cats. I could only assume the smell had attracted them, and they were going batshit crazy with the feathers. I murmured, "Oh no," and ran up the stairs, but the door clicked shut a split second before I reached it. When I jiggled the handle, it was locked.

I knocked, which was stupid. Like the cats were going to answer? Next, I tried knocking on Xavier's door, but the guy who rented the other half of the duplex wasn't home.

I trudged out to the sidewalk and looked up at the house. A gray cat came to a stop beside me and stared at it, too. I told him, "Sorry, you're too late. The cat rave is happening inside, but we can't get in. I hope they're not destroying everything. My roommate is already going to be mad at me for killing his couch, and now this." The gray cat just blinked at me.

I hopped the fence and checked the back door, followed by each window on the ground floor, but everything was locked. When I returned to the front of the house and peered through one of the living room windows, it seemed the cat party was kicking into high gear. I had no idea what it was about the feathers that got them so worked up, but the cats were racing around and jumping all over the furniture.

When one of them knocked over a lamp, I knew I had to get in there and control the situation. The only open window was on the second floor at the front of the house, but it would have to do. After thinking through my options, I returned to the backyard and heaved the patio chairs over the locked gate. Then I stacked them on top of each other to build a rickety scaffold in front of the living room's picture window. A couple of cats stopped frolicking to watch what I was doing.

It was easy to climb the chair ladder. The window opened from the bottom, and I pushed it up as far as it would go, which was only about ten inches. That would have to be enough. I pulled myself up onto the windowsill and stuffed my head and shoulders through the opening. In the process, I knocked over the chair tower. To my relief, it fell onto the tiny front yard, instead of crashing through the picture window.

My entry point was at the end of the hallway that led to the stairs and my room. I put my hands on the wood floor and walked them forward as I shimmied through the window. My torso slid through fairly easily, but when I tried to fit my butt through the opening, I ground to a halt.

Damn it, really? I kicked my legs and tried to wiggle through, but it absolutely wasn't happening. I sighed and slumped in the window, draped over the sill like a rag doll with my hands on the floor and my ass and legs dangling outside.

I was just about to give up and extract myself from the window when a single, piercing blast from a police siren made me jump. Red and blue lights reflected on the white walls to either side of me. I was torn between hoping it was Duke and praying it wasn't.

A moment later, he yelled, "Quinn? Is that you?" I sighed and waved to him with my foot. He called, "Wait there, I'll come upstairs and help you."

I sighed and murmured, "Wait for it."

It was obvious when he opened the front door, because it was accompanied by a booming, "What the hell is happening in this living room?"

Some kind of cat mayhem ensued. It sounded like Duke was trying to shoo them out, but they weren't going without a fight. There was a crashing sound and a muffled yell. A cat screeched, and soon after, two of them ran up the stairs and into my room. Oh man.

Duke came up the stairs a minute later with a few feathers sticking to his hair and uniform. He did something to the window so it would slide open all the way, then grabbed my arms and hauled me inside. I expected him to yell, but instead he asked, "Are you okay?"

I nodded, and then I started rambling, like I always did when I knew I'd fucked up. "Sorry about all of this. I got locked out. Oh, and I'm breaking out in hives. That's why I'm polka-dotted. I have some antihistamine in my bathroom, which should fix me right up. I don't know why the cats went so crazy for the feathers. I came outside when I started having an allergy attack, and next thing I knew, every cat on the block had taken over our living room."

Duke didn't say anything for a long moment, as a little muscle worked in his jaw. Finally, he took my hand and led me to the bathroom. I sat on the toilet lid as he opened the medicine cabinet and popped a couple antihistamines from their packaging, then filled a cup. When he handed me the tablets and water, I looked up at him and asked, "Aren't you mad at me?"

He crouched down beside me and brushed my hair from my eyes. "I know you didn't do any of that on purpose."

I swallowed the pills and returned the cup to the shelf above the sink. When we both stood up, Duke wrapped his arms around me, and I sank into his embrace. After a few moments, I asked, "Do you have to go back to work?"

"Yeah. I had half an hour between shifts, so I thought I'd check on you."

"Is Finn downstairs?"

"No, he went home when his shift ended. I was the only one dumb enough to volunteer to work a double."

"Is the house still full of cats, and if so, are you freaking out about what they're doing down there?"

"I scared most of them out the door when I fell over the coffee table," he said, "but there might be a few stragglers."

"I'll round them up, I promise. I'll also fix the living room."

"Should I ask where all the feathers came from?"

"One of the seat cushions on the couch. I had to know why they were so rock-hard, and I got my answer. The manufacturer somehow managed to pack a metric ton of chicken feathers in there." I plucked a short feather from his shoulder. "At least, I assume this came from a chicken, but what do I know?"

He dusted himself off as he said, "I'll clean them up when I get home from my second shift. You should stay in your room with the door shut, so these allergies don't get any worse."

Duke lightly tapped the end of my nose with his index finger, and I asked, "Did you just do that because I have a red bump there?" He nodded, and I tucked my face into his shoulder. "Ugh, I must look disgusting right now."

"You couldn't look disgusting if you tried, Quinn."

I raised an eyebrow as I scratched my thigh. "Dude, I'm polka-dotted."

"Even so." He kissed my (probably blotchy) forehead and said, "I have to go back to work. Promise me you'll stay upstairs, and call me if your allergies get worse, okay?"

"I will, even though I feel terrible about making you clean up my mess."

"Actually, I like to clean. It's soothing." I pulled him down to my height and brushed my lips to his. He kissed me gently and ran his fingertips over my cheek before leaving the bathroom. I was grinning as I turned on the shower.

"Duke? Is that you?" I sat up in bed and blinked at my surroundings. I'd fallen asleep with the lights on and a comic book draped over my chest and had been awakened by a creaking sound out in the hall.

He stuck his head through the gap in the door and said, "I'm sorry to wake you. I saw your light on, so I came upstairs to see how you were."

I pushed down my Wonder Woman comforter, stuck my arms out, and examined them top and bottom. "I'm still blotchy, but the bumps are gone and I don't itch anymore."

"That's good. Well, I should let you get some rest."

He started to leave, but I tossed my comic book aside and said, "Don't go yet. Come sit down and tell me how your shift went."

Duke came into the room and perched on the edge of my new mattress. He smelled like soap and was dressed in a white tank top and a pair of cotton shorts. My eyes started to wander down his big, sexy body, but then I checked myself and met his gaze as he said, "It was extremely long, but uneventful."

"Uneventful has to be a good thing in your line of work." He nodded at that, and I asked, "Did you find any more cats when you got home?"

"Yup. There were two under the sofa, so I escorted them out."

"I wonder if they were the two that ran from my room when I went to bed."

"Maybe. I got rid of the feathers, too. I tried to stuff a few back into the cushion, but it wasn't particularly successful." I was idly rubbing my ribcage, and Duke asked, "Does your tattoo hurt?"

"Not a lot. It kind of feels like a sunburn, but just over a three-inch area." I pulled up the hem of my T-shirt, glanced at the squiggle, and sighed. It was basically an elongated, upside-down U, with a little flare at just the right place to make it look like a cock. I wondered what Yoshi had actually been drawing when my unannounced flail sent his tattoo gun skittering across my skin. "Damn it, I need to have this fixed. I spend a hell of a lot of time half-naked, and this looks too stupid to just leave it like that. Do you suppose laser tattoo removal hurts in the same way that getting a tattoo does?"

"I really don't know."

"I'd ask Yoshi to tattoo over it, but I don't think I can face another minute of that needle on my skin." I wrapped my arms around myself as a little shudder ran through me.

"Was it really that painful?"

"No. I mean, it didn't feel great, but it wasn't unbearable, either." I studied my blanket, and after a pause, I admitted, "The problem is…it was familiar."

"What do you mean?"

"I guess it almost triggered a memory, something from a long time ago, before my mom and dad adopted me. Maybe I'd been scratched, or burned. Who knows? Most of the scars on my body have totally faded out, so I can't really tell what was done to me. I only remember pain, and being afraid, and when that needle touched my skin this afternoon, that fear came rushing back to me."

Duke pulled me into a hug, and I sank into his arms. After a moment, I asked, "Will you please sleep here tonight? I'm not talking about sex. I just really need you right now."

He murmured, "Of course," and we both shifted around and got under the covers.

I snuggled against Duke's chest, and as he gathered me in an embrace, I whispered, "Thank you."

"You don't have to thank me," he said softly. "I'm getting just as much out of this as you are. Your new bed is really comfortable, by the way. I can't tell you how happy I am that the porn mattress never made it into the house."

I grinned at that as I lightly traced his collarbone with a fingertip, but then I grew serious. After a while, I said, "I don't want to be the weird guy who freaks out while getting a tattoo. Also, I could really do without the random panic attacks about stuff I can't even remember. I try so hard to just be happy and enjoy my life, but every once in a while, something like this happens, and I'm reminded how damaged I am. I fucking hate it, Duke. I hate the fact that even though decades have gone by, the monsters who brought me into this world can still hurt me."

His voice was so quiet when he said, "I totally understand."

I held him tightly and whispered, "I know you do. I understand your pain too, Duke. Maybe better than anyone."

After a long pause, he said, "I had a brother. He died before I was born."

"That's so sad. What was his name?"

"Ulrich."

"Why do you have the same name?"

"I guess I was supposed to take his place, but I was doomed to fail, right from the start. To hear my parents tell it, he was the perfect son and could do no wrong. How could I live up to that? How could anyone?"

After another pause, Duke said, "It's an odd thing, spending your entire life in the shadow of someone you've never even met. I often wonder what Rick was like. That's what everyone called him. I wonder if he and I would have gotten along, or if we would have had anything in common. But that's so stupid. I wouldn't even exist if he hadn't died, so there's no point in wondering what he would have been like as a big brother."

I whispered, "What happened to him?"

"He drowned. It was the night of his high school graduation. He was supposed to go on to the University of

Arizona on a full baseball scholarship. Everyone expected him to have this bright, glorious future. But instead, he got so drunk at a party that he fell into a swimming pool and died, despite the fact that he'd worked as a lifeguard every summer and was an excellent swimmer."

"Oh God."

"It's terrible, I know. I guess you never get over a loss like that. My parents certainly didn't. That part I understand. What I don't get is the decision to have another child, give him the same name, and expect him to somehow step into the giant shoes left behind by a boy who's remembered as perfect in every way. I know I'm a terrible person for resenting Rick, and for thinking things like, how perfect could he have been if he was out partying that hard? He was just a kid, and he died, and nothing that happened to me was his fault. He didn't know our parents would try to replace him with a second-rate facsimile, or that our father's frustration, grief, and disappointment would result in him beating me while our mother turned a blind eye."

I whispered, "Oh no."

Duke stroked my hair, as if I was the one who needed comforting, and said, "It's in the past now. My father can't hurt me anymore. I was seventeen the last time he tried. He went to hit me, and I lunged at him. I was as big as he was at that point, and it must have scared him to realize I was willing to fight back. I stopped myself before I did anything to him, but he got the message and the beatings stopped."

I sat up and tried to meet his gaze. "I don't understand why you allow your parents to be a part of your life now. They're terrible people, and they don't deserve you!"

He shrugged and studied the macaroni Elvis on the wall beside the bed. "They're all I have. I don't make friends easily, and I don't have any other family aside from my grandmother, but she doesn't want anything to do with me."

"Fuck them! You have me, Duke, and you don't need those people!"

"But I don't have you. Not really. We've known each other a matter of days, and even though you agreed to go out with me and I'd love to be optimistic about that, it's hard to imagine this developing into anything long-term."

"How can you say that?"

"Because you're you, and I'm me."

I told him, "That's not an explanation."

Duke sighed and tucked a hand behind his head. "Isn't it obvious? You're amazing, Quinn. You're fun and spontaneous, and so full of life that you light up every room you walk into. As if that wasn't enough, you're also gorgeous, and talented, and fascinating. You're as dazzling as a hundred fireworks going off all at once, and I'm about as interesting as an old piece of cardboard. Maybe that's a novelty for now. Maybe you decided, just for laughs, to take a walk on the mild side. But I can't possibly expect to hold your attention for long. It'd be like a peacock settling down with a pigeon."

"I bet a peacock and a pigeon could be fantastic together! Although in this case, the alleged pigeon has totally failed to realize he's a swan."

"Oh, come on."

"Don't talk yourself out of this before we've even gotten off the ground, Duke."

"I'm not."

"Yes you are, and I hate the fact that you're so down on yourself!"

"For good reason."

"That's your parents talking," I said. "They made you believe you weren't good enough, but they were wrong. You're fucking amazing!"

He laughed humorlessly and muttered, "Hardly."

"You are, and you fascinate me! I want to know everything that's going on behind those gorgeous, sea blue eyes. I want to know what you dream about, and what you want out of life, and what matters to you. I want to know *you*, Duke."

"You're just being nice, which is probably also why you agreed to go out with me."

"I'm going out with you because you're kind, smart, beautiful, and gentle, plus a million more good things. And because of this." I climbed on top of him and kissed him passionately, and he drew in his breath against my lips. I kissed him with all the raw hunger I'd been holding back as I caressed his silky, short hair and straddled his waist.

He held back for only an instant before grabbing me and returning the kiss with an intensity unlike anything I'd ever experienced. His hands slid down my back as he pushed his tongue into my mouth, and my cock throbbed against his belly. I ached for him with every part of me. He flooded my senses, his scent, his taste, the warmth of his body, the sound of the soft moan that slipped from his lips.

He cupped my ass and kissed my neck, and my voice was rough when I whispered, "I'm sorry. I know we're supposed to be taking this slowly. But you need to know how much I want you, Duke."

His eyes were dilated when he looked up at me. "Don't apologize. I only said I need to wait before we have sex." A wicked little grin appeared on his full lips. "There's still so much we can do."

"Really? So you're okay with—"

I didn't get to finish my sentence, because Duke tossed me onto the mattress, pulled off my T-shirt and started sucking my nipple as he caressed my hard-on through my pajama pants. A delighted burst of laughter slipped from me, and I said, "I'll take that as a yes."

After that, there was no need for words. He bit my nipple, just a little, and my cock throbbed in response. Duke slid his hand under my waistband and gripped my shaft as the tip of his tongue played with the double-ended silver stud that pierced my nipple. He stroked me for a few moments, almost experimentally, and then he stripped off my pajama pants, leaned over, and looked in my nightstand.

He found what he wanted right away and squirted some lube into his palm. He then started jerking me off while his lips and tongue explored my body, licking, sucking, and tasting all of me. I moaned and writhed with pleasure as he rolled my nipples between his fingertips, first one, then the other until they were rock-hard.

Duke tightened his grip and started jerking me off harder and faster. I couldn't have held back even if I wanted to. In just a couple of minutes, I groaned and shot all over my chest and stomach. It had been a while, and to say I'd needed release was an understatement.

When he let go of me and sat back, I grabbed my pajama pants with a shaking hand and wiped the cum from my body. Then I threw them aside and launched myself at Duke. Obviously he had to cooperate in order for me to push him onto his back, since he was built like a fortress. I grasped the waistband of his shorts with both hands, looked up at him and said, "If you want me to stop, just say the word."

He grinned at that and said, "I'd have to be out of my mind."

That was all I needed to hear. I stripped him from the waist down and knelt between his legs. Then I just had to take a moment to admire the view. His cock was in perfect proportion to the rest of him. In other words, it was long and thick, and at that moment, rock hard.

I ran my hands up his muscular thighs and licked his cock from balls to tip before taking it in my mouth. He drew in his breath as I slid my lips down his shaft and looked up at him. Duke was propped up on his elbows, watching me, and when our eyes met, the connection was overwhelming.

Everything fell away, except for Duke. I held his gaze as I sucked him, stroking his shaft with one hand while working his balls with the other. His expression was one of pure bliss. I was proud of the fact that I'd caused it.

He reached down to caress my face and hair, and in just a few minutes, Duke moaned as he came, cupping my cheek with his big hand, still holding my gaze as his body shook and he gasped for breath. I swallowed his cum, then gently eased him down. When he finished, I slid my lips from his cock and grinned shyly.

He took me in his arms and kissed me, so tenderly, and then we both climbed under the covers. I turned off the lamp on the nightstand and curled up with my head on his chest. He kissed my forehead, and I smiled when he murmured, "Wow."

"Just to be clear, I didn't have an ulterior motive when I asked you to get in bed with me."

"I know." He tilted my chin up and kissed me again before asking, "Is it still alright if I sleep here tonight?"

"God yes."

He laced his fingers with mine and kissed my knuckle before resting our joined hands on his chest. After a while, he said, "This has been such a surprising evening."

I draped my leg over his and said, "In a good way, I hope."

"In the best way possible. I feel like a different person when I'm with you."

"How so?"

"Well for one thing, I talk."

"Don't you usually?"

"Nope, and certainly not about anything as personal as the stuff I told you tonight. But you just…."

"What?"

He shrugged and looked away. "Nothing. It sounds stupid."

"Say it anyway."

He glanced at me, then looked away again and murmured, "Guys like me shouldn't say stuff like, 'you make me feel safe.' I mean, come on. I'm supposed to be the protector, not the one who needs protecting."

"Who makes these rules? Why can't a guy be big and strong and still want to feel safe? What's so wrong with that?"

"It just doesn't fit."

"That's society talking, but other people don't get to define us, Duke. A guy can be both big and vulnerable, or little and tough as nails. Fuck stereotypes."

He watched me for a few moments in the semi-darkness, and then he grinned and said, "You make me feel safe, Quinn." I smiled at him and curled up in his arms.

Chapter Seven

Duke was the first thing I saw when I raised my lids the next morning. It made me smile. His face was just inches from mine, and he was sleeping peacefully with his arm draped over me.

He looked so young, more so than ever when he was asleep, and he was breathtakingly beautiful. A splash of sunlight filtered in through a gap in the curtains, and it lit up a sprinkling of gold in his short, dark blond hair and in the stubble that shaded his jaw. His thick lashes fanned out gorgeously against his skin, and for the first time, I noticed a few faint freckles across his nose and cheeks, barely visible against his light tan. But his mouth was what really riveted my attention. His full lips curved sensually, and it was so tempting to kiss them, but after that late double shift the day before, I knew I shouldn't wake him.

How could he routinely work sixteen-hour days without it wearing him down? How could anyone? And all because his mother and father had pushed him into buying a house he really couldn't afford.

Anger welled in me at the thought of his parents. The abuse I'd endured had ended when I was adopted, but what he'd gone through had lasted until his late teens. Given the emotional damage I carried with me, even after years of therapy, I could only imagine what he was dealing with.

It broke my heart, and it also put a lot about him into perspective. For one thing, I got why he was so driven to work out and bulk up. I'd felt small, weak, and defenseless when I was a child. He'd probably felt the same way, so he'd made himself strong, to make damn sure no one could ever hurt him again. His need for order made sense, too. I wasn't like that, but I understood it. He probably needed to feel like he was in control of his environment.

It occurred to me that in many ways, ballet did the same things for me. It made me strong, but there was more to it than that. I was always pushing and challenging myself, proving to myself I could do anything I wanted, and that I was in total control of my body. No one else, just me. While the specifics of my abuse had been locked away in my memory, the impression that remained was feeling out of control and helpless. I spent a hell of a lot of time proving to myself I was neither of those things.

I studied Duke as he slept. At first, I'd only seen our differences. But we were the same, in so many ways. Here, finally, was someone who might truly understand me. By the same token, I thought I understood him in a way few people could.

But that connection was actually pretty frightening, because it meant the potential was there for something real to develop between us. I'd made it twenty-four years without ever having a serious relationship, by choice. I got the attention I craved and the intimacy I needed by sleeping with a lot of guys. I'd even dated a few of them, but only for a week or two. That was it.

Letting people get close to me was a challenge. Sure, I had some friends, and I was close to my family, but romantic relationships were another thing entirely. They could start out with the best intentions. The other person might even want to marry you and promise to be with you forever. But since half of all marriages ended in divorce, that meant half those promises were a lie. Relationships failed as often as they succeeded, and people got hurt. Really hurt.

I was a work in progress. I knew that about myself. I wanted to be strong, and in some ways, I was. But deep down, I was still a scared little kid. Hell, just the day before, I'd freaked out over a damn tattoo gun! How did I think I was going to be able to handle a full-blown relationship, even with someone as wonderful as Duke?

For the second time in two days, a wave of panic swept over me, and I took a deep, shaky breath. Fuck! Why did I have to be such a mess? Why couldn't I just be happy and optimistic?

We were just days into this, and I was already falling apart. We hadn't even gone out yet, not that the formality of an 'official' first date mattered. There was definitely something happening between us, and that scared the shit out of me.

I slid out of bed and grabbed some clothes from the clean laundry pile on a chair in the corner. But then I turned to look at Duke, who was still sleeping peacefully, and was overcome with guilt. After our first night together and what was probably one of his first sexual encounters, I couldn't let him wake up to an empty house. He trusted me. He'd even said I made him feel safe. Sneaking out like he was just another one-night stand was *not* okay.

Instead of running, I went into my bathroom and closed the door as quietly as I could. I then spent quite a while in the shower as I tried to get myself together, followed by shaving and getting dressed slowly. By the time I finished, the panic was under control, but just barely.

When I returned to the bedroom, I found a note on my neatly made bed. It said: *I went downstairs to make us breakfast.* Duke had drawn a smiley face beneath the words. It actually broke my heart a little, because I couldn't imagine another time in his life when he would have done something that playful.

Another wave of guilt welled up in me. I'd never get through breakfast without Duke realizing I was freaking out. What if he thought I was having second thoughts about us? That wasn't what was happening, but it could certainly look that way.

I knew I needed to talk to him, but I couldn't do that until I got myself together. To buy myself some time, I pulled a hoodie over my T-shirt and sweats, packed my messenger bag, and put on my sneakers and sunglasses before heading downstairs.

Duke was hard at work in the kitchen, making blueberry muffins from scratch. He was adorable in his glasses and apron. When he saw me, he said, "Hey. You look like you're on your way out."

"Yeah, I have to get to rehearsal." It wasn't for hours. I hated myself for lying to him.

"The muffins are going to take a while to bake, but do you have time for coffee?"

"I wish I did, but I don't want to be late."

He said, "I could drive you. Then you'd have a little more time."

"You don't have to do that." I circled the island and kissed his cheek. "I'll see you tonight."

"Is everything okay?" Damn it. He was way too observant.

I stuck a smile on my face and kept my voice cheerful as I said, "Totally."

"Alright, I'll see you later then. I'll be home around midnight." I felt like an asshole as I headed for the door.

*****

Even though I'd stopped for breakfast on the way there, I was still ridiculously early for rehearsal. I should have gone out and found something to do to pass the time, but instead, I gravitated to the comfort and familiarity of the warehouse. Dare answered my knock with a grin and said, "I appreciate the enthusiasm, but you know we don't start for two more hours, right?"

"I know. Is it okay if I hang out until then?"

He stepped back and held the door for me. Dare was dressed in what I thought of as his uniform, a black tank top and black cotton shorts, which he wore whenever he knew he was going to be dancing, and he said, "Of course. I was going over some bills in the office. Come join me."

As I followed him through the quiet warehouse, past his husband's massive work-in-progress of a head and grasping hands that looked like they were clawing their way up from under the earth, I asked, "Where's Skye?"

"He's in San Francisco, meeting with a potential client. It's kind of odd. They want a sculpture for the lobby of this big office building downtown, but Skye's work isn't exactly corporate, so we're not sure why they approached him."

"He should make them a gigantic sculpture of two guys fucking. It's perfect! Corporate America has been screwing people for years."

Dare chuckled and said, "I wouldn't put it past him."

His office was a ten-foot-square space at the back of the building, with fake wood paneling from the 1970s and a tall bank of windows that were made of some kind of odd, corrugated glass and swung outward with a crank. A purple bougainvillea vine in the alley filled the view, bringing color and beauty to the otherwise utilitarian office.

When I sat down on the burnt orange corduroy couch (which had come with the building), Dare's dog got up from his folded blanket in the corner, flopped onto the couch with his head on my thigh, and wagged his entire butt. I said, "Hey Benny," and scratched the black and white boxer's ears. Then I gestured at Dare's cluttered desk and said, "It looks like you're drowning in paperwork."

He shifted some papers and said, "I wish I could afford to hire an accountant. A lot of these are receipts from the dance classes I teach. I was separating them from the bills for our upcoming show, and then I have to type everything into spreadsheets. Joy."

"Speaking of the show, how are ticket sales?"

"Okay, I guess. We've sold nearly two-thirds of the tickets, so the way it stands now, we'll probably break even. It's too bad the theater rental and advertising were so damn expensive." He sat down on his creaking office chair and pushed his straight, dark hair out of his eyes.

I said, "You know what we need?"

"A miracle?"

"I was going to say we needed a publicist, but a miracle would be good, too."

"That'd be nice," Dare said, "but there's no way we can pay someone. I could barely afford the material for our costumes. Thank God Haley is sewing them for us, because I wouldn't be able to pay a seamstress, either."

I grinned and said, "I just had the best idea. Is it okay if I run with it?"

"Will it cost me money?"

"Since that huge box of flyers in the corner is still half full, nope, not a cent."

"We've already done the flyer thing. They're up in every business in the Castro and beyond. We've also stood on what feels like every street corner in the city and handed them out, over and over again. None of that really boosted sales, even though it's a pretty kick-ass flyer." It really was. Dare had printed it in full-color, and it featured Haley holding me above his head in a dramatic pose, against a vibrant, graffiti art background painted by Skye's artist friend Christian. The name of the troupe, Dare to Dance, was spelled out boldly across the top.

I said, "The problem is, there are hundreds of dancers, performers, and artists vying for attention in San Francisco, so even a gorgeous flyer like ours gets lost in the sea of information overload. But I know someone who's great at thinking outside the box, and I bet she could help us sell the remaining tickets."

"So, who's this miracle worker?"

I smiled cheerfully, pulled out my phone, and selected one of my contacts. When the call connected, I said, "Hi Nana, this is Quinn Takahashi. You know that show I'm in, the one with Dare Evans' dance troupe? We need help selling tickets, so I'm wondering if there might be a way to cross-promote both the show and the upcoming fundraiser for your shelter. Kind of a two-for-one."

She sounded excited. "That's a peach of an idea, Quinn! What we need is a publicity stunt that no one can miss! I'd been thinking I needed to do this anyway for the fundraiser, and now I have two reasons to pull out all the stops. I'll put on my thinking cap and let you know what I come up with."

We chatted for another minute, and when we disconnected, I told Dare, "I should have thought of that sooner. Nana Dombruso knows a ton of people, and she has the resources to do something big and flashy."

"That's true. I just hope she doesn't get us arrested in the process. Nana doesn't tend to play by the rules."

"She does where her shelter's concerned, though. She wants to make sure no one can ever shut that place down, because the residents are going to rely on it. Given that, I bet whatever she comes up with for the cross-promotion will be mostly legal."

Dare grinned a little and echoed, "Mostly."

"Well, it's still Nana we're talking about."

"Let me know what she comes up with."

"Definitely."

I took off my shoes and curled up in a corner of the couch with the dog right beside me. When I hugged my knees to my chest, Dare asked, "Is something wrong? You don't seem like your usual, enthusiastic self today."

"I'm fine."

"Your body language begs to differ."

I leaned against the back of the couch. After a moment, I said, "So, there's this guy."

The corners of Dare's green eyes crinkled as he smiled at me. "Isn't there always?"

"This one's different. Really different."

"You're talking about Duke, aren't you?"

"How did you know?"

"There was something in the way he looked at you when you brought him to rehearsal. It made me think you two were more than friends."

"How did he look at me?"

"Like you were the most fascinating thing in the world."

I said, "He asked me out after that. Our first date is on Wednesday."

"If you haven't even gone out yet, why are you worried?"

"We've been growing closer ever since we became roommates, and we spent last night together. It was fantastic, but this morning, I started to panic. I think this could easily develop into something real, and...."

"You don't know if you're ready for that." I nodded, and he said, "It's perfectly natural to feel anxious at the start of a new relationship."

"Is that how you felt when you met Skye?"

"Actually, I was scared shitless," Dare said.

"Why?"

"I had major trust issues back then, and I was bitter and angry at the world. I couldn't even imagine letting anyone get close to me. When the universe put that beautiful, amazing man in my path, I actually tried to convince myself I hated Skye at first. But that was total bullshit, and he and I both knew it."

"I can't even imagine you bitter or angry."

"I was a much different person before Skye came into my life. I'd only had one other relationship, and it took a huge toll on me, both mentally and physically," he said. "The first time you saw the surgery scar on my knee, you assumed I'd hurt it while dancing, and I didn't bother to correct you. Actually, it was injured when my ex pushed me down a flight of stairs."

"Oh God!"

"When I first met Skye, I hadn't had the operation yet, because I couldn't afford it. I was able to work as a go-go dancer, but the demands of ballet were way too much for my knee. I thought my career was over at twenty-four, and I was furious about what had been done to me."

I murmured, "No wonder you were bitter."

"Exactly." Dare glanced at me and added, "I'm not telling you all of this because I want sympathy, by the way. I guess I'm just trying to say, I get it. It's not always easy letting people get close to you."

"It really isn't. But you managed to let Skye in, despite all of that."

"I had to. I wanted him more than I'd ever wanted anything in my life."

"It still must have been difficult, though."

Dare grinned and said, "I guess it's like skydiving. It was tough to take the first step. But after that, all I had to do was fall. And I fell so hard for Skye."

"I guess in that analogy, I'm still back on the plane, clinging to the seats." After a pause, I asked, "What did you do to get yourself to take the plunge?"

"I guess it ultimately came down to shifting my focus from the past to the future, from what had happened to me to what I wanted for the rest of my life. I knew opening myself up to a relationship meant the possibility of getting hurt, but I also knew Skye was absolutely worth the risk. He's just…everything." The sweetest smile lit up his face.

"This thing between Duke and me feels like it's happening so fast. I think that's part of the reason I'm scared."

"You could tell him you want to take it slower."

"You're right. But the thing is, I don't think I want to slow it down. As much as it terrifies me, I feel like I *need* to take that leap. So basically, I'm causing my own anxiety."

"It was like that with Skye, too. I had to be with him, despite all my fears and worries." He grinned and added, "This'll sound crazy, but I started falling for him even before we met."

"How does that work, exactly?"

"We were both on a dating site, not that I actually wanted to go out with anyone. I was just lonely and needed someone to talk to, and I started chatting online with this funny, upbeat guy, who turned out to be Skye."

"I thought you met at the club where you both worked."

"In a way, we did. While we were chatting online, he mentioned he needed a job, so I told him about some upcoming open auditions at the club. He didn't seem interested, so I changed the subject and forgot all about it."

Dare continued, "The day of the auditions, I was walking down Castro Street on my way to the club, and I was in a terrible mood. My knee was killing me because my prescription for pain medicine had run out, and I was pissed off that I'd gotten roped into working the try-outs. They're so frustrating. Every cute guy with a gym membership thinks he has what it takes to be a go-go boy, as if all you need to do is shake your ass and boom, you're hired!"

I grinned and said, "I've heard the go-go boy wannabe rant before. You're not wrong, by the way."

"I know. It's such a pet peeve. Anyway, I was trying to get to the club, and the Castro was crowded as hell, same as usual. All of a sudden, my path was blocked by what I assumed was a tourist. He was completely oblivious to his surroundings and mugging for photos in front of one of the bars. I totally snapped at him, even though he was fucking adorable."

I grinned and said, "Let me guess. Did he have blue hair?"

"Yup. It was Skye. Later on, he showed up at the audition. He was so cocky, but he was also an excellent dancer, and the club owner hired him on the spot. We started working together after that. I was wildly attracted to him, but I really didn't want to be. It scared the hell out of me to even consider getting close to anyone, after everything that had happened with my ex."

He took a sip from the coffee cup on his desk, then grimaced and exclaimed, "Gross! I guess that's been there awhile." He shuddered and put the mug well out of reach before saying, "At the same time, I was still chatting with the sweet, kind, funny guy online, but I was trying to keep some distance there, too. In fact, we didn't even tell each other our real names."

"How'd you eventually figure out your online sweetie and the hot go-go boy were one and the same?"

"I didn't. Skye pieced it together and showed up at the dance studio where I worked one day. I'd been so conflicted, since I felt this strong physical attraction to Skye at the club and this overwhelming emotional connection to the guy online. When I found out they were one and the same, I knew I couldn't fight it anymore. It wasn't even a conscious decision. I needed him like I needed air. So, we got together, and for the first time in years, I started to feel optimistic again. I guess that's when I started looking to the future instead of the past."

I smiled and said, "That's the best how-I-met-my-honey story ever. I can't believe I never knew all of this."

"You never wanted to talk about relationships before. I guess Duke's getting under your skin."

"He is, and it sucks that I acted like such an idiot this morning. I didn't want him to know I was panicking, so I told him I had to get to rehearsal and left. He was right in the middle of making us breakfast, too."

"The fact that you're roommates does add an extra degree of difficulty. Normally, after a first night together, everyone gets to go home and regroup. But he's right there, all the time."

"Yup."

"What if...never mind."

I said, "You can say it. What if it doesn't work out between us?"

"Exactly."

"I'd have to move. It would be way too awkward to continue living under the same roof. But the bigger question is, what if it does work out? What if we start dating, and everything's great? Then what? Couples usually wait months or years before moving in together, but we're already there! I know living with a roommate and a boyfriend isn't the same thing, but then again, we're already sharing meals and hanging out together, and now we've more or less slept together, so the line between being roommates and being a couple is already blurry."

"More or less?"

"We messed around last night, but we're waiting until we're both ready before we actually fuck." I knit my brows at Dare's quizzical expression and added, "Okay, so we're waiting until *he's* ready. You know I've fucked half of San Francisco, so it's not like I'm saving myself."

"You're in totally uncharted territory here, aren't you?"

"Big time. I've never even met anyone like Duke before, let alone tried to date them."

"But maybe he's exactly what you've needed all along."

"He really might be, and damn it Dare, I'm going to blow it. Hell, I already am! He knew I was lying this morning when I told him I had to get to rehearsal and left him standing there holding his muffins." Dare fought back a grin, and I said, "Literally. He likes to bake, and he was making me blueberry muffins, which is pretty much the sweetest thing ever. And what did I do? I lied to him and ran away, as if he was just another one-night stand."

"You need to talk to him and tell him what's going on with you."

"I will. I just wasn't ready to do that this morning."

Dare said, "I really hope it works out."

"Thanks."

Skye wandered into the office a few moments later and flopped down beside me on the couch. The dog climbed over me and wagged his whole body, and Skye petted him absently. He was dressed up in a royal blue button-down shirt and nice jeans (though he was also wearing his usual, beat up blue Chucks), and he looked dazed. Dare jumped up and hurried over to him as he asked, "Are you okay?"

Skye nodded and blinked at his husband. After a moment, he realized I was sitting there and murmured, "Hi, Quinn."

I said, "Hey. Why are you doing the deer in headlights thing?"

"I had a meeting in the city this morning. This lady had called me. She said she took her daughter to Christian's community art center for painting classes, and she loved the mobile I'd made for the front entrance. She said she wanted to meet with me to talk about doing a project for the lobby of her company's corporate headquarters. So I went, not really knowing what to expect."

Skye shifted a bit and continued, "It turned out to be this newly remodeled, huge building in the Financial District. We were sitting in the lobby so I could see where she wanted the mobile, and it was just utterly sterile. You know that little robot in Wall-e that's constantly cleaning and flips out whenever he sees a mess? I kept expecting him to show up and scrub me to death! Plus, the people were all identical. It was a trip! They reminded me of drones, and she was their queen bee. She introduced me to half a dozen executives during the meeting, and I wouldn't be able to pick out any of them in a lineup."

"Weird."

"Right? So there I was, with the drones, and the sci-fi movie sterility, and this woman, who was like, way too enthusiastic. I was so far out of my element that the whole time she was talking, all I could think about was getting the hell out of there. So, when she asked how much I'd charge to build a twenty-foot mobile for the lobby, I decided to throw out a number so outrageous that it ended the conversation right then and there, and I told her it would cost fifty thousand dollars." He turned to his husband and grasped his sleeve. "She said yes."

Dare's green eyes went wide, and he dropped onto the couch beside his husband and stammered, "Wait, what?"

"That's exactly what I said! Then she told me it was actually less than she'd expected to pay, and she gave me a fifty percent deposit and asked how soon I could start."

Skye pulled a check from his shirt pocket and handed it to Dare, who unfolded it slowly and murmured, "Holy shit."

"This can't really be happening, can it? It's just a dream, right? Nobody just hands you a check for twenty-five grand! Okay, maybe if you're a famous artist, but I'm a total unknown!"

I said, "How does she know you're not just going to cash that and disappear?"

Skye exclaimed, "I asked her that! Apparently she and Christian have gotten to be friends, and he spoke so highly of me that she felt confident hiring me."

Dare blinked at the check, then said, "So…this is real?" Skye nodded. "But do you want the job? You said you didn't feel comfortable there."

"Here's the thing, though. That building *needs* one of my sculptures desperately, something rusty and metal and imperfect," Skye said. "Plus, I'd only have to go back twice, once to measure and take pictures, and then to install it when it's finished. For fifty grand, I'll take my chances with the cleaning robots."

I asked, "Is the company evil? Do they club baby seals, or pollute the environment, or hate gay people?"

"They sell clothes online, and she's a lesbian and the owner of the company, so I think they're probably pretty LGBT-friendly," Skye said.

Dare jumped up and said, "Oh my God, I'm holding a check for twenty-five thousand dollars! Quick, get something to put it in!"

Skye and the dog jumped up too, and Skye dug around on the desk until he produced a big, manila envelope. They sealed up the check like it was a rod of uranium, and a huge smile spread across Skye's face as he scooped up a stack of papers and turned to his husband. "You know what? We can pay all these bills!" He threw them into the air, and as they rained down on us, he said, "We can also give a big chunk to Nana from when she covered those medical expenses for us. Plus, we can buy you those fancy ballet shoes you've had your eye on, and we can get Benny that super nice, cushy dog bed we saw last week."

Dare took Skye's hand and said, "You didn't name anything for yourself."

"Sure I did. All of that's going to make me so happy."

Dare pulled his husband into his arms and kissed him passionately, and then he said, "You're the most wonderful person in all the world."

Skye grinned at him, and then he said, "We need to take the check to the bank before something happens to it."

The two of them rushed to the door, and Dare called, "Make yourself at home, Quinn, we'll be back in time for rehearsal! Bye Benny, keep Quinn company!" The dog wagged his butt, then hopped back up onto the couch, turned in a circle, and curled up for a nap.

I decided to get comfortable too and fished around in my messenger bag for the blanket I'd packed. It was round, white, and printed to look like a giant tortilla, which made me happy. I wrapped myself up in it, then sat on Dare's creaky swivel chair and spun in circles. After a while, I pulled out my phone and called Yoshi. He answered with, "Hey. Are you alright, Quinn?"

"Yeah. Sorry I freaked out on you yesterday."

"It happens. Sorry I drew a squiggle on you."

"My fault. I jumped with no warning."

"Do you want to try again? My schedule's booked solid for the next few weeks, but you can come in after hours if you want."

"I don't know what to do here. I need to fix the mark on my ribs, but something about the tattooing process really unnerved me. I don't know if it was the pain, the sound, the vibration, or a combination of all three, but I can't sit through that again."

Yoshi said, "There are other options besides the tattoo gun. For example, I know this woman from Samoa who tattoos with traditional tools, so there's just a tapping sound and no vibration. It still hurts, but in a different way. She wouldn't be able to draw your original design with her method, but maybe you two could come up with something else to cover the mark. Look online, you'll find some videos of how it's done and can decide if it's for you."

"Thanks for the suggestion. I'll definitely check it out and get back to you." I stopped spinning because I was getting dizzy and said, "Hey, while I have you on the line, your friend Mike Dombruso is an accountant, right?"

"Yup."

"Could you give me his number? My dance troupe is in desperate need of his services." He recited it for me, and I jotted it on a scrap of paper, then said, "Thanks, Yoshi. I'll talk to you soon."

After we disconnected, I snapped a photo of the bills and papers strewn all over Dare's desk and texted it to Mike with the caption, *help me, Obi Wan!* I followed it up with a quick message about wanting to hire him as the dance troupe's accountant, and was surprised when my phone rang less than a minute later. Mike said, "Not to sound completely OCD, but I need to do something about that mess in the photo you sent me. I actually just finished up with a client, so can I come over?"

I grinned and said, "Absolutely. I'll text you the address. Oh, and just so you know, I want your bill to come to me, not Dare. He's the guy who runs the troupe, and that was his desk in the photo."

"Sure. I'll need his permission to access his financial records, obviously, but I have no problem billing you instead of him."

After we disconnected, I sent the address to Mike and a heads-up to Dare. Then I got to work around the office. I washed out the scary mug and the ancient coffee pot in the corner and brewed a fresh pot before starting on the papers.

I'd sorted most of the bills and receipts into tidy piles by the time Dare and Skye returned about half an hour later, accompanied by Mike Dombruso. I could never quite figure Mike out. I'd heard people refer to him as Clark Kent, and that was dead-on. He wore chunky, black-framed glasses, slicked down his thick, black hair, and dressed in drab suits and ties, but underneath all of that, he was tall and muscular with a face like a movie star. He should have had all the confidence in the world, but instead, he was shy and a bit awkward, as if he was totally unaware of how ridiculously hot he was.

Mike and I shook hands, and then I said, "There's fresh coffee, gentlemen. If you need me, I'll be on the roof."

Dare said, "Thanks for doing this, Quinn, but I'll pay the bill. Skye and I have some money now, so we can afford it."

I scooped up my messenger bag and headed for the door as I said, "No way. I really want to give something back, after all you've done for me. Be sure to talk to Mike about that new income, by the way. Maybe he can save you from paying a shitload of taxes."

Skye called after me, "You're awesome, Quinn. Especially because you're dressed like a giant burrito." I grinned at that.

When I reached the roof, I curled up on one of the lounge chairs with the blanket still around me and pulled my phone from the pocket of my hoodie. Then I accessed my photos and changed my screen saver to a picture I'd taken of Duke the night we baked cookies together. I stared at it for a long time, knowing I should call him, but unsure of what to say. It had been relatively easy to discuss my fears with Dare, because there was no pressure there. But what if I said the wrong thing when I spoke to Duke and made everything worse?

I was still clutching my phone when Haley showed up a few minutes later and exclaimed, "Hey! I'm glad you're early too, Quinn. I have some ideas for the finale. Can I teach you a new sequence before Dare and the rest of the guys join us? It'll be easier to show them what I have in mind, instead of explaining it."

I took a last look at Duke's picture, and then I put my phone away and said, "Sure. Are we giving up on that toss and catch?"

"Actually, I'm going to pitch the idea of going another way entirely," he said as he pulled on a stretchy, black headband, which held his short dreads back from his face. "I realized what was missing, not only in the ending, but the whole production. We've been trying to wow the audience by being technically perfect and executing a lot of showy jumps and combinations. But we should be focusing on telling a story. Most of it's already there in the choreography. Two characters meet, are torn apart, and find each other again. But we need to dial it up. There's no sex or passion. When your character and mine come together at the end, we need to make love on that stage!"

"That better not be literal."

"No, we're not going to literally fuck in front of a live audience. But we're going to come damn close."

I muttered, "I'm so glad I invited my mom and dad to this."

"If my family can handle it, so can yours. Although I will say, my mama's a little skeptical about the alterations I'm making to our outfits."

He pulled a tiny scrap of white fabric from his backpack, and I asked, "What is that, an eyepatch?"

"It's your costume."

I sighed and said, "This day just keeps getting better and better."

Chapter Eight

"Dude, I still can't believe you invited your dad to a place like this."

I tossed back my drink, turned to my nephew, and yelled over the pulsating dance music, "Don't start, Max. You know this is a perfectly respectable bar."

"It's called *Thrust*."

"So what?"

"There are two…no wait, three couples dry-humping on the dance floor."

"They're just dancing. Mostly." I chewed my lip for a moment, then said, "Maybe we should have chaperoned Dad's trip to the restroom. Do you think there are people fucking back there?"

"You tell me. You work here."

I thought about it and answered my own question with, "Probably not. It's barely seven-thirty."

"As if there's some rule in San Francisco's gay community that you can't fuck strangers in public restrooms before ten p.m.?"

"The club's still half-empty, and a lot of these people are tourists. I don't think the hookups really get going until later."

Max took a sip from his beer bottle and leaned in so I could hear him. "Do you want me to get your dad out of here before your shift starts? I mean, you don't really want him to see you shaking your ass on a pedestal while wearing next to nothing, right?" He gestured at one of the empty platforms that lined the big dance floor. The go-go dancers didn't start until eight.

"I should have brought him in on my night off. I want Dad to see the other go-go boys performing so he'll realize it's not sleazy, but you're right that I really don't want to get up there and dance in front of him, especially in tonight's outfit. Although, hey, guess what? It turns out I'll be wearing even less when my troupe performs in a few weeks, and the entire family's going to be there for that one." I sighed and signaled the red-haired bartender for another round.

"Seriously?" I nodded, and Max said, "You're the lead dancer, and those guys are your friends. Don't you get a vote on what you wear?"

"I do, but I actually like the costumes and the new direction we're taking. The show needed to be shaken up a bit. It was too safe before, too predictable. My only concern is that Dad's not going to get it, that he'll see sleaze instead of art."

"He's not going to do that. Your parents are super chill."

"They have their limits, though. Plus, my brothers will be there. How do you think skimpy costumes and strong sexual themes will go over with your dad?"

"Oh man." Max frowned and tossed back the rest of his beer.

"Exactly."

"I thought it was just going to be ballet, but now all of a sudden, it's become super awkward. Maybe you should tell our family not to come to the show."

"If I do that, Dad will never believe this dance troupe is the real deal. He'll just think I'm wasting my life and my 'gift' on something I'm ashamed of. And I'm really not ashamed of it, Max. I just need Dad to understand what it is we're trying to do. But he might not, just like he really doesn't get this." I waved my arm to encompass the club. "He's being a good sport and pretending to enjoy himself, but his smile seems a bit forced, don't you think?"

Max traded his empty beer bottle for a full one and thanked the bartender before turning back to me. "I think you're defensive and reading a lot in."

I looked around and said, "Does it seem like he's been in the restroom a long time? Maybe we should check on him."

"Are you proposing we send out a search party? He's a grown man, and he can find his way back from the toilet."

I chewed my lip, then swapped out my empty glass for the newly minted tequila sunrise on the bar and said, "You're right. So, before he gets back, tell me how it went with Yoshi yesterday."

"Dude, what happened with that? I got there and found out you bolted after like, a minute."

"Turns out, tattoos and Quinn are a bad combination. Did you show Yoshi your artwork?"

"Yeah. He invited me to take a seat and wait for you. We both figured you'd come back. Then he noticed the sketchbook and asked to see it. He said nice things about my drawings." Max grinned embarrassedly.

"That's awesome! Did you tell him you wanted to apprentice with him?"

He shook his head. "I couldn't do it. I mean, he's Yoshiro freaking Miyazaki! He's fucking hot, by the way! Holy shit, is he hot! And nice. And insanely talented! Why the hell would someone at his level waste his time with a total novice?"

"Because you're talented too and would be an amazing tattoo artist."

"Well, I chickened out, so I blew my shot."

"Not necessarily."

Max glanced over my shoulder and said, "Here comes your dad. Turns out he found his way back from the restroom all on his own. We should probably change the subject, since you think he'd totally freak out about his grown-ass son getting a tattoo."

"I explained this to you, Max, more than once."

"Yeah, I know. It's basically you thumbing your nose at the major ballet companies and rejecting their uptight, *bourgeoisie* ways, but you don't want your dad to know, because it'll crush his dreams of you becoming the next…insert the name of a famous ballet dancer, because I sure as hell can't think of one."

"I'm pretty sure I didn't say any of that."

"I'm paraphrasing, but that's the basic gist of it." Max leaned around me and said, "Hi, Grandpop. Were you handing out rubbers in the men's room? Quinn was worried about you."

My father grinned and signaled to the bartender as he sat on the stool beside me. "No, although I was glad to see a condom dispenser in there. I stopped to talk to a young man who recognized me."

I asked, "Did you let him believe you were George Takei?"

Dad chuckled at that and said, "He recognized me because I treated him when he was a child. He spent several months in the hospital when he was six years old. Sweet kid. He's studying medicine now. There he is."

He waved at a dark-haired guy across the room named Sergei, who waved and smiled at my dad before glancing at me and frowning. "Nice?" I said. "He works here as a go-go dancer and he's an arrogant, rude, spotlight-hogging diva."

"You should make an effort to get along with him, Quinn," my dad said. "He's a good person."

"I get along with everyone, except for obnoxious people who hate me for absolutely no reason." I gestured at Sergei, and his frown deepened.

"He's had a rough life," my father said. "Try to be his friend. I think he might surprise you."

"Yeah, I somehow doubt that." Dad ordered a cup of coffee from the bartender, which suggested he was planning to stick around a while, and I said, "I start work in less than half an hour, and I'm going to need to get ready soon. You and Max probably want to get home, so…."

"I haven't even seen you dance yet," Dad said.

Without warning, Max exclaimed, "Mikhail Baryshnikov!" When I shot him a look, he said, "I finally remembered the name of a famous ballet dancer. It was bugging me."

I fought back a sigh, then turned to my father and said, "Do you really want to stick around for this? I mean, isn't it kind of embarrassing?"

"Why would it be embarrassing? You've explained to me that this is all perfectly wholesome. You also said you're proud to be a go-go dancer, and I'm here to show you I support you in your chosen line of work." My father had the world's best poker face, and he held my gaze unflinchingly.

"That's not what you're doing," I said. "You're sticking around because you want me to admit I'm uncomfortable with you watching me perform. That in turn must mean I'm ashamed of what I do, right? I mean, if I wasn't ashamed, what difference would it make if my dad was in the audience?"

"I never said any of that. But if you feel uncomfortable with me being here, maybe you should examine which aspects of this job you don't want me to see, and ask yourself why."

Just then, a huge, drunk guy with spiky blond hair pushed in between my dad and me and slurred, "I know you, don't I? We fucked last month, right? You had some weird name. Clint? Cord? I don't remember it, but I remember that sweet little ass."

Oh God. I'd let him take me home five or six weeks ago, though it felt like a lifetime. I was mortified that this was happening in front of my dad, but I kept my voice level as I slid off the barstool and said, "You're thinking of someone else, and you're clearly drunk. You should probably call a cab and head home."

"Don't you remember me? My name's Warren. You sucked my cock so good, and then you let me fuck you like, three times. Your ass was so fuckin' sweet." He grinned at me lewdly. What the hell had I been thinking with this guy?

"I have to go to work, and you need to go home and sober up, Warren." I stepped around him and told my dad, "Stay if you want to, it's your call. I'll be out in a few minutes."

With that, I turned and fled. When I reached the door to the employee dressing room, I looked back over my shoulder and was relieved to see Warren had wandered off toward the dance floor. The very last thing I needed was some drunk-ass one-night stand discussing me with my dad and Max.

When I reached my locker, I rested my forehead against the cool, red metal and sighed. What had I been thinking, bringing my dad to the club? And why hadn't I considered the possibility of running into men I'd slept with while on this little field trip? I used to go home with a different guy every night of the week. Of course the club was going to be littered with them!

I was still in that position when Sergei came into the dressing room a minute later. I straightened up and dialed the combination on my padlock, and as he peeled off his T-shirt, he muttered, "Fucking homewrecker."

I turned to look at him and said, "Excuse me?"

His ice blue eyes flashed with anger, and his muscles flexed when his hands tightened into fists. "I saw you out there with Doctor Takahashi," he growled. "He has a wife and a family, you slut! But I suppose that doesn't matter to a gold-digging little twink like you."

"Dude, gross! That's my *dad*, not my date!"

Sergei rolled his eyes. "Oh, obviously. How did I miss the strong family resemblance?"

"I was adopted, you dick! We've been working together for six months. Do you seriously not know my last name is Takahashi?"

His bravado faltered a bit, and he said, "It is?"

"Fuck you, Sergei, for always being mean to me, for thinking I was dating a married man, and for not even bothering to know my last name!"

He crossed his big arms over his chest and said, "You probably don't know mine, either."

"It's Reznik!"

"Well, congratulations," he said. "You're obviously a saint among men for knowing that! Also, why the hell would you bring your father to a place like this? Are you crazy?"

"Yeah, apparently I am. I was out of my damn mind for thinking I could make him understand why I like this job. He'll never get it, just like he'll never get why I turned down that position with the San Francisco Ballet."

Sergei stared at me like I was the stupidest person he'd ever met. "You turned down the San Francisco Ballet *for this*?"

"No! I didn't turn it down for this! I turned it down because I didn't want the fucking job! Why the hell am I even explaining this to you?" I grabbed my messenger bag, a hat, and a pair of boots out of my locker and stormed into the adjoining employees-only restroom, just to put some distance between myself and Sergei.

As I changed out of my street clothes and into a jock strap and a tight pair of pink satin shorts, I took a few deep breaths. I really needed to get it together. I'd been way too emotional all day, and I missed Duke, but I'd held off on calling him after my awkward departure that morning.

The theme at the club that night was 'Cowboy Up', and I knit my brows as I adjusted my ankle brace, then stuffed my feet into a pair of pink cowboy boots. When I'd first started working at Thrust, we all wore shorts of the same color, which varied depending on the night of the week. But when a go-go dancer named Preston got promoted to manager a few months back, he'd decided to get creative.

I usually had a lot of fun with the themes, but I just couldn't muster any enthusiasm that evening, and I sighed at my reflection as I plunked my white cowboy hat onto my head. The last piece of my ensemble was an oversized belt buckle. I had a few to choose from, most of which I really wasn't going to wear in front of my dad, including the one with a cowboy riding a mechanical bull that looked like a big dick. I ended up going with my Texas-shaped, rainbow-striped buckle and threaded it onto my wide, white belt. It rested about six inches below my belly button in those low-slung shorts.

I applied just a little eyeliner, mascara, and tinted lip gloss, then brushed iridescent body glitter onto a few strategic locations before turning my attention to my pseudo-tattoo. Ugh. It was nowhere near healed, and smothering it in makeup probably wasn't the best thing for it, but the squiggle had to go. I dabbed on concealer until it disappeared, then stepped back and stood on my toes to see how it looked in the mirror above the sink. Mission accomplished.

Sergei was still getting dressed when I went back into the locker room. His cowboy hat, boots, and shorts were all black. He thought he was such a badass with his muscles and tattoos. I ignored him as I crammed my clothes into my locker, then returned to the club.

Max and my dad were right where I'd left them. My nephew grinned when he saw me and said, "That's a lot of look, bro."

"It's western night. There are cocktails to match. You should actually try the Ride Me Cowboy. Jimmy the bartender invented it, and it's damn good."

Max asked, "Are all the go-go cowboys wearing pink?"

"No, they're wearing whatever they want. I happen to like pink."

When I turned toward my dad, he frowned a little and asked, "When did you pierce your nipples?"

Shit. I'd totally forgotten about them. "Four years ago," I admitted.

"You know, you really don't have to keep secrets from me, Quinn."

"You told me piercings were 'unwise' and prone to infection."

He said, "You were fifteen and wanted to pierce your navel with a sewing needle."

Max grinned and said, "I remember that. He did it anyway, and it totally got infected."

"Yeah, and you helped," I said. "In fact, it was your job to disinfect the needle."

"Why would you trust me with something like that?"

"Because you're older than me!"

"Still bro, bad call."

I noticed Sergei had climbed up on the main stage and started dancing, even though it was still a few minutes to eight. Of course he went straight for the featured spot and not one of the identical platforms. "Damn," Max murmured when he followed my gaze. "I never understood the cowboy fetish until this very moment. Can you introduce me to that guy?"

"No. He's evil." My dad started to say something, and I cut him off with, "I don't care if he was nice as a kid. He's gone to the dark side."

I was startled when someone grabbed my ass and slurred, "I knew I remembered you! Your name's Quinn! I need to take you home again tonight, baby. You look good enough to eat!"

I growled, "You need to get off me, Warren," as the big blond wrapped an arm around me.

"Come on baby, it's way too late to play hard to get," he said. "Not after last time. You put out five minutes after I met you!"

I tried to pry his arm off my chest as I yelled, "I said let go of me!" Warren just tightened his grip.

In the next instant, someone pulled him off me and snarled, "He told you to let go!" I spun around and drew in a sharp breath as Duke punched Warren in the jaw. His eyes were blazing, and his big fists were clenched like he was ready to hit him again.

Warren staggered back a few feet, and then he charged at Duke. They exchanged several vicious punches, and when I lunged forward to try to intervene, Max and my dad grabbed me and pulled me back. "Are you crazy?" Max yelled. "Both those guys are built like Optimus Prime! If you try to get in the middle of that, they'll break you in half!"

It took all three bouncers, two bartenders, Preston the manager, and about a dozen bar patrons to break up the fight. Finally, Duke stepped back and wiped his bloody lower lip with the back of his hand. He was wearing his police uniform, and Warren pointed at his name tag and yelled, "I'm going to make sure you lose your fucking badge, Blumenthal! You threw the first punch! I've got a room full of witnesses! You're fucked, asshole!"

Duke pinned him with a steely gaze and growled, "Bring it on."

Warren flinched when Duke took a step toward him, and then he headed for the door, yelling, "You all saw it, he threw the first punch! He's fuckin' toast! I'm calling my lawyer!"

All around us, the crowd started to disperse. The music was off and the lights were up, as if it was quitting time. Someone was talking to me. I didn't care about any of that. All that mattered was Duke.

He turned toward me and started to say something. In the next instant, I closed the gap between us, pulled him to my height, and kissed him passionately. He picked me up and returned the kiss with such raw intensity that I practically dissolved into his arms.

It went on for seconds, or minutes, or days. I didn't know which. When we finally paused to catch our breath, I rested my forehead against his and stroked his short hair. "I shouldn't have done that," he said. "But when I saw that guy grabbing you and heard you telling him to stop, something snapped in me. I never lose control like that. Never. But he had no right to do that to you."

I whispered, "Thank you," and caressed his cheek.

"You're not mad?"

"Why would I be?"

"Because I acted like a caveman."

I grinned and said, "You were defending my honor. I thought it was chivalrous."

He put me down after a minute and murmured, "You look so damn cute."

My eyes never left his as I touched the top of my head and told him, "I had a hat. I don't know where it went."

Duke picked it up from the floor, dusted it off, and put it on me, and then he smiled and said, "There. Now you're perfect."

I ran my fingertips over his cheekbone. It was starting to bruise. "You're going to get in trouble for this, aren't you?"

"Oh yeah. No question. I should probably get to the station and file a report before that jerk does. Not that it'll help."

"I'm sorry, Duke."

"Why? You didn't do anything."

I searched his blue-green eyes as I said, "I slept with that asshole, about a month ago. That's what made him think he could treat me like a piece of meat. If I hadn't done that, none of this would have happened."

Duke cupped my face between his hands and said, "That doesn't make it your fault. Nobody gets to treat you that way, not for any reason."

"But now you're going to get in trouble."

"I don't care."

"Really?"

"I'll probably care tomorrow," he said. "Right now, I'm glad I punched that scumbag."

"What made you drop by?"

"I was on my dinner break, and I missed you. We left things on kind of a weird note this morning. Or did I imagine that? Either way, I was thinking about you all day, and I was worried that maybe you were having second thoughts or something, and I just couldn't wait until the end of my shift to see you."

The lights went down again, and as loud music surrounded us, I leaned in and yelled, "I'm not having second thoughts."

We smiled at each other, and Duke kissed me gently before saying, "See you at home." I nodded and squeezed his hand, then watched as he cut through the crowd, which parted to let him pass.

My smile faded when I turned toward my dad and my manager, who were engaged in a serious-looking conversation. Preston told me, "Come to my office. We need to talk about what just happened, and it's too loud out here." Then he said, "You're welcome to join us, Doctor Takahashi."

Max and I exchanged looks, and then I followed the two men. As soon as we left the main part of the club and the connecting door closed behind us, cutting down the noise, I said, "No offense Dad, but why are you sitting in on this?"

Preston's brows were knit above his dark eyes, and he answered for my dad. "Your father expressed some concerns about your safety when you're working. I tried to assure him that incidents like this one are rare and invited him to join us as a courtesy."

I stopped walking and said, "The bouncers are great, Dad. Even if Duke hadn't shown up when he did, they would have handled it."

My father asked, "Just how often must they handle situations like this?"

I shrugged and said, "Occasionally patrons get drunk, and sometimes they get handsy. That guy today was more aggressive than most."

"I'm sorry, Quinn, but I just don't understand any of this. Why would you want to be in an environment where you're groped and objectified?"

"It doesn't happen that often!"

He exclaimed, "It shouldn't happen at all! You're turning twenty-five next month, and you know as well as I do that the careers of ballet dancers aren't lengthy. This is your time, Quinn, and you deserve so much more than this! You worked tirelessly for two decades, honing your craft, and I know I always say this, but it's true: you have a gift! You're the best dancer I've ever seen in my life, and you don't belong here! You should be principal dancer at a national ballet company, not squandering your talent at a place like this!"

I turned to my manager and mumbled, "Sorry. This is a great club. My dad just got the worst possible impression of it tonight."

Preston sighed and pushed his short, dark hair back from his forehead. "This place is a shithole, Quinn. Please don't tell the owner I said that. I mean, it's nice as far as nightclubs go, but it's still just a meat market. People come here for two reasons: to get drunk and to get laid. Don't make the same mistake I did. I took a job as a go-go boy right out of college, because it was all I could find. Over three years later, I'm still here! Did you know I graduated from UC Berkeley? Every time I write that check for my hefty student loan payment, I tell myself I should really be using that degree for something, after pouring all that time, money, and effort into it. Okay, yes, I'm a manager now instead of shaking my ass out on those platforms, but I wanted so much more for myself. Don't you?"

I exclaimed, "Yes! Even though I actually really like it here, of course I do! That's why I've been working with a start-up dance company for the last year. In just a few weeks, we're staging our debut performance. That little, unknown company might not be good enough for my dad, but I believe in it, and I also believe that show is going to put us on the map!"

My father said, "But it'll never reach the level of the San Francisco Ballet. With that company, you'd be performing for thousands and gaining the national recognition you deserve!"

"You have to let that go, Dad! I'm sorry I disappointed you when I turned down that job. That's the very last thing I ever want to do! But we can't keep having that same discussion, over and over again! Don't you see? I didn't feel safe at that huge ballet company! I'd always be walking on eggshells, just waiting for the moment when I screwed up and got fired. And that would absolutely happen, sooner or later!"

I swiped the back of my hand across my cheek to wipe away my tears and said, more quietly, "Don't you get it, Dad? I'm too damaged for that job. I'm too fearful and insecure. I know you tried so hard to make me whole, but it was already too late by the time you found me. I'll always be broken. But you know what? I'm doing okay, despite that. I found a dance troupe that makes me feel safe. I love Dare Evans like a big brother, and I trust him to take care of me. I also trust that amazing, beautiful man who showed up tonight and probably just lost his job defending me. I'm building a great life for myself! It may not be the one you wanted for me, but please Dad, can you just try to be happy for me?"

He clutched me in an embrace and said, "You've never disappointed me, son. Don't you know how proud I am of you?" I nodded and buried my face in his shoulder, and he told me, "All I've ever wanted was for you to be happy and to live the life you deserve. I guess I had a pretty narrow definition of what that meant. I promise I'll never bring up the San Francisco Ballet again, okay?"

I hugged him tightly and murmured, "Thanks, Dad."

"I love you so much, Quinn."

"I love you, too." After a moment, we let go of each other, and I ran a finger underneath my lashes, then tried to lighten the mood by saying, "Good thing I went with the waterproof mascara." My dad grinned at me, and then we both turned to Preston when we heard him sniff.

My manager was wiping his eyes on the sleeve of his gray dress shirt, and he said, "Sorry. I didn't mean to insert myself into your family moment. But I just have to say, I'd give anything to hear my father say what yours just did, Quinn. Absolutely anything. You're so lucky."

I smiled at my dad and said, "I've always known that."

"I'm the lucky one," my dad said.

I hesitated for a moment, and then I blurted, "Why me, Dad? Out of the countless abused and abandoned kids you must have come across over the course of your career, why did you adopt me? Was it because I was the most broken and pathetic out of all of them, so you took pity on me?"

My father squeezed my shoulder and said, "I adopted you because you claimed a piece of my heart from the first moment I met you. That wasn't because you were pathetic and broken, Quinn. Just the opposite. You were the strongest, bravest little boy I'd ever seen. You were a fighter! Even after everything that happened, there was this spark in you. I adopted you as much for my benefit as yours, because I needed you in my life, with that sweet smile and indomitable spirit. Everything I gave you, I got back ten-fold. You've filled my life with joy and so much love, Quinn, and I'm grateful every day that I get to be your dad."

I kissed his cheek and told him, "I'm grateful every day that I get to be your son."

Preston turned and headed down the hall. "I'm going to go call my father," he said. "Take the night off with pay, Quinn. Go find that hot cop and thank him properly for kicking that douchebag's ass. Damn it, I hate being single."

Chapter Nine

I got home before Duke. Max and my dad dropped me off on their way back to Oakland, and I went upstairs and showered, then stood in front of my closet for a while and tried to pick out something cute to wear. The problem was, I only had two types of clothes: slutty or playful. There was almost nothing in between. Finally, I went with a little of both and pulled on a pair of low-slung red shorts and a cropped tank top with an illustration of Captain America making out with the Winter Soldier. I assessed my overall look in the full-length mirror on the back of my closet door and decided I looked kind of plain, so I applied a little red body glitter to my shoulders and collarbones. It was in the shape of very tiny stars, and it made me smile.

Next, I turned my attention to the living room. Duke had to be worried about his job, so I wanted him to come home to someplace happy and comfortable, and I had plenty of stuff to make that happen. I threw my rainbow-striped beanbag, a soft, fluffy blanket, and all my pillows down the stairs, and then I moved the coffee table aside and built a nest in front of the couch.

I lined up an eclectic rainbow of glass candle holders on the mantel, lit them, and dimmed the lights before heading to the kitchen. After I mixed up a chocolate cake from one of Duke's recipes and put it in the oven, I got worried and thought

I might have forgotten the baking powder, so I found another recipe and made a vanilla cake. If it turned out I hadn't actually screwed up the first one, then he'd have two different varieties to choose from, and that was a good thing.

When the second cake was in the oven alongside the first, I cleaned the kitchen and headed into the backyard with a pair of scissors. Unfortunately, there wasn't much blooming. I heard soft music coming from the other side of the wooden fence that split the duplex's yard down the middle and called, "Xavier? Are you outside?"

"Hi Quinn. What're you up to?"

"I'm trying to make the house cozy for Duke. Do you have any flowers in your yard that I can borrow? And by borrow I mean have, because it's not like you're going to glue them back on when I'm done with them. I would just go out and buy some, but I want to be here when he gets home."

"Actually, yeah. My lilies are in full bloom right now. Let me go grab some scissors."

"I have some." I passed them over the seven-foot-high fence. A minute or so later, Xavier came into view and handed me a beautiful bunch of pink and orange lilies, and I exclaimed, "Oh wow, these are amazing! Thank you."

"You're welcome." He handed me the scissors and said, "I just have to ask. Are you and Duke dating? Is that why you're giving him flowers? Feel free to tell me it's none of my business."

I smiled and said, "Yeah, we are."

"That's shocking."

He started to tip over, but righted himself quickly, and I asked, "What are you standing on?"

"The rim of a wooden planter box. It's a little unbalanced." His shoulder-length blond hair was pulled back in a messy man bun, and he tossed his head to swing an escaped tendril out of his face.

"Please don't hurt yourself."

"That's definitely the plan."

"Why is it shocking that I'm going out with Duke?"

Xavier said, "I just can't imagine two more different people."

"We're not all that different." A beeping sound went off inside the house, and I said, "That's my cake timer, I'd better go. Thanks again for the flowers. Oh hey, are you single and gay?"

"I'm actually bisexual. Why do you ask? And please don't tell me it's because you want to set me up with someone. I'm not into blind dates."

As I headed toward the house, I called, "There's a bachelor auction for an awesome charity coming up, and you should be a part of it. You're super cute, and you'd bring in the big bucks! It's on the last Saturday of the month. Mark your calendar, and I'll get you some information soon!"

"I don't know...."

"I'll take that as a yes."

He called, "Take it as a maybe," and I waved to him as I stepped through the back door.

*****

By the time Duke got home nearly an hour later, both rectangular cakes were frosted (and both looked like I'd gotten the recipes right, so that was a win), the flowers were arranged in a pretty vase on the coffee table, and a few board games were stacked on the lumpy couch. He paused in the doorway to the living room and took it all in, and I looked up from the center of the beanbag and said, "I hope this is okay. I wanted you to come home to some happiness, but I'll put it all away if you don't like it."

"It's fine. I'm going to change, be right back." He seemed distracted as he headed down the hall to his bedroom.

When he returned a few minutes later, he was wearing a pair of gray gym shorts and a T-shirt with a logo of some sort, which combined the letter C and a pissed-off orca. I had no idea what that was about. He settled in beside me on the large beanbag, and I put my arms around him and asked, "What happened at the station?"

"I filled out an incident report and emailed my police chief. He ended up calling me, and we had a long talk. He has no choice but to put me on administrative leave for the next couple of weeks, while the department conducts an investigation. That's standard procedure after something like this. A lot depends on whether the guy I punched decides to press charges, and I'll be meeting with legal counsel. At best, I'll get off with a reprimand. At worst…well, we'll just have to wait and see what happens. I also called Finn and gave him a heads-up. He'll be assigned a new partner until I return."

"What's this going to do to you financially?"

"I'll still collect my base salary during the investigation. The problem is, I count on all that overtime to make ends meet."

"You know, you never cashed that check I gave you for the Hummel figurines. Maybe that could help bridge the gap."

Duke rested his cheek on the top of my head and told me, "There's no way I'd ever cash that check."

"Why not?"

"You donated them to charity. Plus, you were doing me a favor, and I'm glad I don't have to live with them anymore."

"But I shouldn't have done that. Do your parents know they're gone yet?"

"No. They're bound to notice next time they come over, but I haven't brought it up, and I'm not going to worry about that now."

I curled up in his arms and said, "I'm a disruptive influence in your life."

"Yup." I glanced up at him and he grinned at me. "It's not a bad thing. My life needed some disrupting."

"Not like this, though. I never wanted you to get into financial trouble because of me."

"Let's make one thing perfectly clear: punching that guy was my choice. You're not at fault. I obviously could have handled the situation a lot better, especially after all my years of police training. But I didn't act like a cop. I reacted with my emotions instead of my head, and now I have to face the consequences, whatever they may be."

He tilted my chin up and kissed me gently, and I asked, "Do you hate what I did to the living room? Be honest. It occurred to me after the fact that you might actually have preferred things to be calm and orderly tonight, so maybe I should have left it alone."

"I like the fact that you Quinned it up in here. This room was boring and uncomfortable before."

"You seemed less than thrilled when you first saw it."

He said, "Actually, it barely registered when I got home. I was thinking about what I'd do if I ended up losing my job. But that's totally premature, and I need to stop focusing on the worst case scenario. Let's just enjoy tonight. Wait, why are you home so early? Please don't tell me you got fired because of me!"

"No. My manager sent me home with pay. Specifically, he told me to, and I quote, 'go find that hot cop and thank him properly for kicking that douchebag's ass.' Preston's a nice guy."

"What did your dad say? I'm embarrassed that I acted like that in front of him."

"He was upset about that guy groping me," I said, "but it ended up being a great conversation. I feel like he heard me, for once."

I told him what was said, and Duke exclaimed, "That's fantastic! I know how much you needed that."

"I did. And now you and I both have an unexpected night off, so what would you like to do? We could play board games, or watch a movie, or whatever."

"Anything, really."

I reached for the remote, then traced the outline of the logo on his chest and said, "I have to ask what this stands for, because I have no idea."

"A hockey team, the Vancouver Canucks."

"I didn't know you like hockey. Did you ever play?"

"No. I was a total klutz on skates."

"Why Vancouver," I asked, "as opposed to a local team?"

Duke admitted, "When I was a senior in high school, I had a huge crush on a hockey player, this Norwegian guy named Even Eide. He was only on the team for two years, but I watched every game without fail, and that was enough to turn me into a lifelong Vancouver fan. I know that's a stupid reason to like a team."

"No it isn't. We all had teen crushes. Were you always into older guys?"

"He wasn't much older. He got drafted at nineteen, and I was seventeen at the time."

I turned on the TV as I asked, "Whatever happened to him?"

"He got injured and had to retire after a couple of years. Then he actually moved to San Francisco and opened a sports bar with a friend of his who used to play for the Kings. It's called Ellingsen & Eide, and I guess it's a big success. There are two dozen locations throughout the state now."

"I've heard of it. Actually, now that I think about it, I've heard of Even, too. I remember the odd spelling of his name, instead of E-V-A-N like it's pronounced. So, did you ever go to his bar, hoping to run into him?"

"No way."

"Why not?"

"Because that would have been painfully embarrassing." When I grinned at that, he said, "What?"

I settled back onto his chest and said, "I love the fact that you're so shy."

"Why would you like that?"

"Both because it's sweet, and because it makes the fact that you asked me out extra special. I'm guessing you don't do that very often."

He kissed the top of my head and said, "You're right about that."

As I flipped through the on-screen menus, I said, "Maybe we should count this as our first date. I know you were planning to take me out tomorrow night, but you don't need to spend money on me."

"If we were going to count every wonderful afternoon or evening we've spent together, this would be more like our tenth date." Duke touched my cheek as he said, "I know you're worried about me, but my financial situation's not dire. In fact, I shouldn't even have mentioned it, and I have no intention of canceling our plans tomorrow night. I wasn't going to try to impress you by spending a bundle anyway. There's nothing fun about overpriced restaurants and all that fancy stuff."

"Okay, good. So, tell me what you want to watch."

I flipped through Netflix, and after a minute Duke said, "How about that?"

"The Great British Baking Show?"

"I mean, only if you want to."

"Definitely! It'll probably result in you baking something delicious, so I'm all for it."

I was right. After the first one and a half episodes, Duke clicked the pause button and told me, "I want to try making Florentine cookies, like the contestants just did. Do you want to bake with me?"

"I will never, ever say no to that." He hoisted himself out of the beanbag and smiled at me as he pulled me to my feet.

He seemed happy as he moved around the kitchen with confidence, gathered up the ingredients, and went to work. I sat on the counter and watched him, and after a while I said, "Why aren't you doing this for a living? You're so passionate about baking!"

Duke looked up from the recipe on his phone and adjusted his glasses. "I wanted to become a pastry chef when I was a kid, but my father thought that was completely frivolous. I guess I let him influence my decision."

"How is it frivolous to make people happy? I think it's one of the best things any of us can do with our lives."

"That's a nice way to look at it."

"You know, I never asked. How did you end up with a career in law enforcement?"

He picked up a bag of slivered almonds and shook them into a bowl on a small scale as he said, "It started with a high school guidance counselor. He gave me an aptitude test and told me it was the perfect career for me. Apparently I have a strong need for order, and I'm big on following the rules. For lack of any better ideas, I went with his suggestion."

"That exactness is also part of the reason you're such an excellent baker," I said as I watched him remove two almond slivers from the scale and recheck the measurement. "Do you actually enjoy being a police officer?"

He shrugged and said, "Sometimes. I like it when I feel I'm making a difference, but those instances are rare. Usually, we just deal with a lot of hostility and people at their worst. For example, Finn and I arrested a guy for being drunk and disorderly tonight. It's the seventh time we've arrested him. He gets locked up, pays the fine, heads right back to the bars and does it all over again. Every time we arrest him, he calls us every name in the book and pees in the back of the patrol car, just out of spite. That really wears thin. But he doesn't want to get sober, and it's impossible to force people to get help, so nothing ever changes."

I wrinkled my nose and said, "I've been in that back seat."

"Don't worry, we always clean and disinfect it after he's been in there."

"Why do you stay in that job? It sounds awful."

"It's not always that bad."

"That's not a very ringing endorsement."

"I think I just have the wrong temperament for that line of work," he said. "So does Finn, actually. It's tough for us to let all the negatives bounce off without affecting us, and that's what you really need to do to be happy as a police officer. But, it's a job. It pays our mortgages, and it lets Finn take care of his family. I don't want to seem ungrateful, not when there are so many people out of work or barely scraping by."

He started to melt some butter in a saucepan, and when I asked how I could help, he assigned me the task of chopping the almond slivers. As we worked side-by-side, he asked, "What do you see yourself doing once your dance career runs its course?" He thought about that and glanced at me. "Is that an insensitive question? I know it's not going to end for a very long time. I just wondered if you'd thought about it."

"It's not insensitive. No one can do this job forever. Ballet takes a huge toll on our bodies, and every injury has the potential to be a career ender. But I don't know what's next. If I'm lucky, I won't have to answer that question for quite a few years. I think though, once my number's up, I won't take the route so many do and teach ballet. Instead, I'll start fresh and completely reinvent myself, like my mom did. I'll figure out the exact opposite of being a ballet dancer, and I'll do that."

"Please don't reinvent yourself too much," he said. "It'd be a shame if you stopped loving rainbow beanbags and macaroni art, or if you stopped wearing body glitter and making homemade board games. I noticed a stack of them waiting for us in the living room."

"There's a new one. I'm calling it Twist-and-Seek. I just came up with it a few days ago, and you can help me take it on its maiden voyage."

"I look forward to learning what that is."

Once the cookies were in the oven, I found two huge serving spoons and handed one to Duke. He asked, "What's this for?"

"You'll see. Chocolate or vanilla?"

"Chocolate."

"Right answer." I hopped up on the counter, took a big scoop out of the cake I'd baked, and started to eat it like a drumstick. Duke chuckled, and then he took a slightly less heaping scoop of cake and started eating it the same way I was. When I said, "That's the spirit," he grinned at me.

We laughed and chatted while the Florentines cooled, and we made a mess while coating them with chocolate. Then we carried a big plate of cookies into the living room. I made sure they were in reach when I set up my new board game.

"It's basically a cross between Twister and I Spy," I explained, indicating the 6-foot-square, brightly colored, children's play mat I'd spread out on the floor. "There are all kinds of hidden objects in this cartoon cityscape, plus I've added a bunch of stickers. Instead of a spinner, we're using this."

I held up a round child's toy with an arrow in the middle and pulled the string. The arrow spun around, and a mechanical voice told us, "The cow says moooooooo." The arrow stopped on a hand-lettered square that read *left foot, lucha libre wrestler.*

I stepped onto the play mat and looked around, then stuck my foot on a sticker of a masked wrestler that was peeking out of a window in a brightly colored skyscraper. "See? You just do whatever it tells you. I'll show you one more." I stuck a cookie in my mouth and pulled the string. The toy told me what a duck said, and the arrow stopped on: *right hand, scary-looking baby*. I looked around, then pivoted to put my hand on a sticker at the edge of the mat. I took a big bite out of the cookie, then held the remainder with my free hand as I explained, "We'll both be doing this at the same time. If I beat you to a sticker or picture, you have to find another one. First one to fall over loses."

"But you have an advantage. You know where everything is, because you made the game."

"I really don't. I added the stickers to the mat while wearing x-ray specs, so I could barely see. Plus, it's not like I'd remember." Duke grinned and joined me on the mat.

For the next several minutes, we took turns with the pull toy and followed the instructions. At one point, when he and I were totally tangled up and I arched backwards to put my left hand on a rabid squirrel, Duke said, "No fair! You're a hundred times more flexible than I am!"

"But you're eleven inches taller with much longer arms and legs, so it all evens up."

"That's a good point, actually. Pull the string." I ended up pulling it with my toes, because I couldn't reach it any other way. We both shifted around to get our left foot onto a zombie, and Duke and I ended up face-to-face. He told me, "You're a brilliant game designer."

"I'm more of a Doctor Frankenstein. I take bits of other games and cobble them together into some sort of unholy creation."

I could feel the heat from his body as he hovered right above me. His right arm was wrapped around my shoulders, and his thigh was between both of mine. I looked into his eyes and smiled before I stretched up and kissed him. He deepened the kiss, but then he murmured, "Oh crap." I felt his legs start to shake, and a moment later, he tumbled onto the mat and took me with him. Duke kissed me again and said, "Best game ever."

We spent a long time kissing. When we finally came up for air, I asked, "Can we have a sleepover? I have this awesome new Barbie tent I've been wanting to try out."

"A tent for Barbies?"

"No, a tent for people, made to look like a hot pink castle. I'm not sure what that has to do with Barbie, but her name's on the side of it in huge letters. Can we set it up in the living room and spend the night in it?"

He got up and held his hand out to me. "I can't possibly say no to that."

We moved the furniture around and pitched the tent in front of the fireplace. Next, we loaded it with a foam mattress, blankets, and every pillow in the house. When we climbed inside, Duke's feet stuck out beneath the flap, which made us both chuckle.

We curled up in each other's arms, and after a while he said, "If they fire me and I lose my house to foreclosure, will you come and be homeless with me? I'll find us a charming vacant lot, and we can live in the Barbie tent."

"I'll follow you anywhere. We don't have to be homeless, though. We can buy an old hippie bus, load it with beanbags and macaroni art, and stick the tent on top like a second story. It'll be awesome!"

He pulled me closer and said, "It's a plan."

*****

Duke and I awoke around the same time in that little pink tent the next morning and exchanged groggy smiles. He murmured, "Good morning," and brushed his lips to mine.

I whispered, "It's so nice to wake up to you," and kissed him again.

Several minutes later, we were still kissing. I rubbed my thigh against his growing hard-on, and his breath caught. My cock throbbed as I pulled down his shorts and briefs, slid between his legs, and licked his shaft before taking the tip between my lips.

He moaned softly as I sucked him. I held his gaze and really got into it, sliding my mouth up and down his cock, working on taking him a bit deeper down my throat with each pass. But then, without warning, the front door slammed open.

It made me jump, and I accidentally bit down. Duke yelped, and I sat up and stammered, "Shit, I'm so sorry!"

My heart raced as a booming voice demanded, "What's going on in here?" We were fully concealed by the tent, so the man must have been talking about the condition of the living room and not what we'd been doing moments before.

I looked at Duke, and he mouthed the words, "My father." He pulled up his shorts and winced.

Anger welled up in me. I burst out of the tent and was confronted with a man who was nearly as big as Duke. He sported a thick, dark beard, which made him look like a lumberjack, and I got the impression the deeply-etched scowl on his face was a permanent feature. I demanded, "Have you ever heard of knocking?"

The man glared at me and sputtered, "Who the hell are you?"

Instead of answering, I told him, "This is Duke's house, not yours! You have no right to barge in here like that!"

The man squared his shoulders and growled, "I have seventy thousand dollars wrapped up in this place, so that gives me the right to come and go as I please!"

"Oh, you mean the high-interest loan you gave Duke when you pressured him into buying this house? He's the one busting his ass every week to not only pay the mortgage, but to pay you back *with interest*, so spare me that bullshit!"

Duke untangled himself from the tent and asked, "What are you doing here, Dad?"

"I found out you got suspended from the police force, so I came over here to see what was going on. Now I find this!" He swung his arm to indicate the living room.

Duke crossed his arms over his chest and said, "I'm on administrative leave. Who told you I was suspended?"

"I called the station this morning to talk to a golf buddy who works in HR, and he told me the paperwork had just come across his desk." He looked around and asked, "Where are the Hummels? I told your grandmother you couldn't be trusted with anything of value!"

Duke snapped, "To hell with the Hummels! That conversation with your buddy in HR was a serious violation of my privacy, and so is bursting into my home unannounced! When I gave you a key, it was for emergencies, not so you could barge in here on a whim and interrupt my boyfriend and me!"

"Your boyfriend!" His father glanced at me with disgust and told Duke, "He looks like a prostitute. I don't know what's come over you, but all of this is totally unacceptable!"

Duke's voice was a low growl when he said, "You know what's unacceptable? The fact that you think you can let yourself into my home, insult my boyfriend, and talk to me like I'm a child!"

His father turned to me and bellowed, "I bet you're to blame for all of this! Duke has always been weak, so it must have been easy for a cheap little hustler like you to insinuate your way into his life! Did you get him hooked on drugs? Is that why he's acting like this?"

"Listen, Hagrid's evil twin," I snapped, "if you think for even a minute that amazing saint of a man is weak, then you're not only an asshole, you're also really fucking stupid!"

The man turned bright red and hissed, "How dare you speak to me that way, you piece of trash!"

Duke yelled, "I want you out of my house and out of my life! I've put up with way too much for too long, and this is the last straw. Get out!"

His father snapped, "This is totally unacceptable! You're to address me with respect!"

"You don't deserve respect!" Duke's eyes blazed with anger.

"Somebody needs to teach you some manners, you worthless disappointment!" His father balled his hands into fists and looked like he was about to lunge at him, but Duke stared him down unflinchingly.

After a moment, his father backed down. But he made no move toward the door, so I snapped, "Duke told you to go! Now are you going to get out of here, or do I have to make you leave?"

The man narrowed his eyes and snarled, "I'd like to see you try!"

With that, I ran to the couch, picked up the bucket of miniature beanbag crabs from one of my games, and started pelting him with them as I yelled, "You don't deserve Duke, not after the way you treated him! You should be ashamed of yourself!"

The crabs completely threw him off. He shielded himself with his hands as he stammered, "You're crazy!"

Duke marched to the door and held it open as he told his father, "We're done. Don't bother coming back, because I'm changing the locks."

I kept up the constant barrage of crabs, chucking one after another at him until he turned and fled the house. Duke slammed the door behind him and leaned against it, and I murmured, "Wow, what a dick."

"Yup." After a moment, he grinned a little and said, "I can't believe you pelted him with crabs."

"Well, he wouldn't leave."

"It was very effective."

As I put down the bucket, I said, "I'm so sorry I bit you. Are you okay?"

"Don't worry about it. I'll be fine." He crossed the room to me and pulled me into a hug. Then he kissed the top of my head and said, "I'm going to get a shower. I'll be back in a few minutes."

When I nodded, he headed down the hall to his room. I knit my brows with concern as I watched him go. The only thing I could do for Duke at that moment was feed him, so I went to the kitchen, got a pot of coffee going, and gathered the ingredients for breakfast. On a whim, I also quickly mixed up a batch of blue icing and used it to write a message and draw a picture on the vanilla cake I'd baked the night before. Then I got busy mixing up some batter.

By the time Duke joined me maybe twenty minutes later, I'd turned the kitchen into our own, personal pancake house. I transferred the last batch from the griddle to the heaping platter I'd kept warm in the oven and told him, "You have your choice of banana, chocolate chip, and party explosion pancakes. Feel free to mix and match."

I took a pot from the stove and poured a stream of warm blueberry syrup into what was meant to be a cream dispenser. The white, ceramic vessel was in the shape of a cow, and the syrup flowed out of its mouth, which I thought was hilarious. I put it between the two place settings on the kitchen island, and as Duke took his seat, he asked, "What does a party explosion pancake involve?"

"Sprinkles, chocolate chips, bananas, edible glitter, and chopped up peanut butter cups. They're pretty freaking awesome."

Duke glanced at the vanilla cake, then rotated it around to face him and chuckled. I'd written, 'I'm sorry I bit your dick,' and added a drawing of a penis with a sad face. "I really am sorry," I said.

"It was an accident. You don't have to keep apologizing."

"Did I break the skin?"

"Yeah, but just a little."

I exclaimed, "Oh my God! Do you want an icepack?"

He grinned at me. "I really don't."

"Oh. Right. That would actually suck."

Duke thanked me when I handed him a cup of coffee, and he stacked a few pancakes on his plate as I turned off the stove and joined him at the kitchen island. Instead of eating anything, he began to fidget with his fork, and after a while he said, "I'm sorry you got caught in the middle of that."

"I'm not. You needed backup."

"My father was totally out of line with the things he said to you."

"I've been called worse."

"That doesn't make it okay." He stared out the kitchen window and was quiet for a while before saying, "My father and I have argued before, but never like that. I wonder what the upshot will be."

"What do you want to happen?"

"I don't know." He ate a bite of the party pancake and said, "This is really good." But after a minute, he pushed back his barstool and said, "Sorry, but I don't have much of an appetite right now. Can you save some of these for me?"

"Of course."

"I'm going to go out for a while and try to clear my head."

"Sure, no worries. I'll see you later."

He kissed my forehead and left by way of the garage. I sighed quietly and climbed up on the counter with a big pancake in my hands. It made me sad that he was hurting, and I couldn't do anything about it.

The garage door rattled open, then closed. I wondered where he'd go. He said he wanted to be alone, but if he changed his mind, who did he have to turn to?

I tore off a bit of pancake and ate it, then jumped a little when the connecting door to the garage swung open. When Duke stepped into the kitchen, I said, "I thought you left."

"I started to, but then I got to thinking." He came up to me and slid his hands around my waist, and I wrapped my legs around him. "I've always dealt with everything by myself. That's all I know. But I realized I don't have to do that anymore, because now I have you." That was one of the best things I'd ever heard. I set the pancake aside and draped my arms around his shoulders, and he said, "Everything feels so uncertain right now. Everything but this."

"What can I do to help?"

"You're already helping, so much more than you know." Duke kissed me, and then he picked up the platter of pancakes and said, "Come on, let's try again with breakfast."

Chapter Ten

I called Duke as soon as I got off the bus that evening, and he answered with, "Hey! Where are you?"

"About three blocks away. Rehearsal ended a little early, so our choreographers could regroup. Want me to stall for time?" We'd agreed that I'd come home for our date at seven. It was about six-forty, so I started walking in exaggerated slow motion, which earned me a bunch of funny looks from the people at the bus stop.

"Nope, everything's ready. Come on home."

"Okay, great." I started walking at a normal pace and said, "I'm going upstairs to shower and change as soon as I get there, but it won't take long."

"I figured you'd want to do that. See you soon."

Duke was waiting on the front steps when I reached the duplex about five minutes later. He was dressed in a white T-shirt, khaki shorts, and flip flops, and he greeted me with a new set of keys because he'd changed the locks that day, and a single, hot pink Gerbera daisy. I kissed his cheek and thanked him for the flower, then asked, "Should I go by what you're wearing and dress accordingly?"

"I'm sure you'll put your own, unique spin on it, but yes. The date is taking place in our backyard. I know that sounds lackluster, but I hope you like what I have planned. Oh, and try not to peek back there, okay? I want to surprise you."

"I gotta be honest here," I said as he held the door open for me. "I'm terrible when it comes to stuff like that. It's not that I want to ruin the surprise, but I'll be drawn to the view outside my bedroom window like a moth to a flame."

"I thought that might be the case," he said with a smile, "so I did something to help you out. You'll see what I mean."

When I reached my bedroom, I burst out laughing. Duke had hung a sheet over my window from the outside, and had decorated it with a rough approximation of my usual view of the yard, rendered with colored markers. I was still smiling as I headed to the shower.

About ten minutes later, I bounded downstairs barefoot and dressed in a romper printed to look like the universe. On the front of it was a picture of a cat surfing on a huge burrito. I'd decided to default to playful instead of sexy on the Quinn's-closet-continuum, because Duke was dressed casually and I didn't want him to think I was coming into the date with any expectations.

Duke was waiting for me in the living room. He'd added a red Hawaiian shirt and a lei of purple orchids to his ensemble, and he slipped a matching lei around my neck and grinned shyly. "Oh, sweet," I exclaimed, "a Hawaiian theme! The lei is gorgeous, thank you. How did you find such a thing in San Francisco?"

"You can find anything in this city, including leis and Quinn-worthy cocktail garnishes." He stepped aside to reveal a pair of hollowed-out pineapples on the coffee table, each overflowing with umbrellas, skewers of tropical fruit, swizzle sticks, and little plastic toys. I squealed with delight, and he chuckled at my response and said, "I thought you'd like that."

"I love it!" He handed me one of the pineapples, and after I took a sip from the coiled, purple straw, I told him, "It tastes as good as it looks, which says a lot because this is the greatest beverage I've ever seen." Duke seemed pleased by that.

We carried the pineapple drinks through the kitchen and paused at the back door, which was covered with a sheet. He looked a little nervous as he held the makeshift curtain open for me. My mouth fell open as I stepped into a tropical paradise.

The yard had been completely transformed. The first thing I saw was a pair of eight-foot-tall palm trees. Duke had cut them out of plywood, painted them, and outlined them with Christmas lights. They arched toward each other, forming a gateway to wonderland. A metal fire pit blazed near a beautiful tiki bar on the patio, and the lawn was rimmed with a dozen tiki torches and dotted with inflatables, including a dolphin, a palm tree and a few colorful inner tubes. Duke said, "I hope it's okay that I raided the box labeled 'pool toys' that you'd stashed in the garage." I nodded as I wandered wide-eyed across the patio and stepped onto the lawn.

The two show-stoppers were a six-foot-wide children's wading pool, which was home to half a dozen little plastic boats traveling in a circle, and a big, metal swing set, which looked like it belonged in a city park and spanned the width of the lawn. As I stood there with my mouth hanging open, Duke explained, "You'd mentioned how much you loved that sushi restaurant with the little boats. This is my version. The sushi looks clunky, but it tastes okay. I tried to make it like you showed me that one time."

We walked over to the turquoise plastic pool, which was printed with cartoon fish and seashells, and I saw that each of the toy boats was carrying a different variety of sushi. He'd covered them with little sheets of plastic wrap and added a couple edible flowers between the sushi rolls. A straw beach mat, topped with two place settings and strewn with more flowers, waited for us beside the pool. I put my pineapple drink on the mat, and Duke did the same before we walked back to the swing set.

As I blinked at it in wonder, he explained, "You said you missed the swings you used to have at your parents' house, so when I saw this for free on an upcycling website, I thought you might enjoy it." A tear tumbled down my cheek, and when I turned to Duke and crushed him in an embrace, he asked, "Are you crying?"

I pulled him down to my height and kissed him, and he gently wiped the tears from my cheek as I whispered, "Thank you."

"You're welcome."

"You did so much for me. I'm overwhelmed."

"You're the most amazing person I've ever met, Quinn, so I couldn't just take you out to dinner or something ordinary. You deserve a first date as fun and unique as you are."

I held him tight and asked, "How did you do so much in a single day?"

"I actually found the swing set on Monday. Finn let me store it at his house, and he came over right after you left this afternoon and helped me install it. He invited us to dinner next week, by the way." Duke looked around and gestured at the plywood cutouts. "I made the palm trees on Monday and Tuesday, and I actually found the bar last week. Someone had put it out on the sidewalk with a 'free' sign. I refinished the wood and added the wicker panels and bamboo trim. It's lucky you rarely go into the garage."

I looked up at him and said, "Last week? You hadn't even asked me out yet."

"It was just going to be a present, but then I ended up theming our first date around it. Right after you moved in, you asked if you could put a tiki bar in the living room, and I totally shut you down. Later on, I realized how unfair that was. It's important to me that you to feel at home here, so after tonight, we can set up the bar near the fireplace."

"You're the kindest, most thoughtful man in all the world, Duke."

He lightly ran the back of his hand over my cheekbone and murmured, "I just want to make you happy."

"Mission accomplished. Nobody's ever done anything like this for me. It makes me feel so special."

"Good, because you are."

"Can we use the swings yet, or does that cement around the legs need to dry?"

"It was actually really stable even before I embedded it in quick-drying concrete, so I think it'll be just fine." Three swings with black rubber seats were suspended by thick chains from the metal crossbar. I took the one in the center, and Duke gingerly sat on the one to my left and said, "Finn tried it out, but I haven't yet. Let's hope it actually holds my weight."

"I'm sure it will," I said as I started to glide back and forth. "Did this come from a park? It's super sturdy."

"It's from a private school in South City that's putting in a new playground. I would have gotten the slide too, if I thought there'd be room for it." He pushed off with his feet and grinned as he sailed through the air. "This is fun. I haven't been on a swing since I was about seven years old."

"It's fantastic!"

We laughed as we swung higher and higher. Eventually, we both stopped propelling ourselves and joined hands as we gradually slowed. When we were nearly at a standstill, I jumped onto the lawn and stood in front of him, and when Duke swung up to me, I grabbed the chains to stop him and kissed him deeply. Then I climbed onto his lap and wrapped my legs around his waist, and Duke grinned at me and started swinging both of us. "I'm amazed that you installed this permanently in your backyard," I said as I draped my arms over his shoulders.

He held my gaze and murmured, "I guess it's my way of saying I hope you're around for a very long time."

"I'm not going anywhere." I leaned in, and he licked my lip playfully before kissing me.

We spent a long time on the swing, kissing each other as we swayed back and forth. But after a while, I shivered a little, so Duke carried me across the yard and put me down beside the cozy fire on the patio. As I held out my hands to warm them, I gestured at the round, brass fire pit on its metal stand and asked, "Is this new, or did you have it in the garage?"

"Actually, I borrowed it from Xavier. He made me promise not to throw it out."

"Why would he say that?"

Duke grinned and said, "Every time he uses it, I get nervous and tell him not to burn the house down. He probably figured I was sick of worrying about it."

Once we'd both warmed up a bit, he tilted his head toward the wading pool and asked if I was ready to eat, and I exclaimed, "I'm hungry enough to eat an entire fleet of sushi!"

We settled in on the straw mat, and he draped a blanket over my shoulders before plucking the little squares of plastic wrap from the boats as they motored past. The sushi procession was led by a radio-controlled speed boat, which towed five brightly-colored bath toys. "Here's where it gets a little awkward," he said. "There's only one speed on the motorized boat, and it's a bit faster than I would have liked. Also, I looked it up and saw that the little boats at the sushi restaurants carry small plates, which is what you grab when you see something you want. But every plate I tried ended up capsizing the boats, so I left them out. Now we have to do this."

Duke picked up a set of chopsticks and leaned forward, then made a quick grab for a sushi roll as it floated past on the bow of a red and white tug boat. He lost his grip on it, but ended up catching the roll with his free hand before it hit the water. On the next lap, I plucked a roll from a plastic yacht with my fingers and said, "In Japan, it's perfectly acceptable to eat sushi with your hands. Your way looks fun, but I think I'll skip the chopsticks. That way, more sushi will end up in my belly, instead of at the bottom of the deep blue sea." I tossed the California roll in my mouth, then murmured, "Mmmm," and gave him a thumbs up.

"Really? Is it okay? I ended up overcooking the rice and made another batch, but I thought maybe I'd overcooked that one, too."

"It's delicious. Thank you again, Duke, for all of this." I caught another California roll and tossed it in my mouth.

"You're welcome. I enjoyed putting it all together. My motto was 'think like Quinn' so that's why it turned out to be fun."

I leaned against him and said, "Actually to me, this is all pure Duke. It's clever, considerate, and completely exceptional, just like you."

He glanced at me and asked, "You really think I'm exceptional?"

"Of course I do."

"Nobody's ever said that about me. Just the opposite. The guys I dated in the past thought I was uptight and boring."

"Well, then they didn't know you at all."

Duke grinned a little and said, "It's nice to feel appreciated."

I rested my head on his shoulder and said, "You can tell me it's none of my business, but I'm curious about your love life before I came along."

"It was a slow-motion train wreck. For the most part, I dated guys I met at this gym I belonged to. I didn't want to try dating anyone at work or church, and I don't go out much, so that ended up being my main social outlet. But I guess that gym was basically a meat market. Most of the men I went out with were only interested in sex, and they couldn't begin to understand why I'd possibly want to wait. I thought the last guy I went out with was different. This was about a year ago. He said he was fine with waiting, but on our third date, he tried to get me drunk and force himself on me. I already started out with trust issues, and that was the last thing I needed. I took a big step back from the singles scene after that. I also stopped going to that gym. Instead, I bought some equipment and started working out at home, and my life became a lot less complicated."

"I'm so sorry that happened to you."

"It is what it is." He picked up his pineapple and took a sip from the twisty straw, then said, "By the way, these are nonalcoholic. I wasn't going to liquor you up on our date."

"It'd be fine if they were boozy. I know you'd never take advantage of me."

"Yeah, but still."

I ate another sushi roll, and then I glanced at Duke and said, "It sounds like you were pretty isolated for most of the last year. Did you get lonely?"

"I wasn't really alone. I'm usually at work, and Finn has become a good friend. When I was off duty, my roommate Cole kept me company. We'd often have meals together, which was nice. Sometimes we'd invite Xavier to join us."

"I'm glad they were there for you," I said. "But I guess what I'm asking is, didn't you miss the intimacy?" I ran my hand down his arm to show him what I meant.

"You can't miss what you never had. Even when I was going out with people, it was never like this. Honestly, I felt more alone when I was dating than when I decided to take that year off." When I straddled his lap and wrapped my arms around him, he murmured, "Please don't feel sorry for me."

I hugged him tighter and said, "I'm not, I promise. I'm just filling the well."

"What does that mean?"

"You didn't get enough hugs and touches and kisses before. It was like a drought. So now, I'm going to hold, kiss, and caress you so much that it fills you up inside."

"So I'll be ready for the next drought?"

I rested my forehead against his and grinned. "No. Totally not what I meant."

I ran my hands over his short hair and kissed him, and Duke smiled against my lips before whispering, "You're so good for me."

"Ditto."

I leaned back and caught a sushi roll as it motored on by, then fed it to him. On the next lap, I got one for myself. We proceeded like that until all the sushi was gone, and then he asked, "Ready for dessert?"

"Literally always."

I relocated to one of the patio chairs beside the fire pit, and Duke draped the blanket over my legs before heading to the kitchen. A few moments later, he called, "Close your eyes." I slapped my hands over my face to keep myself from peeking and could hear Duke moving around close beside me. Finally, he said, "Okay, you can open them."

I pulled my hands away and whooped with delight at what was waiting for me on the patio table. Duke had turned a batch of his big, fluffy sugar cookies into a bouquet by mounting them on skewers, then arranging them in a vase tied with a wide, rainbow-striped ribbon. Tulip- and daffodil-shaped cookies mingled with cats, a couple of Totoros, dragons, crabs, and a single Santa Claus, who was wearing a Hawaiian shirt. Each cookie was bright, colorful, and meticulously decorated, fanning out in a dazzling display, and I yelled, "Oh my God, it's amazing!"

He grinned and said, "I tried to include stuff I knew you liked. The Santa and dragons are a reminder of the first night we baked together."

"And the crustaceans are from when we played crabs in my pants."

"Exactly."

"Where did you get a Totoro cookie cutter?"

"I made my own with a pair of pliers and a snowman shape."

"Wow." As I studied all the little details, I said, "You need to sell these. Not to get all capitalistic on you, but seriously. This is absolutely jaw-dropping."

"I didn't invent the cookie bouquet. Lots of places sell them."

"Not like this they don't! I've never seen one so whimsical and totally personalized. Plus, your decorations are perfect and your cookies are the best I've ever had!" I carefully framed up a shot of the bouquet with my phone and snapped a photo.

"You really think people would pay for something like that?"

"They'd be lining up and begging you to take their money! I'm posting this on Facebook and Instagram. Just watch, people are going to go crazy over it." I uploaded the photo and a quick caption, then watched my post for a moment and grinned. "It got a like already. And there's a love."

"Really?"

"Yup. Duke, you have to start baking for a living. Not only are you fantastic at it, but it's what makes you happy! No matter what ends up happening with your job on the police force, you owe it to yourself to give this a shot."

He studied the cookie arrangement and murmured, "I'd love to, but I wouldn't even know where to start."

"Well, with a commercial kitchen, I suppose. Cole and River rent one for their catering business, and you could do the same thing. Or, you know what? Maybe you could work out a time share with them and split the rental cost! You tend to bake at odd hours anyway, and I bet their kitchen is sitting empty at three a.m."

"That's a good idea," Duke said. But then he shook his head. "There's just no way, though. I'd never be able to run a business on my own."

"You won't be on your own! I can be your delivery boy, baking assistant, salesperson, whatever you need. Hey, you know what you should do? Bake a few big centerpieces and donate them to Nana's charity auction! That's a total win-win: delicious treats for her guests and lots of exposure for your new business! We just need a name. Duke's Delectable Delights? Bangin' Baked Bouquets? Oh man, I have an alliteration fixation."

He said, "We can't start a business."

"Why not?"

"Well, for one thing, it takes a lot of capital to get a company off the ground. I don't have very much in savings, and if I end up getting fired, I'm going to need every penny to live on until I find a new job."

"You know what you do have, though? Me. I believe in you, Duke, and I have plenty in savings to get this business off the ground. We don't just have to limit it to bouquets, either. What if we packaged individual cookies and sold them at some of the local coffee houses? Lots of bakeries already do that, but no one is out there selling rainbow-colored sparkly dragons! Look how amazing that is!" I pointed at the perfect dragon in the center of the bouquet, which glistened with edible glitter. "These cookies are made for the Instagram generation. Plus, they're absolutely crave-worthy. Oh hey, Craveable Cookie Creations! Damn it, I need an alliteration intervention. What would we need to get this business off the ground? A license obviously, a kitchen, and a ton of ingredients, but what else?"

Duke thought about it as he sat down beside me, and then he said, "A commercial mixer, I guess, and ways to package the products, including labels. If we were selling locally, we'd need a delivery van, and if we were going to be shipping from a website, we'd need to figure out how to package them so they wouldn't break in transit." He exhaled slowly, and then he said, "But people don't just up and decide to start a company. It takes planning, market analysis, a business plan, and a hell of a lot more."

"That's not the only way to launch a business. Look at River and Cole. They're running a successful catering company in an incredibly competitive market, and I know for a fact they didn't start out with anything but a love of cooking."

"I'm probably not going to get fired though, and when I go back to working sixty hours a week, I won't have enough time to devote to a business."

"So quit! You'd be so much happier if you were baking for a living."

"I'd never be able to pay my mortgage. Selling cookies wouldn't turn enough of a profit, especially not at first."

I took his hands in mine and said, "Right now, this house owns you, not the other way around. Why don't you sell it and get that weight off your shoulders?"

"And then what? You know how expensive it is to rent just about anything in this city. If I quit my job and started a business, it could be years before it became profitable. What would I do in the meantime?"

"We'd figure something out."

He shook his head. "That doesn't work for me, Quinn. I'm not like you. I don't have it in me to take a leap and trust that everything will work out. I don't have a safety net like you do, either. My parents and I were already on thin ice, and after that fight with my dad, I'm on my own."

"No, you're not. Like I said, you have me! That means you also have my family. If you end up selling the house and quitting your job to start a business, they'll make sure we're okay. Both of us, you and me."

"That's sweet, but I have to be able to take care of myself."

"Come on, Duke, go after what makes you happy! You're worried about what might happen if you fail. But what if you succeed? What if you take a leap and soar?"

"It's so easy to say: quit your job, sell your house, start a business and follow your bliss. But I'm not that guy, Quinn. I can't live with that kind of uncertainty. I need to know I have a steady paycheck coming in, and a roof over my head, and that I'm going to be okay."

He paused for a moment, and then he said, "Just so you know, I'll probably always be like this. I'll keep doing what's safe and avoid taking risks. You should think about whether you can see yourself with someone like that. Even if it doesn't bother you now, will it, somewhere down the road? You have so much freedom. You can act on a whim and go anywhere and do whatever you want. Now imagine us as a couple, one or two or ten years in the future. Imagine me in the same job, still struggling to pay the same bills, and still living the same quiet little life. Would you feel tied down? Would it drive you crazy? Or worse, would you end up resenting me for all the fun you missed out on by settling down with someone like me?"

I met his gaze and said, "God, I hope I'm lucky enough to still be with you ten years from now. You're talking about these hypothetical things I'd be giving up, but look at all I'd gain!"

"Like what?"

"Like you, Duke! Ending up with you wouldn't be a burden like you're trying to make it out to be, not by a long shot. It'd be the most amazing gift imaginable!"

After a pause, he grinned a little and said, "We suck at dating."

"How so?"

"We both keep talking about the future and making all of this so complicated, instead of just enjoying today. Why is that?"

"It's because we both feel something real developing between us," I said, "and we can't help but wonder how your life and mine are going to fit together."

He thought about that, and after a few moments he nodded. "You're right. That's exactly why we keep doing this." Duke leaned in and kissed my forehead before plucking a crab-shaped cookie from the bouquet and handing it to me.

It was absolutely adorable with its blue eyes, glossy orange shell, and little smile, and I felt guilty about eating it. But my sweet tooth won out, so I bit off a claw and savored it, and then I murmured, "These really are fucking awesome."

"I'm glad you like them." Duke went over to the wading pool and shut off the boat parade, then straightened up and stuck his hand out, palm-up. A moment later he said, "Well, crap. There was only supposed to be a twenty percent chance of rain."

A few raindrops landed on me, and I exclaimed, "Oh no, save the cookies!" I rushed inside with the bouquet, then returned to the yard to help Duke. The bar was on wheels, so we rolled it to the door and lifted it over the threshold, and then he placed a mesh grate over the fire pit and went around and extinguished the tiki torches. Meanwhile, I brought in the blanket, dishes, and pineapple drinks. By the time we unplugged the palm trees and fit them into the house, we were both pretty soggy.

We stood just inside the kitchen doorway and watched the rainfall for a minute, and Duke said, "It actually rains a lot in Hawaii, so technically, the theme's not ruined." He turned to me and added, "I was going to hang up a bedsheet and project movies onto it for the next part of our date, but we can do that indoors, too. Right now though, we need to dry you off. You're shivering."

He took my hand and led me to his bedroom. We both hung our leis over a chair in the corner, and he brought me a fluffy, white towel. I scrubbed my hair with it before unbuttoning my romper and stepping out of it. That left me in nothing but a pair of Superman briefs with a short, red cape over the rear. I'd selected them specifically because I was trying not to make the date about sex and had planned to keep my clothes on. But I decided I'd probably swung way too far in the opposite direction, so I plucked off the detachable cape and tossed it aside before running the towel down my arms and legs.

Duke chuckled at that, then came up behind me and kissed my shoulder. When I handed him the towel, he ran it over his face and hair, then stripped down to a pair of wonderfully snug navy blue briefs and finished drying off. He was mind-blowingly sexy, but I tore my gaze from all of that bare skin and tried to think about pretty much anything else besides climbing him like a tree and doing all sorts of nasty things to him.

He began massaging my shoulders, and when I sighed with pleasure and leaned into him, he said, "Why don't you lie down so I can do this properly?"

"Yes please!" I took a flying leap onto his bed and landed face-down with a bounce. Fortunately, that position hid the growing bulge distorting Superman's emblem on the front of my briefs.

Duke straddled my thighs and grabbed some lotion from the nightstand, which he squirted into his hand. He rubbed his palms together and went to work on my neck and shoulders, and I told him, "That feels fantastic."

"Glad you like it."

In an effort to stop thinking about sex, I began rambling aimlessly. "We built some set pieces before rehearsal today and it was surprisingly strenuous, so this massage is just what I needed."

"Is there much more to do?"

"Tons. Dare wants the set to keep evolving throughout the performance. Some of that'll happen with colored lights and panels of fabric, but then there are also the giant plywood canvases."

Duke kneaded my right shoulder as he said, "I can help if you want. I'm pretty good at building stuff."

"I'll definitely take you up on that."

"I'm planning to contact your friend Darwin to see about helping with the shelter fundraiser, too. I figure I should do something useful with all this free time."

"That's great! I'm volunteering, too. This weekend, I'm going around to a bunch of local businesses to see if they'll donate items for the silent auction." My eyelids slid shut as he began working his way down my back, and my rambling ran out of steam. I murmured, "You're so damn good at this," before making a weird little sound that was just this side of a purr.

He massaged my lower back for a couple of minutes before running both hands all the way up my spine. I'd been doing a decent job of calming the hell down, but when Duke leaned forward, his cock grazed my ass, and it was like flipping a switch from 'perfectly innocent' to 'do me now.' I had to force myself not to shudder with pleasure, or squirm as his big hands ran over my body and his bare thigh rubbed against mine.

I was less than successful at hiding my reactions though, because Duke said, "You're shivering again. Want me to turn on the heater?"

I cleared my throat and managed, "No thanks. I'm good." Then I started doing long division in my head, in a desperate ploy to kill the back-with-a-vengeance hard-on that was pinned against the mattress. It felt like it was about to raise me up from the bed like a jack under a car. I accidentally let a quick burst of laughter slip from me at that mental picture, probably because all the blood had rushed from my brain to my dick, leaving me borderline delirious.

Apparently Duke was growing accustomed to my randomness, and he took the laughter in stride. He slid down a bit and worked on one leg, then the other before rubbing my feet. But then he ran out of things to massage and said, "Why don't you flip over, so I can keep going?"

"Um...."

"Or we can be done if you want. Feel like watching a movie?"

"Sure, let's do that."

When Duke climbed off the bed and started to leave the room, I got up, glanced down at myself, and sighed. My cock was sticking out at a sharp angle and straining against the fabric of my briefs. I looked like a sun dial.

He turned back to me and asked, "Everything alright?"

"Oh yeah. I'm good," I said as I kept my back to him. "Top notch. A-okay."

"Except for that huge boner."

I glanced up and noticed both of us reflected in the window to the left of the bed. Duke was smiling at me with his arms folded across his chest. I colored slightly and murmured, "Except for that." I turned to him and tried in vain to push it down as I said, "Tonight wasn't supposed to be about sex, and I know we're taking it slowly and all that, but you look really fucking sexy in those briefs, and I have the self-control of a hormone addled fourteen-year-old."

Duke crossed the room and surprised me by picking me up and tossing me back onto the bed. Lust shot through me, making me shake as he pushed my legs apart and licked my inner thigh. He glanced up at me with a wicked grin and said, "So that's why you were shivering."

He climbed up beside me and draped his leg over both of mine, and when he claimed my mouth with a demanding kiss, it made my cock throb. He stroked my erection through my briefs before stripping both of us. I started jerking him off, and when he pushed his cock against mine, I tried to get my hand around both of them. But Duke was much better suited to the task, and he grasped his cock and mine in his big hand and jerked us off together. His lips found mine again, and I moaned and bucked into his hand, totally lost to the sensation.

I clutched him as I started to cum just a few minutes later. My lids closed automatically, but when he whispered, "Look at me, Quinn," I did as he asked. As we locked eyes, I cried out, thrusting into his palm as cum sprayed my body and his.

A moment later, a moan slipped from him, and Duke started cumming, too. He kept stroking both of us as he wrapped his other arm around my shoulders. His cock was still pressed to mine, rubbing up and down my length, and I grasped his ass with both hands as wave after wave of that overwhelming orgasm forced every drop of cum from my balls.

When it finally came to a shuddering end, I slid my hands up Duke's back and held on to him. A tremor went through his big, powerful body, and for some reason, it triggered a protective instinct in me. I held him tighter and stroked his back, and when his orgasm ebbed and he let go of our cocks, I crawled up and dotted kisses on his cheeks, his lips, even his eyelids.

He grinned drowsily, and I murmured, "That was intense." Duke nodded and wrapped me up in his arms. "We're all sticky," I whispered as he settled in comfortably beside me. "Want me to get the towel?"

"No, because that would mean letting go of you."

We spent a long time kissing tenderly. Given his usual tendency toward keeping everything neat and clean, I was kind of surprised he could tolerate the fact that we were both such a mess. But he seemed perfectly relaxed as he leaned back a bit to look at me and murmured, "You're so beautiful, Quinn."

"No I'm not. I'm cute, but I'll never be beautiful."

Duke knit his brows and said, "You're also extremely cute, but you can't honestly believe you're not beautiful. You're just being modest, right?"

I shook my head. "That's just not a word that applies to me, and I'm fine with that. It's enough to be cute."

He reached across me to the nightstand and picked up his phone, then held it at arm's length and snapped a picture of both of us. He pulled it up on his screen and showed it to me as he said, "Tell me what you see."

"A stunningly beautiful man."

"Right."

"And me."

Duke sighed at that and said, "Come on. Really look at yourself and tell me what you see."

I frowned at the screen and said, "I should go back to bleaching my hair. It looked better when it was white-blond, but now that I let my natural color grow in, it looks mousy."

"Do you think my hair looks mousy?"

"Not at all. It's a gorgeous shade of dark blond, and when you're in the sun, it's shot through with gold."

"My hair is about half a shade darker than yours, so how can you think yours is mousy and mine's not?"

"I think in my case, there's just an overall mousiness." I pushed my ears up with both hands and wiggled my nose, and Duke grinned and looked at the photo. Then he tapped his screen a few times and made it his wallpaper.

He said, "Maybe it's good that you don't know how gorgeous you are. It could only lead to the inevitable conclusion that you're totally out of my league." He returned his phone to the nightstand and rolled out of bed, taking me with him.

I grinned as he hoisted me over his shoulder and said, "I like it when you carry me around."

"Good."

"Where are we going?"

"To the bathroom to get cleaned up. I wonder if we'd both fit in my tub."

"I think we definitely need to find out."

The answer, as it turned out, was kind of. Duke was a big guy, and the standard-size tub/shower combo fit him alright, but with little room to spare. We made it work anyway. I straddled his lap, and we took turns lathering each other, then soaking as best we could in the warm water.

As we dried off afterwards, Duke asked, "Are you still up for a movie?"

"Definitely."

"Great. Let's make some popcorn. If you want to watch in bed, we could project the film onto that empty wall in my bedroom. This might be one of the only times when having blank, white walls actually comes in handy."

"Speaking of which, would you absolutely hate it if I painted the living room? It's such a pretty space, and with a little color it'd be amazing."

He mulled that over, then said, "I guess it depends on the color. I think it'd probably make me jittery if you painted the walls hot pink and covered them in glitter, like you did in your old apartment."

"How'd you know I did that? Did Cole tell you?"

"Yeah, but not to warn me off you or anything. I asked him why you were covered in glitter the first time I saw you, and he told me about your decorating efforts. Apparently, it also included a disco ball. Please don't put one in the living room." He thought about that for a beat, then said, "Okay, if you really want one, you can hang up a disco ball. I can learn to live with it. I don't think I can manage neon pink walls, though. Or neon orange. Or neon green. Basically, no neon anything, alright?"

"I can work with that." I turned from the bathroom mirror, where I'd been finger-combing my hair, and said, "I always wondered if you remembered the day we met." I'd gotten a birdcage stuck on my roommate's head in an effort to armor him up against an attack cat, and then I got my hands trapped in there too when I tried to get him out. We'd been headed to Oakland so Skye could cut us loose when we ran into Duke and Finn, who were out on patrol. Really not my finest hour.

Duke smiled at me and said, "You were dressed in rain boots, goggles, and a skimpy pair of briefs, and you were coated in hot pink glitter. There's absolutely no way I could ever forget that."

"Good point."

We went into the bedroom and pulled on our underwear, and Duke glanced at me and said, "I'd wondered if you remembered meeting me that day."

"Dude, seriously? You're six-eight with muscles that would give Thor an inferiority complex, and you were wearing a cop uniform. How could I possibly forget you?" He grinned at that.

I started to head to the kitchen, but Duke said, "Hang on, you're not dressed properly."

I looked down at my Superman briefs. "Oh, I thought we were going in our skivvies. My bad. I'll run upstairs and grab some clothes, since my romper's still wet."

"That's not what I meant." He scooped the short, red cape from the floor and reattached it to the back waistband of my briefs, and then he said, "Now you're ready." I flashed him a big smile, and we headed to the kitchen hand-in-hand.

A few minutes later, as the rain tapped against the windows, we returned to Duke's bed with popcorn and big boxes of candy that he'd bought just for the occasion. He hooked a little projector to his laptop, and as one of my favorite Miyazaki movies started to play on the wall of his bedroom, I curled up comfortably in Duke's arms and said, "Thank you again for everything you did for me tonight. It was absolutely magical. In fact, it was the best date in the history of dating."

He touched my cheek and murmured, "I'm glad you had fun."

I glanced up at him and said, "Just so you know, I'm going to start referring to you as my boyfriend now, and I'm going to do it *a lot*. I'll be asking everyone, 'have you met my boyfriend Duke?' And I'll be telling our friends, 'my boyfriend is better than your boyfriend,' and stopping total strangers on the street and going, 'hey, see that tall, handsome man over there? That's my boyfriend.' If you have a problem with that, you'd better speak up now, because otherwise, the boyfriend train is pulling out of the station."

He held me tight and said, "I have no problem with that whatsoever."

Chapter Eleven

Christian George leaned over the edge of the scaffolding and said, "Do me a favor, Quinn, and hand me the midnight blue." He was working on one of the backdrops for my dance troupe's upcoming performance, and I was supposed to be helping, but mostly, I was just loitering and watching the painting unfold. The nighttime cityscape took up one vertical six-by-twelve-foot panel of a three-sided set piece on wheels, and it was breathtaking.

I rummaged around in a big cardboard box, which was loaded up with well-worn cans of spray paint, and took my best guess at midnight blue based on the lid color. When I held it up to him, he said, "That's indigo." I tried again and was told, "That's navy." I held up another can, and he said, "That's denim blue."

"Oh, come on!" I straightened up and pulled the red bandana off the lower half of my face, which I'd been wearing to keep from breathing the paint fumes.

"It's darker, almost black."

"This would be a lot easier if the cans weren't all paint-smudged, so I could actually read the labels."

Christian gracefully leapt off the platform and rummaged through the box himself. A minute later, he pulled the black bandana off his nose and mouth and grinned at me. "I guess I used it up. Can you add it to the shopping list?"

"Yup."

I pulled out my phone, added the color to the notes I'd been keeping for him, and texted him the list. Meanwhile, Christian flexed his fingers and shook out his hands before wiping them on his torn jeans. He'd survived a brain tumor and the surgery to remove it a few years back, and I'd heard he still had a few problems as a result of all of that. I wondered if that was why his hands were bothering him. When he saw me watching him, he said, "You can go ahead and ask. Everyone always does."

"That's why I didn't want to say anything," I said. "It's annoying to answer the same question over and over."

He peeled off his ragged T-shirt, with the word 'Ramones' so faded out it was almost illegible, and used it to wipe his face. He was tall and slim, with a big, black and gray mandala tattooed on his stomach, and between the ink, the clothes, and his fondness for black eyeliner, Christian looked like a rock star. He was actually a graffiti artist, which was pretty close, but he'd also founded a nonprofit community center that offered free art and music classes to kids, so there was a lot more to him than met the eye.

"Come on, let's raid Skye's fridge. I need a break." He tossed his shirt aside and began to cross the warehouse, and as I fell into step with him, he said, "To answer your unasked question, the brain tumor left me with a few lingering issues with my hands. I worked my ass off in physical therapy and regained more than ninety percent of what I'd lost in terms of coordination and fine motor skills, but some of the damage was permanent. It's not a big deal, though. I can paint, and I can walk. That's what's important. As for the rest of it, I've learned to adapt. It's become my new normal."

The warehouse was crowded. Skye's huge sculpture of a man who looked like he was clawing his way up through the floor had been pushed against the far wall, to make room for the giant metal jellyfish he'd been constructing for his corporate client. When I'd asked him why he went with jellyfish, he'd said it was because they were the most organic, free-form things he could think of, and just what the sterile lobby of the downtown office building needed. Each bell-shaped jellyfish was made out of rusty, reclaimed metal and was about six feet tall, not counting the surprisingly delicate-looking rope-like tentacles and lacy arms. One completed jellyfish hung from the twenty-foot ceiling, and its tentacles grazed the cement floor. As if all of that wasn't enough, half a dozen of the towering, triangular set pieces crowded the warehouse, and we had to weave our way to the small refrigerator in the corner.

Once we'd retrieved a couple of sodas, we sat on the workbench beneath the tall windows, and I asked, "Do you worry about the tumor coming back?"

Christian considered the question as he pushed a chin-length tendril of light brown hair out of his green eyes. He'd shaved the sides and back of his head to about a quarter-inch in length, and the part he'd left long had been gathered into a short ponytail. A scar was just barely visible behind one ear. It curved up until it disappeared into the longer hair on top of his head.

"Worrying about things you can't control doesn't get you anywhere. It just eats you up inside and keeps you from enjoying the here and now." He took a sip from his soda can before saying, "I had a fantastic surgeon, and he's positive he removed the entire tumor. I go in every six months for a scan, just to be sure, and it always comes out clear. I'd be lying if I said it didn't cross my mind occasionally, but I refuse to be ruled by fear. Instead, I make a point of being grateful for and cherishing every single day I have with my husband Shea. I'll never take our time together for granted, not after what I went through. I guess that's the one positive that came from nearly dying. It put everything into perspective." Christian smiled when I threw my arms around him, and he asked, "What's that for?"

I squeezed him a little harder and said, "I'm just so glad you're still here, making beautiful art. I also think you're amazing for going through something like that and coming out on the other side so strong and positive. I feel lucky to know you, Christian."

When I let go and grinned at him, he said, "I'm lucky to know you, too. You're a lot of fun, Quinn. The four of us should hang out sometime."

"I'd love that. I know Duke would, too."

"So would Shea. He keeps saying he's shocked at how much Duke has opened up. Maybe that's your influence. I guess your boyfriend used to be pretty quiet and reserved."

His husband was actually Finn Nolan's kid brother, and Duke had worked with him before Shea quit the police force. I got the impression they hadn't known each other very well when they were coworkers, but Duke and Shea had been bonding over the last few days, while helping my troupe with the backdrops for our show. The two men were currently on a hardware store run and had taken over the job of finishing construction on the set pieces. Meanwhile, Dare and Skye had gone out to rummage for scrap metal to use in the jellyfish mobile, leaving Christian and me to paint (or more specifically, leaving him to paint and me to gawk in wonder at his ability).

"I'm glad they've had a chance to get reacquainted," I said. "What's Shea been doing since he left the police department?"

"He draws comic books, and he's taking art classes at my old alma mater, Sutherlin College."

"God, I wish I could convince Duke to do that."

"Go to art school?"

"No, follow his passion. He's a fantastic baker, and it makes him so happy. But he doesn't think it'll pay the bills."

Christian's full lips curved up at one corner, and he said, "I remember one of the first times I met Duke. It was Christmas, and I was visiting Shea at the station. Your boyfriend brought us a plate of cookies, and it seemed so incongruous because he's built like a fortress, and yet he produced these delicate little confections. They were damn good, too."

"Baking is his art." I pulled out my phone and showed Christian the cookie bouquet Duke had made me a week ago, on our first 'official' date.

"Wow, that's fantastic."

"Isn't it? I posted this picture to social media, and everyone went crazy for it and asked where they could buy the cookies. But he still doesn't believe he can make a living at it."

"Well, give him time. It took Shea a while to make the transition, too. So many people dismiss comic books as trivial, which is total bullshit. He's as much of an artist as I am, but he was hesitant to quit his day job at first, not only because he thought he'd never make a living with his art, but because he believed the assholes who told him there was no real value in drawing comic books. Duke probably heard the same shit about baking."

I said, "Yeah, especially when he was growing up. I've tried to tell him producing something that makes people happy is always worthwhile."

"That's exactly right. Just keep encouraging him. Hopefully he'll take the leap when he's ready."

"Definitely. I think Shea is a good influence on him, too. He's the perfect example of following your passion, especially since he started out in the same profession."

"It's interesting, a lot of Shea's family started out in law enforcement," Christian said as I took a drink. "It was basically the family business, going back two or three generations. Shea and his brother and several of their cousins became police officers right out of school, because of pressure from their family. But over the years, almost all of them have changed careers. Finn is the last holdout. I think he actually likes the job though, unlike his brother and cousins, who just went along with it because it was expected of them."

"It's not easy to let go of expectations like that."

"Did your family pressure you into becoming a ballet dancer?"

"No, that was my idea," I said. "But my dad really wants to see me succeed, and he's been less than thrilled that I've devoted the last year to this start-up dance troupe, instead of a nationally recognized company. I think we finally had a breakthrough a few days ago, and he's trying to see things from my perspective. But there's a lot of pressure on this upcoming performance. I need him to know I made the right call with Dare's troupe."

"Is your dad coming to the show?"

"My whole family is." Christian raised an eyebrow, and I asked, "Why do you look surprised?"

"I watched part of the rehearsal today. Skye told me there were some last minute changes to make the show more passionate, but I hadn't quite expected such raw sexuality. Don't get me wrong, I think it's fantastic. But I think if I were in your shoes, I'd have a hard time doing that in front of my dad."

"Is your father kind of uptight?"

Christian grinned and said, "No. Not even a little. He's actually a rock star, and I suspect he probably slept with hundreds of men and women before he finally fell in love with his boyfriend Gianni and settled down. Even still, I'd be embarrassed to get up onstage in front of him and just go for it the way you guys are, but then I'm in no way a performer."

"I really believe in what Dare and Haley are trying to do here. They want to portray a relationship between two men in the most honest way possible. The sexual aspect is just one component of the bigger picture."

"They're definitely achieving that." Christian took a sip of his drink, then asked, "Out of curiosity, what does your boyfriend think about all of this?"

"I warned him ahead of time that we were changing the show, and that Haley and I would be kissing and would have a lot of body contact onstage. He's watched us rehearse three times this week, and he hasn't said anything, so I assume he's okay with it."

"Would he tell you if he wasn't?"

"Yeah, definitely." Wouldn't he?

Shea and Duke returned to the warehouse a few minutes later. They were talking animatedly as they carried several sheets of plywood through the huge loading door, which we'd left open to air out the smell of spray paint. They'd both volunteered to move the sets during the show and were debating how best to rotate the three-sided displays, since the backdrop was going to change in front of the audience while we were dancing.

Though not quite as tall as Finn, Shea was a big, muscular guy with the same dark hair and bright blue eyes as his older brother. Those eyes lit up when he spotted his husband. As soon as he and Duke put down the plywood, Shea wound his way across the warehouse, and when he reached Christian, he wrapped his arms around him and kissed him before saying, "That cityscape looks fantastic. Have you talked to Dare about what he's going to do with the set pieces after the show?"

"Actually, Quinn had a great idea. He suggested auctioning off the individual panels at Nana's charity fundraiser next week, with the understanding that the winning bidders won't be getting them until after the show in mid-October. We just need to take some photos of them, so people know what they're bidding on."

Duke reached me a moment later and cupped my cheek as he said, "I'm glad to see you actually sitting down. You seemed sore after rehearsal, and then you went straight to helping with the backdrops."

"I'm fine. My ankle aches a little, but it's no big deal. I'm planning to ice it before we go to Finn's house tonight, and then I'll be good as new."

I'd stopped wearing a brace at the beginning of the week on the advice of my physical therapist, and I was doing twice-daily exercises to help strengthen my ankle. While it had healed well, there was still some lingering soreness. With just three weeks until the show, we'd been practicing twice as long and twice as hard. Since I was onstage for the entire ninety-minute performance, I was actively involved in almost every aspect of rehearsal. I felt it not just in my ankle, but my entire body. I planned to take a few days off after our debut to recuperate, but until then, I needed to keep pushing myself.

Duke asked, "You sure you're up for dinner? We could always reschedule."

I smiled at him and said, "I'm fine. You don't have to worry about me."

He wrapped his arms around me and said, "You danced for four hours today, with minimal breaks. Yesterday, you rehearsed for five hours, then went to work at the club and danced some more. How long can you possibly keep this up?"

"As long as it takes."

"But you have to be hurting."

"Sure, but these long rehearsals are necessary. There have been a lot of changes to the routine, and Dare and Haley will probably continue to fine-tune it right up until the curtain rises, so we'll keep rehearsing as much as we possibly can."

Duke looked like he wanted to argue with me, but instead, he said, "Let's go home so I can take care of you for a couple of hours before dinner."

"But I was going to help you and Shea build the next set piece, so Christian can start painting it."

Shea said, "Don't worry about us, we got this. Go get some rest, Quinn. We'll see you tomorrow."

"Well, okay. Take care, guys." Duke said goodbye to our companions and picked me up, and I told him, "You don't have to carry me."

He kissed my forehead as I wrapped my legs around his waist. "I know, but let me have my fun."

We scooped up my backpack on the way out, and when we were in his truck and headed back to San Francisco, I said, "Thanks for helping out today, Duke."

"You don't have to thank me every day."

I grinned at his profile and said, "Let me have my fun."

He smiled at that. "It's fun to thank me?"

"It's fun to let you know you're appreciated. Between building sets and volunteering with the shelter's fundraiser, you've been going nonstop these past few days."

"I like feeling needed." I rested my hand on his denim-clad knee, and he glanced at me and asked, "Are you sure you don't want me to reschedule our plans for tonight? Finn and Chance will understand."

"Please don't cancel. I'm looking forward to it, and I'm not nearly as broken down as you seem to think I am."

"Is there any part of you that doesn't hurt right now?" When I hesitated before answering, he added, "Be honest."

"My arms don't feel too bad. I haven't had to do much hammering and sawing since you started helping us build."

"Why isn't the rest of the troupe helping? There are a dozen dancers in all, but usually it's just you and Dare staying after rehearsal and working on the sets."

"Because they all need to get back to their jobs. It's already tough for them to make a living while devoting so much time to rehearsal. Take Haley, for example. He looks after his disabled mom and his three younger siblings, works two part-time jobs, and still makes time for the troupe, including choreography and sewing our costumes. Dare and I have the most free time, since he cut back on teaching classes to get ready for the show, and I just work a few evenings a week. We're all doing as much as we can."

"Not everyone. A couple of those guys are clearly doing the bare minimum."

"But that's fine, too," I said. "They're already taking a lot of time out of their lives for rehearsal, and they're not getting paid a cent. If they don't want to build sets or sew costumes or whatever else on top of that, it's understandable."

"But it just leaves more work for the few who volunteer for everything, like you."

"It's okay though. Like you said, it's good to feel needed."

A minute later, Duke said, "I knew you overdid it today. I could tell by the way you were carrying yourself." I'd been absently massaging the top of my right thigh through the red sweats I'd pulled on after rehearsal.

"Okay, yes, my muscles are sore. But hey, at least I'm not working tonight."

"What do you think about taking a leave of absence from the club, just until after the show?"

"I'd hate to leave Preston short-handed. Some of those dancers don't have the best work ethic, so he relies pretty heavily on the handful of us who he knows will actually show up when we're supposed to. The club owner gets down on him when there are a lot of empty platforms around the dance floor, and I don't want him to get in trouble."

"It's frustrating that you never put your needs first," he said. "If Preston can't get enough go-go boys to show up for work, that's his problem, not yours. Something has to give, and it's not going to be the dance troupe, especially with just three weeks left before your debut. That leaves the job at the club. With your savings, you could afford to take some time off."

"I'll think about it. I'd still have to finish out this week, though. I can't give my manager zero notice, that's not okay."

"I suppose you're right." I glanced at his profile two or three times as he was merging onto the Bay Bridge, and after a minute he said, "Is there something you want to ask me?"

"Are you really okay with the changes to the routine? Haley and I haven't actually kissed yet, because we didn't feel like we needed to rehearse that over and over again. But there's a lot of touching now, and there will be a kiss when we're onstage, so I'm wondering how you're feeling about all of that."

"I'm enough of a grown-up to get that you're both performers, and that you don't have romantic feelings for your costar."

"But still," I said, "does it make you uncomfortable?"

"I'm trying not to let it get to me. You've only rehearsed the finale in bits and pieces, so it doesn't seem all that sexual yet. But...."

I guessed, "But you still kind of want to punch Haley in the face, right?"

"The thought had crossed my mind. That's not okay, though! I've turned into such a caveman since I met you. I used to think I was a lot more evolved than that, but apparently not."

"We all get a little primal when it comes to the people we care about."

"But you'd never think like that, if the situation were reversed," Duke said. "I can't even imagine you getting jealous and possessive."

"I've never really been the jealous type, but that doesn't mean I'd enjoy watching you making out onstage with some guy."

Duke said, "I'm trying to be an adult about all of this. So, seriously, just keep doing what you're doing, and don't worry about Fred Flintstone over here." I smiled at him and kissed his cheek.

*****

We pulled up in front of Finn and Chance's place at seven sharp. Beforehand, I was treated to two hours of pampering by Duke, including a full body massage. I'd also taken a long, hot shower and iced my ankle, so I was feeling worlds better. But still, I was glad the most strenuous thing I'd have to do that evening was sit around a dinner table and hoist a cocktail.

Finn and his family lived in a boxy, converted warehouse in an industrial part of town. While the outside could best be described at minimalistic, the interior was warm and welcoming. The majority of it was one big room, with high ceilings, honey-colored hardwood floors, and an open, industrial kitchen off to the right, tucked beneath a balcony that fronted a row of small offices-turned-bedrooms. The back wall of the building was all glass, overlooking a spacious patio and an unobstructed view of the bay, while the brick wall to my left held a huge, colorful mural. I knew it was Christian's even before I spotted the name 'Zane' in the corner, which he used to sign all his artwork.

Finn's husband Chance was a beautiful brunet with a slender build, pale skin, and soulful blue eyes. He worked as a professional photographer, and dozens of his gorgeous photos decorated their home. He was also his kid brother Colt's legal guardian. When we arrived, the dark-haired teen was playing a video game on a laptop with a red-haired, freckled kid named Cory, who was Chance's half-brother, or something like that. I got a little lost in the branches of their elaborate family tree.

And then there was Elijah. I'd been told the tiny, blue-eyed blond was nineteen, but he looked much younger. He sat off by himself with his knees pulled up to his chest, reading a thick textbook, and he glanced up and nodded when Chance introduced us. On the drive over, Duke had explained that Elijah and Colt used to date, and that Finn had become Elijah's legal guardian, because the kid had been a runaway with no one else to turn to. That had to be awkward, living with his ex-boyfriend's family.

Elijah seemed completely isolated, even in a room full of people, and I found myself wanting desperately to be his friend. I knew Finn and his family cared about the kid, but he just looked so fragile, and his eyes were haunted, in a way that resonated with me, deep down. Even without knowing the particulars of what he'd run away from, I understood, and I wanted him to know I did.

At the same time though, I knew at a glance that it'd be way too easy to overdo it and freak him out. So I reeled in the urge to give him a huge hug, and instead, I plucked three cookie pops from the bouquet I'd begged Duke to make for our hosts. I gave two of them to Colt and Cory as I joked about ruining dinner, and then I crossed the room to Elijah and said, "Please accept this raccoon on a stick, from one hot blond to another." When he grinned, it felt like a total win.

He took the treat from me and asked, in a soft voice tinged with a faint southern accent, "Where'd you get the raccoon cookie?"

"I coerced my boyfriend into baking them for tonight," I said as I sat down in the club chair beside his. "It's part of a woodland-themed cookie bouquet. There are also bears, pine trees, and a ton of squirrels. But I happen to think the raccoons are the best, because of those little masks. They're like, nature's Hamburglars."

When Elijah burst out laughing, I wanted to do a fist-pump. Apparently it was fairly unusual, too, because every member of his family stopped what they were doing to glance at him. Fortunately, he didn't seem to notice, and he asked, "Why a woodland theme?" He started to raise the cute critter to his lips, but then he took pity on it and chose to save it.

"My thought process basically consisted of, 'well, who doesn't like squirrels?' Later on, I realized my logic was faulty, because anti-squirrel prejudice is actually rampant in our society. But by then, Duke was fully committed to the woodland theme, so it was too late to bail out."

Elijah grinned and said, "Did you buy the sweater to match the cookies?"

I looked down at my snazzy red sweater with a raccoon knit into the front of it and said, "Oh no, I already owned this."

"Seriously?"

"Dude, do you have something to say about my righteous raccoon sweater? Because this is bad-ass!"

"If you say so. Where'd you find it?"

"At a yard sale! Oh my God, they're so much fun! They're like, a huge scavenger hunt, except you don't know what you're looking for when you start off."

He grimaced a bit. "So, that's a used raccoon sweater."

"Yeah, but it still had the tags on it, because who on earth besides me would ever wear such a thing?"

"I have absolutely no answer to that."

"Yeah, me neither, actually."

After a pause, he said, "Finn mentioned you're a ballet dancer when he was talking you up earlier. I'm curious, are you able to stand *en pointe*?"

"Yup."

"I've always wanted to ask, doesn't that hurt? Because it looks incredibly painful."

"Hell yes it hurts! Here's a little secret about ballet: it *all* hurts."

"So, why do you do it?"

"Because some things are worth suffering for."

"Is it, though?"

I said, "I think I love ballet in part *because* it's difficult, and because it pushes my body to its absolute limit. It's hard to explain, but I get a deep sense of satisfaction out of excelling at something so challenging."

"That makes sense."

"I also happen to think ballet is one of the most beautiful things in all the world." I lowered my voice and admitted quietly, "And when I dance, I feel beautiful. It's the only time I do. Or it was, before I met my boyfriend. He makes me feel beautiful, too." I grinned shyly and glanced at Duke across the room, who was chatting with Chance and Finn around the long, stainless steel bar that fronted the kitchen. "Ballet also makes me feel powerful, and in total control of my body. I needed that desperately when I was a kid. I guess I still do."

Elijah met my gaze, and a look of understanding passed between us. I knew right then he'd been hurt, the way I had. Or possibly far, far worse.

After a moment, he said, "I've never seen ballet performed live. I'm curious now."

I said, "I'm doing a show in three weeks, so I'll send you and your family some tickets if you want. Just be forewarned, the show gets a bit adult in parts."

He reached up to tuck a strand of hair behind his ear, and the sleeve of his huge, pale blue cardigan fell back to reveal a delicate charm bracelet. His voice grew even softer when he said, "That, um...that might be a bit uncomfortable for me."

"Okay. Then how about coming with me to watch the San Francisco Ballet perform?"

"I don't know. I don't do well with crowds."

I got up and bowed deeply, then said, "In that case, I cordially invite you to the patio for an uncrowded and family-friendly performance of one of my very favorite routines."

Elijah's eyes went wide, and he stammered, "Um, you really don't have to do that."

I'd obviously crossed the line from friendly person to scary lunatic as far as Elijah was concerned. I tried to tone it down a little by dropping to one knee, so I wasn't standing over him, and I said softly, "I'm a lot, I know. When I meet somebody I want to be friends with, like you, I usually try too hard and just make it awkward. But there's one thing I can do well, and that's dance. Yeah, I know it's weird to want to dance for you, but weird is kind of what I do."

"Why do you want to be my friend?"

"Because you laugh at my jokes, and because you think that cookie is too cute to bite its head off, which makes me think we have a lot in common."

He glanced at the cookie pop in his hand and said, "I'm actually considerin' shellacking it, so it'll last forever."

I tilted my head toward the patio at the back of the building and said, "Come on, let me show you what ballet is all about. I already embarrassed myself with the raccoon sweater and the bizarre request to dance for you. Let me achieve the trifecta of awkwardness by actually going through with it."

Elijah stared at me for a moment, and then he grinned a little and said, "It's nice not being the weirdest person in the room for once."

I jumped up and exclaimed, "That's a yes, isn't it?"

He got up too and said, "Sure. Why not?"

A few minutes later, Duke, Elijah, and the rest of his family were lined up in chairs on the edge of the patio, which had been cleared of furniture. I'd done some stretches, stripped down to just my jeans, and cued up a song on Finn's stereo, which he'd very accommodatingly relocated to just inside the back door. I stood facing the bay and my little audience, lit by the strands of white bulbs which rimmed the cement patio, and said, "I wanted Elijah to experience ballet first-hand, so thanks for humoring me. This is the routine I performed when I auditioned for the San Francisco Ballet. I hope you like it."

Colt and Cory looked bored, while everyone else had a politely interested expression fixed in place. They were probably expecting the death scene from Swan Lake, or some tired shit like that. I grinned a little and pressed a button on the antiquated stereo.

Everyone's eyes went wide when Bohemian Rhapsody started to play, even Duke's, and he should have known me well enough by that point to guess I wasn't going to do anything conventional. During the *a cappella* introduction, I swung my arms around and leaned so far backwards that my fingers grazed the concrete. Then I moved deliberately around the patio, executing a series of pirouettes, arms up, toes pointed, head back, in perfect form, just like I'd been taught.

When the tempo picked up, I brought it. I leapt high into the air and spun, dropped onto the deck and rolled across it, then pushed off, arching my body. For the next few minutes, I reacted to the music, I became it, forgetting everything but how to move. I executed a flawless series of *grand jettes*, wide, soaring leaps across the stage. I felt so alive! My body responded with everything it had. It knew that routine so well, every note, every moment. I swirled across the stage, bending, twisting, and leapt into the air again, defying gravity, completing two complete rotations before I landed. I reached out, elongating my body, then jumped and spun again. It was as natural and familiar as breathing. It was strength and beauty, power and grace. It was everything.

As the final notes of the song faded out, I slowed, then stilled with one arm raised overhead and my right leg stretched behind me. All was silent for a moment. I'd forgotten where I was. Then someone exclaimed, "Holy shit!"

I looked up and remembered my little audience beside the bay. They were still staring at me with wide eyes. In the next instant, Elijah leapt to his feet and started clapping wildly. The rest of the group followed his lead, and I grinned embarrassedly at my standing ovation and took a bow.

Duke crossed the cement patio to me, dipped me back, and kissed me passionately. Then he looked deep into my eyes and whispered, "You astonish me." I smiled at him and touched his lips, and after a moment, he pulled me upright and ran the back of his hand down my cheek.

Finn and his family gathered around us, and he said, "I can't believe the San Francisco Ballet didn't hire you after that."

Duke traced my jaw, still staring at me with wonder as he said, "They did."

Finn said, "Oh. So…what happened to the job?"

Duke murmured, "Quinn turned it down. They weren't good enough for him." Then he peeled off his dark blue sweater, wrapped me up in it, and told me, "Come on, beautiful boy. Let's go inside, before you get cold." I grinned at him and let him lead me indoors.

Once I was dressed again, we gathered around the big dining room table. Duke sat beside me on my right, and Elijah slipped into the chair to my left and said, "Thank you, Quinn. That was amazing. If the offer still stands, I'd love those tickets to see you perform onstage. I have some money, so I can pay you for them."

I said, "It's my treat. I was given a whole stack of tickets for my friends and family, so I'll send you five of them, if everyone wants to go."

I was surprised when Cory asked, "Could you make it six? My dad's out of town on business right now, but I don't want him to miss out."

I looked across the table at the teen, who was studying his place setting, and said, "Absolutely." He murmured a thank you.

Colt joined us at the table, tossed his shaggy, dark hair out of his blue eyes, and exclaimed, "That was bad-ass! I had no idea ballet could be like that. I thought it was all tutus and prancing around on your tiptoes. But dude, that rocked!"

"Ballet can be all kinds of things, from classical to contemporary and everything in between. My troupe is trying to use dance to evoke emotion and tell a story. *Our* story. Everyone in the troupe is gay or bi. We're not the only all-LGBT troupe out there, but I still feel like we're doing something special. Dare and Haley, the choreographers, have this vision, and we have a fantastic original score by an incredible composer. He's this twenty-two-year-old kid who's still in college, and he's so gifted. It feels just magical, with all of us coming together and making something beautiful." I looked around the table and smiled. "Sorry, I'm totally monopolizing the conversation. I should never talk about ballet. Once I get going, I just don't stop."

Finn placed a big bowl of pasta in the center of the table and said, "Don't apologize. I for one happen to love passionate people." He glanced at his husband as Chance put a huge salad on the table, and the two exchanged the sweetest smile.

We all talked animatedly over dinner, and we were halfway through coffee and dessert when I got a text. I read my screen, then asked everyone, "Do you guys feel like a field trip?"

Colt said, "Always. I don't even care what it is."

Elijah asked, "But what is it, though?"

"Here's all I know: Nana Dombruso spent the last few days arranging some kind of publicity stunt to draw attention to her upcoming fundraiser and my dance troupe's debut. She says she's ready to let it rip, her words, but we have to go now, because she only has the truck for a couple of hours. I have no idea what truck she's talking about, or what she has up her sleeve. But she wants me to meet her in the Castro ASAP, and she told me to bring along as many people as I possibly can."

Colt pushed back from the table and said, "I'm definitely in. Do we need to bring anything?"

Chance got up too and said, "Probably just bail money, knowing Nana. I'll get my coat. And my wallet."

Elijah said, "Despite my better judgement, I'm in. If it brings in a bigger audience to watch Quinn's troupe perform, then I'll help in any way I can. And I don't know what fundraiser y'all are talkin' about, but I'm down for helping with that, too."

I turned to Duke and asked, "What do you say? Want to go commit some crimes in the name of art and charity?"

He flashed me a smile and said, "Only for you, Quinn."

*****

When we arrived at the designated meeting spot in the Castro maybe half an hour later, I couldn't help but smile. A truly unique crowd was gathering. People in all types of costumes mingled with about two dozen radiantly beautiful drag queens, members of my dance troupe, a group of burly leather bears, and a bunch of senior citizens.

Nana rushed up to me and asked, "Where's Dare? He's supposed to bring the flyers for your show! We gotta get moving, before the fuzz shows up and rains on our parade!"

It took me a minute to process what she'd said, since she was dressed in an opaque body stocking, a rhinestone bikini, and a huge, Vegas-style feathered headdress, which she'd paired with comfortable sneakers. Finally, I snapped out of it and looked around. I noticed Skye's blue hair weaving through the crowd and spotted his husband a moment later, and I told Nana, "He's here."

Her little husband Ollie rushed up to her when Nana yelled, "It's time!" He was dressed in black leather, from his captain's hat to his vest and chaps. Ollie handed Nana a children's walkie-talkie, and my eyes went wide when he spun around. Fortunately, the senior had opted to wear a pair of baggy boxers printed with hearts under his chaps. Nana yelled into the little red and yellow device, "Alpha team! Bravo team! Charlie team! Converge on the Castro! We're lighting this candle!"

Beside me, Duke murmured, "Um, what's happening right now?"

Nana turned to me and said, "Spread the word, Quinn! When the truck rounds the corner, you and your troupe need to climb onboard and start dancing! Dare, there you are!" He and Skye appeared at our side with a box of flyers, and Nana yelled into the walkie-talkie, "Mr. Mario, where are you?"

Her friend appeared a moment later, dressed in a glorious drag ensemble. He looked like a square dancer in his sequined gingham dress, which had so many petticoats underneath that the skirt puffed out like an umbrella. He also wore silver boots and a matching tiny cowboy hat, which was perched in a sea of auburn curls, and he said, with a thick Spanish accent, "I am here, Nana, along with the entire cast of Drag Queen Does

Dallas! The show just let out. Tell us what you need and consider it done!"

"We have to get two flyers in the hands of every single person in the Castro, one for the dance show, one for the Rainbow Roost fundraiser," she said. "Could you be a love and take that box from Dare? He needs to dance. The other flyers are with Josh and Darwin. Has anyone seen my great-grandsons? Never mind, there they are!" The teens were making their way down the crowded sidewalk, handing stacks of flyers to every drag queen they came across.

Duke murmured, "I still don't know what's happening here, but if this crowd gets any bigger, it's going to overflow into the street and shut down traffic."

Nana turned to him and exclaimed, "That's the whole idea! Oh hey, I remember you. You're that stripper! Get on the truck with Quinn and the boys and shake your money maker, hot stuff!" Before he could reply, she called, "Alpha team, welcome! You're leading us off, ladies! Go on now and strut your stuff!"

We were joined by a group of ten middle-aged women with drums and camouflage clothing. A woman of about fifty with short silver hair blew a whistle and yelled, "Greater Bay Area Lesbian Drum Corps, let's fucking do this!" She returned the whistle to her lips and blew three sharp blasts. A thunderous beat filled the air as the women all started drumming in perfect unison and stepped into the road. I finally got it: we were going to parade right the hell down Castro Street.

As the drum corps started their march, a group of Asian senior citizens rushed up to Nana. They were wearing some kind of bizarre costume, and Nana told them, "Mr. Wong and Bravo Company, move out!" A little old man gave her a crisp salute, then donned a huge Chinese dragon head. The rest of the bright orange dragon formed behind him and snaked into the street, following the drum corps and gyrating wildly. I laughed with delight and clapped my hands. The drag queens and several members of Nana's family fanned out on both sides of the street and thrust flyers into the hands of the astonished crowd, most of whom were recording with their phones.

"Here's my ride," Nana announced as a parade float rounded the corner. "Yours is up next, boys! Be ready!" I sent a quick group text to everyone in my troupe, alerting them to climb onto whatever showed up after the float.

Nana's grandson Dante was out in the intersection of Castro and 18th, directing traffic like a pro. He held his hand up to stop the cars while waving his arm to bring the float to his grandmother. The big, pink contraption was ringed in clouds and rainbows and made to look like Cinderella's castle. Kind of. Whoever had built the float (and it definitely looked homemade) had run into trouble making the turrets, so they looked an awful lot like a bunch of huge, pink cocks. Or maybe that was on purpose. The float already held five little old ladies dressed just like Nana in opaque body stockings, glittery bikinis and Vegas headpieces. I recognized Nana's bestie Kiki among them. Nana, Ollie, and the leather bears all climbed onboard and started dancing, and the floating dick castle began rolling again and fell in line behind the twenty-foot-long Chinese dragon.

When a giant semi truck rounded the corner, I was disappointed at first, because it just looked ordinary. But then the cab lit up inside and out with purple neon, and techno music began blasting from hidden speakers. It towed a long, open flatbed, which had been draped all around with rainbow streamers and a hand-lettered banner that read 'Dare to Dance.' I grabbed Duke's hand and yelled over the music, "Let's go!"

"You want me to come along?"

"Of course I do!"

Dare and Skye raced ahead of us and climbed on first, then began pulling up members of our troupe. We'd lost Finn and his family in the crowd, but we spotted them once we were up on the flatbed and gestured at them to join us. They all scrambled onboard, and Elijah was grinning a little as he leaned against the cab of the truck and held on.

Dare made his way to me and said, "Why don't you take center stage and perform act one from our show?"

But I shook my head and said, "You should represent us, brother. Go show San Francisco how amazing you are." He smiled at me, then moved to the open section in the center of the flatbed and started to perform a classical ballet routine, which paired surprisingly well with the techno music.

Duke and I began slow-dancing, while our friends danced all around us. I stopped noticing the crowd and the noise as I looked into his eyes. When he leaned down and kissed me, my heart skipped a beat, and I wrapped my arms around him and held on tight. I never wanted to let go.

The spell was broken and our lovely, magical parade vanished when we got to the end of Castro Street. It reminded me of Cinderella's coach turning back into a pumpkin. The drum corps fell silent and ran off into the night, and the dragon dancers shed their costumes and vanished into the crowd. Nana and her friends jumped off the float and piled into a row of waiting SUVS, and the dick castle turned right on Market Street and soon disappeared. Meanwhile, we all jumped off the flatbed. The driver shut off the music and the neon lights, and the truck merged into traffic, transformed in the blink of an eye from spectacular to ordinary.

Beside me, Elijah murmured, "That was amazing. It felt like a dream."

Chance said, "I'm sad it's over."

I waved to my troupe, and Duke and I fell into step with Finn and his family as we headed back into the Castro. The sidewalk was still crowded with people, who were saying things like, "Only in San Francisco."

Finn said, "That was fun. You know though, it is actually possible to get a permit and conduct a parade legally. Just saying."

"There was no time for that," Duke told him. "The fundraiser is next week, and the troupe is performing in mid-October. You know how slow the permit process is."

Finn raised an eyebrow and exclaimed, "Wow! Mr. by-the-book, actually condoning an illegal act! I never thought I'd see the day!"

"The only illegal act I saw was a few people jaywalking, who happened to be sporting drums or dragon costumes. Then a couple of vehicles drove slowly down the street," Duke said with a grin. "They tied up traffic a bit, but so what? The whole thing took fifteen minutes, and it made a lot of people happy. Maybe not the cars stuck behind us, but they'll get over it. And maybe it'll do some good. Maybe more people will attend the fundraiser and donate money to the shelter, then show up to watch my gorgeous, amazing boyfriend set the dance world on fire."

I hugged Duke's arm with both of mine and beamed at him as Finn muttered, "Seriously, who are you?"

*****

Later that night, when Duke and I were curled up in his bed, he whispered, "What an extraordinary day. One of many, since you've been around."

I pulled the blanket up over his bare shoulder and grinned contentedly. We'd spent every night since our Hawaiian-themed date sleeping in the same bed, alternately his or mine, in addition to spending all day, every day together, apart from when I was at work. In many ways, it felt like the date had never ended.

I said, "Thank you for being such a good sport with the impromptu parade. I know that wasn't the night you'd planned."

"It was better. We still had dinner with our friends and rounded out the evening with them, and in between we got to do something totally unexpected." We'd ended up accompanying Finn, Chance, and the boys to a diner in the Castro, where we had a second round of dessert and coffee and talked until midnight.

"They're such nice people. I'm glad they're a part of your life."

"Our lives," Duke murmured drowsily. "You totally won them over tonight, including Elijah, and that's not easy to do."

"He's such a sweet kid. He thought I was insane when I asked to dance for him, but then he really seemed to enjoy it. I thought that was awesome."

"Why'd you do that? Not that I'm complaining. It was spectacular."

I thought about it, then said, "I guess I wanted to give him something, and that was all I had to give."

"He reminds you of yourself at that age, doesn't he?"

"Yeah, aside from the fact that he's a math genius. Did you know he's attending a prestigious university on a full scholarship?"

Duke nodded as his eyes lost the battle to stay open. "Finn's so proud of Elijah. He brags about him all the time."

After a pause, I said, "When the time is right, I want to adopt a kid of my own, someone who just needs a chance, and a family to love him and take care of him."

"Like your dad did with you."

"Yeah." I searched his face in the semi-darkness as I asked, "Have you ever thought about becoming a parent?"

He murmured, "I definitely want a family of my own someday, a husband and a bunch of kids who I can give what I never got, all the unconditional love in the world."

Duke fell asleep a few moments later, and I kissed his forehead and whispered, "I hope I'm a part of your someday."

Chapter Twelve

"This place is packed!" I loosened my tie, then reached behind me and cracked a window. It was the last weekend in September, and Nana's charity event seemed to be off to a great start, if the size of the crowd was any indication.

Darwin and I were hanging out in the DJ booth with my lavender-haired friend Ash, who turned to us and said, "But that's good, right? It's what you wanted."

"As long as they're bidding on the auctions, this is definitely what we wanted," Darwin said. "Do you think we're violating the fire marshal code, though? It looks like half of San Francisco is here."

"They're taking tickets at the door," I said, "and we sold a set number, so I think we're okay. It just seems like a lot with everyone crammed into the ground floor of the firehouse."

Darwin nodded. "You're right. I'm going to check on River and Cole, see if they need help with anything." Our friends were providing the catering, and a dozen waiters circulated with drinks and trays of gorgeous-looking appetizers. I was sure they had everything well in hand, but it was probably good for Darwin to keep busy, since he seemed anxious. The teen tossed his long, dark bangs out of his eyes, straightened his red bowtie and tugged at the rolled-back cuff of his black dress shirt. Then he took a deep breath and waded into the throng. Introverts and crowds weren't the best combination.

There were two parts to the sold-out event, first the cocktail reception, then a dessert bar after the bachelor auction, with the silent auction running throughout. Duke and I had baked and decorated over two hundred sugar cookies to add to the treats River and Cole had prepared. We'd made brightly colored, glittery rainbows and little nests with birds (since the shelter was called Rainbow Roost), and we'd arranged them into three big bouquets. I thought they looked spectacular.

We'd also spent a lot of time over the last week helping Darwin put the finishing touches on the silent auction. An impressive selection of gift baskets and other prizes were displayed on a long series of tables spanning the far wall, and it looked like a lot of people were bidding. I was proud of myself for getting some great last-minute donations from a few local businesses to add to the bounty.

Ash hit a couple of keys on his laptop as he held his headphones to his ear, and one song transitioned into another. The music was upbeat, but he was keeping it in the background, so people wouldn't have to yell over it. He draped the headphones around his neck and smiled at me as he said, with a slight southern twang, "Your boyfriend definitely stands out in a crowd, Quinn."

I looked across the room and spotted Duke instantly. It was true that at six-foot-eight, blending in was never an option, and I grinned as I watched him. He looked so handsome in his pearl gray suit. It was one that he wore to church, and I'd jazzed it up with one of my pink ties. Nana had recruited him as her personal assistant of sorts the moment we'd walked into the fundraiser that night, and while I couldn't see the tiny senior amid all those people, I guessed by Duke's quick pace and amused expression that she was probably right in front of him and towing him through the crowd.

Ash chuckled and said, "Wow, you're one love-sick puppy."

"What? He's a handsome guy, and I was just admiring him."

"Oh no honey, you were doing more than that. If you were a cartoon character, your eyes would be heart-shaped, and your tongue would unfurl out of your mouth and hang on the ground." I grinned at that, and he said, "What's it like, dating someone you're living with?"

"Fantastic. He's been off work, so we've been spending almost all our free time together and really getting to know each other."

"And how's the sex?"

"It's the best I've ever had." I didn't mention the fact that we hadn't actually fucked yet, both because it was none of my friend's business and because it really didn't matter. Duke and I had an incredibly intimate relationship. At times it was also intensely sexual, even without going as far as anal. I definitely looked forward to the day when he was ready to take that final step, and the desire to feel him inside me was an almost physical craving at times. But Duke was absolutely worth waiting for.

"Now I'm jealous."

I squeezed Ash's shoulder and said, "I should see if I can help out anywhere before the bachelor auction gets going. Can I bring you anything?"

"A hot guy."

"Maybe one will bid on you tonight."

Ash shook his head and told me, "I won't be going onstage, since it's my job to provide the soundtrack. Want me to play stripper music when it's your turn on the auction block?"

"Please don't."

"Wait, why are you getting auctioned off if you have a boyfriend?"

"Duke and I promised Nana we'd participate before we were a couple, but even then we made a pact and agreed to be each other's winning bidder. That way, Nana's happy, the shelter makes money, and there's a nice, full roster of bachelors to generate interest."

Ash had stopped listening. His pale blue eyes went wide as he stared past me and murmured, "Hey Quinn, can I borrow a million dollars?"

"What for?"

"The hottest guy I've ever seen just walked in, and I hope to God he's one of the bachelors. If he is, I'm smashin' the hell out of my piggy bank and throwing down every cent to get a piece of that."

I turned to see who he was talking about and asked, "The tall, dark-haired guy?" The man had to be just about Duke's height, given the way he towered above the crowd. He was built like him too, with broad shoulders and big muscles, all wrapped up in a dark suit.

"Uh, yeah, the tall, dark-haired guy. Sweet baby Jesus, he's stunning! And he's coming this way! How do I look?"

I turned back to Ash and assessed him critically. He was my height with a slim build, and like me, he looked younger than his mid-twenties. He tried to smooth down his wild shock of pale lavender hair, which matched his form-fitting T-shirt, and I said, "Don't do that, you're making it worse."

He stopped trying to fix his hair and murmured, "Why does he look familiar? Is he on TV or something? With that face and bod, I wouldn't be surprised if he was an actor." Then Ash bounced on his toes and exclaimed, "Wait, no! Now I remember! He used to be a hockey player, and now he's some big shot entrepreneur. I've seen his picture in the newspaper. His name is Evan something."

I glanced over my shoulder and murmured, "Oh my God, that must be Even Eide." He'd been stopped by a big group of people, who were taking selfies with him and shaking his hand. Apparently he was more of a celebrity than I'd realized.

"Yes! That's it! I wonder what he's doing here."

"I think he's here because I invited him."

"Seriously?"

I nodded and said, "He owns that famous sports bar, Ellingsen & Eide, which he turned into a successful franchise. I was going around to local businesses last weekend trying to get last-minute donations for the silent auction, and that was one of the places I visited. I didn't speak to him personally, but I left two tickets and a note inviting him to attend the fundraiser. I guess he took me up on it."

"Well done! Did you invite any more insanely hot men here tonight?"

"No, and I actually had no idea what Even looked like. I just thought to invite him because Duke was a huge fan back when that guy played hockey, and I thought he'd enjoy meeting him."

"Aw, that's so sweet."

"He was also Duke's first crush."

Ash exclaimed, "For fuck's sake Quinn, what's the matter with you?"

I turned back to my friend and raised an eyebrow. "What are you talking about?"

"Are you *trying* to get Duke to leave you for another man?"

"No! Of course not. Duke had a crush on him ten years ago, when he was in high school. I'm sure he's gotten over it by now. Besides, I don't even know if Even Eide is gay."

"Of course he's gay! He's totally out, too. In every photo I've ever seen of him, he's had a different hot guy on his arm. Don't you read the society pages?"

"No, I don't read the society pages! Do you?"

"Duh! How else am I supposed to find out about the hottest, most eligible bachelors in San Francisco?"

"Is this a southern thing? Because all of a sudden, I'm getting a real Scarlet O'Hara vibe from you."

My friend shot me a look and said, "Could you just not with the Gone with the Wind references? It's bad enough that my mama named me after one of the characters."

"That's why your name is Ashley? I had no idea. Come to think of it, there's a lot I don't know about you, since you never want to talk about your past."

His accent became twice as thick as he drawled, "I will someday regale you with the very long, very dramatic story of my torturous upbringin' on a decayin' plantation in the swampy back woods of Louisiana. But today is not that day."

"Did you really grow up on a plantation?"

"Yes. Now act casual! The hottie's on the move again, and I do believe we're his destination! Lord, please let him be into skinny, purple-haired DJs!"

Even Eide reached us a moment later and asked, "Which one of you is Quinn Takahashi? The fellow at the door told me he was in the DJ booth." He had a very slight, unfamiliar accent. What had Duke said, that he was Finnish? Or Norwegian? Something like that.

Ash and I said in unison, "I am," and I frowned at my friend.

"He's kidding," I said. "I'm Quinn. Thank you for coming, Mr. Eide."

He smiled at me as he shook my hand. "Please, call me Even. I wanted to thank you for the tickets."

"You're welcome. It's amazing that you showed up, since you must get all kinds of invitations to events like this."

"It's a wonderful cause. I took a look at the shelter's webpage and was impressed. I do a lot of work with LGBT youth." When his smile widened and his green eyes crinkled at the corners, a little knot formed in my stomach. He really was exceptionally handsome, and obviously wealthy, if his flawless, custom-made suit was any indication. I suddenly felt like a kid playing dress-up in my vintage, royal blue thrift store suit and floral tie. Ash's words echoed in my mind: *are you trying to get Duke to leave you for another man?*

But this really wasn't the time or place for a major bout of insecurity, and I said, "I'd love to introduce you to Stana Dombruso, the woman responsible for this shelter. She's around here somewhere." Ash kicked my shoe, and when I glanced at him, he opened his eyes as wide as they would go, in a look that clearly said, *introduce me or die*. I turned back to Even and said, "Oh, and this is my friend Ash Landry. He's a big fan."

Even shook his hand and said, "So, you like hockey?"

Ash unleashed a flirtatious smile and said, "Absolutely. Anything with sticks and balls, and I'm all over it."

"Good to know, although we use pucks." Even grinned at him and said, "Pleasure to meet you, Ash," before we ventured into the crowd.

It took forever to cross the room, since he kept getting stopped for photos. I eventually pieced together that he wasn't really famous for his two years as a professional hockey player, but for an award-winning documentary that had been made about him. That was certainly news to me.

After what felt like hours, we finally found Nana in the kitchen, where she and Duke were chatting with a handsome couple. Duke's eyes lit up when he saw me, and then he glanced at the big guy behind me and his mouth fell open. Well, shit.

I introduced him to Nana first, and she beamed at Even as she shook his hand. "Well now, you're a tall drink of water, about as big as my boy Duke here! I've heard of you, too. You do a lot of charity work in the city. I'm surprised we hadn't crossed paths sooner."

"It's a pleasure to meet you, Mrs. Dombruso," he said. "Congratulations, it looks like the fundraiser is a huge success."

"I hope so," she said. "We gotta do right by the kids who are going to be living here, and that takes money. There's a gay homosexual bachelor auction happening in just about fifteen minutes, and I tell you what, we got some real hotties! That should loosen up people's purse strings!"

Even said, "I'm sure it will." Then he smiled flirtatiously at Duke and ran his gaze down his body as he asked, "Are you participating in the auction?"

Duke swallowed hard and nodded, and then he blurted, "I gotta tell you, I'm a huge fan. Your rookie season with the Canucks was epic. I'll never forget that time you scored three consecutive goals against L.A. It was one of the greatest moments in sports history!"

Even's smile became even more radiant. "I'm flattered you remember that. It's actually the game I'm most proud of when I look back at my career."

Duke told him, "There's no way I could ever forget."

I was relieved when Nana interrupted their little love fest with, "Where are my manners! Even, that's Duke Blumenthal. He's a stripper."

Duke muttered, "Actually, I'm a police officer."

But Nana was barreling ahead with the introductions. She indicated the handsome, sophisticated-looking blond at her side and said, "This is my dear friend Alastair Spencer-Penelegion. He's an angel! He partnered with me so we could buy this building and fix it up real good for the young people who are going to be calling it home. He and his honey Sawyer MacNeil flew in from London for the fundraiser and the grand opening, which is happening in just a couple of weeks! Aren't they the cutest couple?" The two men grinned at her, and Nana turned to me and asked, "Quinn, have you met Alastair and Sawyer?"

Even and I both shook hands with Alastair and his dazzling partner and exchanged the usual pleased-to-meet-yous. Sawyer was a tall, muscular guy who was absolutely striking in his tailored black suit, which he'd paired with red lipstick, a leather corset, and a pair of fierce stilettos. Normally, I would have gushed over Sawyer's look and begged him to go shopping with me, but right then, I was a little too busy worrying about the giant hockey stud who was most definitely eyeing my boyfriend flirtatiously.

Duke, meanwhile, was still doing the deer-in-headlights thing. It was hard to gauge his reaction, aside from *oh my God.* But was that an 'I've just met my sports idol' oh my God, or an 'I've just met the man I've lusted after for a decade' oh my God? I really couldn't tell.

Darwin appeared a moment later and said, "It's time to assemble all the bachelors for the auction. Can you give me a hand, Nana? I think a couple of them are about to chicken out."

Nana hiked up the neckline of her silver cocktail dress and said, "Not on my watch! Come on Duke, we gotta make like it's the old west and do a roundup of those varmints! Where's my grandson Dante? He was supposed to be keeping an eye on his bachelor friend Cameron Doyle, who was looking real squirrely last time I saw him. I bet ol' Cam's trying to make a break for it!" She grabbed Duke's hand and towed him into the crowd as she yelled over her shoulder, "Pleasure to meet you, Even! Have a good time, and be sure to try the mini taco appetizers. They're the shit!"

He chuckled at that, then asked us, "Does that mean they're good? Because it sounds like a warning."

Sawyer craned his neck and scanned the room as he said, "They're awesome. In fact, I could go for about twenty more of them. Next time I spot a waiter, I'm going to hijack an entire tray."

Alastair smiled at me as he said, with his posh English accent, "I'm craving another of those delightful biscuits. I know they're meant for the dessert buffet, but I snuck one earlier. Nana told me you and Duke made them. Do you sell them locally?"

"Biscuits?"

"That's Brit speak for cookies." Sawyer flashed Alastair a teasing smile.

"Oh. Um, no. We don't sell them yet, but we've talked about it."

"When you do, give me a call," Sawyer said. "I own a couple of coffee houses in London, and I'm about to open one here in San Francisco. I'd love to carry those delicious rainbow cookies. I already ate two of them."

"You ate four," Alastair said with a grin.

Sawyer clicked his tongue and told him, "That was supposed to be our secret." Then he pulled Alastair close and kissed his forehead.

"I'm glad you like them," I said. "I'd better go, since I'm supposed to be in that auction. It was nice meeting all of you."

The bachelors had been told to meet on the second floor at nine sharp. When I went upstairs, Nana's grandson Dante greeted me and checked my name off on his clipboard, then turned to an auburn-haired guy who was trying to slip away and bellowed, "Don't even think about it, Doyle! You agreed to be a part of this thing, and you're not going to disappoint my grandmother."

"I was off my rocker when I agreed to it," Cameron Doyle told him. He spoke with a faint Irish accent, and held open the flaps of his tan trench coat as he said, "Who the hell's going to bid on this? Tell you what, I'll just write your gran a nice, fat check and we'll call it even, alright?" Cam was probably in his early thirties and around six feet tall, with soulful blue eyes and a nice build. He was actually a good-looking guy, but the rumpled suit and overcoat could have used a little help.

Dante's expression softened, and he handed me the clipboard and crossed the room to his friend. "You need to get back out in the dating world, Cam. You and I both know it. Give me the trench coat, and let's straighten your tie."

"It's going to be damned embarrassing if nobody bids on me," Cameron said, as he handed over the coat and finger-combed his hair.

"That's not going to happen. But if it did, I'd bid on you myself," Dante told him. He brushed off the shoulders of Doyle's wrinkled, navy-blue suit and said, "What have I told you about sleeping in your clothes?"

"I didn't! And you can't bid on me. You're married! What would Charlie say?"

From across the room, Charlie called, "I'd say my husband has excellent taste! Don't stress out, Cam. This is going to be great! You'll see." Doyle didn't look convinced.

A few moments later, someone tapped my shoulder, and I turned to face a gorgeous guy of about thirty with shoulder-length dark hair, a short beard, and a wicked grin. "Ignacio Mondelvano," he said. "Checking in to be auctioned off to the highest bidder. It makes me hard just thinking about it!" He had a Spanish accent and wore several long, exotic-looking necklaces with his white shirt and ripped jeans. When he pushed back his sleeves, he revealed two full sleeves of tattoos, and he winked at me flirtatiously. Okay, that guy was going to bring in a king's ransom.

Loud music began to play on the ground floor, and the crowd cheered. Nana's friend Mr. Mario was our MC for the evening, who'd donned a slick-looking gold suit for the occasion. He announced the start of the auction just as Duke ran upstairs. We were supposed to make a big entrance by sliding down the brass poles, a remnant of the building's firehouse past. As the first two guys slid down to thunderous applause, Duke came up to me and asked, "Why am I so nervous?"

I stretched up and kissed him, then said, "There's no need to be. You know who you're going home with tonight." He grinned at that as another pair cued up.

Dante hurried over to us, took the clipboard and told me, "Quinn, go next with my friend Cameron. He's nervous, so try to help him out if you can, okay?"

I promised I would, and then I winked at Duke and said, "Have fun," before taking my place at the top of a pole. Cameron looked like he wanted to throw up as he grasped the one next to me. When Mr. Mario introduced us (as Randy Salami and Miles Long), we slid down to the stage that had been constructed for the event. I waved to the audience, grabbed Cam's clammy hand, and guided him to the row of bachelors. A few more pairs made their entrance, and finally it was Duke and Ignacio's turn. My boyfriend looked pale and wide-eyed as he took the last spot in line.

The auction moved at a brisk pace. Ash played a different song and Mr. Mario read an outrageous, totally fake bio for each bachelor, while the audience laughed and applauded. The first few guys fetched between five hundred to eight hundred dollars each. Everyone seemed to be thoroughly enjoying themselves (except Cameron).

I was the fifth one up. According to my bio, I was a billionaire turnip mogul from Delaware, who collected sexy underwear and enjoyed long, romantic walks to the sex shop. When I paraded up and down the stage, Ash played 'Me so Horny,' which got a good laugh from the audience and an exasperated look from me. I was surprised when a couple guys bid on me right away. Then Duke called, "I bid a thousand dollars," and everyone cheered. That was double what we'd talked about, and while I was worried about him spending that much money, it still made me all warm and fuzzy inside.

Mr. Mario brushed back his salt-and-pepper hair and called, "Going one time! Going two times!" Then he brought down his gavel and yelled, "Sold!"

Cameron was next up, and he was practically shaking as he stepped forward. After the fake bio and theme song ('I Wanna Sex You Up' by Color Me Badd. Really, Ash?) the bidding began. I called, "Two hundred dollars," just to get the ball rolling.

A couple of people in the audience shouted their bids and brought Cameron's total to a very respectable four hundred dollars. But then, Ignacio Mondelvano called, "Two grand!" Mr. Mario's mouth fell open along with Cameron's, and he struck the podium with his gavel. Cam looked dazed as he got back in line. After a moment, he leaned forward and took a peek at Ignacio. The Spaniard licked his lips flirtatiously, and Cam straightened up again and swallowed hard.

Over the next half hour or so, eight more guys were auctioned off. Then it was Ignacio's turn. He sauntered over to the podium, plunked down a big wad of hundred dollar bills, and said, "I bid whatever that is for myself, and I give me to the handsome man I purchased earlier." He smiled at Cameron over his shoulder, then told the audience, "That is all the money I have, so be kind and don't bid against me, *bueno*?"

Everyone cheered, and Mr. Mario banged the gavel and yelled, "Sold!"

Ignacio crossed the stage to Cameron and planted a big kiss on his lips, while the audience whistled and applauded. Then he tucked a slip of paper in Cam's jacket pocket and said, "That is my private number. Regrettably, I am flying home to Barcelona on the red-eye in a few hours, and what I intend to do with you will take a great deal of time, so our date will have to wait until my return. But when I get back, I'm going to rock your world."

Ignacio caressed Cam's cheek before returning to his place in line, and Cameron whispered, "What just happened?"

Finally, Duke was up. He glanced at me nervously as he took center stage, and I flashed him a smile and a thumbs-up. According to his bio, he was a porn star and astronaut whose hobbies included rope bondage and knitting. As he self-consciously walked back and forth a bit, Ash played Sir Mix A Lot's 'Baby Got Back' while I coughed to cover my laugh.

I wasn't the least bit surprised when the bidding took off. Two guys were going back and forth, and they got the amount up to eight hundred dollars before I called, "A thousand!"

"Two thousand!"

I looked around to see who'd joined the bidding, and my stomach dropped when I realized it was the rich hockey stud. I yelled, "Three thousand."

Even Eide countered with, "Five thousand!"

Damn it! "Six thousand!"

He came right back with, "Ten thousand." A murmur went through the crowd.

I muttered, "Fuck a duck," then held up my finger to indicate I needed a minute and pulled my phone from my pocket. I quickly accessed my savings account on my banking app, checked the balance, and yelled, "Twelve thousand, two hundred sixty-two dollars and thirty-three cents." That was every penny I had.

Even Eide grinned at me from across the room and called, "Twenty thousand dollars." The crowd actually gasped. Okay, yes, it was for charity, but I felt like punching him in the face.

Duke glanced at me over his shoulder, and I mouthed the word, "Sorry," and raised my hands in surrender. Mr. Mario yelled, "Sold for twenty thousand big ones," and slammed down the gavel. The crowd went absolutely wild.

Duke crossed the stage to me as everyone started talking all at once, and he said, "Okay, that was terrifying. What if he hadn't outbid you?"

"Huh?"

"Your last bid was your entire bank balance, wasn't it?"

"Well, yeah."

"Why would you bid so much? That could have had serious repercussions."

"Because I promised you I'd win. I'm sorry I failed you."

"You didn't! No one could have predicted what just happened, and I'm so glad you don't have to drain your bank account."

Nana and Ollie rushed up to us a moment later, and Nana tackled Duke in a hug. "Hot damn," she exclaimed, "I knew a big sexpot like you would bring in a lot of dough, but twenty grand! That's just mind-boggling. Thanks for being a part of the auction, Duke. You too, Quinn. Both you boys did a lot to make tonight a success. Speaking of which, they're bringing out the dessert buffet now. Everybody's been pilfering your cookies, I hope there are some left!" Nana looked around and announced, "Someone's calling my name, I'd better go see what's going on!" She rushed off again, and Ollie flashed us a thumbs up and hurried after her.

Mr. Mario picked up the mic and said, "All the winning bidders, please make your way to the podium for payment! I accept cash, checks, Visa, Mastercard, and offers of sexual favors! I am only kidding. I do not take Mastercard."

Duke smiled at me and said, "I'm going to go pay. I'll see you in a few minutes."

I tried to stick a smile on my face, even though I felt sick to my stomach. I'd just thought Duke would enjoy meeting Even Eide when I'd left those tickets. I never imagined he'd end up going out with him, and I'd basically set up the whole thing!

I made my way to the stairs at the end of the stage, because of course *I* didn't have a winning bid to pay off. When Even Eide and I crossed paths, he smiled at me with just a hint of smugness and said, "No hard feelings, mate."

Oh no. Hard feelings. *Definitely* hard feelings. I muttered, "Uh huh," and kept walking.

When I reached the main floor, I looked back at the stage, and the knot in my stomach tightened. Even and Duke were chatting and laughing, and Even's hand was on Duke's shoulder. They looked absolutely perfect together, like two gods visiting from Mount Olympus, there among the puny humans.

The room felt stifling all of a sudden, just way too hot, loud and crowded. I waded through the mass of bodies and left by the front door. Once outside, I took a deep breath and pressed my eyes shut. After a few moments, a soft voice with a southern accent asked, "You alright, Quinn?"

I turned to Elijah and said, "I'm fine. I just needed some air."

His hand was under the cuff of his oversized, dark blue sweater, and I caught a glimpse of his slender fingers fidgeting with his charm bracelet. "Same here. It's way too crowded inside. I should have predicted that and stayed home, but Finn and Chance were so excited about the fundraiser, and I didn't want to be a spoil sport." He glanced up at the building and added, "I don't think I can go back in there."

"Me neither. Want to share a cab?"

When he nodded, I stepped off the curb and looked in both directions. As we waited for a taxi, he said, "It seems like a real nice shelter, don't you think? Nana's friend Alastair showed us around."

"Definitely. It's going to make a real difference to a lot of people when it opens in a few days."

After a pause, he told me, "Alastair said they were looking for tutors, because some of the residents will be studying for their high school equivalency diplomas, and others will be enrolling in college. I volunteered to help them with math. Do you think I made a mistake?"

"No. Do you?"

"Maybe. I've never taught anyone before."

"That's okay. Everyone has to start somewhere, and I bet you'll be great at it."

A cab rounded the corner, and I stuck my arm out. When it pulled up in front of us, we slid into the backseat, and I gave the driver Elijah's address. My friend said, "Your house is closer, she should stop there first."

"Yeah, but I want to make sure you get home okay."

"Thanks, Quinn." I texted Duke to let him know where I was, and Elijah asked, "You sure you don't want to go back inside to your boyfriend?"

I shook my head and murmured, "I doubt he's going to miss me."

*****

After dropping off Elijah and driving back across town, the cab pulled up right behind another one in front of my house. Xavier got out of the backseat, dressed in scrubs and a baggy fleece jacket. While he waited for me to pay, he stretched his back, and when I stepped onto the curb he said, "Hey. You're home early."

"Yup."

"You got my message, right? I'm sorry I couldn't make it to the bachelor auction. We were short-handed at the hospital, so I had to work a double."

"It's fine. We had a good turnout."

"Glad to hear it," he said. "So, where are you taking Duke on your date?"

"What date?"

"Wasn't that the point of the auction, to win a date with a hot guy? You said you and Duke were going to bid on each other."

"Some rich dude outbid me."

Xavier exclaimed, "Poor Duke! Was he totally freaked out? He's so shy and awkward around guys, and I know the only reason he agreed to participate was because he was sure he'd end up with you!"

"Actually, I think Duke's just fine. And I tried, Xavier. I really did. I literally bid the entire contents of my bank account. But then Even Eide came back with a bid of twenty thousand dollars and shut me down."

"Even Eide the former hockey player?"

I raised an eyebrow and said, "Because there are loads of guys walking around with that name."

"Well, maybe in Norway. But really? Even Eide was the winning bidder? That's crazy, since Duke's totally in love with that guy." I don't know what Xavier saw in my expression, but he quickly backtracked with, "Not literally! I just meant he had a crush on him and owned two or three hockey jerseys with Eide's name on them. But all of that was before he met you, Quinn!"

"Yeah, well, now he gets to go on a dream date with the guy he's been lusting after for a decade. So, yay to that. And yes, I know I'm an asshole for not being thrilled about the shelter getting that huge donation. But damn it, I think I just lost Duke, and it's all my fault, because I was the one who invited Eide to the fundraiser!"

My neighbor asked, "Why would you do that?"

"Because I knew Duke was a fan, and I thought he'd enjoy meeting his idol."

"Or maybe subconsciously, you were testing him. I assume Duke told you about his crush on Eide. Maybe some part of you wanted to see what would happen when the two of them met, because you needed proof that Duke wanted you above all else."

I frowned and asked, "Did you take a lot of psychology classes in nursing school?"

"A few. I could be wrong, but it might be something to think about."

After a pause, I said softly, "What if I lose him, Xavier? Duke is the greatest guy I've ever met. What am I going to do without him?"

He gestured at his front door and said, "Want to come inside and have some tea? Or vodka? Whatever works."

"Thanks, but I just want to go to bed and hide under the covers."

"Okay. Text me if you need anything. I'll be home all night."

I told him I would. After we said good night and went inside, I leaned against the front door and texted Duke to let him know I was back at the duplex. He replied after a minute with: *Oh, I assumed you were returning to the party after escorting Elijah home.*

I wrote back: *I was tired.* That wasn't a lie. I felt almost painfully weary right then.

He texted: *I'm planning to stay until the end. I told Nana I'd help clean up.*

I said out loud, "Great. Be sure to fall in love with the man of your dreams while you're at it." Then I texted: *Have fun. I'll be asleep by the time you get home, so I'll see you in the morning.* I kind of hated myself for the 'have fun' part, since I couldn't stop picturing him and Eide dancing, chatting, laughing....

I trudged upstairs and exchanged my stupid, nerdy suit for a pair of flannel pajamas. Then I did exactly what I'd told Xavier I was going to do by climbing under the covers and pulling them over my head. Sleep was out of the question, though. As the minutes and hours moved in ultra-slow motion, I tortured myself by imagining the fun my boyfriend and that rich, handsome jerk were probably having together.

*****

Duke got home close to three a.m. I heard him moving around in the kitchen before going back to his bedroom. I knew I should go downstairs and talk to him, but I just couldn't make myself do that, since the conversation was bound to start off with him gushing, "Oh my God, I can't believe I just met Even Eide!" He'd probably be nice enough to spare me the details, like how gorgeous Eide was in person and how incredibly generous he was for donating all that money to the shelter. But he'd be thinking it. Who wouldn't?

Eide was a fucking rock star. He was tall and attractive, rich and famous, and extremely generous, and he could give Duke things I could only dream about. If they ended up together, all Duke's financial stress would disappear in the blink of an eye. He could move into Even's palatial mansion, quit his job, and spend all day blissfully baking cookies in a magazine-perfect kitchen that was probably bigger than the entire duplex.

Damn it. How could someone like me possibly compete with someone like Even Eide? How could *anyone* compete with that?

Chapter Thirteen

I stalled for time before going downstairs the next morning. I was pretty sure I'd be able to keep my raging insecurity under wraps, but I still didn't want to have the 'wasn't Even so great?' conversation. Hiding in my room forever wasn't an option though, so after I showered and pulled on a lackluster T-shirt and jeans, I went and found Duke.

He was in his bedroom, dressed in a dark blue suit and folding towels with an odd degree of precision. Each was creased just so, aligned, folded, and folded again, so it was absolutely identical to every other towel in the stack on his tidy bed. It made him seem vulnerable, in a way I wouldn't have predicted. Continually striving for that degree of perfection had to be exhausting.

I came up behind him and wrapped him up in a hug, and as I rested my head on his back, he said, "Good morning. How'd you sleep?"

I'd probably slept less than two hours, but I murmured, "Fine. Are you going to church?"

"Yup."

"By yourself?"

Duke nodded. "I haven't heard from my parents since the fight, so I decided to go back to our old church in South San Francisco, the one that now has a progressive pastor."

"Well, that's good. Aren't you going to be late, though?"

"There are two services. I'm going to the one at ten-thirty, and I'm leaving in just a minute. Would you like to come with me?"

I said, "Some other time, okay?"

"I know it's not really your thing. Just thought I'd offer."

"I am curious to see what it's all about, but I'm not really feeling up to it today."

Duke turned to face me and kissed my forehead. Then he draped his arms over my shoulders and said, "You're upset, aren't you?"

"No."

"Yes you are, I can tell. You feel you let me down with the auction, don't you? It really is okay, I'm not upset about it. I know you promised you'd be the winning bidder, but like I said last night, neither of us could have predicted what ended up happening."

That wasn't what was troubling me, but I decided to go along with it, because it sounded a hell of a lot better than admitting I was jealous and insecure. "You're right. So, when is Eide taking you out?" In my mind I added, *that bastard.*

"Tonight. He's picking me up at eight and taking me to a restaurant called Elixir. It's supposed to be nice, real fancy."

"That sounds great." *That sounds really, really awful.*

"I figured this would be a good evening for it, since you're working anyway. I'll probably get home about the same time you do, and then we can spend the rest of the night together."

"Definitely." *Please don't leave me for that rich, handsome hockey player, even if he is perfect.*

"Want me to meet you at rehearsal? I'm going to stay for the church social afterwards, but I'll be done by about one."

"You don't have to. We can't build anything today, because Skye needs the whole warehouse to lay out a bunch of twenty-foot-long tentacles." I couldn't help but grin a little, because that sounded awesomely weird.

"Alright. Well, I guess I'd better get going." He turned to the towels and folded the last one with the same precision as all the rest, carried the stack to his shelves in the bathroom, and put them away. As I walked him out, Duke asked, "Are you going straight from rehearsal to work?" When I nodded, he said, "I'll see you tonight, then."

I pulled him to me and kissed him. Then I tried to make myself say, 'have fun on your date,' but I just couldn't do it. My heart ached. I wanted to believe Duke would choose me over Even Eide, but why would he?

My only hope was that the date sucked, and sucked bad. Maybe Even Eide would chew with his mouth open, or pick his nose at the dinner table, or hit on the bartender, the waiter, the busboy, and a group of seminary students at the next table. Maybe he'd turn out to be the biggest fucking dick in the history of big fucking dicks, and maybe that twenty-thousand-dollar date would crash and burn ten minutes in, preferably ending with Duke throwing a drink in Eide's face.

I knew none of that would happen, though.

I shook myself out of my little date disaster fantasy as Duke left by way of the garage. It wasn't news to me that I had to get a grip. But I was jealous and heartbroken and angry, all at the same time. I needed a drink, but it wasn't even ten a.m.

I settled for coffee instead, which I carried into the living room with a piece of buttered toast. I flopped down on the horrible, unyielding couch and sighed at the white walls. Duke had given me an okay of sorts to paint them, but when I showed him some samples, he'd balked at all of them. The only one he liked was an almost nonexistent pale, pale blue at the very top of a paint chip. The color I'd actually been showing him on that little paper rectangle had been the rich indigo at the very bottom.

After a minute, a thought occurred to me. I finished the toast and licked my fingers, and then I got up and went to take a look at Duke's tiny movie collection, which was in the cabinet beneath his modest TV. I sat cross-legged on the area rug and frowned as I dealt the DVDs out like playing cards around me. Most of them were sports-themed. There were baseball movies, hockey movies, and football movies, with names like 'Any Given Sunday' and 'Miracle'. I hadn't seen any of them.

Near the bottom of the stack, I actually found what I was looking for. It was a documentary called 'Inspiration: The Even Eide Story.' There was a portrait of Eide on the cover, looking handsome and sun-drenched with an idyllic, possibly Norwegian fishing village in the background. I turned the box over and discovered the movie had been released just three years ago. Since Duke had bought it, his crush obviously hadn't been left in the distant past.

Even though I knew I was just rubbing salt in the wound at that point, I stuck the DVD in the player on the shelf beneath the TV and settled in to torture myself. I fast-forwarded through the part about his childhood in Norway. Oldest of eight kids, son of a poor fisherman, okay we got it, humble beginning. The next section was all about his hockey career. I flopped down on the rug and sighed dramatically while the narrator rattled off Eide's accomplishments: one of the few people to play both offensive and defensive positions, recruited at nineteen, scored a bagillion goals, brought his team to victory...awesome. There were lots of clips from various hockey games, featuring Eide doing bad-ass stuff on the ice. Whatever.

But then the music took a turn for the dramatic, and I sat up and watched the screen. Footage of ambulances and hospitals accompanied a voice-over talking about the accident that ended Eide's hockey career. His body was shattered when his Porsche was T-boned by a truck. The other driver had fallen asleep behind the wheel. Though the doctors told Eide he'd never walk again, he defied the odds. He spent the next two years in intensive physical therapy and fought his way back, but his injuries were so severe that he had to retire from the sport he loved.

There was one more chapter in Eide's story. The last part of the documentary talked about how he'd opened a sports bar with a fellow hockey player. Then they'd franchised it, and the cash started pouring in. He went on to donate great, big, heaping boatloads of money to children's charities and LGBT organizations. Eide was also supporting his parents and younger siblings. And why? Because he was fucking awesome.

I rolled over so I was face-down on the area rug and groaned. No wonder Duke had a crush on that guy. As if it wasn't enough that he was rich and handsome, apparently Eide was also the nicest person ever and was going to be canonized into sainthood (I added that last part, but it seemed pretty goddamn likely).

And damn it, Eide had to be attracted to Duke, too. He'd paid a fortune to spend one evening with him! When he saw how determined I was to win that auction, he could have just let it go, then handed Nana a big, fat check, if all he'd wanted was to support the shelter. That way, she would have gotten my money and his, and the kids would have come out way ahead. He also could have contributed by buying up every damn thing in the silent auction if he'd chosen to, or dropping a bundle on the world's most expensive gift basket, or whatever.

But no. He'd wanted Duke. And apparently, rich people always got what they wanted.

By the time the documentary ended, I was in a total funk. I rolled onto my back and stared at the blank, white ceiling for a while, but the longer I did that, the more depressed I became. After a while, I gathered up the movies and put them away, then decided to perk myself up with a little fresh air and sunshine.

I went into the backyard and sat on one of the swings. At first, I just rocked back and forth a little. But then I grasped the chains and started swinging as hard as I could, under the theory that no one could be unhappy when they were swinging. I kept that up for quite a while, until I finally had to admit my theory was unsound and stopped propelling myself forward. My path of motion got smaller and smaller, until I was at a standstill.

Storm clouds were moving in, which suited my mood. The only positive thing was a big, gray squirrel that came into the yard looking for a place to stash an acorn. I said, "Hey, buddy," and watched him for a while as he scampered around, then found his ideal spot in the flowerbed and buried his prize. "Hang on," I told him. "I think I have some nuts in the kitchen."

I went inside and looked in the cabinet. All I had were chocolate-covered peanuts, but Duke had some dry-roasted, unsalted almonds (ugh, where was the fun in that?), and I raided his stash. When I stepped out the kitchen door, I found the squirrel darting around on the patio with his nose twitching. I sat on the stoop and rolled an almond over to him, and he grabbed it with his tiny hands, sat back on his haunches, and made a quick meal of it.

I placed the next almond right in front of me and was delighted when the little animal approached in fits and starts, then finally sat at my feet and ate the nut. He seemed friendly, so I put the last one in the palm of my hand and held it out to him. The squirrel sat up and stared at me for a long moment with his beady black eyes.

In the next instant, the squirrel jumped at me, grabbed the nut, and scampered up my arm. I yelped in surprise and shuddered, because his tiny squirrel feet felt horrific as they skittered over my bare skin. He used my shoulder as a springboard and took a flying leap into the kitchen, and I yelled, "Oh, come on!"

I leapt to my feet and spun around, just in time to see the fluffy-tailed little jerk bounding down the hall. Great! I left the back door open to give him an escape route and ran into the living room, but I didn't see him anywhere. I dropped onto my hands and knees and looked under all the furniture. Still nothing. After running upstairs and conducting a thorough search, I jogged back downstairs and looked everywhere. Twice.

I kept that up for a good half-hour, but the creature had vanished. Maybe it had run off when I wasn't looking. I stuck my head out and looked around the backyard before closing and locking the kitchen door. Since I didn't want to be late for rehearsal, I had to abandon my search.

Damn it! I scrubbed my hands over my face, then located a pad of paper and left Duke a note on the kitchen counter. It said: *There may or may not be a squirrel in the house. Sorry.* He was going to be thrilled. I sighed and went upstairs to get my backpack.

*****

It was raining when rehearsal ended, and I gratefully accepted a ride back to the city with Skye and Dare and their dog. We'd practiced for hours. I was pretty sure Dare and Haley were going to keep fine-tuning the choreography right up until the night of the performance. As a thank you for putting us through all of that, they'd bought the whole troupe beer and pizza afterwards, and we all ate together in the office before heading home. Or in my case, to work.

They dropped me off a few minutes after seven. Since I didn't start until eight, I had a couple of drinks before I went back to the locker room to change. Appropriately enough, the theme that night was 'Raining Men'. Preston had hung rows of silver streamers from the ceiling, and when the white and blue lights hit them, they really did look a bit like raindrops.

I'd been so happy when I pulled together my outfit for the Raining Men theme a few days earlier, but as I took the pieces of my costume out of my locker, I frowned. What I'd intended to be cute and playful just looked childish. I didn't have anything else to wear though, so I had to go with it.

I stripped completely and pulled on a jockstrap, then shimmied into a pair of tight, yellow shorts, which were made out of the same plastic material as my matching raincoat. I stood in front of the mirror and tied the white laces that crisscrossed the fly, and then I bent and twisted to make sure I could actually dance in them. Good thing the answer was yes, since I hadn't thought to pack a back-up pair. The shorts were a lot skimpier than I'd anticipated, too. They barely covered my ass and were cut so low in the front that I had to tuck in the jockstrap.

The next step was a pair of knee-high rain boots. They were bright blue and printed all over with yellow rubber ducks wearing rain hats. It was surprisingly difficult to slip them on. I ended up grabbing the top and jamming each foot in. I wondered how I was going to get them off again, but figured I'd worry about that later.

I grabbed my cosmetic case and went back to the mirror to apply a hell of a lot of iridescent body glitter. While I was doing that, three more dancers came in and changed into their outfits, which basically just consisted of tiny shorts and boots. One of them chuckled when he saw what I was wearing and said, "Only you, Quinn."

Another said, "You're only encouraging Preston and his stupid theme nights. Maybe if you stopped using it as an opportunity to play dress-up, he'd realize none of us want to do this shit and give up on it already." I frowned at him in the mirror's reflection, then leaned in to apply some lip gloss.

They left the locker room a couple of minutes later, while I stepped back, examined myself critically, and decided I needed to punch it up a bit. I applied black liner along my upper lashes, then some mascara, followed by a sweep of royal blue glitter eyeshadow, which matched the boots. That added a bit of pizzazz.

Sergei came in while I was doing that. He knit his brows and said, "You know this isn't a drag show, right?"

I muttered, "Bite me," and put on even more glitter before slicking my hair with gel to make it look wet.

The last two pieces of my outfit were a cropped yellow coat that barely grazed the hem of my shorts and a matching rain hat. When I put them on, Sergei said, "What are you, five?"

I ignored him and went to assess myself one last time in the full-length mirror. The overall look was fun, which had been the goal. I tried to smile at my reflection and failed miserably.

It was a few minutes before eight p.m. Duke would be getting ready for his date. I'd been trying so hard not to think about it, but there it was. Did he have butterflies in his stomach? Was he shaving for a second time that day and applying his cologne, which he reserved for special occasions?

Did he change his shirt three or four times before finally selecting one, and did he fret over which suit to wear?

I muttered, "Fuck," and rested my forehead against the glass.

Sergei appeared beside me and checked his reflection in the wide mirror. He was dressed all in black, as usual. The one good thing I could say about him was that he always embraced Preston's themes. Along with his leather shorts, he was wearing combat boots, a long, black trench coat, and a fedora. He shot me a look and said, "You're sad because you just realized you look like a slutty kindergartener, right?"

I whirled on him and snapped, "Could you give me a break, just for one night? Next time we're both working, you can hate me and make fun of me all you want. But not today!"

I stormed out of the locker room just as two more dancers came in to change. Then I climbed up on the first empty platform I came to and started dancing with all I had. I usually toned it down at the club, but that night, I just went for it. I needed the distraction.

A minute later, Sergei took the platform directly across from mine and started dancing. He was making far more of an effort than usual, working the coat like a prop, dropping it off his broad shoulders, tipping the brim of the fedora while he swayed his hips. What the hell did he think, that this was a fucking musical and I'd challenged him to a dance-off?

I turned my attention from him and just danced. The club was pretty empty on a rainy Sunday night. There was no one to try to impress, but that didn't matter. I danced to tire myself out and to try to stop thinking.

Good luck with that.

My brain was firing off questions like a game show host: was it eight o-clock yet? Had Eide arrived at the house? Did he bring Duke flowers, and was he invited in for a drink? Did Eide rest his hand on Duke's back as they walked to the curb, then hold his door for him? What kind of car did he drive, and was Duke impressed by it? Was Eide being charming and witty? Did Duke laugh at his jokes, and did his heartbeat speed up when Eide smiled at him?

Damn it!

By the time Preston signaled me to take a break maybe an hour later, I was glistening with sweat, exhausted, and on the verge of tears. I jumped from the platform, not bothering with the steps, and was caught off guard by a round of applause. I'd been totally unaware of the small crowd that had gathered to watch me dance.

I ignored the offers of drinks and hurried to the locker room, where I threw aside my hat and coat and leaned against my locker as I caught my breath. Sergei burst into the room a moment later and growled, "What the hell was that?"

"What are you talking about?"

"The way you were dancing! Are you so desperate for attention that you have to make sure all eyes are on you and nobody else?"

I turned to him and yelled, "Oh my God! Do you think I was dancing like that to take the spotlight away from you? Newsflash, I forgot you were in the room! And I don't even sort of care if I had the attention of every man in the club. None of those people matter, not even a little! There's only one person who does, my boyfriend Duke. And he's not here, because—"

Without warning, I burst into tears. Sergei hesitated, and after a minute he asked, "Are you having some kind of nervous breakdown?"

"Probably!" I slid down with my back against the locker as jagged sobs shook me.

Sergei muttered, "Shit." He paced around a bit, then crouched down in front of me and said, "I'm sorry. I didn't mean to make you cry. It just annoyed me that you were grandstanding, that's all. Come on Quinn, stop."

I yelled between sobs, "I'm not crying over that, and I wasn't grandstanding! I was trying to take my mind off the fact that my boyfriend is on a date with a hot, rich, handsome hockey player right now! How am I supposed to compete with that? I'm just this weird, skinny guy who periodically infests the house with cats and squirrels!"

"You…what?"

"Nothing."

"Are you trying to say your boyfriend's cheating on you?"

"Of course not. He would never do that!"

"I'm confused." Sergei looked around, then brought me a towel and said, "Here, dry your eyes. You're making a mess of yourself." I scrubbed my face with the towel before tossing it aside, and he muttered, "Yikes."

I took a deep, shuddering breath and demanded, "What?"

"You were wearing a lot of eye makeup, and now it's all smeary. You kind of look like a homicidal clown." When I started sobbing again, he exclaimed, "Shit, sorry. Come on, stop crying, will you? I don't know what to do."

"You don't have to do anything! Just go away." I wrapped my arms around my knees.

"I can't leave you like this."

"Sure you can. You hate me, so it should be easy."

"I hate everybody. You shouldn't take it personally." I frowned at him and dragged my hand over my eyes, and he said, "Now your makeup's really fucked."

"Good!"

"You should try to calm down."

"I am!"

"Would a drink help?" When I nodded, he ran from the room.

While he was gone, I retrieved the towel and wrapped it around myself like a shawl. Then I put my head on my knees and took a few deep, shuddery breaths. Damn it. I hated the fact that I'd lost it at work, and in front of Sergei.

He soon returned with a big to-go cup and a straw, and when he thrust it at me, I murmured, "I don't want to sound ungrateful, but I meant alcohol, not a soda."

"That's a hell of a lot of vodka over ice, with a splash of cranberry juice. I told the bartender you were having an emotional breakdown, so he hooked you up."

I accepted the cup from him and said, "You probably could have skipped the part about telling Rico I was having a breakdown, but thanks for the drink."

I took a sip from the straw and coughed a little. It was strong enough to make my eyes water, but I kept drinking until it was gone. After a few moments of making loud slurping sounds as I tried to vacuum up every last drop, Sergei snatched the cup away from me and asked, "Feel better?"

"Not even a little."

"Tell me what's wrong."

"Why should I?"

"Because you obviously need someone to talk to, and I'm the only one here."

"That's not enough of a reason."

"It's going to have to be, because this," he gestured all around me, "needs to stop."

I said, "If it's bothering you, just go away."

"Tell me what's going on. Why is your boyfriend on a date with someone else?"

Sergei sat on the bench across from me, and as concisely as I could, I told him about Duke's decade-long crush, and how Even Eide had outbid me at the charity auction. Then he asked, "Is Duke the really tall guy who punched out that drunk, the night your dad was here?"

"Yeah, that's him."

"Damn it, Quinn, that's a man worth fighting for! Why are you just sitting here and letting this happen?"

"What can I do? Eide paid a fortune for the date, the money went to a good cause, and Duke is going out with him willingly."

"But look what it's doing to you!"

"I'm probably being stupid. Maybe it's totally innocent, and they're just going to have some food, talk about hockey, and never see each other again."

Sergei asked, "Did it seem innocent when Duke and Eide met?"

"Actually…no. Duke was almost too stunned to speak, but Eide was definitely flirting and checking him out."

"Did Eide know you were Duke's boyfriend when he bid against you at the auction?" I shook my head, and he said, "But you told him afterwards, right?"

"Actually, I just left. I was reeling after it was all said and done, and I needed to get myself together. Obviously, I never actually achieved that."

"I understand needing time to regroup, but why wouldn't you make sure that rich fucker knew the score before you took off?"

"I thought I might be overreacting," I said. "I mean, the auction was supposed to be fun, and it raised money for a good cause. I wasn't supposed to feel threatened or jealous."

"Who cares how you were 'supposed to' feel? If you were unhappy, you should have said something! And it's not too late. You can still speak up."

"How? Am I supposed to march into Elixir and announce that Duke is mine, then slap Even Eide with a white glove and challenge him to a duel?"

"Oh shit. He took him to Elixir?"

I nodded and asked, "Have you eaten there?"

"Hell no. I couldn't possibly afford it. But I bussed tables there for a few weeks, before they fired me for telling an obnoxious customer to go fuck himself," he said. "Nobody, and I mean nobody, goes there on a casual date. The entire place is designed to do two things: impress and seduce. If this rich guy took your man to Elixir, it's because he really wants to get in his pants."

"You're making this all so much worse."

"I'm just telling you what I know. The kitchen staff would joke about it, like, 'table three just ordered the fifty-seven dollar fuck-me-now *pommes frites*.' That's French fries, by the way. Or, 'table five is sealing the deal with the ninety dollar blow-me-crème-brulee.' That's a little dish of custard."

"I know what crème brulee is, and Duke's not going to sleep with him."

Sergei asked, "How can you be so sure?"

"Because he's not a slut."

"But you just told me he's been crushing on this guy since he was a teen."

"Still." I frowned and said, "You're probably making this out to be way worse than it actually is. Like I said, it could all be perfectly innocent."

"Wake up, Quinn. That rich fucker paid twenty thousand dollars for one night with your man. If all he wanted was to donate to the shelter, he could have easily cut them a check. But he didn't do that. Instead, he made a point of outbidding all his competitors. He staked a claim on Duke. And then he didn't take him on a bro date for pizza and beer, he took him to one of the most romantic and expensive restaurants in town. People don't go there with friends, family, or business associates. They only go to Elixir because they're trying to wine and dine their way into someone's pants."

The conversation was pushing my anxiety through the roof. I jumped up and started pacing around the locker room. "I wish I could be a fly on the wall during their date. If I could see them for myself and confirm Eide isn't trying anything, I'd feel so much better."

Sergei got up too and said, "Actually, if you really want to do that, I know how to make it happen."

"Seriously?" When he nodded, I asked, "How?"

"I used to work there, remember? I know a spot where you can look directly into the dining room without anyone seeing you."

"I couldn't spy on him. It'd basically be saying I don't trust Duke, but I do. It may not sound like it right now, because I'm so angry and jealous I can barely think straight. But I definitely trust him."

"Yeah, but it's that rich fucker you shouldn't trust," Sergei said. "Besides, you're not going to be spying on them. You're just going to take a quick look at whatever's happening on their date, so you can gain some peace of mind. You obviously need that, since you're a total fucking disaster right now."

"Thanks."

"Well, you are. Want me to take you to Elixir? It's not all that far, and we can be back here in less than half an hour. Preston adores you, so he'll totally sign off on this, especially since the club is dead tonight."

"I don't get why you're helping me. We've worked together for six months, and all I've ever gotten from you is hostility."

He crossed his big arms over his chest and said, "Maybe I want you to owe me a favor."

"Or maybe my dad is right, and you're secretly a nice guy who just wants everyone to think you're an asshole."

"No, I'm an asshole who wants everyone to think I'm an asshole. Now are we doing this, or what? Because they're not going to be at Elixir forever."

"Alright, let's go. I think I'll feel better once I see with my own eyes that the date is perfectly innocent."

"And if you see Eide trying to hit on your boyfriend?"

"Then I'm going to kick his ass."

"Really?"

"They've been on their date for over an hour. Duke must have told him by now that he has a boyfriend. If Eide is hitting on him anyway, then he's a dick, and he deserves a swift ass-kicking."

Sergei frowned as I turned to my locker and dialed the combination on the padlock. "You told me this guy is six-foot-eight and used to be a professional hockey player. If you start something, he's going to snap you like a twig."

"I don't care."

I grabbed my jeans and sat down on the wooden bench, but when I tried to pull off my tall rain boots, they wouldn't budge. I struggled with them while Sergei changed into a pair of jeans, a T-shirt, and a leather jacket, all black. He turned to me when he was fully dressed and asked, "What the hell are you doing?"

"My boots are stuck. I think it's because they're all sweaty inside after dancing in them, so the rubber won't slide over my skin."

He rolled his eyes and grabbed a boot, then tried his damnedest to yank it off my foot. It wouldn't budge. Finally, he dropped it and said, "Just pull your pants on over them."

I tried to do that, but there was no way to cram the boots through the legs of my jeans. I threw my clothes back in the locker, retrieved my yellow hat and raincoat, and said, "Fuck it. Nobody's going to see me anyway."

Sergei's frown deepened, and he grabbed the towel. When he came right up to me and took hold of my chin, I exclaimed, "What are you doing?"

"Trying to downgrade you from a class five natural disaster to a class two." He dragged the towel over each cheek, then held it up to show me the smears of mascara, eyeliner, and blue glitter. "Just so you know, you still look horrific. But if I try to wipe your eyes, I have a feeling I'm just going to smear everything more than it already is."

"It doesn't matter. Let's just go."

He tossed the towel into the laundry hamper as we headed to the door and muttered, "At least you look slightly less like a homicidal clown now."

Preston intercepted us on our way to look for him and said, "I was just coming to find you, Quinn. Rico said you were having a mental breakdown. Are you alright?"

I sighed at that. "I'm not having a breakdown. I'm just upset, but Sergei is going to help me with something that should calm me down. We'll be back in about twenty or thirty minutes, is that alright?"

Preston nodded. "Go ahead. The club keeps getting emptier with each passing minute, so you won't be missing much."

I pulled on my yellow slicker and jammed the matching floppy hat on my head, then turned to Sergei and said, "Let's do this."

He grimaced and asked, "Is the hat really necessary? You look like a preschooler on a whaling expedition."

"Yes it's necessary, because it's still pouring outside!"

"But we're travelling by motorcycle, so it'll just fly off." I held his gaze as I reached under the hat, pulled out the elastic strap, and snapped it under my chin. Sergei sighed and headed for the door.

*****

Driving to Elixir on Sergei's ancient, beat-up motorcycle pretty thoroughly sucked. I held onto him tightly and buried my face between his shoulder blades, both to keep from getting pummeled by the rain, and because I'd never been on the back of a motorcycle before and it was scary as hell. Finally, he parked in a back alley, and as we both ducked under an awning, he asked, "Was that really necessary?"

"Was what really necessary?"

"Crushing me in a vice-like grip the whole way over here." He pulled off his black helmet and rubbed his ribcage. "I can still feel it."

"You'll live. Where are we, exactly?"

"That's Elixir." He pointed to a one-story structure that must have been built around a courtyard, since a huge tree outlined with white lights rose from the center of it like a mushroom cloud. "Just get up on the roof, then walk around and look through the skylights until you find your boyfriend and the rich fucker. They obviously won't be on the patio in this weather."

"What if they aren't seated near a skylight?"

"They will be. The restaurant is fairly narrow and the tables are spread out for privacy. There's a skylight over just about every table, so the patrons have a view of the tree branches and the lights while they're dining."

I said, "Sounds romantic."

"That's the whole idea. Like I said, that place is all about seduction. So, here's what you're going to do: climb the fire escape on the side of this building, then circle around on the second-floor balcony. It's an easy step down onto Elixir's roof."

"How do you know this?"

"I liked climbing up there on my dinner breaks and sitting amid the branches."

I smiled at him and said, "That's sweet."

"Shut up."

"You can stop trying to make me think you're an asshole, Sergei. You spent the last half hour comforting me, then driving me here in a rainstorm, so I know you're a good person."

"If I was a good person, I would have given you the helmet. Now would you hurry up and do this? We need to get back to work."

"Why does it sound like you're not coming with me?"

"Because I'm not coming with you."

"Why not?"

"This is your rodeo, Quinn, not mine. I'll wait here for you, under this nice, dry awning."

"But this whole thing was your idea!"

"You're welcome for thinking of it!"

"Come on," I cajoled. "I need a partner in crime."

"No you don't. I'm freezing my balls off in these rain-soaked jeans, so could you fucking hurry?"

"See? You were making fun of my outfit, but I'm actually nice and toasty. In fact, I'm a bit overheated in this plastic coat."

He shot me a look and said, "Congratulations."

"My thighs are cold, though. So are my hands." I rubbed my palms on my bare legs to warm them up a bit.

"If you don't go right now, I'm leaving you here."

"Please don't do that. I didn't bring my wallet or bus pass, and it's a long walk back to the club."

"Then go!"

"Just come with me! Please? I'll beg if I have to, and that'll be awkward for everyone involved."

"Oh my God! Fine."

He attached his helmet to the motorcycle, and then we jogged around to the side of the building. I jumped up, caught the bottom of the fire escape and pulled it down, and we made our way to the balcony. When we reached Elixir's roof, I said, "Um, there's a problem," and gestured at the row of big skylights. Each was covered with a layer of wet leaves from the huge tree that stretched out above us.

"I didn't anticipate that," Sergei said. "Someone comes up here and cleans the skylights every other day or so. They must have just fallen in this rainstorm."

"So what are we supposed to do, go around and squeegee off every one of these until we find Duke and his date?"

"Pretty much. Let's start over here," he said, making his way to the west side of the restaurant. "That's the most desirable seating, and if the hockey dude is as rich as you say, he would have slipped the manager some cash to make sure he ended up in a prime spot."

The five-foot-square skylights were spaced eight feet apart all around the building, which in turn framed a pretty courtyard on all four sides. I reached over the wide, metal rim of the nearest skylight and brushed some leaves from the corner of the glass panel, then said, "So, there's another problem." The glass was fogged up from the inside.

Sergei swore under his breath and looked around. Then he ran back to the balcony next door and returned a moment later with a flattened cardboard box, which we'd passed on the way in. "I forgot that the skylights tend to fog up when it's cold and damp," he said. "It's a gradual process, though. It starts on the edges and works its way to the center, so if we're lucky, maybe part of it is still clear. Get on the other side of the glass, and let's scrape off the leaves."

I followed his instructions and grabbed one end of the big box while he held the other, and we pushed all the leaves aside as we dragged it over the skylight. This uncovered an eighteen-inch space in the center of the glass that had yet to fog over. It was still hard to see through it, between the film left behind from the leaf litter and the rain dripping off the branches, but I crouched down and peered through that little vantage point at different angles, and after a minute I announced, "I think I see them!"

We carried the box to another skylight and repeated our squeegee trick, and I said, "They're directly below us! That's lucky. I'm glad it's not all that dark in there. But damn it, I need to get a better view! I can make out shapes and colors, but I can't see their expressions. Help me run the box over it one more time." When we did that, it actually made it worse, since the cardboard tracked a smear of leaf residue over the glass.

"This was a terrible idea," Sergei said as he let go of his side of the box. "I should have thought about the effect the rain would have on the skylights. I also should have just gone with getting you drunk to cheer you up, instead of operation I-spy. This really is one of the dumbest things I've ever done."

"It was a great idea," I said as I swung the cardboard around to find a clean edge. "We just need to give it one more sweep." I stepped up onto the ledge around the skylight and held the box out so Sergei could grab an end.

But in the next instant, my rubber boots slipped on that slick, metal edge and I fell forward. My heart raced as I landed on my hands and knees atop the big piece of cardboard in the center of the skylight. I gripped the edges of the box and exhaled slowly, and then I looked up at Sergei and asked, "Do you think Duke and his date heard that thud?"

Without warning, the skylight swung open, and I yelped as I dropped into the restaurant. There was the clatter of glass shattering and dishes breaking as I landed with a sharp jolt. It rattled my teeth and sent pain radiating from my knees, which took most of the impact. Around me, a few people cried out in alarm.

I'd pressed my eyes shut as I fell, and when I opened them, I found I'd landed directly on Duke and Even's table. I was still clutching the edges of the box with white-knuckled tenacity, which was lucky, because it had provided protection from the broken plates and glasses beneath me. I glanced at Even, who'd leapt to his feet directly in front of me, then looked over my shoulder at Duke and said, "Hey. How's it going?"

Both men were absolutely stunned. So were the people at the other tables and the waiter who'd frozen in mid-pour. Everyone was staring at me. Because I didn't know what else to do, I quipped, "I was just in the neighborhood, thought I'd drop by."

A glob of wet leaves landed on my shoulder, and when I realized it was raining on me, I looked up at the high ceiling. The skylight had swung open on its hinge, and Sergei was peering through it with a horrified expression. I gave him a little wave, then climbed off the table and tried out my arms and legs. Nothing appeared to be broken.

All of a sudden, Even Eide burst out laughing. He laughed so hard that his entire body shook, and he had to wipe tears from his eyes. Meanwhile, I dusted myself off, and when he finally got his laughter under control, Eide told me, "That was a hell of an entrance, Quinn." Duke still hadn't said anything. He got up and looked down at himself, then brushed a splatter of something or another from the lapel of his dark blue suit jacket.

The manager rushed up to us a moment later with an expression that could best be described as pinched and demanded to know what was going on. Even pulled a stack of hundreds from his wallet, which he handed to the manager as he said, "Just a little accident. This should cover our meal and the broken dishes, plus a little extra for you and your staff for the inconvenience."

The manager was still ruffled (even though he pocketed the money) and was threatening to call the police, but Eide took him aside and spoke to him in hushed tones. Whatever he said seemed to calm the man. While that was happening, a busboy hurried over with a long pole and used it to close and latch the skylight, so at least it stopped raining inside the restaurant. I turned to Duke and said, "I'm sorry for ruining your twenty-thousand-dollar date."

He looked at the skylight, then at me and asked, "Were you spying on me?"

"No?"

"Why is that in the form of a question?"

I flailed around and finally came up with, "Maybe it was more checking to see how things were going?"

His voice rose a little. "But instead of texting me and asking, you climbed up on a roof in the pouring rain and watched me through a skylight? I thought you trusted me, Quinn!"

"I do! But I don't trust him!" I pointed at Eide, who glanced at us over his shoulder.

"Based on what, the fact that he outbid you at a charity auction?"

"I saw the way he was looking at you beforehand! Then he decided to bring you here for dinner, and this is hardly a let's-be-friends kind of restaurant!"

"None of that should matter," Duke said. "Even if you didn't trust him, and even if you were worried he'd try to hit on me, you should have believed in me enough to know I'd turn him down!"

"I wanted to believe that, but I knew you had a crush on him."

"*Had*, Quinn! What the hell do you think I've been doing with you the last month, biding my time until something better came along?"

"Yes!" I shouted it and fought back the tears that prickled behind my eyes. "That's exactly what I thought! Why would you settle for me, when you could have that?" I gestured at Eide with a shaking hand.

"You think I'm settling?"

I lowered my voice and said, "I've always known I'm not good enough, all my life. That's why I pushed myself so hard in ballet. I tried and tried until I became better. But I can't do that with you. This is all I have to give."

Duke's expression softened, and he asked, "How could you possibly think you're not good enough?"

"Because I'm not! But Eide is. He's so fucking special that they made a documentary about him, and you bought it, less than three years ago!"

"Is that supposed to mean something?"

"It proves your infatuation didn't end when you were seventeen!"

"You're right, it didn't."

Eide came over to us and said, "Sorry to interrupt, mates, but the management would like us to take this outside. There was an implied 'or else'. Also, I believe these people want to get back to their overpriced dinner."

I looked around. The eyes of everyone in the restaurant were on me. All those rich, elegant couples glared at me with contempt, as if I was something disgusting they'd found stuck to the bottom of their shoe.

Fuck those assholes.

I held my head high as I pulled off my floppy hat and ran a hand over my slicked back hair. Then I strutted to the exit, as if I was working the runway at New York fashion week. If they wanted something to look at, I'd fucking give it to them.

But my bravado dissipated as soon as I got outside. It was still raining, and I shivered a bit and clutched the front of my coat to hold it closed. I was in a beautiful neighborhood, full of charming shops and restaurants. Several trees lined the sidewalk in front of Elixir, each wrapped in white lights. It was magical, but all I could think was, *so this is where it ends.*

My heart was breaking. I was sure I'd blown my chances with Duke. He thought I didn't trust him and was probably about to break up with me. Then I'd get to watch him drive off with Even Eide. I'd practically pushed Duke into his arms.

The two of them exited the restaurant a few moments later. They'd both put on stylish, dark overcoats and looked like they'd stepped from the pages of a magazine. Eide leaned in and said something to Duke, and then he went to speak to the valet.

Duke joined me under the sparkling canopy of one of the trees, and he said, "To finish what I was saying, I did still have a crush on Even when I bought that DVD, but I don't anymore. Do you know when it ended?" I shook my head, and he said, "When I met you."

"Really?"

"What did you think you'd find when you came here tonight? Did you expect Even and me to be making out at the dinner table and getting ready to run off together?"

"No…but why wouldn't you run off with him?"

"Because I'm completely, utterly, madly in love with you, Quinn!" I looked up at him, and he said, "I know I haven't said those words before today, but it can't be news to you, can it? You're everything to me. Absolutely everything! I wake up thinking about you, and you're on my mind every minute of the day. I'm happier than I've ever been! In fact, I've smiled more this past month than I have in the last twenty-seven years combined! Don't you see all the love I have for you?"

He cupped my face in his hands, and I whispered as I met his steady gaze, "No one's ever loved me like that. I didn't know what it looked like."

"It looks like this." I dropped my hat and slipped my arms around him as Duke kissed me. It was deep and tender, passionate and gentle, and it made my heart stumble over itself.

When he rested his forehead against mine, I said, "I love you too, Duke. God, I love you." His smile was glorious.

He stepped back after a moment and took my hand as he looked me over. "Did you hurt yourself when you fell through the skylight?"

"No. I got lucky."

"I have to say, this is the cutest rain gear I've ever seen."

"It was for tonight's theme at the club. That reminds me, I wonder what happened to Sergei." I looked around and saw him jogging up to us on the sidewalk, just as the valet pulled a big, black SUV to the curb. Eide came up to us, and I told him, "I'm sorry I ruined your twenty-thousand-dollar date."

He said, "On the contrary, you made it even more fun. And it's not over yet! Duke was telling me about the club where you work, and I think we should all head over there and keep this party going. Can I give you a ride?"

"Thanks, that'd be great. My friend and I actually need to get back to work." I turned to Sergei as he came to a stop beside us and assessed Even with a wary expression. "Even, I'd like you to meet Sergei Reznik. Sergei, this is the famous Even Eide."

Sergei raised his chin a little and narrowed his pale blue eyes as he met Even's gaze. "Am I supposed to be impressed?"

Eide unleashed a sexy, flirtatious smile as his gaze slid down Sergei's body, and he said, "Not yet. But by morning, I bet you will be." Sergei actually grinned at that, despite himself.

I said, "You should ride with us, Sergei, and come back for your motorcycle later. The rain's starting to pick up."

After a moment's hesitation, Sergei nodded in agreement. Duke and I piled into the backseat of the SUV as it started to pour, and Even held the passenger door for my friend as thunder rumbled overhead. The two men exchanged a smoldering look as Sergei slipped past him.

*****

Preston had made himself comfortable at the bar with a cup of coffee and a stack of paperwork, since there were no customers whatsoever. He glanced up at us when we came in and said, "I sent all the dancers home, since the storm killed what little business we had tonight. I texted you, Quinn, to let you know you and Sergei didn't have to come back."

I introduced Even to Preston and Rico, and after they exchanged greetings, Even asked, "Is there a bar menu? I'm starving! The food at that fancy restaurant was miniscule." When Preston told him we didn't have a kitchen, Even offered to order pizza for all of us and pulled out his phone. My manager cheerfully signed off on that idea.

Meanwhile, I stepped behind the bar and found a big pair of scissors, then carefully sliced down the inseam of my rain boots. I was sorry to see them go, but I really needed to get them off me. Then I called, "Be right back," and went to the locker room.

I'd washed my face and was fully dressed and tying my purple sneakers when Even came into the locker room a few minutes later. He asked, "Can I speak with you a minute, mate?"

"Of course."

"I wanted you to know I had no idea Duke was your boyfriend when I outbid you at the auction. He told me when we chatted afterwards. He also said you'd both planned on being each other's highest bidder. I'm sorry for mucking up your plans."

"No need to apologize. You had no way of knowing."

"Still though. I feel like an asshole for shutting you down the way I did."

"I'm curious. How high would you have been willing to go in your bidding?"

Even grinned and admitted, "I'm extremely competitive, so I would have done whatever it took to win. That's the former athlete in me, I suppose."

I pulled a sweater from my backpack as I appraised Even. He was leaning against one of the lockers with a friendly half-smile on his face, and I asked, "If Duke told you he had a boyfriend right after you outbid me, why did you take him to such a romantic restaurant?"

"My personal assistant made the reservation. I told her to pick someplace nice, which she interpreted as romantic and ungodly expensive. She hasn't been working for me very long and didn't realize I prefer far less pretentious restaurants."

"Okay, but you must have been attracted to Duke to bid on him in the first place."

"Of course I was. Your boyfriend is gorgeous yet humble, which is such an appealing combination. But my competitive nature doesn't extend to breaking up happy couples. Duke talked about you all evening, and it's obvious that man is madly in love. I have to say, I'm envious of you." I grinned a little as I shut my locker. Even Eide was envious of *me*. What a concept. Even stuck his hand out and said, "No hard feelings?"

I shook it and nodded. "No hard feelings."

When we returned to the club, Duke smiled at me and asked, "Is that new?"

I looked down at myself and patted my stomach. The sky blue sweater featured a unicorn rearing up on its hind legs, with a rainbow arching out of its back end. "Yeah. It's a bit understated, so I was thinking about gluing on some rhinestones. What good is a rainbow-pooping unicorn without some sparkle?"

Duke chuckled at that. Then he led me to the empty dance floor and pulled me into his arms. The DJ had turned down the volume a bit, compared to the usual roof-rattling decibel level, and he was playing a fairly slow song.

I looked up at my boyfriend and said, as I swayed in his arms, "I really am sorry about wrecking your date. You were probably having fun talking about hockey with your sports idol."

"Actually, we mostly talked about you. I invited him to your dance troupe's debut."

"Did you really?"

Duke nodded. "He says he'll be there. He also invited you and me to his house next weekend to watch the hockey game."

"You two really bonded in an hour."

"We did. He's a nice guy. Is it going to be weird for you though, if Even and I end up as friends?"

I glanced at Eide across the club. He was toasting Sergei and said something that actually made him laugh. "It won't bother me. I don't see Even as a threat. Not anymore."

"What changed your mind?"

"Hearing you say you loved me was a big part of it. Knowing you feel the same way I do means everything to me," I said, and he gently caressed my cheek. "Plus, I believed Even when he told me he didn't intend to come between us. And here's the other thing: I thought I was going to lose you tonight, because of my own insecurity. It was the worst feeling in the world, and I never want to experience that again. So that means putting aside my fears and jealousy and believing in this amazing thing that's happening between us."

"You know, not that long ago, you told me you weren't the jealous type."

"I didn't really know what I was. This is all uncharted territory for me."

"Me, too."

I looked up at Duke as we danced. Overhead, the metallic streamers sparkled, looking more like stars than raindrops. After a while, I said, "That seemed like a pretty amazing restaurant. Too bad I'm probably banned from it for life."

"It was alright. Nothing special."

"But it seemed so romantic!"

Duke smiled sweetly. "Right now, this is the most romantic place in all the world, because you're here with me."

I whispered, "I adore you, Duke."

"I adore you, too."

A minute later, I asked, "Did you see my note about the squirrel that might or might not be in the house?"

"I did. Should I be alarmed?"

I said, "Nah. Just keep dancing," and he picked me up and spun us around the dance floor.

Chapter Fourteen

I stood at the edge of the dance studio in my parents' house and took a deep breath. Then I ran toward Duke, leapt high into the air, and spun before landing in his arms. My little audience applauded, and my dad said, "That was perfect, and a great stopping point. Save some energy for tonight's performance, son."

My boyfriend kissed my forehead before putting me down and accompanying me to the seating area in the corner of the room, where my parents and Max had settled in to watch me practice. Duke had been reinstated with only a reprimand at the beginning of the month, and even though he was back to working a lot of overtime, he'd been devoting every spare minute to helping me rehearse. He jokingly called himself Haley's stunt double.

My mom got up and smoothed out her colorful caftan as she said, "Come on, let's have lunch. Your dad made one of your favorite dishes, Quinn, so you can fuel up before the show."

I reached for a towel and wiped the sweat off my forehead as I said, "Thanks, but I doubt I'll be able to eat anything. I'm a bundle of nerves."

We'd done a full dress rehearsal in the theater the night before, and it went off without a hitch. But there was so much riding on our debut performance. The show had ended up selling out, thanks to our little parade down Castro Street, and Dare had gotten a few media outlets to cover the event, so a lot of people were about to watch us succeed or fail. We'd all worked so hard for the past year, and it all came down to that night.

I knew my part and knew I could dance the hell out of it, but I just couldn't keep the what-ifs at bay. What if I messed up? What if I let down Dare and all the guys? What if, what if, what if? I was the lead dancer, onstage for the entire show, but it was my first professional performance. Maybe I wasn't ready for this. Maybe Dare had been wrong to put so much faith in someone so inexperienced.

Duke must have seen the panic in my eyes, because he gently drew me into his arms and whispered, "Just breathe, Quinn. You've got this."

"But what if—"

He interrupted me with a gentle kiss, then said, "You're going to be amazing. You need to eat though, because you barely touched your breakfast, and you must be starving. Come on, let's go see what's for lunch." I pulled a big sweatshirt over my tank top and shorts, and Duke and I followed my family to the kitchen.

My dad had made chili and cornbread, perfect for a cloudy, mid-October afternoon. I removed the lid from the big pot on the stove and asked, "Did you sneak some healthy stuff in here? Is this quinoa chili?"

Dad grinned and said, "Not as far as you know."

It smelled great, and since my stomach was rumbling, I decided eating really was a good idea. We sat at the round table at one end of the kitchen and dug in, my nerves temporarily forgotten. Duke had two big bowlfuls and asked for the recipe, which thrilled my father to no end. After the meal, we helped clean up, and then Max turned to me and said, "Still want me to draw on you?"

"Yes please."

"Alright, let's do this thing." Instead of covering my tattoo mishap with makeup, I'd decided to get a bit more creative and asked Max to freehand a temporary tattoo onto my skin. I had an ulterior motive. Yoshi Miyazaki was going to be at the performance, and I thought it'd be a good opportunity to showcase Max's skills. But I also just wanted to do something fun and interesting for my big night.

We all relocated to the living room, a beautiful, open space with rich wood tones, a huge slate fireplace, and elegant, modern furniture. I thought it was one of the most soothing rooms in what was already a very tranquil home. My parents settled in with tea and books on a loveseat beside the blazing hearth, and I stripped from the waist up, stretched out on the couch and put my head on Duke's thigh.

Max perched on the edge of the square coffee table with the set of temporary tattoo pens I'd bought him and leaned in close. Then he paused with a black pen poised right above my ribcage and said, "Dude, I just flashed back to when we were kids and used to give each other tattoos with felt tip pens."

"See? You were always meant to be a tattoo artist." I grinned and added, "Oh man, remember the time we accidentally used permanent markers? Your dad was so mad."

"Like I can forget." He studied my side as he asked, "Any final requests before I start drawing?"

"Just do what we talked about. Make it big and bold, and don't go dark on me with like, the illusion of peeled away skin or anything like that."

Max pushed his long hair behind his shoulder and said, "Got it. Although you should let me do that some other time, because it'd look rad."

He began to draw with big, bold lines, while Duke idly stroked my hair. Across the room, my parents leaned against each other while they read. After a while, my mom finished her novel, put her head on her husband's shoulder, and started reading his book along with him. They were so sweet together, still so in love after half a century together, and I whispered, "Relationship goals."

I looked up at Duke, and he smiled at me and said softly, "That'll be us in fifty years."

"You're right."

"The main difference is, we'll be living in your Barbie tent, because I've decided to sell the duplex."

I sat up abruptly, and Max pulled back and exclaimed, "Come on, bro! That's how you got a tiny dick drawn on you!"

I ignored him and asked Duke, "Are you serious?"

He nodded. "I've been thinking about it for weeks, and I know I need to make a change. I could never really afford that house, and my entire life has been centered on trying to keep up with the payments. That has to stop. Hopefully it's built up some equity, so I can pay back my parents with a little left over. That's another big reason for selling it, to get myself out from under that debt."

"You were dead-set against it, the last time we talked about it. What made you change your mind?"

"A lot of soul searching," he said. "I've been spending all this time watching you and the rest of the guys in your dance troupe pursuing your passion, and I started asking myself, is owning a house really worth it, if it means my dreams have to be put on hold indefinitely? That doesn't mean the next step is quitting my job. But if I find more affordable housing, then I won't have to keep working sixty to seventy hours a week, and I'll have time for things that make me happy."

"Wow, Duke, this is a huge step! I think it's fantastic, and it goes without saying that I'll be there every step of the way."

He said, "I'm counting on it. That's what gave me the confidence to go ahead with this, knowing I'm part of a couple now, so I won't be facing all these changes alone."

"You're not just part of a couple, you're part of a family," my mom called from across the room. "And if you kids need someplace to stay after you sell the duplex, you're always welcome to move in here. We have much more room than we need."

Duke murmured, "Thank you, Doctor Takahashi."

My mother clicked her tongue and said, "I told you to call me Toshiko or Mom, whichever you're comfortable with." He smiled at that.

A thought occurred to me, and I turned to my parents and said, "Please tell me you'll never sell this place and downsize."

My dad shook his head. "No chance. This is your home as much as ours, and we'd never sell it out from under you. Besides, it may be bigger than we need right now, but we see a lot more grandchildren and great-grandchildren in our future, so we'll need the room."

"If you're counting on me for the great-grandkids, you're going to have a hell of a long wait," Max told them. "First, I need to find a J-O-B. Then I need to move out of my parents' house and find a big, strong, handsome man to knock me up. It's all outlined in my forty-year plan."

I chuckled at that as I returned my head to Duke's thigh. As my nephew started drawing again, I said, "You never know, Max. Life has a way of surprising you, and all of that might happen a lot sooner than you think. Except for the part about you getting knocked up. But hey, with a forty-year plan, maybe modern medicine will catch up to you."

"Or not." Max leaned in and concentrated on a spot on my side as he said, "Have you guys talked about having kids?"

I glanced up at Duke and said, as he went back to stroking my hair, "Yup. We definitely want to start a family, when the time is right."

Max asked, "How will you know when that is?"

"I think we'll just know."

My nephew shook his head and murmured, "It's weird. You look and sound like the same old Quinn. But then this super grown-up stuff comes out of your mouth, and I'm like, who is this dude?"

*****

Dare stared at me as I pulled off my shirt and asked, "Holy shit, did you go out today and get a huge tatt?"

"No, it's just temporary," I said as I turned toward the mirror in the threadbare dressing room and admired Max's handiwork. He'd drawn a gorgeous, Japanese-inspired pattern of colorful peonies interspersed with life-size koi, framed by branches and fanciful swirls. It extended from my chest to my knee, all along one side of my body, and it was so beautifully rendered that I was sad it'd fade out in a few days. "I'm still planning on getting a traditionally applied tattoo over the squiggle on my ribs, but I wanted to wait until after tonight. I didn't think it would heal well with all the rehearsing we've been doing, especially since that's right where Haley's hands end up every time he catches me."

"Speaking of Haley, I wonder where he is," Dare said. It was a little over an hour until curtain, and the rest of us had arrived early to warm up before the show.

"I thought he'd be the first one here," a dancer named Oz said, looking up from his spot on the floor, where he was stretching his hamstrings. "Did you try texting him?"

"Yeah, and I haven't heard back, but I'm not worried. I'm sure he'll be here," Dare said as he pulled on his costume, which was a tiny pair of skin-tight shorts, made out of a stretchy material. For the first act, everyone was dressed in black, except me. I remained in white throughout the show, and pieces of my costume tore away, so it kept getting smaller.

A minute later, Duke, Skye, Christian and Shea joined us in the dressing room. They were all wearing black pants and long-sleeved black T-shirts with the troupe's logo, 'D*to*D', printed on the front in red. They were acting as our ushers before the show, along with some of Dare's former students. Then they were changing into solid black shirts and knit caps and coming out onto the stage during the performance to switch out the sets. The performance was in three acts, each thirty minutes long with no intermission, so our crew would become part of the show.

Skye said, "The tech guys wanted me to let you know everything's good to go. The sound and lighting checks went off without a hitch."

"That's good news." Dare pulled his husband into his arms and asked, "Did you see Milo out there? He was here, but then he disappeared." The twenty-two-year-old college kid who'd composed the original score was more nervous than we were.

Christian took a seat at one of the makeup tables and said, "He's pacing in the back alley, which is probably a good place for him, because he looked like he was about to throw up. Way better than puking in the theater." He checked his reflection in the mirror and ran a fingertip below his lower lashes to either clean up or smear his black eyeliner. I wasn't sure which.

Duke came up to me as I wriggled into my costume. It looked a bit like a very short sarong over a Speedo. The spandex material draped one hip and was cut high over the other, so the left side of my body with the temporary tattoo was almost totally bare, aside from a narrow strap spanning my hipbone. I put on the tight tank top that went with my costume, and I'd already applied a bit of makeup, so I was totally set after that. As I pulled on a hoodie and slipped my feet into my sneakers, I announced, "I'm going to find a quiet corner to warm up and calm the hell down, and I'm taking my boyfriend with me, so you'll have to make do without him for a while."

Duke and I left the dressing room hand-in-hand and ran into Haley in the hallway. I said, "Hey. Dare tried to call you."

He grinned at me. "I know. I was burning off some energy before the show, so I couldn't exactly get to my phone."

I grinned too and asked, "What was his name?"

Haley brushed back his short dreadlocks as he thought about that. "Gavin, maybe? Or Guillermo? Something with a G. Or maybe a C?"

"Seriously?"

"Don't even think about acting shocked, Quinn. You used to be just like me, before you fell madly in love with your hot cop." That was very true, although my days of sleeping with pretty much anyone felt like a lifetime ago.

He winked at us before continuing to the dressing room, and Duke and I made our way to the cluttered backstage. The theater had been built in the 1920s, and it seemed as if every show that had graced its stage over the last century had left behind a dusty prop or two. For the last twenty or thirty years, it had become a venue for adult entertainment. I wasn't sure if that meant screening dirty movies, or some kind of live show. Either way, its new owners were trying to turn things around for the faded theater and gain some legitimacy. I had to wonder if our somewhat avant-garde performance was going to help or hinder their efforts.

Duke and I settled in on a faded, red velvet couch in a forgotten corner of the big backstage. It had a few questionable-looking stains on it, so I said, "I was just wondering if this theater used to feature live adult entertainment. If so, do you think this couch was part of the act?"

He grinned and said, "I refuse to give that too much thought."

"Remember my used porn mattress when I first moved in? You were so freaked out by it that I was pretty sure you were germ-phobic. But now here you are, willingly sitting on a possible sex couch with stains of unknown origin!"

"For the record, that bed was disgusting, on multiple levels." He thought about it and said, "How was that only a month and a half ago? My life is so different now."

I put my head on his chest and said, "Mine too."

He began to massage my shoulders. "You're still nervous, aren't you?"

"Oh yeah. It's not stage fright, I just really need everything to go perfectly tonight. Dare and the rest of the guys have so much riding on this."

"So do you."

"Not like they do. I could always come up with a plan B, but…."

He finished the sentence for me. "But for a lot of those guys, this is their last shot." He wrapped his arms around me and said, "They're why you chose this troupe. I never fully got it until just now. I know you really didn't want that job with the San Francisco Ballet, but any one of a hundred other dance companies, including plenty of independents, would have hired you in a heartbeat and offered a good salary. And yet, you chose Dare's troupe because they needed you, and because you could bring the spotlight to them, right? You sacrificed your career for their sake."

"It won't be a sacrifice if the show is a success."

He said, "No wonder you've been nervous. It must feel like the future of every guy in the troupe is riding on your shoulders."

"That's exactly what I feel like, but I can do this. I've trained for most of my life, and now I just need to go out there and give it everything I've got."

Duke kissed the top of my head and said, "That audience is so lucky, because they're about to find out how amazing you are."

*****

My heart was pounding in my ears as the curtain rose at eight sharp. The set pieces displayed the dark cityscape Christian had painted. The audience was hushed.

As the music built, I took a deep breath. Duke squeezed my hand, and I looked up at him. He held my gaze for a long moment, and there was so much love in his eyes. Beyond him, Dare and the rest of the troupe fidgeted with nervous anticipation.

I exhaled slowly. It was time. Right on cue, I walked out onto the enormous stage by myself. I couldn't see the audience beyond the bright, white lights, but I knew they were there. Four hundred pairs of eyes were on me.

Twenty years of my life had built to this moment. I spun slowly, then extended my arms overhead and stretched out to the right. When I raised my head, I caught a glimpse of Duke. He didn't look nervous. He just looked proud.

The tempo picked up, and I threw myself into my routine. I ran across the stage and leapt into the air. I stopped thinking and worrying and just danced.

For ten minutes, I was alone on the stage. I poured everything I had into each moment. The score built and built. I leapt and spun, then did it again and again, until the music reached its crescendo, and I dropped onto the stage.

All was silent for a moment. Then the audience exploded with applause. I could actually feel it vibrating through me, as my heart pounded from the sheer exertion of what I'd just done.

As the music began to build again, Dare and Cleveland joined me on the stage, and we began to dance in perfect unison. Every few minutes, two more dancers joined us, until I was flanked by five dancers on each side. We executed a perfect series of jumps, and then we spun around. I was the axis, and the dancers coiled around me. They all came in close, forming a cocoon of sorts. I could feel the warmth of their bodies as they closed in.

The music rose, and the other dancers fell away as Haley strode onto the stage. I stepped over and around them and held Haley's gaze as I approached him. We circled each other at center stage. I stopped moving, and Haley orbited me, coming closer on each pass. He stopped right beside me, and then he reached out and touched my cheek. End of act one.

As the audience applauded again and the lights dimmed, long strips of fabric unfurled from the ceiling. Duke and the rest of the crew crossed the stage, turning the giant, three-sided set pieces to display colorful graffiti panels. Act one had been about two men meeting. The second was about our courtship, and for the first half of act two, Haley and I were alone on the stage. Our movements were gentle, tentative, as if we were getting to know each other. We kissed at the halfway point as the score paused, almost as if it was taking a breath.

Then the tempo picked up. I ran across the stage and leapt, and Haley caught me around the waist, lifted me high overhead, and spun. The rest of the troupe joined us. They were all dressed in red. Haley and I stepped back as they took center stage. He and I kept dancing, but slowly. Adrenaline coursed through me. I caught my breath and hit my mark as the music changed again.

We acted out jealousy as the score turned harsh, discordant. Haley crossed the stage and ran his hand across

Dare's bare chest. I tried to drag him away. When Haley and I began to dance again, our movements were sharp and aggressive. Red light bathed the stage. The white banners acted as movie screens, and jagged, abstract imagery was projected onto them. The graffiti backgrounds became garish, almost nightmarish as the colored lights brought some elements to the foreground and dropped others back. We used our bodies to act out our argument, and Haley tore my tank top from me and cast it aside.

At the end of act two, Haley and I were on opposite ends of the stage with our backs to each other. The rest of the troupe was divided, half on his side, half on mine. He and I remained fixed in place as our friends danced around us, then stilled. The music stilled with them. Once again, applause filled the theater.

Act three began quietly. Soft blue lights replaced the red. The other dancers left the stage as our crew rotated the set pieces to the third side. The paintings were abstract and reminded me of an indistinct reflection on water.

Haley and I glanced at each other, then approached slowly. Our movements were tentative as we danced together. I reached out and touched his jaw, and the lighting became brighter.

Over the next half hour, we acted out falling in love through dance. Small movements became bold. The other dancers took the stage in white costumes smeared with bright colors and swirled around us. Haley and I executed a flawless series of *grand jettes* across the stage, soaring together.

The score swelled, became joyous, and we kissed. All around us, the dancers grabbed handfuls of colored powder and threw them into the air. Spotlights flickered and brought the abstract backgrounds to life, creating the illusion of movement, as if a gentle tide was ebbing and flowing.

Haley and I came together at center stage. We grabbed at each other, acting out desire. I tore away his costume, leaving him in just little, white briefs. He did the same with my sarong.

The rest of the troupe paired off as we danced. Our movements conveyed joy and passion, love and sex. Clouds of bright color bloomed on the stage as the pairs swirled around us and pelted us and the white banners with powder, transforming us. Haley grabbed some blue powder and smeared it across my chest, and I took a handful of hot pink powder from the little bag Cleveland held out to me and ran it down Haley's back. Then we joined together, dancing across the stage in perfect unison.

It was meant to be a celebration of love. It ended up being so much more than any of us ever expected. The music and the dancing, the lights and the color, combined into something ethereal. It transcended all of us. We created magic on that stage, something beautiful and true, raw and honest. I knew that because all I could think about was Duke, and how much I absolutely adored him. I felt like I was showing the world what the contents of my heart looked like, and it was glorious.

As the final notes of the score faded out, Haley and I knelt at center stage, our bodies intertwined in a passionate embrace. The other pairs of dancers did the same all around us, freezing in different poses. The music ended, and silence filled the theater as the clouds of color settled in slow motion. My heart was pounding, and Haley and I both gasped for breath.

In the next instant, cheering and applause rose to meet us like an avalanche, thunderous and overwhelming. Haley and I both looked a bit dazed as we let go of each other and stood up. I turned to face the audience. They were all on their feet, every last one of them. I was stunned by the standing ovation.

The troupe lined up across the stage and took a bow, and then Dare dragged Milo out from behind the curtain. The composer quickly tried to smooth down his unruly, dark hair and pulled off his glasses, and then he waved self-consciously. When Dare did the same thing to Christian, the artist grinned and curtseyed.

Dare gestured at me, and for a moment I was too overwhelmed to think straight. Duke appeared at my side and handed me a huge bouquet of red roses. Then he leaned in and told me, "Take your bow, Quinn. You've earned it."

When I stepped forward, the cheering and applause doubled in intensity. I squinted against the lights and looked for my family. They were right there in the first row. My father looked like he was crying as he smiled at me and applauded wildly. I kissed my fingers and stretched my arm toward him, and then I took my bow and stepped back in line.

Haley stepped forward next. He took his bow, and then he reached for me, pulled me to the edge of the stage again, and raised our joined hands in a gesture of triumph. We then rejoined the troupe, and we all took one more bow. The audience was still on its feet, still clapping.

I looked around for Duke. He'd left the stage, and I ran to get him, because I needed to share that moment with him. He dug his heels in when I tried to pull him onto the stage and said, "This is your moment, Quinn. Go enjoy it."

I pulled him close and told him, "You were a part of that. You're my muse and my inspiration, Duke. Don't you see? I know what it means to be in love because of you. If we'd never met, I would have just been going through the motions, but you made it genuine." He smiled at me and joined me at center stage. When we kissed, the audience cheered.

Finally, the red velvet curtain came down, and Dare and the rest of the guys gathered around me. I tried to shield my beautiful rose bouquet as they hugged me and raved about how well I'd done, and I told them, "All of you were amazing. Absolutely flawless."

Someone handed me a towel, and I quickly wiped the sweat and colored powder from my face and body as people began flooding the stage. Skye ran to Dare, and the two men kissed passionately. My family appeared at the edge of the crowd that was forming, and Duke took the roses and towel and said, "Let me hold these for you." I thanked him and rushed over to my family.

Max reached me first and hugged me as he exclaimed, "Dude, you were awesome!"

My brothers and their wives all raved about how well I'd done, and then my mom grabbed me in a crushing embrace and gushed, "You were fantastic, Quinn, absolutely fantastic! So was the show! It was beautifully staged, and so artistic! And that standing ovation was the longest I've ever seen!"

When I turned to my dad, his eyes were bright with tears of happiness. He beamed at me and pulled me into his arms as he said, "I'm so proud of you, son."

I had to ask. "Still think I should have accepted that job with the other ballet company?"

He shook his head. "You're right where you belong, with a talented, cutting-edge company that was smart enough to build the whole show around you. The troupe is going places after that performance, mark my words!"

I shivered a little as the sweat started to cool on my skin. Just as my dad said, "You're cold," my boyfriend appeared beside us with a hoodie and sweatpants. He held the jacket for me, and while I slipped my arms into the sleeves, my father said, "You're a good man, Duke. It's reassuring to know you're always looking out for our boy."

Dozens of people came up to congratulate me, friends and strangers alike. Even Eide was there with Sergei, which was a pleasant surprise, and Elijah braved the crowd to give me a hug and tell me, "You're an inspiration, Quinn."

Haley introduced me to his mom, who kissed my cheek, and his younger brothers and sister. A few people took photos with me or of me, including someone from a local LGBT+ newspaper. Yoshi Miyazaki shook my hand and raved about my temporary tattoo as much as my dancing. I pulled up my hoodie to show him the details before dragging Max over and saying, "You know, my nephew has been looking for an apprenticeship. I think you two should talk." Max panicked a bit, but I just smiled at him, and Yoshi led him to a less crowded part of the stage and did exactly what I'd suggested.

After about half an hour or so, Skye climbed up on a chair and yelled over the noise, "Don't forget, everyone, party at Dare's and my apartment tonight! Bring your friends and your appetite! We'll get going at about eleven, so the dancers have time to run home and get cleaned up. Or just come sweaty. We don't care, but our dog might lick you to death!"

As Skye jumped off the chair, I turned to my dad and asked, "Want to come to a party?"

"That's a bit late for this old man, but you and Duke are still planning to come to Sunday dinner, right?"

"You're not old, and we'll absolutely be there."

Once my family headed home, I took Duke's hand, and we returned to the dressing room to get my stuff. When I sat down to put my shoes on, my legs started shaking. I'd been running on pure adrenaline, but as it ebbed, pain and exhaustion crept into every part of me.

I'd practiced the ninety-minute routine several times beginning to end, but I'd always held a bit back. That night, I'd left it all on the stage. Every jump was as high as I could possibly go, and every spin, kick, and turn was as sharp and precise as it could be. I gave everything I had, and I was feeling it.

Duke draped my backpack over his shoulder, and then he surprised me by picking me up. I murmured, "You don't have to carry me," even as I wrapped my arms and legs around him.

He kissed my forehead and said, "I know. Humor me." I was grinning as we headed to the door.

*****

When we got home, he carried me into the house and left me on his bed while he filled the tub. Then he stripped me and bathed me gently, while the hot water soothed my aching muscles. Afterwards, he wrapped me in a big, fluffy towel, returned me to the bed, and asked, "Are you hungry? I made you some homemade macaroni and cheese, and there's a cake for dessert."

I grinned at him and held out my arms. "That sounds fantastic, but come here first."

Duke climbed up onto the bed and gathered me in an embrace. Then he rubbed his cheek against my hair and told me, "You were breathtaking tonight. I didn't realize you'd been holding back during rehearsal. That had already been incredible, but seeing what you're really capable of absolutely blew me away. I'm in awe of you, Quinn."

"All the guys danced their hearts out, not just me."

He said, "You're going to take some time off now, right? A couple weeks maybe, to rest and relax?"

"God yes. I think I might spend the next few days right here in this bed, aside from that party tonight."

"Are you really up for that?"

"No, but I'm going anyway." I flashed him a tired smile and added, "Please don't ask me to dance."

"I promise I won't." He reached behind him and took something out of the nightstand, and then he curled up with me again and handed me an envelope. "I got you a present, speaking of R and R." He watched with anticipation as I parted the flap with my fingertips and looked inside.

"Plane tickets to Las Vegas at the end of the month! We'll be there on our birthday!"

He nodded and grinned at me. "I booked a hotel and got us tickets to a big Halloween costume party. It seemed like something you'd enjoy."

I threw my arms around his neck and said, "This is amazing! Can I pay for half of it, since it's your birthday, too? That way, it'll be a gift to both of us."

"Nope, it's on me, and you don't have to worry about whether I can afford it. Not only am I back at work, but since I decided to sell the house, I don't have to be quite so careful with every penny. I won't suddenly start living like a tycoon, but three nights in Vegas is definitely in the budget."

I kissed him before saying, "Thank you, Duke. This really means the world to me."

Duke smiled at me and caressed my cheek. "I love seeing you so happy." I felt exactly the same way about the joy that lit up his eyes.

Chapter Fifteen

Two Weeks Later

"It's a love grotto!"

Duke looked stunned as he followed me into our Las Vegas hotel room and murmured, "Um, this wasn't intentional."

I ran across the suite and took a flying leap onto the round bed, which was in a sunken recess off the living area. "It's the used porn mattress's twin! Oh my God, come here. The bed has a control panel!"

He climbed onto the bed with a concerned expression. It started to vibrate when I pushed a button, and I whooped with delight. The next button made it rotate slowly, and I exclaimed, "This is the best hotel room ever!" I flopped onto my back and burst out laughing. "There are mirrors on the ceiling! That's so great!"

Duke gripped the red velvet bedspread as he glanced upward and told me, "The room pictured in the online reservation form looked normal. I didn't plan on bringing you to the set of a 1970s porno movie. I just clicked the box to upgrade us to a suite with a spa tub for two. Who knew that included mirrored ceilings, a vibrating bed, and whatever's happening over there?"

He gestured at a golden cherub nestled in a bed of plastic flowers. It was in what looked like a cylindrical cage with diagonal, clear plastic strings in place of bars. I jumped up to take a look at it. When I flipped a switch, the interior lit up, and after a moment, rows of what looked like tiny glass beads began to travel down each of the strings, creating the illusion of rain. I grinned and touched one of the beads, then rubbed my thumb and forefinger together and said, "Oh weird, that's actually oil. I don't know what's happening here, but I love it!"

I returned to the bed and bounced up and down, while Duke studied me and asked, "Do you really like this place, or are you just being nice? Because we can move to a newer hotel on the strip if you want to."

"This is a million times better than a regular hotel room!" I poked the control panel a few times and flopped onto my back. I'd revved up the vibration as far as it would go, and it was so vigorous that when I said, "Ahhhhhh," it came out in a staccato rhythm, kind of like a machine gun.

He grinned and said, "I picked this place because it has an original 1950s tiki bar downstairs, and I thought you might enjoy that. Since you appreciate kitsch more than any other person alive, it looks like I accidentally found the perfect hotel."

"A tiki bar? Epic!" I turned off the spin and the vibration because I was getting dizzy, and Duke stretched out on his side with his head propped up in his hand. I leaned in and kissed him, and then I said, "Thank you for this birthday trip. It's the best vacation I've ever had."

He smiled at me and pointed out, "We've been in Las Vegas less than an hour."

"I know."

"Also, I'm sure your parents took you on all kinds of fantastic trips when you were growing up."

"Yeah, but this is better, because I'm here with you, we're in such a fun hotel, and in just a few hours, we're both celebrating a birthday! How great is that?"

Duke reached out and ran a fingertip over my earring. I'd swapped out my usual silver studs for a new pair that looked like miniscule Captain America shields. "One of the many things I love about you is your unwavering ability to see the positive in any situation."

"Well, that's pretty easy to do when everything is amazing!" I kissed him again before climbing off the bed and saying, "Let's see what other wonders await us in the love grotto." When I pulled back the heavy, dark red curtains, I murmured, "Oh wow."

We had a fantastic view of the strip, which lit up the night in the middle distance. I opened the glass door and stepped out onto a narrow balcony. A warm breeze stirred my hair and carried the faint sound of Mariachi music. Duke came up behind me and wrapped his arms around my shoulders as he said, "The one good thing about being so far from the strip is actually getting a great view of it. That said, I thought we'd be closer. I've never been to Las Vegas before, so I didn't know how it was all laid out."

I turned to face him and reached up to cup his cheek. "Please tell me you're not disappointed."

"I'm not. I just wanted everything to be perfect this weekend. I also wanted to show you how much you mean to me, and a funky, old hotel about five miles from the strip doesn't really convey that message. You deserve the best, Quinn, and this…." He shook his head.

"It's perfect! We have a huge suite with a killer view and a vibrating bed, and somewhere there's even a tub big enough for two. How great is that?"

"You promise you're not just pretending to be excited to make me feel better?"

"I promise, and here's proof. If you were going to design the perfect room for me and you had to choose between elegant or fun, which would you pick?"

"Fun, no question."

"Exactly!" The frown line between his brows eased, and Duke grinned a little. I smiled at him and said, "Let's go find that tub. I'd love a soak before we head down to the tiki bar."

Duke seemed a lot happier as he let me tow him through the suite. A seating area with plush, red velvet furniture and gold accents was complemented by gold-toned wallpaper, and on the other side of the room, a pair of double doors led to a cavernous bathroom. It featured a huge shower, double sinks with a faux-marble vanity, and the best bathtub I'd ever seen in my life. It was glossy red and heart-shaped, and big enough to easily hold four people. I squealed with delight, and Duke chuckled and said, "Okay, that tub is totally you."

I flipped the lever to plug the drain and turned on both water spigots full-force. Then I peered over the edge of the giant tub and said, "What do you want to do for two hours, while the tub fills up?" I was only slightly exaggerating.

"Hmm, let me think." Duke's grin turned devilish, and he scooped me up and tossed me over his shoulder while I whooped and laughed. He carried me back across the suite, then down the four steps to the sunken bedroom, where he pulled the bedspread aside and tossed me onto the black satin sheets.

He stripped me quickly and efficiently, which made my cock throb. It was just so sexy when he took control. Once I was naked, I wiggled around on the silky bedding and said, "We totally need to get satin sheets at home. This feels amazing."

Duke met my gaze as he began to undress, and I stopped wiggling so I could watch. He unbuttoned his pale blue shirt slowly and deliberately, then slid it off his broad shoulders and let it fall to the floor. He pulled off his shoes and socks and tossed them aside, and my gaze ran down his smooth skin and landed on his hands as he unfastened his belt. He pushed down his khakis and briefs in one motion and stepped out of them, and then he stood before me for a moment and let me look at him, probably because I was rock hard by that point and squirming for another reason, besides the feel of satin against my skin.

His cock had started to stiffen, and I spread my legs shamelessly and massaged my erection as my breathing sped up. Duke climbed up onto the round bed and pushed my thighs even farther apart before sliding his lips over my swollen cockhead. Pleasure rolled through my body as he started to suck me. I watched him for a few minutes, and when he looked up at me with my cock in his mouth, my breath caught.

After another minute, I flipped around and took him in a sixty-nine, sucking him almost feverishly as he picked up his pace. He paused just long enough to lick his finger, then went back to sucking my cock as he massaged my hole. In the last week, he'd started fingering me whenever we were doing anything sexual, and I absolutely loved that. He hadn't fucked me yet, but it seemed like he was building up to it, and I was enjoying the anticipation.

When he slid his finger into me, I moaned around his cock. I'd cleaned myself thoroughly right before we left San Francisco in anticipation of exactly what was happening, and I'd even worked a little lube into myself, so his finger slipped in fairly easily. He added a second one, stretching me slightly. I bucked my hips and rode his fingers, thrusting just a little into his warm, wet mouth.

He started massaging my prostate as his other hand cupped my balls, and the pleasure was so intense that I came just a few moments later. I kept sucking him hard, bobbing my head as I slid my mouth up and down his thick shaft. Duke came a minute after I did, shooting into the back of my throat as he pushed into my mouth.

His fingers slipped from me when we were both done, and we fell back onto the mattress with huge, satisfied grins on our faces. He laughed when I said, "Viva Las Vegas." Once we caught our breath, I said, "We'd better check the tub," and we slid off the slick sheets. On the way to the bathroom, I retrieved my toiletry bag from my suitcase, then dumped a travel-size bottle of body wash into the water to make bubbles.

The huge tub was a little more than halfway full, so we climbed into the warm water, and I curled up on Duke's chest. "I have a new goal for the apartment we rent after we sell the duplex," he murmured. "A bathtub big enough for both of us. I don't really care if the rest of the place is a hovel, as long as it has a giant tub."

"I totally agree with that." I reached over and shut off the water, and then I sat up and said, "Oh no, I just remembered the swing set! We don't have to leave it behind, do we? It means too much to me!"

"Maybe your parents will let us put it in their side yard. I know they took down the swings you had as a kid, but if you tell them you really want this set, I bet they'll agree to it."

I nodded and rested my head on his chest again. We'd started researching the real estate market over the last couple of weeks, but since Xavier was out of town, we hadn't gone as far as putting the house on the market yet. We wanted to give him plenty of advance notice before that happened.

After a moment, I asked, "Do you think we can find an apartment that allows pets?"

"For the squirrel that's possibly still living somewhere in our house?" That had become a running joke with us. The squirrel that had invited himself in a few weeks before had probably run back outside that same day. But every time we heard an unexplained sound, we both looked at each other and said, "Squirrel." We found it endlessly amusing.

I grinned and said, "No, not him. I've always wanted a pet. Actually, I've always wanted a lot of them, and my life's finally settled enough to be able to take in a shelter dog or cat, or rabbit or guinea pig, or you know, one of each."

"So a menagerie, basically."

"Pretty much. It obviously won't be until after we move, but I'd like that to be one of the criteria for our new apartment."

He kissed the top of my head and said, "If that's what you really want, then sure."

After a minute, I asked, "Are you going to miss the duplex when you sell it?"

Duke said, "If I'm being perfectly honest, then yeah. I'm going to miss it a lot. It was a financial burden, but it was also my home. I went straight from living with my parents to the duplex, and it meant a lot to me. It made me feel safe and secure, which I'd never felt growing up. But giving it up is the right call, because I just can't afford it. Once we move someplace cheaper, we can fix up our new apartment and really make it feel like home, and it's going to be wonderful, because you'll be there."

I smiled at him before settling comfortably on his chest again. After a minute, I noticed a switch on the rim of the tub, and when I flipped it, a dozen jets whirred to life around us, churning the water like a tropical storm. Immediately, the body wash I'd dumped into the water started foaming up. Duke and I looked surprised when it quickly reached our shoulders. Then we both burst out laughing as we disappeared into a bank of fluffy, white bubbles.

*****

Duke's ringing phone jarred us awake the next morning. Or technically, afternoon. After our bath, we enjoyed the hell out of the tiki bar until it closed, then moved to an after-hours dance club on the strip. We'd finally fallen into bed around dawn.

Duke stabbed the speaker phone icon on his screen and murmured, "Hello?"

Xavier said, "Duke? Is that you?" When he muttered something like, 'mmm' our neighbor asked, "Did I wake you…at three p.m.?"

"Yeah, but that's fine. What's up?" Duke rolled onto his side facing me and rested his hand on my belly.

"Can I come over once you're fully awake? I need to speak with you about the note you left under my door about selling the duplex."

"Actually, Quinn and I are in Las Vegas for our birthday," Duke said. "And don't worry. We're not going to sell it out from under you. I spoke to a real estate agent last week, and she told me we might be able to make your tenancy a condition of the sale. In other words, we'd only sell it to someone who agreed to keep renting your apartment to you. Apparently that's fairly common, especially when multi-unit buildings are sold. Whoever buys it will probably want to rent out half the duplex anyway, so this way, they already have a tenant."

"Are you sure you want to sell it?"

"Yeah, just because I need to move someplace more affordable."

"Do you mind telling me what you're going to ask for it when you put the house on the market?" Duke repeated the figure the real estate agent had quoted us, and Xavier murmured, "Holy shit."

"I know that sounds exorbitant, but after I pay off the bank and my parents, it's not like I'll be making a huge profit or anything."

"No, I know," Xavier said. "It's perfectly in line with San Francisco housing prices. I'm just surprised, because it's exactly what I hoped you'd say."

"What do you mean?"

"I got an inheritance last year when my father died. Actually, these last two weeks, I finally went back home to Seattle and cleaned out his house so I could sell it, and someone made an offer the day I put it on the market. I'd been thinking about buying a condo with the money I'll have coming in from the sale of his house, but I really love where I am now and wasn't looking forward to moving."

"I'm sorry to hear about your dad, Xavier. I had no idea that'd happened."

"I didn't mention it at the time. He and I weren't close, and I've been having a hard time processing it." Xavier sighed and said, "In fact, he'd be so angry if he knew I'd inherited his assets. He never planned on dying at fifty-seven, so he didn't have a will in place. Otherwise, my father would have made sure it all went to anyone but me. Anyway…." His voice tightened, as if he was fighting back a strong emotion.

Duke and I sat up, and he said, "Cleaning out his house must have been upsetting."

"It really was. But the reason I'm telling you all of this is because after taxes, the money I'll be making on the sale of my father's house is almost exactly half the amount you just quoted me. So, I have to ask, would you consider accepting a cash payment for my half of the duplex, then maybe refinancing the remaining amount and staying where you are? Or I could buy the whole building when you put it on the market and finance the balance, which I guess would make me your landlord if you chose to stick around. I'm just thinking out loud here, but I'd love it if we could work something out."

Duke looked at me, and when I nodded enthusiastically, he told Xavier, "Actually, one of those two scenarios might be perfect, since we really didn't want to move. Let's talk about this when we get back to San Francisco on Thursday and run some numbers, see what we come up with."

They spoke for another minute, and after they said goodbye, he tossed the phone onto the mattress. Then Duke pulled me into his arms, kissed me passionately, and said, "Happy birthday, Quinn."

I beamed at him and said, "Happy birthday, Duke. I've never gotten to repeat that back to someone before."

"Wait here, I have something for you. Let's hope it survived the flight." He went to find his luggage, then returned a minute later with two plastic forks and a little, sky blue cake.

It was delicately decorated with white icing, sprinkled with edible iridescent glitter, and topped with a lit candle. "It got a little dented in transit, but you get what I was going for."

"It's so cute! Thank you!" I closed my eyes and made a wish, which had to do with the answer to a certain question I'd be asking later that day. After I blew out the candle, we sat cross-legged on the bed and shared the tiny confection. "I assume you made this," I said, "since it's absolutely delicious." The chocolate cake really was perfection.

He nodded. "Not that we couldn't have found something in Las Vegas. I just really wanted to be the one to make your birthday cake. I have a present for you, too, but I'm saving it for later."

"Ditto. I also kind of brought you a birthday cake, but it's just a Twinkie and a candle. Your version is way better." I fed him a few more bites, and when the cake was gone, I licked the little plastic plate.

Duke smiled at me and asked, "What do you want to do once you finish licking that?"

"Let's explore the hotel. There are all kinds of crazy things listed in the directory, and I want to see them for myself, including the swim-up bar in the pool. But first, we need a huge breakfast. Think we can find that at this time of day?"

"It's Vegas," Duke said. "I think we can find absolutely anything."

*****

He wasn't wrong. We stuffed ourselves with French toast at a twenty-four hour diner right inside the hotel, then tried our luck at the casino for about ten minutes, before we both decided it wasn't fun to lose money. Next, we visited the gift shop and bought each other a bunch of souvenirs. Because the hotel was inexplicably called the Polynesian Princess Resort and Casino, most of it was Hawaiian-themed. We ended up with matching T-shirts that said 'I got lei'd at the Polynesian Princess', straw hats, shot glasses, rainbow-colored silk flower leis, and giant foam hands with the pinkies and thumbs extended and the words 'hang loose' on the palms. I wore both of them and strode through the hotel lobby with my arms over my head on the way to the pool. Duke laughed and hurried after me.

The sprawling grounds were framed on three sides by the hotel's towers. Clusters of palm trees swayed in the warm breeze, and grass-roofed cabanas lined the far side of a huge, sparkling pool. The best part was a twenty-foot volcano, which dominated the landscape. Fake lava glowed orange, and red lights shone out of the caldera, illuminating a steady vent of steam. There was even a miniature village at its base. I exclaimed, "Volcano selfies," shook off my foam hands, and pulled out my phone. Duke and I mugged for the camera, pretending to look terrified as fake Kilauea loomed menacingly in the background.

"I'm proud of you," I said as I stuck our foam fingers in the shopping bag, and we continued our walk.

"Good to hear. Why, exactly?"

"You totally went along with the super crazy selfies. I particularly enjoyed your level of commitment with that Blair Witch-style close-up. Your fake fear was palpable!"

He chuckled and said, "Why, thank you. It's nice to be appreciated."

At the back of the tropical oasis, we came to a tiny, white church with a pointed steeple, lots of stained glass, and a huge, neon sign proclaiming it 'The King's 24-hour Aloha Wedding Chapel.' There was a wedding in progress right in front of it, under an arch covered in silk hibiscus flowers. The bride and groom were probably in their late fifties, totally decked out in tattoos and black leather, and were being married by an Elvis impersonator in a Hawaiian shirt. Their witnesses were two pit bulls wearing bowties and a man with a camcorder who looked a hell of a lot like Christopher Walken. We stood back and watched the ceremony, along with a few other hotel guests. When Elvis pronounced them husband and wife, the crowd applauded, and I told Duke, "That was literally the best wedding I've ever seen."

"Me too, actually. Want to cool off in the pool? I just spotted the swim-up bar down at the far end, near the…are those llamas?"

I followed his gaze and spotted the animals in the far corner of the sprawling outdoor area. They were in a temporary corral, under a big, white canopy. "Actually, those are alpacas."

"Why do you know that?"

"Because alpacas are awesome."

"What do they have to do with the Polynesian theme?"

"Nothing, but there's a convention for alpaca enthusiasts at the hotel this week. I saw a sign in the lobby. We just got lucky that they're here at the same time we are," I said as I dropped our shopping bag onto a lounge chair, peeled off my T-shirt, and retied the drawstring on my swim trunks.

Duke deadpanned, "That is lucky."

I kicked off my flip flops and walked to the edge of the pool as I told him, "Prepare to be impressed by the world's best cannonball!" I launched myself high into the air, hugged my knees to my chest, and plunged into the cool, sparkling water.

A moment after I bobbed to the surface, Duke landed with a tremendous splash right beside me. Then he popped up, shook the water from his short hair, and said, "Nice try, but my cannonball rules them all." I was laughing as he pulled me into his arms.

Chapter Sixteen

"This is what happens when I let you dress me," Duke said with a grin. We were in an elevator on our way up to the Halloween party at The Venetian, a lavish hotel on the strip, and my boyfriend was checking his reflection in the mirrored walls. He adjusted the utility belt on his little black shorts, then tried to pull down the cuffs before resigning himself to the fact that they weren't going to get any bigger.

"You should let me dress you more often, because wow." The Batman and Robin costumes I'd put together for us were definitely sexy. Duke wore a black cowl with a built-in mask and pointed ears, along with black gloves that nearly reached his elbows, combat boots, and a shiny black cape, in addition to the aforementioned shorts. I'd also drawn the bat symbol in a yellow oval on his bare chest with temporary tattoo pens.

"You're pretty wow yourself," he said. "I'm trying not to stare. If I get turned on, I'll immediately be arrested for indecent exposure, because these micro-shorts aren't going to keep the situation contained." My costume was composed of a black mask, yellow cape, boots, and tiny green shorts with a red waistband. An 'R' in a circle drawn on the left side of my chest completed the look. I grinned at him and playfully brushed my ass against his bare thigh just as the elevator doors slid open, and he groaned and adjusted the front of his shorts.

Like the rest of the hotel, The Venetian's grand ballroom was elegant, golden and sparkling, with giant chandeliers and ornate frescoes on the high ceilings. But it had been transformed with flashing lights, pulsating techno music, and a huge throng of costumed partygoers, who were moving to the beat like one giant, living organism. A wave of excitement surged through me as we joined hands and waded into the crowd.

*****

We'd been dancing for a couple of hours when Duke leaned in and asked, "Want to show off a little?" The crowd had stepped back to create an open circle on the otherwise packed dance floor, and couples were taking turns in the center, busting out their best moves.

I grinned and called over the music, "The answer to that is always yes."

"In that case, act three, fourteen minutes in, beginning with the lift." My grin turned into a smile, and I nodded.

As soon as a pair of dancers cleared the circle, Duke strode into the center of it and turned to face me. I ran at him, leapt high into the air and spun twice before he caught me. The crowd actually gasped. When he put me down, I danced around Duke while he pivoted with me. Our movements synched surprisingly well to the pulsating beat of the techno music.

He'd chosen one of the most intense scenes from my recent performance, one he'd rehearsed with me dozens of times, and the crowd was riveted. For the finale, I reached up and dragged my hand down the side of Duke's face, and he grabbed my arm and spun me around, tossed me into the air, and caught me a foot above the floor. We kissed as our fellow partygoers whooped and applauded, and then we got up and held hands as we took a bow.

We decided to get some air after that and left the ballroom by a side door. It was much quieter in the hallway. Duke pulled off his cowl and gloves and stuck them in a pocket hidden inside his cape, and as he ran the back of his hand over his sweaty forehead, he said, "I have to admit, I fantasized about being the person dancing with you the night of the performance. And yes, I know that's nuts, because I'm not a dancer. But being with you in the spotlight just now was really satisfying."

"It felt like you were with me onstage that night."

He kissed me and caressed my cheek. Then he smiled mischievously and said, "Let's go downstairs to the gondolas. I want to take you for a ride."

"Yes, please!" He laughed as I practically dragged him to the elevator.

I'd been looking for the right moment all day to give Duke his birthday present, and once we were seated in the long, black gondola on the indoor canal, I realized it was my perfect opportunity. As the gondolier standing at the back of the boat propelled us through the water, I slipped the gift from a hidden pocket in the waistband of my costume. Nervous energy crackled through me.

Duke was looking to his right, away from me, and taking a few deep breaths. I figured he was winded after all that dancing. As we glided past make-believe Venetian buildings under a painted sky, I took a deep breath too, picked up his hand, and said, "I want to ask you something."

When he turned to face me, I blurted, "I adore you, Duke. Whenever I think about my future, whether it's a year from now, or five, or fifty, I always see you right there, by my side. This might seem crazy since we've only been together two months, but I'm asking you to take a chance on me, and on us." I opened my hand to reveal a silver ring and asked, "Will you marry me?"

Duke stared at me for the longest moment of my life. He looked totally stunned, and I couldn't tell what he was thinking. My heart was beating so quickly that I thought I might pass out. I really hoped I didn't land in the canal water.

Finally, he blurted, "I had a whole speech prepared!" He pulled something from the little pouch on his utility belt, then held up a gorgeous silver ring, inlaid all around with a rainbow of square stones. "I can't believe you beat me to it, by about ten seconds!"

"Wait, you were going to ask me to marry you?"

"It's why I planned this entire trip, so I could get you here, in a gondola on our birthday, and propose! I even went to Oakland last week and asked for your hand in marriage. Your parents started crying, and your mom kissed my cheeks. It was so sweet. They made me promise we'd call them tonight, no matter how late it was. But then, as I was building up enough nerve to pop the question, you snuck right in there and beat me to it! You even had a ring and everything!"

Behind us, the gondolier chuckled and murmured, "That's a new one."

I burst out laughing and threw my arms around Duke's shoulders as I said, "I want to hear your speech. Tell me what you were going to say."

He hugged me tightly. "I can't remember all the words now because you totally threw me for a loop, but here's the important part: I adore you, Quinn, and I need to spend the rest of my life with you. I know we've only been together a couple of months, but I'm asking you to take a chance on me and be my husband." He leaned back to look at me and added, "I didn't copy the 'take a chance on me' part. It was in my original version."

"Yes! Of course I'll marry you, Duke!" He slipped the sparkling rainbow ring onto my finger, and I murmured, "It's beautiful."

"It made me think of you."

As I slid the carved, silver band into place on his left hand, I said, "This ring has been in my mother's family for five generations. She gave it to me last week, when I went to visit her and Dad to tell them I was going to propose."

"What day did you go see them?"

"I was there Tuesday morning. What about you?"

"Tuesday afternoon. You beat me again."

I smiled and said, "It just goes to show this was meant to be."

"It really was."

I grabbed his hands and exclaimed, "Marry me, Duke!"

That made him smile. "I figured my yes was implied in my proposal."

"I mean tonight! Let's go to the Elvis chapel at our hotel and get married while it's still our birthday."

"I'd love that," he said, "but what about your family?"

"What do you think about getting married again when we return to San Francisco? It doesn't have to be anything fancy, just a small ceremony with the people we love. I really want tonight to be fun, spontaneous, and only for us. But we can still include everyone by doing it over again once we're back home."

"That's a great idea."

"I wish I could call my mom and dad and tell them what's going on, but my phone didn't fit in my pockets."

The gondolier said, "Here, use mine," and leaned forward to hand it to me, while juggling the long pole he used to push the boat through the water.

Duke and I both thanked him, and I dialed the number. When my father answered, I blurted, "He said yes! This is Quinn, by the way. We're in a gondola, and I had to borrow a phone so I could call you right away!"

"That's fantastic!" My dad sounded emotional. "Who proposed first?"

"I did, by less than a minute. Way to keep it a secret that we were both planning the same thing!"

The call was on speaker, and my mother yelled, "We're so happy for both of you! Congratulations!"

"Thanks, Mom. And guess what? We're getting married tonight! We don't want to leave you out though, so we're going to plan a second ceremony with the whole family when we get back to San Francisco. Are you okay with that?"

My mother said, "You've always followed your heart, Quinn, and if it's telling you to get married tonight, then you go right ahead and do that with our blessing. We'll celebrate together when you get home."

"Thanks for being so understanding."

"We love you, son," my dad said. "We love you too, Duke! Welcome to the family!" Duke was smiling as he murmured a thank you.

My mother added, "Oh, and happy birthday to you both! You certainly found a fantastic way to celebrate!"

We spoke for another minute, and after we said goodbye, Duke placed a call to the Elvis chapel. The only remaining timeslot of the night was in less than half an hour, and we added our names to the list. I handed the phone and a big tip to the gondolier as he pulled up to the dock, and he said, "I see a lot of proposals at this job, and I have a good feeling about you two. Congratulations, boys!"

We thanked him and stepped off the boat. Then Duke raised my hand to show off my engagement ring and yelled to the people waiting in line, "He said yes!"

I held up his left hand and exclaimed, "He said yes, too!" Everyone cheered and applauded as Duke and I joined hands and took off running.

*****

We tumbled out of the cab at the Polynesian Princess, ran through the hotel, and arrived at the wedding chapel just as a young brunette with a bouffant hairdo and a clipboard yelled, "Blumenthal-Takahashi party, last call!"

"We're here," Duke said as we came to a stop right in front of her and gasped for breath. She was chewing gum and wore a nametag that said 'Priscilla.' That had to be a part of the Elvis theme, and I idly wondered what her real name was.

Not-Priscilla said, "Welcome! Come on inside. There are a just few formalities to get through, won't take but a minute."

Duke and I sat across from her at an ornate, gold-painted desk. We handed over a credit card and our IDs, filled out a couple of forms, and paid extra for the deluxe video and photo package, so we could share it with my family. Then she asked, "Do you have any witnesses, or any special requests?"

I glanced at Duke, who smiled at me and said, "Go ahead, put a Quinn spin on it. I wouldn't have it any other way."

I told the woman, "We'd like to get married at the base of the volcano. As for witnesses, I'll be right back." I got up and dashed from the chapel while Duke chuckled.

A group of alpaca enthusiasts were checking on their animals before bed, and I ran over to them and said, "Hi everyone. Would you and your alpacas like to be the witnesses at my wedding? I'm Quinn, and about to marry an amazing man named Duke. You'll like him."

A short woman of about sixty-five with a curly, red wig exclaimed, "We'd love to! Oscar's never been to a wedding. Hey, you know what? I think I still have his parade top hat packed, let me run and get it!"

I had no idea who Oscar was, but I said, "Great! Meet us at the volcano in five minutes!"

She called, "You got it, sonny," as she scurried to some storage boxes beneath the canopy. The rest of her friends chattered excitedly and bustled after her.

Duke and the woman with the bouffant were waiting outside when I returned to the chapel. 'Priscilla' adjusted her off-the-shoulder Hawaiian print dress as she told me, "We'll get going in just a minute. Elvis has left the building." She looked around to make sure her coworkers weren't watching and pantomimed taking a drink. Then she said, "Don't worry, he's a pro, so he'll be back. We'll meet you at Kila-fake-a. That's what I call the volcano. You know, like Kilauea, but not?" I liked her.

Duke took my hand, and he and I walked to the edge of the pool. It was vivid turquoise and lit with underwater lights, which cast interesting reflections all around us. I looked up at my fiancé and asked, "Do you want to call your parents and tell them you're getting married?"

"No. I went to see them last week, on the way back from your parents' house, and...well, let's just say it's official now. They're no longer a part of my life."

"What happened?"

Duke's voice was low and steady as he picked up my hands and ran his thumb over my rainbow ring. "I told them I was getting married and asked them to come to the wedding. They were furious. My mother said I was going to hell unless I changed my ways, and my father told me until I repented, I wasn't welcome in their home. Loving you isn't a sin. It's just not. But I know they'll never be able to overcome their bigotry, so instead of trying to argue with them, I said goodbye and left. I doubt I'll ever see them again."

"Oh God Duke, I'm so sorry."

"I'll be alright. It hurts, but it's also a relief in a way. That relationship was beyond toxic. All my parents ever did was make me feel less-than, but no more. There's just the loose end of paying back the loan, and then I'll truly be free of them." He pulled me close and said, "But this isn't the time for looking back and being sad. Just the opposite! Today is a new beginning. It's my birthday, and I'm marrying the love of my life! You make me feel like anything is possible, Quinn, and I'm so excited to begin our lives together and see what the future holds for us."

I wrapped my arms around him and asked, "Are you really okay with marrying me right now, like this? I know it all happened really fast, and it's alright to change your mind about the rushed Elvis wedding. We can go home and plan a proper ceremony if you want to. You know, the way most people do it."

He said, "You're not most people, Quinn. This is fun and unexpected, and beyond anything I could have imagined. In other words, it's exactly you, and that makes it perfect."

I pulled him down to my height and kissed him, just as the woman with the big hair called, "It's time, boys! Save the smooching for the honeymoon!"

Duke smiled at me and said, "Oh hey, the honeymoon! I hadn't thought about that."

"Do you think you're ready for the final step?"

"Oh yeah. I'd been planning on that tonight anyway. Looks like our first time will actually take place on our wedding night."

I chuckled and said, "So old-fashioned."

He leaned in and licked my earlobe, then whispered in my ear, "There's nothing old-fashioned about what I'm planning to do to you." A shiver of pleasure skittered down my spine as we went to join our makeshift wedding party.

*****

I never in a million years could have come up with anything more perfect than our wedding. Duke and I were married just before midnight on our Halloween birthday, while dressed as Batman and Robin. The ceremony took place at the base of a fake, glowing volcano, surrounded by alpacas in top hats and neckties, their enthusiasts, and a ragtag group of hotel guests. Two people were in bathing suits. A few others wore Halloween costumes. One guy was dressed like a giant lobster, which delighted me to no end.

The ceremony was short and sweet. Priscilla took pictures, and the man we'd seen earlier, who for all we knew really was Christopher Walken, filmed it with a small camcorder.

Hawaiian Elvis, with his mighty pompadour and big, gold sunglasses, asked, "Quinn, do you take this man to be your hunka hunka burnin' love, and do you promise to love him tender, for better or worse, for richer or poorer, in sickness and in health, all the days of your life?"

I squeezed Duke's hands and looked into his eyes as I said, "I absolutely do."

Elvis said, "Duke, do you take this man to be your lovin' teddy bear, and do you promise to love him tender, for better or worse, for richer or poorer, in sickness and in health, all the days of your life?"

"I do." I was overwhelmed by the love in Duke's eyes when he spoke those two little words.

"Then by the power vested in me by the great state of Nevada," Elvis swiveled his hips, swung his arm around three times, and gestured at us with both hands, "I pronounce you married. Go on now and kiss your husband."

Elvis broke into a fantastic rendition of 'Can't Help Falling in Love' as Duke picked me up and kissed me. One of the alpacas sneezed, and our audience applauded as cameras flashed around us. Afterwards, a lot of people shook our hands and congratulated us, and then we signed the marriage certificate. It was witnessed by the assistant with the bouffant, whose name turned out to actually be Priscilla, and the woman in the red wig, who signed her name 'Glenda Farbernugen and Oscar the Amazing Alpaca'. I couldn't have been happier.

Finally, Priscilla said, "Mazel tov, boys! I'll be assembling your photos, wedding video, and documents in a keepsake box. You can pick it up anytime tomorrow, since I know y'all are going to be busy tonight."

Duke grinned and murmured, "Definitely."

He took my hand, and as we headed to the side entrance of the hotel, I smiled at him and exclaimed, "We just got married!"

"We did!"

"That means we're now…wait, what are we going to call ourselves? Duke and Quinn Blumenthal-Takahashi?"

He thought about that, then said, "If you're okay with it, I'd like to take your last name. Seems fitting, to go with my new family and the whole new life you and I will be building together."

"That'd be amazing! Duke Takahashi. You sound like a movie star!"

He chuckled and held the door for me. "I don't know about that, but it does have a nice ring to it."

As we started down the long, quiet corridor that led to the lobby, I changed the subject with, "Since we're headed to our hotel room to begin our honeymoon, maybe this is a good time to mention that I brought along condoms, and if you want to use them, I won't be offended or anything."

He stopped walking and turned to me with a puzzled expression. "Why would we do that? We both got tested a few weeks ago, and we know we're going to be monogamous, so there's nothing to worry about."

I'd used condoms without fail in the past and got tested regularly. The results had always been negative, including my most recent screening, and Duke had gotten tested with me to show his support. There was no reason for concern, but I still found myself saying, "It just, you know…might give you peace of mind."

"Where's this coming from?"

I shrugged and murmured, "I don't know."

"Yes, you do."

I studied the peach-colored tile floor, and after a moment I said, "I just thought the idea of fucking someone with my track record might make you a little uncomfortable. Maybe that's part of the reason why you put this off as long as you did. I mean, we said we loved each other weeks ago, and you still didn't fuck me. If you're nervous about doing this without protection, that's totally understandable. I don't want you to feel like you can't bring up the idea of using a rubber, just because my STD test came back negative."

Duke's voice was gentle when he said, "Look at me, Quinn." I glanced at him from beneath my lashes, and he cupped my cheek in his big hand. "The reason I've waited this long is because I wanted our first time to be special. I'd been planning this trip since the beginning of October, and I latched on to the idea that this would be when it happened. And then, I have to admit, I freaked myself out a little, because I started building it up so much in my mind. I began overthinking where we'd be when it happened, what the hotel room would be like, what I'd say and do. I have a problem with feeling like everything always has to be perfect. I'm sure you know that, given how rigid I was when you first moved in. But I'm trying to change, and I spent the last couple of weeks working on letting go of those expectations and trying to take some of the pressure off."

I asked, "So, how are you, now that it's about to happen?"

"A lot less nervous than I thought I'd be. That 1970s porn palace of a hotel room threw me for a loop, but you know what? It's actually good that it ended up being so different than what I'd imagined. It helped me let go of the last of my preconceived notions about what our first time is supposed to be like."

"That's great."

"It is, and I know I have nothing to worry about. I trust you, and you accept me as I am, so there's no pressure to try to act suave, or cool, or manly, or whatever. I can just let go and have fun." I smiled at him, and he added, "Now, as far as the condom question, we're monogamous and we've been tested, so we don't need them and I'm not worried."

"Okay."

He rested his hands on my shoulders and added, "I want you to know I don't care that you have a past, Quinn. So I'm not the first guy you slept with. So what? I'm the last, and that's all that matters."

I said, "I like that perspective."

Duke pivoted me so my back was to the wall and ran his hands down my arms as he said, "Any other comments or concerns? Speak now or forever hold your peace. Hey, you know what? Our wedding ceremony didn't include that part."

"Who was going to object, one of the alpacas?"

"Possibly. I felt like Oscar was judging me."

"He did seem a bit judgmental," I said. "It was probably the top hat. It made him think he was better than everyone else."

"Nothing worse than an alpaca with attitude." He looked in my eyes and lowered his voice. "That was a serious question, though. Are you worried about anything else, and if so, should we talk about it before I take you upstairs and fuck you?"

I grinned and said, "I've never heard you say fuck before."

Duke surprised me by running his hands down my chest, then pinching my nipples and rolling them between his fingers. I drew in my breath and looked around, even though I knew we were alone in the long hallway, and he leaned against me and said, "That word is overused. It should be reserved for what I'm about to do to you." I shivered with pleasure, and he pushed his leg between mine and rubbed his thigh against my swelling cock.

"Not that I'm complaining," I murmured, "but we have to make it all the way up to the tenth floor, and as you pointed out earlier, these shorts don't hide much."

"You're too sexy to resist," he said, "and I've been wanting to play with your nipples all night. I've seen you shirtless many times, but never without those little silver studs. It's surprisingly erotic, kind of like I'm seeing you naked for the first time."

"Is it?" He nodded, and then he shifted his gaze to my chest and circled both nipples with his thumbs. As he grew bolder, I started to feel shy, almost as if the universe was trying to maintain our usual equilibrium. I stammered, "It's just, you know, the nipple rings didn't go with the Robin costume, so I...oh God." Duke ran his tongue down my chest and sucked on my left nipple, and my cock jumped as a jolt of electricity shot directly to my balls. "We should wait until we get to our hotel room," I murmured, even as I rubbed my cock against his thigh. "What if we get in trouble?"

He kissed his way back up to my neck, then said, in between nibbling on my earlobe, "I'm pretty sure we're not the first couple to make out in public in Las Vegas."

"True." It was becoming tough to focus as lust clouded my thoughts, and I whispered, "Why do I feel like it's my first time?"

"Well, it's *our* first time, so...."

"Only technically. Even if you've never fucked me, we've done plenty of other stuff." I moaned quietly as he grazed the tip of my cock through my clothes. When he licked my neck, pleasure radiated through me and I murmured, "How are you so good at this?"

His breath was warm on my ear as he cupped my ass and told me, "There are advantages to taking it slowly. It's almost as if we've spent two months on foreplay, so I've had time to memorize your body. That's how I know this makes you weak in the knees." He licked my nipple and blew on it, and the surprisingly intense sensation really did made my legs shake.

I slid my hands down his back and told him, "We have to go upstairs, because I need you in me more than I've ever needed anything in my life."

He glanced to his left, then said, "In a minute. We're about to have company."

Duke braced his hands on the wall and leaned against me to hide our erections as a couple came in from the pool area. They were all over each other. The guy's shirt was totally unbuttoned, and the woman gripped her high heels with one hand and her boyfriend's ass with the other. When they passed us, they stopped kissing long enough for the guy to acknowledge us with a quick bro nod. Once they disappeared into the lobby at the far end of the hallway, Duke ground his cock against mine and said, "See? It's Vegas. Nobody cares what we do."

I flashed him a big smile as I slid my hands down to his ass. "And here I thought I'd married such a nice, quiet boy."

"Oh, I'm very nice. But I'm not planning to be quiet tonight." He tossed me over his shoulder, and I burst out laughing.

Duke carried me down the hall, but instead of cutting through the lobby, he ducked into the empty stairwell. I made him put me down, because I really didn't want to tire him out before we got to our room. We jogged upstairs, pausing on every second or third landing to make out wildly. When we reached the tenth floor, we caught our breath, and as Duke kissed me, I slipped my hand into his shorts and massaged his thick cock while he kneaded my ass. Both of us were shaking with desire.

We burst out of the stairwell and rushed to our room. He pulled the key from one of the little pouches on his utility belt and jammed it into the lock, and then we tumbled inside, kissing feverishly. As the door swung shut behind us, I dropped to my knees, totally consumed by lust, and pulled down the front of Duke's shorts. I sucked his cock as I pushed my shorts to mid-thigh and jerked myself off, and after a few minutes I gripped his shaft and looked up at him as I rasped, "I need you in me."

Duke scooped me into his arms and took me with him when he hurried to the bathroom to find the lube. He put me down in the center of the long vanity before rifling through my toiletry case. Meanwhile, I tossed my shorts aside, slid my ass to the edge of the counter and leaned back against the mirror. When he raised the bottle triumphantly, I smiled at him and swung one leg up and over his head, then planted my boots on the lip of each of the sinks, so far apart that I was almost doing the splits.

He grinned and said, "What an awesome bonus to have a husband who's that flexible."

"Husband," I repeated as he tore the seal off the new container of lube. "That has such a nice ring to it."

"Doesn't it, though?" Duke dumped way too much lube into his palm and said, "Woops." He shook some of the excess into the sink, set the bottle aside, and pushed two very well-lubed fingers inside me, which made me moan and arch my back. While he worked the lube into my hole, he pushed his shorts down with his other hand and stepped out of them, leaving both of us in only a cape and boots.

I retrieved the lube, squirted some into my hand, and jerked him off as I rode his fingers. After a while I asked, around my labored breathing, "Where do you want to do it? Here? The bed? The balcony?"

"All of the above over the next few hours, but let's start with right here, right now." He slid his fingers from me and wiped his hand on a towel before grasping his cock and pointing it at my hole. When he leaned forward, the tip pressed against my opening. I bore down to open myself up for him, and the pressure increased. For a moment, it seemed like he wasn't going to fit. But then my body yielded just enough, and the tip slid into me.

Duke eased his length into me as our eyes met. He murmured, "You feel amazing," and then he rocked his hips a little, sliding his cock in and out of me. It was a tight fit because he was so thick, and I exhaled slowly and bore down again. He kept going until he bottomed out in me, and I shifted my hips a little, getting used to the way he filled me up.

He kissed me as he grasped my butt. When he began thrusting into me, I moaned against his lips and started moving with him, and he took me harder. I threw my arms around his neck, bracing myself against the edge of both sinks with my feet, and rode his cock as he fucked me. Wave after wave of pleasure radiated through me, and my cock throbbed as it rubbed against his stomach.

When Duke reached between us and started jerking me off, I knew I wouldn't last long. In just a couple of minutes, I cried out and started to cum as I clutched his big, powerful body. A tremor went through me, and I drove myself onto him as his hips slammed against my ass. He came in me moments later, with a primal, almost animalistic growl. It was the sexiest thing I'd ever heard.

When it was all over, we fell against each other, gasping for air, and Duke murmured, "Wow." I grinned and wrapped my arms and legs around him, holding on tight as my heartbeat gradually returned to normal. When he caught his breath, Duke said, "You know, I'd been thinking about our first time for weeks and trying to picture what it would be like. Never once did I imagine we'd both be wearing capes."

I burst out laughing, and Duke chuckled, then carefully eased his cock from my body. As he washed up, I untied my boots and let them fall to the floor, followed by my socks. I hopped off the counter and looked at myself in the mirror while I cleaned up at the other sink, and I asked him, "Whatever happened to my mask?"

He grinned at my reflection and said, "You took it off in the cab on the way back to the hotel. That was the last I saw of it."

"Was I wearing it when we proposed to each other?"

"Yup. It was very cute." He dried his hands and checked the pocket on the inside of his cape, but he produced only a single glove. "I guess my cowl got lost too, maybe when we were running to our wedding. Oh well." Duke untied his laces and deposited his boots and socks on the bathroom floor. Like me, he kept wearing the cape.

When I finished cleaning up, I turned to him and asked, "Do you want to go out? I'm sure Vegas will keep partying until dawn, and there's still a lot to see."

"Actually, for the remainder of this trip, all I really want to see is the inside of this hotel room." He flashed me a mischievous smile.

I smiled too and said, "In that case, onward, caped crusader, to the porn bed! I'll race you."

We both ran across the suite. Duke took a flying leap at the bed a moment before I did, and we both went sliding across those slick, satin sheets. He landed on the floor with a yelp, and I landed on top of him. We both looked startled for a moment, and then we howled with laughter.

Duke tossed me onto the bed, and then he crawled up beside me and kissed me tenderly before saying, "What an epic birthday."

I laced my fingers with his and slid close to him. "It really was."

He said, "We should return to Las Vegas every Halloween and renew our wedding vows in different costumes."

"We totally have to do that!"

"Maybe next time, we can dress as Captain America and Bucky," he said. "Or anything, really. I'd marry you dressed as a ham sandwich, or a giant bottle of lube. I don't care, as long as I get to say I do over and over again. In fact, I'd marry you a thousand times if I could, because that's how much I love you."

"I feel exactly the same way."

We settled in face-to-face, sharing the same pillow, and he said, "I'm totally serious about this. I want us to be standing in front of that fake volcano when we're in our nineties, getting married yet again while dressed like shriveled-up superheroes with walkers."

I kissed him and said, "Then that's what we'll do." His smile was glorious.

Epilogue

Two months later

Sawyer MacNeil's new coffee house was a thing of beauty, especially with its sparkling holiday decorations. An elegant Christmas tree with a thousand white lights cast reflections onto the highly polished wood floor, and the warm brick walls and brass fixtures made the reclaimed warehouse seem warm and cozy on that chilly December morning. Most of the tables were full, and I smiled and nodded to Sawyer and his partner Alastair, who sat side-by-side with twin laptops in their booth at the back of the large café. I got a matched set of smiles and waves in return.

I stepped around the long line of customers and put the box I was carrying behind the counter. The assistant manager greeted me with, "Hey Quinn, you're just in time. We're down to our last rainbow, and the holiday cookies totally sold out."

Since he and the five baristas were busy, I offered to fill the case for him and exchanged my wool gloves for plastic ones. I took a moment to admire the oval label on the box, which read, 'Duke & Quinn Takahashi' above the line 'Artistic Edibles, San Francisco, California'. The clean, modern font was colored in a rainbow, the red letters on the far left blending into orange, then yellow, and so on across a white background.

I slid open the door to the huge bakery case and restocked the top shelf with sugar cookies, which sparkled under the bright lights shining down from the top of the cabinet. In addition to our usual bestsellers, the cheerful rainbows, we'd also been making Christmas trees, menorahs, presents, and dragons wearing Santa hats for the holiday season, all perfectly iced and lightly dusted in translucent edible glitter. As soon as I put them out, the customers in line began ordering them, which made me smile.

Duke still worked as a police officer, but he'd recently been able to cut back to just a four-day work week. Not only was our cookie company beginning to take off, but our mortgage was far more affordable now that Xavier owned half the duplex. That took a lot of the financial pressure off and allowed my husband to pursue his passion, instead of worrying about making ends meet.

The cookie business's overnight success was thanks in large part to Sawyer. From the moment his newest coffee house opened in a prime location near the Castro, he'd prominently featured our products. That in turn brought in even more business, since he and his crew were always quick to hand out our business card whenever a customer raved about our cookies. Plus, he was in the process of renovating three more buildings around the city and had already contracted with us to provide baked goods for all of those locations once they opened.

Life was hectic with both Duke and me working two jobs, but it was invigorating, too. We'd been sharing an industrial kitchen with our friends Cole and River and spent most evenings there, baking around their catering schedule to fill the next day's orders. The timeshare had been a great way to start out, but we were looking into renting our own kitchen, and that was going to help normalize our hours.

I'd quit my job as a go-go boy, since I was so busy with the dance troupe and the cookie company. Dare to Dance had six shows coming up over the next twelve months. Our first show had been a critically-acclaimed smash hit, so we'd signed a contract with the theater we'd used for our first performance and set up a website with subscriptions and advance ticket sales. That meant we all had a little money coming in, and it was wonderful to see Dare, Haley and the rest of the guys so happy.

Once the case was filled, I switched out my gloves again and carried a small, pink box back to Sawyer and Alastair. Both men were wearing elegant cashmere sweaters, and since one of Sawyer's long legs was sticking out from under the table, I noticed he'd paired his with a miniskirt, tights, and sexy thigh-high boots, all in black. I loved the way he totally owned his personal style. "Hey," I said as I handed Sawyer the box. "I brought you a batch of Florentine cookies. Duke's been baking them by the hundreds, and he thinks he's close to perfecting the recipe."

Sawyer said, "Thanks for these, and for coming back with a second batch of sugar cookies to get us through to closing. They sold out in record time today."

"Which is awesome," I said.

"It is! Can you stay and have a cup of coffee with us?"

"I wish I could, but I have an appointment in a few minutes. Next time for sure. How late is the coffee house staying open tonight?"

"Just until two, so our employees can get home in time for Christmas Eve dinner with their families." Sawyer pulled a thin, lacy cookie from the box and took a bite, then exclaimed, "That's delicious! Tell Duke it's perfect and to stop tinkering with it. You're going to start selling these to me, right? They'd go so well with a latte."

I grinned and said, "I'll add it to your wish list for our expanded product line. I'd better get going. Merry Christmas, you two! I'll see you at Nana's party tomorrow."

From there, I drove Duke's truck a few blocks to Yoshi's tattoo studio. Duke, Max and Yoshi were all waiting for me in the lobby, and Max said, "You're really gonna do it this time, right?"

"That's the plan."

Duke took my hand and we went back to Yoshi's station, where a woman named Kes with long, black hair, a beautiful, deep skin tone, and some fierce tattoos was setting up her traditional, Samoan instruments. They were basically a series of tiny metal combs of various widths on long, wooden handles. I'd met with her ahead of time and she knew exactly what I wanted. Now it was just a question of making it through the procedure.

I stripped off my gloves, T-shirt, and awesome tacky Christmas sweater with a light-up tree on the front, then settled in on the black leather chaise. As Yoshi prepped my skin, he said, "There's no shame in tapping out if you need to, Quinn. This is definitely going to hurt, and like I mentioned before, the ribs are one of the most sensitive areas on the body."

"I know. I really want this tattoo, and I now have the added motivation of covering the finely rendered dick you drew on me."

I smiled at him, and Yoshi grinned and said, "You drew that on yourself, Jumping Jack Flash. If you decide to leap up this time, give Kes at least a second's notice, okay?"

"Definitely."

Yoshi and Kes switched places, while Duke sat down on my right and took my hand. Max asked me, "Are you disappointed that you won't be getting Totoro, like you originally wanted?"

"Not at all. The design Kes and I came up with is gorgeous," I said. "Plus, Totoro's services are no longer required. I wanted that tattoo so he'd always be with me. But now, I have my gorgeous husband by my side, so I never have to worry about being alone."

Duke asked, "Is that really why you wanted the tattoo?" When I nodded, he said softly, "I promise I'll always be right here, Quinn."

I smiled at him and said, "I know."

"I'm ready to get started if you are. Remember what we talked about," Kes said. "It's going to hurt, and it's going to bleed. Maybe don't watch if you think the sight of blood will bother you." Max sat down beside her and pulled on a pair of gloves. He was there not only to observe the procedure, but to help Kes by stretching my skin taught while she worked and by wiping away the blood and excess ink.

"Yeah, I'm definitely not watching." I focused on Duke as I told Kes, "Go ahead and do it. I'm as ready as I'll ever be."

Max put both hands on my ribcage, stretching and framing the spot where the tattoo would go. I braced myself as Kes pressed an ink-laden tool to my body and struck it with a second implement, which pushed the black pigment into my skin. The sharp poke definitely didn't feel great, but it didn't trigger any bad memories, either. I knew right away that I could do this.

It took her about two hours to apply the four-inch tattoo. I kept my eyes on Duke. Max helped pass the time by chattering animatedly about all he'd learned in the last month as Yoshi's apprentice.

Finally, Kes sat back and said, "I'm done. Take a look."

I glanced at the gorgeous design on my ribcage, and a huge smile spread across my face. The letters D and Q were integrated into a geometric pattern that formed a beautiful, artistic heart. It was even better than I'd envisioned it.

Kes covered it in plastic and repeated the care instructions she'd mentioned during our consultation. I thanked her and got dressed, and as I settled my bill, I asked Max, "You're coming to dinner tonight, right?"

"Of course! Your dad's been cooking for two days, and it's going to be a feast! I don't even think it's all healthy this time. Although it's good that you and Duke are bringing dessert, so at least I can gorge on that if it does turn out to be a health food extravaganza." He turned to Yoshi and said, "I meant to ask earlier if you have plans for Christmas Eve. If you don't, you're welcome to join my family and me." Then he told Kes, "You too, ma'am."

She peeled off her black latex gloves and said, "Thanks for the offer, but my husband and I are expected at my in-laws' tonight. That pretty much blows, but it's the holidays, so what're you going to do?"

Yoshi stretched his back as he said, "Thanks for asking, but I have plans, too. I'm having dinner with my friend Mike and his boys. After the kids go to bed, I'm supposed to help him play Santa and put together this elaborate train set. He went completely overboard. It's so big that it laps his entire living room, which is so decked out for the holidays that it looks like the set of ten Christmas movies rolled into one."

Duke said, "He sounds like a great dad."

Yoshi smiled sweetly. "He really is."

I asked, "Do you want a ride back to Oakland, Max? We're heading over early to help Dad cook."

"Thanks," he said, "but I need to hit a few shops before I head home."

"Please tell me you're not planning to do all your Christmas shopping in a single afternoon."

He grinned at me and said, "Of course I am, dude. Why break with tradition?" Some things never changed.

After we all said our goodbyes, Duke and I headed to his truck, and he asked, "Are you in a lot of pain? I was surprised by how much that bled."

"It's definitely sore, but nothing major."

"Are you happy you got it done?"

"I really am, not just because the tattoo is amazing. It was important to me, because I didn't want to let fear keep me from something I really wanted." I thought about that and added, "I guess I didn't really face my fear, because I got it done a different way, but it still feels like an accomplishment."

Duke turned to me when we reached the truck and said, "You not only faced your fear, you climbed over it, and then you found a new path forward. I think that tattoo is a total victory. Oh, and by the way, it looks incredibly sexy."

"You think so?"

"Oh yeah. Believe it or not, I'm actually considering getting some ink myself now."

"You should totally do it! What would you get?"

"Something super manly, obviously. Right here." He made a fist and curled his arm up across his chest, then slapped his huge bicep, which strained the sleeve of his dark blue sweater. "I'm thinking a gingerbread man would be good, or a unicorn sugar cookie flying over a rainbow made of sprinkles."

I flashed him a huge smile and said, "I know you're kidding, but that would be epic."

"Yeah, I really wouldn't go with that, but I'm serious about getting a tattoo. I'd probably do something old-school, like a simple red heart with D+Q inside it. In other words, my own version of your tattoo."

"That would be amazing." I unlocked the sleek, white camper shell, which we'd added to the back of Duke's truck so we could use it for deliveries, and double-checked to make sure I'd packed all six dessert boxes we were taking to my parents' house. Once I locked it again, I stepped onto the curb to make myself taller, draped my arms around Duke's shoulders, and gave him a kiss. Then I said, "Have I mentioned how excited I am that we're spending our first Christmas together?"

My husband grinned at me. "Yes. Probably six hundred times this week, as a matter of fact, but I never get tired of your enthusiasm."

"Well, that's a good thing, because," I broke into song and flung my arms wide, "it's the most won-der-ful time of the year!" I'd been serenading him with loud, tone-deaf Christmas carols all month.

Duke shook his head, but he was smiling as he pulled me into his arms. Then he asked, "Do you think your friend's still planning to join us? He was supposed to meet us at the tattoo studio fifteen minutes ago."

I said. "I'm sure he'll be here. He's probably just running late."

Sure enough, Sergei jogged up to us two minutes later and said, "Sorry to keep you waiting. I stopped off to get some wine, and the shop was overrun with last-minute holiday shoppers. I didn't know if Doctor Takahashi likes red or white, so I got both."

"Both is always the right answer," I said.

He swung his backpack off his shoulder and adjusted the collar of his black leather jacket as he asked, "Are you sure I'm not intruding? Christmas Eve is a time for family…."

"Dad is super excited that you're joining us. So am I." Sergei and I had become good friends over the past few months. He and Even Eide were still seeing each other off and on, but the former hockey player had gone home to Norway for Christmas, and Sergei's family had moved back to the Ukraine a few years ago, so I'd asked him to have dinner with us. I thought he was secretly happy about the invitation, even though he wasn't really the type of person to let it show.

Sergei mumbled, "Yeah, okay," and we all piled into the truck.

As my husband pulled away from the curb, I exclaimed, "Let's sing Jingle Bells to pass the time on our drive!" Sergei groaned and Duke chuckled as I started belting out the first verse.

*****

After a huge, delicious meal and a great visit with our family, we dropped Sergei off at his apartment and drove to Duke's church. I'd been accompanying him every Sunday for the last few weeks, ever since we held our second wedding ceremony there for our family and friends. I'd been doing a lot of soul-searching and didn't really know if I believed the way my husband did, but I still enjoyed the comfort and the ritual of going to church, and I really liked the young, friendly pastor and the welcoming congregation. Most of all, I loved sharing that time with Duke, since it was an important part of his life.

The Christmas Eve service was fantastic. The church was lit by candlelight, and the choir wore white robes with gold trim and sang beautifully. The sermon was about the importance of treating everyone with kindness, and how we should all make that a goal in the coming year. I could totally get behind that message.

We had one final stop that night. It was close to midnight when we parked in the alley behind Rainbow Roost. Duke and I unloaded three big boxes of muffins, cinnamon rolls and pastries, which we'd baked for the residents' Christmas breakfast, and lugged them to the back door.

Sixteen young people from eighteen to twenty-four called the transition shelter home. They'd either been homeless or had aged out of foster care, and all of them landed somewhere on the LGBTQ+ rainbow. Duke and I volunteered there every week and conducted baking classes for anyone who was interested. We also regularly brought over baked goods, which was as fun for us as it was for the residents.

Darwin answered our knock, and he looked delighted when he saw what we were carrying. As he held the door open for us, I said, "You're here late."

"I know. The counselors already went to bed, and Nana left an hour ago, but I just wanted to do a final check to make sure everything's perfect for tomorrow."

"You're amazing," I told him as we put the boxes on the buffet table that would be brimming with food in the morning. "You've done so much to make the holidays special for the residents." The ground floor featured both a big, brightly lit Christmas tree with a mountain of presents and an elegant menorah. The entire room was ringed in lights, decorations, and tinsel, and sixteen full stockings hung from a clothesline near the brass fire poles.

"I've tried my best," he said as he pushed back the sleeves of his form-fitting red sweater. I loved the fact that he no longer hid in dark, baggy clothes. "Some of these guys have never had a real Christmas or Hanukkah, and I really wanted them to get to experience that."

Duke said, "Well, it looks like you're ready."

"I think so. I just finished wrapping a few last-minute presents." Darwin turned and assessed the room. "The stockings are stuffed, the refrigerator is full of food for Christmas brunch, and everyone's asleep but me. I guess that's it."

I asked, "Do you want a ride home?"

"No thanks. I set up a cot in the counselors' quarters, and I'm planning to spend the night. I want to get up before the residents, so the buffet will be ready when everyone comes downstairs."

"Want us to come back in the morning to help?"

"Between the two counselors and me, I think we've got this," he said, "but thank you for the offer."

After we said goodnight and Darwin locked up behind us, Duke pulled me into his arms and whispered, "Do you hear that?"

"Hear what?" We were bathed in light from the fixture over the back door, and I looked around the dark, quiet alley.

"Nothing. It's perfectly still. That's so rare in this city."

I smiled and said, "You're right. Normally, I'd burst into a heartwarming rendition of Silent Night, but then it wouldn't be silent anymore, so I'll save it for later."

I was startled when a small voice in the darkness asked, "Do you work at the shelter?"

A tiny blond boy stepped out of the shadows, dressed in a filthy ski jacket and jeans with a backpack slung over his shoulder. I said, "We're volunteers. Can we help you?"

"I need a place to stay," he said. "I went to six other shelters like this one, but they were either full or just for grownups. This is the last one on my list."

Duke crouched down so he was at eye level with the kid and said, "I'm Duke, and this is my husband Quinn. What's your name?"

"Aiden."

"Can I ask how old you are, Aiden?"

"I'm twelve. People never believe me, because I'm so small. I hate being the shortest kid in my class."

Duke asked, "Do you have a family, or someone we can call for you?"

The boy shook his head. "My parents kicked me out, so I came to San Francisco. I'd heard all these great things about it. It's different than I thought it'd be, though."

Since he'd come to an LGBT shelter, I asked gently, "Did they kick you out because they found out you were gay?"

The boy looked at the ground and muttered, "I never should've told them."

"I'm sorry to say this shelter is full, and it also only accepts kids who are at least eighteen, so this wouldn't be the right place for you," Duke said. "But I'm a police officer, and I can call a friend of mine who works in social services. She'll find you a bed for tonight and something long-term after that."

"You're talking about foster care, right?" When Duke nodded, Aiden said, "No way. The first thing they'll do is separate me and Mrs. Nesbitt."

Duke asked, "Is that a friend of yours?"

The kid took a step back. "She's my pet, and I'm not giving her up for anything. I'd rather sleep on the street than lose my best friend."

He looked like he was about to bolt, so I said, "Hang on. We don't have to call Duke's friend if you don't want to. I know a place where you and your pet would both be welcome." Duke glanced at me, and I told my husband, "It's Christmas, and we have a spare room...."

He smiled at me before turning back to Aiden and saying, "If you want to, you and Mrs. Nesbitt can come and stay with us."

The boy narrowed his blue eyes and said, "Show me your badge, so I know you're a real cop and not some scuzzball kidnapper." I grinned at that, and Duke pulled his identification from his back pocket and held it up so Aiden could read it. The kid said, "Okay, that looks legit. I guess I'll go with you. But you have to swear to me that you're not going to change your mind about Mrs. Nesbitt, no matter what. If you kick her out, I'm gone too! And don't even think about getting rid of her when my back is turned and then claiming she ran away, because I know how you grownups operate!"

Oh man, I loved that kid. I held up my right hand and drew a big 'X' over my chest as I told him, "We promise we won't get rid of your pet, cross my heart. I love her name, by the way. That's one of my favorite scenes in Toy Story."

He studied me for a moment, then said, "Most people don't get it. They ask me why I gave her an old lady name, and then I'm like, duh! I guess I'll go get her and we'll come home with you for tonight. I know I'm not supposed to get in a car with strangers, by the way. I'm not stupid. But the big guy really does look like a cop, and I literally can't picture you as a kidnapper. Especially not in that sweater."

"It's great, right? The tree lights up, but I turned it off because the blinking lights were making me dizzy."

"It's super ugly, but that makes it kind of awesome," he said. "I'll be right back. I tied Mrs. Nesbitt's leash to a pole at the end of the alley. I was going to sneak her into the shelter after everyone went to bed."

As soon as Aiden walked away, I turned to Duke and said, "It's a Christmas miracle! That boy found us on Christmas Eve, because there was no room at the inn!" I gestured at the shelter and Duke got up and grinned at me. "We talked about adopting a kid someday, and I think he just walked into our lives."

Duke rested his hands on my shoulders and said gently, "I love your enthusiasm, but you're getting ahead of yourself. We don't know his whole story. Maybe he has relatives somewhere who'd be willing to take him in. Or maybe he's scamming us. We might wake up in the morning to find him gone, along with all our valuables."

"What valuables?"

"Your macaroni Elvis."

"Funny."

"You know what I mean, though. There's no saying this will work out."

"I know, but I just have this overwhelming feeling that Aiden was meant to find us tonight."

"If you're right, then I'm totally open to the idea of adoption. We knew we wanted that to happen someday. But let's just take this slowly and see what happens. I'd hate it if you ended up disappointed."

Aiden came walking down the dark alley with his black and white dog behind him on a long leash, and he called, "I could hear every word you said. Sound totally carries in this alley. The rest of my relatives are even worse than my rotten parents, so there's no way I'd agree to live with any of them, not that they'd want me anyway. And it's sweet that you guys want to be my dads, but I need to check out your qualifications and think about it before I decide anything. Just so you know though, I'm not going to rip you off, and I have no idea what a macaroni Elvis is, but I hope you can eat it because I'm really hungry." He came to a stop a few feet from us and wiped his nose with the back of his hand.

"Well then, let's get you and Mrs. Nesbitt home and make you both some dinner," I said.

Duke unlocked the truck and got behind the wheel, and I slid in right beside him to make room for Aiden. The kid picked up his pet and climbed in after us, and I got my first good look at Mrs. Nesbitt and exclaimed, "She's so cute!"

She also wasn't a dog. Duke's eyes went wide, and he stammered, "Um, you should put that outside, Aiden."

The kid stroked her white back and scowled at him. "You said she could stay!"

Duke exclaimed, "But that's a skunk!"

"I know that, but you promised!"

"It might have rabies, Aiden. You need to put it down."

The boy looked like he was about to cry. "She doesn't have rabies! I bought her from a breeder in Oregon, and I bottle raised her since she was a baby. She's had her shots, and she's been to the vet a bunch of times for checkups, and she's perfectly healthy. I know having skunks as pets is illegal in California, but that's a dumb rule, especially because they're legal where I used to live. And I told you we're a package deal, so if you don't want her, then you don't want me either!"

Aiden started to get out of the truck, but Duke said, "Wait." The kid looked at him over his shoulder, and my husband asked, "Is she de-scented?"

"Of course! You think I'd be carrying around a fully loaded skunk?"

Duke sighed and said, "Fine. Bring the skunk. After Christmas though, we're going to have to find an underground vet who won't report us, so we can get her a checkup and make sure she's current on all her shots. That's the responsible thing to do, as illegal pet owners."

I smiled at my husband and whispered, "I absolutely adore you."

*****

When we got home, we found Xavier outside in a ski jacket and pajama pants, wrestling with a light-up snowman. After buying his half of the building, he really took his new role as a homeowner to heart, especially when it came to holiday decorating. The three of us had gone a bit crazy, and the duplex was festooned top to bottom in a dazzling array of colored lights, while the tiny yard was crammed full of whimsical, light-up figures.

But the wire-framed snowman kept falling over and breaking into three pieces, despite our best efforts to secure it. Duke pulled into the garage, and when we went out into the driveway, he called, "Haven't you learned, Xavier? The snowman will always win!"

Our neighbor pushed his long, blond hair out of his face and said, "I refuse to accept that. He's going to stand here and be merry, whether he likes it or not!" He turned to look at us and asked, "Who's your friend, and is he holding a skunk?"

Duke pushed the button on his keychain remote. As the garage door rattled shut, he headed for the front steps and said, "That's Aiden. He's going to be staying here, hopefully for a long time. And of course that's not a skunk! They're illegal, and I'm an officer of the law! Now go about your business, citizen. And also, give up on that cheap snowman already and stuff his lopsided butt in the garbage can!"

"Never!"

When we went inside, Aiden looked around appraisingly, and I did, too. The Christmas tree was decked out with a truly insane number of lights and ornaments, and the new medium-blue wall color (halfway between the dark color I wanted and the pale color Duke wanted) looked so pretty with the super comfy blue couch and matching chairs I'd found at a yard sale. But my favorite thing in the room was the cluster of framed wedding pictures on the mantel. Three were from our Vegas wedding. The rest had been taken at our second ceremony and the big party afterwards at my parents' house. The best one was a shot of Duke and me totally surrounded by the people we loved.

Aiden murmured, "This place is nice." Then he turned to me and asked, "Is it okay if I take a shower? I just spent the last seven weeks sleeping in abandoned buildings with no running water, and I'm pretty much grossing myself out."

"Of course. Go upstairs to the bedroom at the end of the hall," I said. "It used to be mine, but I sleep downstairs with Duke now, so it's yours for as long as you want it. There are clean towels in the bathroom, and you can help yourself to anything you want in the closet. It's all going to be too big, but when the stores open after Christmas, we can go buy you some new stuff."

"Thanks, that's nice of you." He hesitated before asking, "Will you take care of Mrs. Nesbitt while I'm in the shower?" I thought that showed a lot of trust.

Duke said, "Absolutely. She can hang out with Quinn and me in the kitchen while we make you both some dinner. What does she eat?"

"Pretty much anything, but apples are her favorite."

Aiden handed her to me and climbed the stairs, and I scratched the top of Mrs. Nesbitt's head as Duke and I went to the kitchen. The skunk and I had bonded on the ride home, but Duke was still eyeing her suspiciously. I figured he'd warm up to her in time, though.

While my husband heated up some leftover lasagna and assembled a plate of cookies for Aiden, I took off Mrs. Nesbitt's pink leash and put her down so she could explore her new environment. I filled a bowl with water, and when I sliced an apple for her and put it on a little plate on the floor, and she came right over and started packing it away. The skunk seemed very well-behaved, and she was spotlessly clean. It looked like Aiden had taken wonderful care of her, even when he could barely take care of himself.

I returned to the living room and took off my shoes and sweater, while Duke plated the dinner and put a ceramic bowl over it to keep it warm. As I hiked up the hem of my T-shirt and checked my new tattoo, the water shut off upstairs. After a minute, the floor creaked as Aiden headed for the closet. I wondered what he'd make of my offbeat wardrobe.

A moment later, there was a thud in the kitchen, followed by a yelp. It took only a moment for the overpowering odor of skunk to reach me. I pinched my nose shut, ran into the kitchen, and yelled, "What happened?"

"The skunk's fully loaded, that's what happened!" Duke had taken a direct hit of skunk spray, and his hands where clamped over his nose and mouth. "I tripped over the water bowl, and I guess I startled her. This is the worst smell ever!"

My eyes were burning. I ran to the back door and opened it, and Mrs. Nesbitt cheerfully padded out into the backyard. How could anything smell that bad? I flipped on the kitchen fan and grabbed a big garbage bag as I yelled, "Strip off everything including your shoes, and put it in here! I'll take it out to the trash. Then you need to head straight for the shower!" I didn't know why I was yelling.

Duke emptied his pockets as fast as he could and stripped down to just his briefs. He kept trying to hold his breath, but that only lasted so long. The stench was overpowering, and so strong I could taste it.

Aiden appeared in the kitchen doorway a moment later. He was pinching his nose with one hand and fanning the air with the other. His shaggy hair was wet, and he was dressed in one of my rompers, the one printed to look like the universe, with a cat surfing on a burrito. It reached mid-calf on him.

He exclaimed, "Where's Mrs. Nesbitt? Is she alright?"

"She's fine," I told him. "She went into the backyard, and it's fully fenced. Duke tripped over her water bowl and startled her, so she let it rip."

"I'm sorry I lied about her being de-scented," he said as he hung his head. "She hadn't sprayed before, not once in the two years I've had her, so I thought you'd never find out. I'll go change back into my clothes, and we'll get out of here."

He turned to leave, but Duke said, "Nobody's going anywhere. See if you can figure out what to do to get rid of this horrible smell while I take the world's longest shower. And just so you know, we're getting her de-scented as soon as we find that illegal, underground vet I mentioned earlier. That's not open for discussion."

Aiden's eyes went wide. "You mean you're letting us stay, even after that?"

"Of course you can stay. It was an accident," Duke said. "I'll be back after I get cleaned up. Don't feel bad about this, Aiden. The smell is punishment enough." He hurried to the bathroom while I tied off the bag with his sprayed clothes, triple-bagged it, and carried it outside, where the skunk was happily patrolling the yard.

As I crammed the bag into the trash can, Xavier called from the other side of the fence, "I may not have seen anything earlier, but I'm definitely smelling something now. Tell me this isn't going to be a regular occurrence."

"Nope. One-time thing. Maybe go inside and shut your door, and keep reminding yourself this too shall pass."

"Very Zen of you," Xavier called before the patio door clicked shut behind him.

I went back into the kitchen and saw that Aiden had found a pair of swim goggles in a drawer, which I'd stashed there for slicing onions. He'd also tied a dish towel around his mouth and nose like a bandit. It was exactly what I'd planned to do, and I murmured, "It's like looking in the mirror."

The smell was much less intense now that the drenched clothes were out, and the fan was helping too, but it was probably going to be a long time before it was completely gone. Aiden looked up at me and asked, "Did Duke mean it? Are you really letting me and Mrs. Nesbitt stay, even after she sprayed him?"

I crouched down to his height and said, "Here's the thing about Duke. He's the kindest, gentlest man you'll ever meet, and he's also the most honest and sincere. If he says you both can stay, you can absolutely believe it."

Aiden smiled at me and threw his arms around my shoulders. Then he stepped back embarrassedly and said, "I'll get the kitchen cleaned up. Don't worry. It'll all be good as new."

"Let me worry about that. Go get Mrs. Nesbitt, and let's find you someplace not so stinky to eat. I know you're hungry."

After I got him and the skunk set up in my old room with his dinner and dessert, I started to leave, but Aiden called, "Hey Quinn?" When I turned to look at him, he said, "Thanks for bringing me home with you."

"You're welcome."

He was wearing the dish towel around his neck, and he pushed the swim goggles up to his forehead and ran a fingertip along the edge of the desk. After a pause, he said, "It's weird. My real family doesn't want me, but right after you met me, you called me a Christmas miracle and talked about adopting me. Maybe...I dunno. Maybe I was supposed to find you and Duke or something. What do you think?" As he was talking, the skunk waddled over and flopped down right on Aiden's bare feet.

"I think you really were."

He was quiet for another moment as he bent down and petted his skunk. Then he said softly, "This is the first time since I got kicked out that I haven't been scared." My heart shattered when I heard that. I'd already known I'd do anything in my power to help that kid, but hearing those words made me feel fiercely protective of him.

"I promise everything's going to be alright now, and just like Duke, I always keep my promises." He took a bite of a rainbow cookie, and I said, "Call me if you need anything. I'll be right downstairs."

I closed the door behind me and went to find Duke. He was still in the shower, so I tossed my phone and wallet on the vanity and climbed in there with him. My husband smiled at me as the water soaked into my T-shirt and jeans and asked, "What are you doing?"

I threw my arms around him and said, "I couldn't wait another minute to tell you I adore you. The way you handled that situation in the kitchen was amazing. Anyone else would have screamed and yelled and been furious, but not you."

He hugged me and brushed his cheek against my hair. "He shouldn't have lied, but Aiden needs us, and it's scary for little kids when adults yell at them. I know that from experience.

Maybe that's the only good thing about the way I grew up: it taught me exactly what not to do as a parent."

"God, I hope this works out with Aiden," I said, "not only because he's an amazing kid and he really does need us, but because you're going to be a sensational dad."

"So are you."

I glanced up at him and asked, "You really think so?"

"I know that for a fact."

"I feel like my life just came full-circle," I said, "from a scared little kid who needed a home, to an adult who can provide one."

"Exactly."

"This is the best holiday ever, except for that horrible smell. Do you think you'll ever be able to get out of this shower?"

"Nope."

"Yeah, I don't think so either." I held him tight and rested my head on my husband's chest. "Merry Skunksmas, Duke."

He kissed my forehead and said, "Merry Skunksmas, Quinn."

The End

Duke's famous sugar cookie recipe follows.
The Firsts and Forever Series will continue
with Mike and Yoshi's story.

For more by Alexa Land

Please visit her Amazon author page,

find her on Facebook

or on Twitter @AlexaLandWrites

Or visit her blogt:

alexalandwrites.blogspot.com

Bonus Recipe: Duke's Sugar Cookies

1 cup butter, softened
1 ½ cups sugar
1 large egg
3 cups all purpose flour
½ teaspoon salt
½ teaspoon baking soda
1 teaspoon cream of tartar
2 teaspoons vanilla extract

Beat butter with an electric mixer at medium speed for two minutes, or until creamy. Gradually add sugar; beat well. Add egg and beat until combined. Combine flour and next three ingredients. Add to butter mixture, beating at low speed just until blended. Stir in vanilla.

Roll dough to a quarter-inch thickness on a lightly floured surface. Cut into awesome shapes with cookie cutters. To help them hold their shape, refrigerate the cut-out cookies for at least an hour before baking (optional).

Place cookies one inch apart on ungreased cookie sheets. Bake at 350F for 9-10 minutes, just until the cookies begin to turn golden around the edges. Cool completely on a wire rack before decorating as desired. Quinn recommends using lots of icing in bright colors, and of course edible glitter.

Made in the USA
Columbia, SC
27 February 2019